CAT DECK
THE HALLS

ALSO BY SHIRLEY ROUSSEAU MURPHY

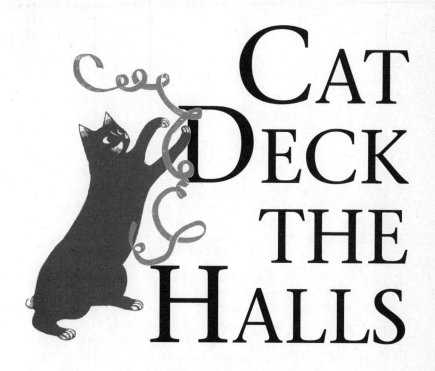

CAT DECK THE HALLS

A JOE GREY MYSTERY

Shirley Rousseau Murphy

WILLIAM MORROW

An Imprint of HarperCollins*Publishers*

This book is a work of fiction. The characters, incidents, and dialogue are drawn from the author's imagination and are not to be construed as real. Any resemblance to actual events or persons, living or dead, is entirely coincidental.

CAT DECK THE HALLS. Copyright © 2007 by Shirley Rousseau Murphy. All rights reserved. Printed in the United States of America. No part of this book may be used or reproduced in any manner whatsoever without written permission except in the case of brief quotations embodied in critical articles and reviews. For information address HarperCollins Publishers, 10 East 53rd Street, New York, NY 10022.

HarperCollins books may be purchased for educational, business, or sales promotional use. For information please write: Special Markets Department, HarperCollins Publishers, 10 East 53rd Street, New York, NY 10022.

FIRST EDITION

Designed by Nancy B. Field

Library of Congress Cataloging-in-Publication Data has been applied for.

ISBN: 978-0-06-112395-5
ISBN-10: 0-06-112395-1

07 08 09 10 11 ID/RRD 10 9 8 7 6 5 4 3 2 1

For Patrick

I think, you know, it is the innocence. A violent dog-eat-dog world, a murderous world, but one in which the very young are truly innocent. I am always amazed at this aspect of creation, the small Eden that does not last, but recurs with the young of every generation. . . . We lose our innocence inevitably, but isn't there some kind of message in this innocence, some hint of a world beyond this fallen one, some place where everything was otherwise?

—Loren Eiseley, *All the Strange Hours: The Excavation of a Life*

1

H<small>E REACHED THE</small> village half an hour before midnight, cutting over from San Jose to Highway One, on the coast, the child tucked up warm in the seat behind him. She slept soundly, her faded doll clutched close to her, one of its angel wings tucked beneath the seat belt. He had made a wide nest for her, had filled the floor well with the cheap pillows he'd bought in the first drugstore he came to, and with their two duffel bags. With the blanket laid over, the backseat of the rental car was just like a regular bed. She had a new drawing pad and crayons and a picture book back there, but she hadn't touched them much. Any other six-year-old would be raging for action, bored out of her mind, wanting to run and work off steam—as she once had, he thought sadly, seeing a sharp picture of her when she was smaller, laughing on the park swings and chasing a ball in their walled garden.

Above the highway, the night sky was black, he could see no stars, no moon. The only illumination came from flashing car lights racing north on the freeway as he and the sleeping child headed south from the airport. The car was rocked periodically in bouts of wind and rain, the storm raging and then easing off only to return every few miles. He was worn-out from the trip, from the long waits going through security, the delayed schedules and plane changes. He'd made the call from San Jose but had to leave a message, said the flight was delayed, that he'd just swing by and if he saw no light he'd get a motel and they'd be there in the morning. It was too late, tonight, to get anyone out of bed.

He was hungry, though. Their simple supper seemed ages past. He hoped the child would be hungry—if she woke at all. At last, heading downhill into the small seaside village, he left the heavy traffic, passing only three cars, all coming uphill as if maybe going home to the hillside houses behind him. The streets were slick from rain. He rolled his window down and could smell the sea. With the wind easing off, he could hear the surf, too, crashing half a mile ahead; that would be at the end of Ocean Avenue, he remembered from the map.

Driving halfway through the village, he turned up into gentler hills among close-set cottages. Molena Point had no street lamps, its narrow streets were dark beneath the trees. Shining his headlights on street signs, he found the house he wanted, but not by an address, there weren't any house numbers in the village. He wasn't able to see much on the dark streets, but he found his destination by its description and he slowed, looking. Yes, everyone was in bed. He started to get out, to see if there was a note on the door, but something made him pause.

Parking for just a minute, studying the house, he thought he saw movement in the shrubbery, something dark and stealthy. Puzzled, he watched uneasily, then decided it was nothing, just shadows. What was wrong with him? Tired. Tired from the trip, and from tending to the child. Her malaise dragged him down real bad. Though the shifting of shadows was not repeated, still he felt edgy, and did not leave the car; he didn't feel right again until he'd moved on, made a U-turn in the black, empty street and headed back down to the village.

Even in the small business section, the streets were lit only by the soft illumination from shop windows shining down onto the wet sidewalks, and by the softly colored lights of motel signs reflected on the slick, mirroring surfaces. He saw two motels with their vacancy signs lit, but first he moved on, looking for a café. Each shop window gleamed like a small stage set with its own rich wares, diamonds and silver, expensive leather and cashmere, imported china, Italian shoes, oil and watercolor paintings and bronze and marble sculpture, a feast of riches for such a small village. Windows stacked with children's books, too, and with toys, and brightly wrapped Christmas boxes to entice a child with imagined surprises. The quaint restaurants were all closed for the night, their windows dark, nor were there any moving cars on the streets, though it wasn't yet midnight. Just parked cars, maybe left overnight by tourists already asleep in their motel rooms. On this stormy night, even so near Christmas, the whole town had buttoned up early, and he thought of bed with longing. He really was done in after the long flight and then the drive down from San Jose, bone tired and achingly hungry. But most of all, he wanted to get some food into the child before he checked in to a motel and put her to bed. He had not expected all of the village to be closed, not a restaurant lighted, not even a bar, and he passed only a couple of those. Cruising the narrow, tree-sheltered streets not finding what he sought, he parked beside a small shopping plaza and got out. Stood listening, hoping to hear the echo of voices from some unseen café within. He was eager suddenly to hear another human voice, but he could hear nothing but the surf, and the dying wind—as if he'd stepped into some kind of time warp, as if everyone on earth had vanished except himself and the child, as if all the world was suddenly empty.

No voices. No canned Christmas music. No sound of another car on the streets until one lone vehicle turned on to Ocean and approached, moving slowly toward him and then speeding up and going on, the dark-clad driver invisible within the dark interior. A bicycle swished past, too, and turned left, and that made him feel less isolated.

But then, only the surf again. And the constant drip of water from the roof gutters and the branches of the oaks and pines that caressed the roofs of the cottagelike shops. Lifting the sleeping child out of the backseat, he tucked her doll in the crook of her arm, knowing she'd wake without it. Snuggling her against him, he turned in to the small but exclusive-looking shopping plaza hoping to find a coffee shop open, catering to late-night tourists. He had hardly entered when he saw the Christmas tree.

He stopped, longing to wake her, longing to see a gleam of delight kindle in her somber eyes. A two-story Christmas tree, brilliant with colored lights and oversize decorations and a tangle of large toys jumbled beneath the laden branches. It stood in the center of the plaza surrounded by flower gardens and brick walkways, the gardens enclosed on four sides by two stories of shops, in a rectangle that must fill the whole block. The colored lights of the lavishly decorated tree cast a phantasm of brilliant reflections across the windows of Saks and Tiffany and the small boutiques and three small, closed cafés. Nothing moved, not a soul was there. Standing among the deserted gardens, he wondered, if he woke the child, if the sight of the wonderful tree would bring her alive, would be enough to stir her blood and excite her, maybe stir her hunger, too? Thin as a little bird, she was, frail and infinitely precious. And there was no medicine that could help this condition.

Around six this evening, he'd gotten her to eat half a peanut-butter-and-jam sandwich and drink half a small carton of milk, and that was a victory; then soon she'd slept again. He longed to see her dark eyes wide with wonder, as they used to be—wonder at the magical decorations and the fairy lights and the brightly painted toys and the rocking horse beneath the laden branches, longed to hear her laugh with pleasure and reach up to the magical tree.

He looked above him to the upper-floor veranda and additional shops, where an open stairway led up, but there was no little coffee shop tucked in there, either. Turning, he looked back toward the street and his car thinking he'd better go on, get checked in to a motel. With the help of a motel coffeepot, he could heat a cup of the instant soup he carried in his suitcase, something hot if not very filling. Get the child tucked up safe for the night, and then drop into sleep, himself. As he turned to leave the plaza and return to his car, he saw that they were not alone. A man stood behind him, had approached without sound, and light from the tree caught his face.

"Well, hey!" He laughed, clutching the child tighter, glad to see his friend, but then puzzled. "How did you . . . ?

Where did you come from? Why didn't you . . . ? Is this a surprise? How did you get here? And when?" When the other didn't speak, he stepped forward, reaching out to clasp his shoulder.

When the man moved he glimpsed the weapon. "What . . . ?" He twisted away, shocked, ducking and shielding the child, but he wasn't quick enough. A jolt caught him and light exploded and he felt himself reel off balance. He fell, shielding and cushioning the child. Why? Why would he . . . ? She had awakened, struggling and clutching him, she caught her breath staring up into the face of their attacker then drew back against him, trying to hide herself. She made one gasp, no other sound. He couldn't see right, couldn't see at all, felt himself falling into blackness, the child clutching him. He could only imagine her little white face, couldn't see her, felt her shivering against him as deep darkness swarm over him.

THE KILLER BENT over them, pressing the gun against the victim's throat. The weapon felt awkward with the silencer on it. Well, he didn't need it now, the man was limp, gone. He was going through the fallen man's pockets when a cop car passed and slowed, he caught a glimpse of their uniform caps, heard their radio, and he ducked and froze in place as a spotlight shone in.

But it was just a routine patrol. The white Buick sedan moved on again slowly, the cop in the passenger's seat sipping coffee from a white Styrofoam cup as he scanned the shop fronts that faced the street, scanned what he could see of the plaza and gardens.

The minute the law had gone he finished searching, made sure he had the billfold, the airline tickets and rental car keys. The child huddled away from him, staring at him white with shock. He didn't speak to her. Rising, he rearranged some of the oversize toys so the body wouldn't be visible from the street, then headed away through the plaza to the back, keeping to the darkest doorways and to the gloom beneath the small, ornamental trees. The cops would be back. Would most likely circle the block, checking again before they went on. He hoped to hell they wouldn't walk the plaza, walk right past the tree to look in the individual stores. They would if they had any feeling of unease. He'd planned for more time. He'd have to hustle to move the body, he hadn't planned it this way, and he hated to hurry.

He'd waited for his quarry beside that house, cold and wet from the storm. When the car appeared at last, and stopped, and he could see the driver's profile, then it turned around and took off, he'd expected them to head straight to a motel. He'd followed silently on the bike, keeping to the shadows, drew back when his victim went into the plaza maybe looking for a café. And wasn't this ironic. This was too good. Shot beneath a Christmas tree, his death fitting right in with the season.

Not that he'd wished his victim any special bad luck. He just couldn't have him around.

Watching for the cops, he knew they couldn't have heard or seen any disturbance, couldn't have heard the faint pop of the silenced weapon. He waited until they returned, shining their light in again across the lighted tree and the toys and rocking horse but missing the dead man where he lay in the dark behind the big toys. Missing the silent child

7

cringing against him, hidden among the tangle. She was so scared she likely wouldn't run. And she sure wouldn't cry out for help. The minute they'd gone he slipped across the wide street, retrieved the old bicycle that was his transportation tonight, and wheeled it toward the empty store, one of a dozen dark retreats that he'd scoped out weeks earlier, scattered around the village.

He waited inside the dark store until the cops moved on down Ocean. He was returning for the body, entering the plaza, when he heard a soft noise like someone running; he melted into the shadows and was gone again fast, heading for the backstreet.

THE BODY WAS discovered only a few minutes after the killer fled. It was glimpsed by a lone and silent prowler looking down from the roof of a plaza shop. By a four-footed wanderer trotting across the steep shingles enjoying the lull in the storm, a lone adventurer out to discover what might be new in the night. By a tortoiseshell cat out on the prowl, to see what she could see.

Below the darkly mottled cat, the streets were deserted. The only movement was the police unit making its way slowly up Ocean—out on the prowl, too, she thought companionably.

As she crossed the plaza roof, she smelled blood, and then cordite. Startled, she approached the plaza below her, and was suddenly shaken by the smell of death. Nose twitching, she padded to the edge of the roof's rounded tiles and looked down into the enclosed gardens.

Here atop the single one-story shop at the front of the complex she was below the rest of the building, and below the top of the plaza's Christmas tree, below its crowning star. For a moment the colored lights blinded her. As her pupils contracted, she saw the body under the branches and she hissed and backed away. But then she crept to the edge again, looking.

The man lay unnaturally twisted, his body angled awkwardly between the tangle of oversize toys, his face whiter than paper except for the dark blood spilling from a wide and gaping wound down the side of his forehead and cheek. He was dead, no question, the sour smell of death filled the night. He was beyond help now, beyond any help in this world—but the little child who clung to him was alive and shivering, a little girl lying curled against the dead man, clutching him tight, her face pressed against him and her little tense body shivering with silent sobs.

Crouching and still, the tortoiseshell cat looked out to the street. The deepest shadows were pitch-black, impenetrable even to feline eyes. The smell of death was so sharp it made her draw back her lips, her teeth bared, her whiskers flat against her darkly mottled cheeks. She lifted a paw but didn't back away, she stood watching the dead man and the little silent child with her arms tight around his arm and neck, her face burrowed into his shoulder, her little white sweater soaked with his blood.

She thought the child might be five, maybe six years old; it was hard to tell with humans. Beneath her bloody white sweater she wore little blue tights, and little white boots with fake white fur around the tops. Her hair was jet-black, her skin milky. A ragged cloth doll lay forgotten beneath her, a doll that seemed to have little padded wings, a homemade angel doll.

Kit studied the black shadows of the plaza but did not see a lurking figure. She was crouched to leap down to the child when the little girl choked out a tiny, thin sob, a small, lost sound perhaps too faint for a human ear, and that sob frightened and hurt Kit all the more deeply. This child had been abandoned in a way no child should ever be abandoned, this child should be laughing and reaching up among the laden branches and golden bells and ribbons, not hovering terrified against a dead man, filled with incomprehensible loss; and a terrible pity filled Kit, and an icy fear.

The dying wind carried the scents of Christmas that lingered from the village shops, of baking, of nutmeg and ginger and hot cinnamon, all mixed, now, with the stink of death. Away across the roofs behind Kit, the courthouse clock struck midnight. Twelve solemn tolls that, tonight, were death tolls.

This afternoon the village and plaza had been crowded with hurrying shoppers, the park across the street filled with white-robed carolers and with the velvet soprano of Cora Lee French, ". . . rest ye, merry gentlemen, let nothing you dismay . . ." And now there was no one but a little abandoned child and, somewhere unseen, a killer with a gun, for surely that was a gun shot wound. What else could it be? Kit was alone in the night with a dead man and a lost little girl, and an unseen killer. Nervously she washed one mottled black-and-brown paw, trying to get centered, trying with calming licks to soothe her frightened inner cat.

And then she spun around and bolted away across the rooftops racing to bring help.

2

CORA LEE FRENCH heard the sirens shortly after midnight as she undressed in her upstairs bedroom. She had arrived home late from choir practice, driving slowly on the wet streets although the storm had almost passed. As she pulled into the drive, the house was dark above her, one of her housemates gone for the holidays, and Mavity most likely having read herself to sleep with a romance novel. Gabrielle was probably out on a date with Cora Lee's cousin, and that made her smile, that Donnie had found someone to console him and ease his hurt. Gabrielle was good for him, and no one said you couldn't have a hot romance at sixty-some. Whatever the outcome, Cora Lee was pleased that Gabrielle's charm and attentions took Donnie's mind off his loneliness, even if only for a little while.

Letting herself into the main house, she had turned on a lamp and gone upstairs to make sure young Lori was safe, in her third-floor room next to Cora Lee's. Lori didn't wake, but the two big dogs looked up at her—knowing the sound of her car, and her step, they hadn't barked. She spoke softly to them, and they wagged and smiled and laid their heads down again. If she'd been an intruder, they would have raised all kinds of hell; the deep voices of the standard poodle and the Dalmatian, alone, would drive away a prowler, thundering barks that would be backed up with businesslike teeth and powerful lunges.

There weren't many twelve-year-olds Cora Lee would leave alone for the evening, with only Mavity downstairs. But Lori had the dogs, and she was a resourceful kid, a child who would be quick to call 911 at anything unusual, and she knew how to use Cora Lee's canister of pepper spray, too, if she needed more than canine protection.

Going back downstairs to the kitchen, Cora Lee saw that Gabrielle's bedroom door was closed, so maybe her housemate was home after all. She fixed a mug of cocoa, and brought it upstairs with her, setting it on her nightstand beside her bed. The big white room was filled with the bright colors of her paintings and of the handwoven rugs she liked to collect, and the bright covers of a wall full of favorite books, among them many dog-eared picture books from her childhood. Cora Lee had never had children, but she treasured her own tender past. And now, of course, she had Lori, the kind of child who, though she was reading adult classics, was never too old for good picture books—she had Lori, she thought uneasily, until the child's father got out of prison. Cora Lee dreaded that parting, and tried not to think about it.

Cora Lee was a tall woman, still slim for her sixty years, her black short hair turning to salt and pepper but her café au lait complexion still clear and smooth as a girl's. As she undressed, slipping on a creamy fleece gown, she heard a rescue unit heading out from the fire station, and then the higher scream of police cars. She paused, listening, dismayed by the possibility of some disaster so near to Christmas.

This was a quiet village, where any ugliness seemed more shocking than in a large city, seemed far more startling than on the crowded streets of New Orleans's French Quarter, where she grew up. And now, during the gentle, homey aura of Christmas in the village, the prospect of violence was all the more upsetting.

The sirens whooped for some time, then the night was shockingly quiet. Before slipping into bed, Cora Lee removed Donnie's three letters from the drawer of her nightstand and set them beside the cocoa. Because the sirens had unnerved her, she checked on Lori again, then moved down the hall to the high-raftered room filled with her paintings. Builder Ryan Flannery had added the tall studio, designing it in such a way that it lent a finishing charm to the flat roofs of the original house.

Looking out the bay window, down the hills toward Ocean Avenue, she could see the red lights flashing, and again she shivered—but maybe it would turn out to be a wreck with no injuries, or an overexcited call about a bear up a tree. That had happened one evening right in the middle of the village, a disoriented young bear with no territory of its own, wandering down from the open hills, lost and afraid.

Or maybe the sirens were responding to a false alarm, she thought hopefully. She wanted Christmas to be peaceful, wanted to see around her only renewal and joy. Saying a little silent Hail Mary in case someone out in the stormy night might be hurt, she returned to her room and slid into bed beneath her down comforter. But the violence of the sirens, though silenced now, echoed in her head for some time, mixed with the Christmas carols she had practiced earlier, sending a cold chill through her own soprano solos.

Propping three pillows behind her, she opened Donnie's creased, linenlike pages that bore the logo of a Days Inn in Texas. And as she reread his letters, the sirens and the carols all vanished, and she felt again only his terror and the pain of his shocking loss in the hurricane.

Donnie's letters said far more to her than Donnie himself had even told her, since his arrival a month ago, more than he wanted to talk about, and she understood that. In the aftermath of Hurricane Katrina, his loneliness shone far more clearly in the letters he had written to her than he let anyone glimpse in his daily banter and quiet good cheer—perhaps this was why, though her cousin had been in the village for over a month, she still found herself returning to his written words to make real for her that shocking time—an entire population homeless; injured, sick, or dead; or escaping the city like rats from a doomed ship.

Donnie's letters stirred too realistically the thunder of hurricane winds and the crashing of gigantic waves, the rending of collapsed levees and of twisted, falling buildings. It was all there in his careful handwriting, so vivid that it frightened her anew each time she read his words; but she was glad she had the letters when she saw how difficult it was for him to talk about that time—as if the gentle cousin who had come to spend Christmas with her could be known, truly, only by the anguish of his written words, never by the quiet and cheerful facade he so carefully nurtured for others to see.

Until three weeks ago, she hadn't seen Donnie since they were young children. Since Donnie's family left New Orleans for the coast of Arkansas, when she and Donnie were nine. To little kids who were best buddies, Arkansas had seemed continents away; and they hadn't been in touch since. The ugly row had parted their families irrevocably.

Never borrow from relatives, the old adage went. But she and Donnie had been only children, they hadn't been responsible or really understood about bankruptcy and inability to pay, and the resulting bitter feelings.

But now, in their sixties, suddenly Donnie had needed her again, had needed her badly enough to write his first letter to her in over fifty years. Had needed to reconnect with the only family he had left, after his children died in the flood, and with his wife already dead from cancer. Had needed to be with the only close blood relative he had left.

She could hardly bear to think about those three little children drowning before he could reach them, before he could race from the restaurant where he worked, through New Orleans's chaotic, flooding streets, battling the surging waters to the school that had been, he'd been promised by city authorities, completely floodproof and safe. He arrived as the building collapsed beneath pounding waves and surging debris, the top floor of the classroom imploding, drowning more than two dozen children—little children huddled in a refuge they'd been assured by grown-ups was secure against any storm.

Setting the letters aside, she snuggled down beneath the comforter, trying to dispel the coldness of spirit that filled her far deeper than the chill of the stormy night. Softly, she could hear the waves breaking on the shore, a strongly aggressive high tide, but not waves of hurricane force; not here on the Pacific.

Yet even as that thought comforted her, a sharper gust of wind and rain moved suddenly across the rooftops, rattling the widows.

But this was only a minor winter storm, nothing like the violence of an East Coast hurricane.

When Hurricane Katrina hit, she'd tried to reach Donnie, but she'd had no phone number or address. She'd tried through the rescue units, through the Red Cross and Salvation Army and the police, but had been unable to obtain any information. For over a year she'd tried, and then this fall, when Donnie called her, the shock of that phone call had sent her heart pounding.

He had followed up with a letter, and then two more. And now here he was, under her own roof, and safe.

But, Cora Lee thought uneasily, life was never safe.

Nor was it meant to be. Anything could happen, any life could take a disastrous turn, just as any sea could turn violent. Even the tamer Pacific could flood the land, she supposed, under the right conditions. Listening to the heavy waves of the full tide, she wondered how far up the sand they were breaking tonight, and she imagined them lapping up onto the street, at the end of Ocean Avenue where the asphalt ended at the sand beach. But *not here*, she thought stubbornly, willing herself into a sense of security, yet at the same time wondering perversely if, in the distant future, the seas would indeed take back the West Coast.

That was the way the world worked, she thought sleepily, in gigantic cycles of change.

But that would be centuries from now, she thought as she dropped away into sleep; everything about the earth was ephemeral, each in its own time and cycle, nothing on this earth was meant to be forever.

Except, Cora Lee thought, our own spirits. Our spirits never die, they simply move on beyond the earth's cycles, to a realm we can't yet see. And in the deep, windy night Cora Lee slept.

3

THE GRAY TOMCAT lay on his back, his four
white paws in the air, his sleek silver body
stretched out full length across the king-size
bed, forcing his sleeping human housemate to
the edge. Clyde Damen's left arm hung over the side, his
knuckles resting on the cold hardwood floor; all night Joe
Grey had been nudging him away from the center; all night
Clyde had unknowingly given, inch by inch, to the tomcat's
stubborn possession. Now, as Joe lay contentedly snoring,
pressing his paw against Clyde's shoulder bidding for ever
more space, suddenly he jerked wide-awake and flipped
right side up, intently listening.

The sound was soft.

It came from the roof above. The rhythmic thumping
of an animal racing across the shingles.

The next instant, the running paused. He heard a small
window slide open just above him. Then the familiar flapping of his plastic cat door that led from his rooftop cat

tower down through the ceiling onto a wide rafter in the next room of the master suite.

Whoever had entered was now inside the house. Cat or raccoon, poised on the rafter above Clyde's desk in the adjoining study.

No strange cat came into Joe's personal territory without serious damage. A raccoon or possum entered only at risk of its life.

The flapping of the cat door slowed and stilled. Then a hard thump as the intruder dropped down from the rafter onto Clyde's desk. Joe crouched to leap, his gray fur bristling, crouched to do battle when he saw her . . .

Her yellow eyes were huge as she leaped from the desk, her dark, fluffy tail lashing and switching as she came racing into the bedroom and hit the bed leaping over Clyde wild with panic and fear, talking so fast that he could understand nothing. Before he could make sense of what she was trying to tell him, she was off the bed again in a froth of impatience and back onto the desk, where she hit the speaker button, shouting into the phone.

"A dead man, dead with a shot in his head in the plaza under the Christmas tree and a little child in his arms scared and crying. Hurry! Oh, hurry, Mabel, before the killer comes back! Tell them to hurry!" And even as Joe leaped to the desk beside her, hearing the dispatcher's familiar voice, they heard the first siren leave Molena Point PD, and then the beeping of a rescue unit careening out of the fire station. Kit's eyes were black with fear, she trembled against him crying, "The child, Joe. The little child . . ."

"Tell me on the way," Joe said as he sailed to the rafter.

Together they crowded out Joe's cat door and through his tower to the roof—where Kit bolted away, Joe racing after her across the shingles, down to Clyde's back patio wall and up again to the two-story wall that separated their patio from the shopping plaza.

When the plaza was originally planned, both Clyde and the tomcat had fumed because the wall proposed along their back property line would block their view of the green hills that rose to the east of the village and hide the sunrises they both enjoyed. Clyde had said the wall would destroy property values along the entire street, but that hadn't happened.

With Ryan Flannery's innovative design and construction, their scruffy backyard had been transformed into a handsome outdoor living area, a private retreat clearly defined and sheltered by the white plaster wall along which Joe and Kit now raced, at last dropping down onto a roof of the plaza shops. Kit never stopped talking, blurting out the details of the dead body in such a garble that Joe had a hard time making sense of what she was trying to tell him. For a moment he saw the plaza as it had been late that afternoon, hours earlier, when he and Kit and his tabby lady, Dulcie, had sat atop the wall watching the procession of white-robed carolers come up Ocean Avenue from the Community Church, gliding regally in their long robes to the little park across from the plaza. In the last rays of winter sun, they had stretched out on the roof tiles enjoying the Christmas carols, and the Christmas tree that rose beside them, its decorations a bright feast of color, the rocking horse and oversize toys richly painted. But now, just after midnight, the little park was dark and deserted, and the lights of the tree shone even brighter—though not as bright as the red strobe lights that pulsed atop the rescue vehicle that had backed in among the gardens, and the half-dozen squad cars parked at the entry to the plaza—and all across the shadowed gardens, uniformed cops moved fast, the beams from their flashlights swinging into shop entries and in through shop windows, picking out rich wares and searching the shadows within.

The ambulance stood with its back door open facing the Christmas tree. A stretcher stood on the sidewalk. Both were empty.

"So where's the victim?" Joe said, studying Kit. "You said there was a body under the tree, and a clinging child."

"It *was* there! And the child was there. Maybe in the ambulance?" Kit said hopefully, crouching to peer deeper in through the van's open door.

"You can see there's no body," Joe said flatly, just the usual medical equipment, cots, oxygen tanks, who knew wat else? He looked at her patiently. Two medics stood beside the van with Dallas Garza as the detective spoke on his radio. As the cats drew closer, Garza clicked off and stood studying the green plastic cloth beneath the wooden toys where it was rumpled and awry, the toys knocked roughly aside. There was no body there and no child, and the tomcat looked at Kit with narrowed yellow eyes, his silver ears back, the white streak down his nose drawn into a harsh feline scowl.

"What the hell are you up to, Kit? You called them out here on a ruse? Some kind of . . ."

But the space beneath the tree *was* disturbed, and was splattered with blood; Joe could smell the blood, and he could smell death. And he said no more. They watched Dallas Garza study the short trail of blood, seeing where it led, and then look away at the plaza gardens, his dark eyes taking in the shadows beneath the small trees. Joe glared at Kit.

"There was a body, Joe! I swear! There was a child! A scared little girl with the dead man's blood on her sweater! I suppose it was his blood," she said. "Or was it the child's blood? Oh, was the child hurt, too?" Crouching at the edge of the roof, Kit peered down into the windows of the squad cars, still looking for the victims. She could see no one, no glimpse of long black hair and dark eyes, no little white sweater. She looked at Joe forlornly. And even if his nose hadn't told him, Joe would know she hadn't made this up—Kit did not make up disasters.

"What will Garza do now?" Kit whispered. "Will they all go away, will they *think* it's a hoax? But the blood . . ."

The paramedics had sat down on the back bumper of their vehicle, waiting for someone to come up with a victim. Detective Garza, stepping carefully around the tree, began to take photographs. Beyond the Christmas tree in the darker reaches of the plaza, officers continued to search, and on the dark streets beyond the plaza, squad cars slipped along like silent, hunting hounds, their sudden spotlights sweeping into sheltered doorways and down narrow walkways—and before Joe could stop her, Kit leaped off the roof into a pine tree and down to the plaza gardens to disappear among the flowers and shadows in her own search for the frightened child.

• • •

The moment the running footsteps had ceased and the dark street had grown silent again, when he'd been able to see no one watching among the shadows, the killer had hurried around to the main street to the rental car parked in front of the plaza—if someone *had* seen the shooting, and had called the cops, he had only seconds to get the body out.

Backing quickly in over the curb between the plaza gardens, and stepping out, he'd seen that the kid was gone. That scared him. Where the hell? Well, he had no time to look for her, and anyway, she wouldn't talk. He'd dragged the body up the walk and into the front seat, pushing it down partially under the dash, and at the last instant he'd grabbed the ragged cloth doll—it was obviously handmade, and might be traced, and he didn't need that kind of evidence. Swinging into the driver's seat, he'd sped away from Ocean heading for the nearest hiding place of the seven he'd pinpointed earlier, this one just two blocks away. All these residential streets were dark, no streetlights to deal with in this quaint little town. Pulling into the drive, he'd heard the first siren, and he'd backed the car around behind the row of tall bushes. The house was empty and dark, the part-time residents were in China for the holidays—he read the Molena Point *Gazette* religiously, at least the society column, to get a fix on the planned vacation schedules of the village's well-to-do residents.

He'd thought of pulling the body out of the car and shoving and rolling it under the bushes, covering it as best he could with dry leaves and dead branches. The bushes were thick there, heavy with shadow. But then he'd changed his mind, in case he might have to move in a hurry—it would take a while to get the ID out of the car, remove the VIN number, and get the plates off.

He'd waited a long time until he thought they'd quit searching. When all seemed quiet, he silently opened the empty garage, folding the old hinged doors aside, and pulled the car inside; he knew there were tools in there.

Shutting the doors without sound, he got to work. He worked nervously, worrying about that kid and if they'd found her, wishing he'd had time to look for her. Maybe she'd be so scared she'd stay hidden, scared of what she'd seen and then of the flashing red lights and dark figures milling around. He imagined her crouched somewhere frozen like a frightened rabbit. Did a rabbit ever die of fear? he thought hopefully.

If they found her, she couldn't tell them anything—and yet . . .

He'd better go back. As soon as he took care of the car's ID. See if the cops had her. Maybe hear where they were taking her—then it would be a cinch, he'd take care of her later, if needed.

4

Racing away from Joe into the dark plaza looking for the vanished child, the tortoiseshell cat didn't care that the body had vanished, she thought only of the terrified little girl, afraid that the killer had taken her—or had the child run before he could grab her? Had the sirens scared him away before he could snatch up the frail witness? A little girl like that, could she get away from a grown man? Maybe hide where he wouldn't find her? If she'd seen the shooter's face, she was surely marked for death.

Trying to find the child's scent among all the cops' trails as they'd quartered the plaza sent Kit doubling back again and again, sniffing at every brick, at every patch of earth, scenting around every bush trying to catch the smell of the little girl over the sharp trails of shoe polish, testosterone-heavy sweat, gun oil, and the pungent odors of geraniums and Mexican sage that seemed to want to drown out all else. Though Kit could track as no cop could, as only a dog could do, this morass of fresh scents was indeed daunting.

And was the killer still nearby, watching the police? Maybe even watching her, wondering what that cat was doing?

The day had begun so happily amid all the Christmas bustle. As Kit had trotted out of the house that morning through the dining-room window onto her favorite oak branch, behind her the dining table was strewn with wrappings and boxes; in the living room, the tree lights glowed; and in the kitchen her two human housemates had been chopping nuts for fruitcake, the tall, eighty-some newlyweds as happy as a couple of kids, laughing and teasing each other, surrounded by the delicious smells of baking, of vanilla and almond flavoring and ginger and candied cherries. Racing away toward the village over the familiar tangle of rooftops, Kit had found Joe Grey and Dulcie on the tiled roof of the Patio Café, the big silver tomcat having a morning wash while tabby Dulcie waved her darkly striped tail, caught happily in the milieu of delicious Christmas smells and of taped Christmas music that rose up to them from the small shops, and listening to the villagers' cheerful greetings as they hurried from one small store to the next. The cool morning had been jewel bright, almost balmy for December, a day to roll on warm concrete or, for a human, to abandon the house for the sunwashed village and seashore. After a week of icy winds and lashing rains, everyone had seemed to be out and about, as busy as field mice emerging from their holes on the first nice morning. But then, by late afternoon, the weather had turned stormy again, dark clouds rolling in and the wind whipping up foam off the ocean. Since early November, the weather had been wildly unpredictable, the central California coast awash with bright sun one day, battered by dark rain and heavy winds the next. Kit's human friends hardly knew, when they got out of bed in the morning, whether to dress in shorts and a light shirt, or sweaters and rain gear. Even the newscaster on TV seemed unable to predict heat or cold, rain or sun, his broadcasts so uncertain that he should be embarrassed to show his face on the big screen. In six weeks' time, the Pacific Coast had been hit by five gusting storms that ripped away tree limbs, tore off shingles, and made everyone as grouchy as if the weather's tantrums were personal assaults. Then would come a few days of sunshine that made everyone smile and laugh and go out Christmas shopping before another storm hit, the pre-Christmas temperatures as crazy as if the weather gods were binging on catnip.

WHILE KIT SEARCHED the dark gardens, deftly avoiding the fast-moving hard shoes of the uniforms, across the street from the plaza, inside the empty store that he had scoped out earlier, James Kuda stood among sawhorses and stacked lumber, looking out, watching the dark-clad cops searching the street. Because the store was undergoing extensive renovation, he had wandered in there days ago, out of curiosity. Investigating the back room, he had found only a simple, punch-type lock on the backdoor, which, tonight, he had easily jimmied. Now, wearing a black sweatshirt and black pants, and a black stocking cap that amused him, he stood among a half-dozen upright rolls of black construction paper, his face turned away into the shadows—black on black to the cops' lights that flashed like explosions through the glass, picking out bare stud walls, stacked plywood and two-by-fours, and sliding over Kuda, who stood like another roll of strong-smelling building paper.

From this vantage he couldn't see much inside the plaza. An abbreviated view through its side entry, part of the Christmas tree, a half-dozen cops clustered around, and the back end and open doors of the EMT van. Body or no body, it looked like they were running the scene. A Latino detective taking photographs. Next thing, he'd be dusting for prints, taking particle and blood samples, then walking the grid. Kuda wasn't worried about prints, not with cotton gloves—generic gloves whose fibers they probably couldn't trace. He still had the gun and silencer, though, and was debating where to dump them.

Well, not likely they'd find the body. The car was well hidden, and not even a window in that garage; and he wouldn't be pulling out again until the uniforms cooled off, had gone off duty or back to their regular rounds. Glancing above to the plaza roof, he glimpsed something dark and small slipping along the tiles, some animal or maybe an owl; maybe that was what he'd heard earlier, an animal running across the roof.

Except, there'd been a person, too. Someone had called the cops, no animal could do that.

FROM THE ROOF, looking down on the dark gardens as the officers searched, Joe Grey caught only glimpses of the tortoiseshell kit prowling among the flowers and bushes, her darkly mottled coat hardly visible against the night-dark patterns of leaf and shadow. She'd been down there a long time. Had she found nothing? Restlessly, he dropped down a tree to join her, and together they sniffed and shouldered through the darkest, back portions of the garden, as deeply intent as a pair of tracking bloodhounds.

They found not the faintest scent of the child. Until . . .

Joe stopped and reared up. Sniffing. Listening. His white paws and chest and the white stripe down his nose gleamed in the night as he spun around toward the center of the plaza—and swiftly Kit leaped to join him.

"There," he said softly.

They approached a tangle of flowering shrubs where a tiny pond and waterfall had been built, set aside as a special drinking fountain for visiting canines. No one had thought to dedicate anything to the village cats! "There! Do you smell her?" Joe hissed.

Kit's nose twitched. Smell of water, of dog and dog pee, all so heavy around the little pool that she had missed the child's scent. Now she caught it, and they circled the pond to where the smell was sharpest—scent of child. Scent of blood.

Behind the rocky waterfall, the fountain's pump was enclosed in a small shed some two feet high. The child's smell came from there. Approaching the little closed door, fearful of what they would find, they caught no scent of death. But now, on the door handle, another smell. The smell of peanut butter.

And then, listening, the rhythm of soft, ragged breathing.

Pawing and fighting the door handle, then hooking their claws underneath the door itself, they were able to pull it open.

• • •

At the back of the shed, the little girl was crouched in a dark niche between the small water pump and the rough wall, her face pinched and white, her dark eyes huge with fear, eyes as black as obsidian—but when she saw that it was only cats, she drew in her breath with startled relief.

Kit approached her softly. When the child didn't cringe away, Kit nosed at her, then stepped into her lap. Standing with her paws on the child's shoulders, Kit licked her on the nose. Shyly the child stroked Kit, drawing in a tremulous breath. Behind them, Joe Grey managed, with stubborn claws, to draw the door closed again. And in the dark, small space the two cats snuggled close to the little girl, nosing at her as they tried to see if she was hurt, tried to find a wound.

The blood on her sweater was drying. They found no fresh blood, and there seemed to be no physical hurt, and they decided this was, indeed, the dead man's blood. They didn't want to discuss the matter, didn't want to speak in front of the child, their commitment to secrecy was far too important. Even a six-year-old could tell tales. They simply curled up on her lap and smiled up at her, purring—and wondering if they could nudge her into leaving her hiding place, if they could lead her back to Detective Garza; the child was so rigid with fear that they didn't think she'd follow, didn't think she'd leave her tight little refuge.

Joe thought the fastest way to bring help was to race home and phone the dispatcher, tell Mabel where the child was so Dallas Garza could come and get her. He was about to push outside when footsteps came pounding up the walk straight toward the shed, heavy steps that paused, then began to circle the fountain. The child cringed deeper in, shivering. The cats, leaving her huddled, crouched by the door, tensed to leap in the face of whoever entered, their claws flexing with predatory lust. Beyond the door, the man stood inches from them. The child swallowed, her thin body rigid with fear—but then a radio mumbled softly, and they caught the man's scent.

5

THE LOW DOOR to the pump house flew open, and a gun was thrust in at the cats and child, and a dark, crouching figure peered in, the black automatic held in his meaty hand. The cats didn't breathe, the child didn't breathe. He switched on a light, blazing in their faces. And suddenly he laughed. Brennan, Officer Brennan, his belly protruding over his belt as he bent lower and reached in. Brennan's gruff voice was unusually soft.

"Come on, honey, it's all right. It's all right now. I'm a police officer, I won't hurt you."

But the child pressed away from him, pushing so hard against the metal pump that she was surely embossing its imprint into her thin arm. Brennan drew back so as not to frighten her further, and for an instant his brown eyes met the cats' eyes in a surprised, searching look that sent a shock of wariness through Joe and Kit.

While Joe thought fast—and came up with no logical excuse for being there—Kit looked at Brennan with big round eyes, gave a soft little mewl that would charm the hardest cop, and rubbed against the child, purring and waving her tail. Taking Kit's cue, Joe snuggled closer, shaken by the child's trembling.

Brennan's voice softened even more, and slowly and gently he reached to stroke Kit, then tried to entice the little girl out to him. She only stared at Brennan, her eyes as glazed as those of a trapped deer.

Brennan had been on the force for as long as Joe Grey could remember, and he had never hurt or been harsh with a child; he had never touched Joe or Dulcie or Kit except gently. But the child's fear of the stranger did not ease. Watching them, Joe longed to speak, to tell the cowering child that this officer would never hurt her.

Once, when Brennan, answering a security alarm late at night, had discovered Joe and Dulcie inside Sicily Aronson's art gallery, when they had stared out at him fearfully from beneath Sicily's desk, face-to-face with the startled cop, Brennan had not snatched them up and thrown them out as some patrolmen might do. But there had been more embarrassing moments, the most recent when Kit leaped from a rooftop onto a thief's head, knocking him straight into Brennan's arms. That kind of caper did make a cop wonder. Now, with Brennan finding the cats at another scene just after the snitch's call, they trembled at what that good officer might be thinking.

Well, hell, Joe thought. Clyde and I live beside the plaza. Our house backs up to it. Of course Clyde's cat would prowl the plaza gardens. And as for our being in here with the kid, everyone knows that cats and children have a natural affinity. Wandering neighborhood cats come on a child in the plaza gardens at night and make friends with her. So what's the big deal?

It all seemed reasonable to Joe. He spent a long time trying to convince himself it was reasonable while Brennan tried to get the little girl to trust him and come out. The officer rose at last, defeated, and backed away, speaking into his radio.

"The little girl's here. She seems all right, but scared, won't come to me. She's in that little pump house behind the dog fountain. I don't want to drag her out. Maybe a woman . . . You got a woman out there?"

"Davis," came Garza's reply. "She's on her way."

Joe and Kit didn't know whether to make themselves scarce, or whether running would tweak further the big cop's sense of suspicion. They heard Garza tell Davis to bring a blanket, and then in a moment heard Detective Juana Davis's familiar footsteps approaching, her black regulation oxfords making a sharp, quick rhythm along the brick walk—and all they could do was snuggle closer to the child in dumb innocence.

Davis emerged from the shadows, her dark uniform separating itself from the night. Juana Davis was squarely built, and was always on a diet, which she found any number of excuses to circumvent. She had short graying black hair and dark expressive Latino eyes that could burn a hole through a felon, or could fill with gentle understanding, as they did now as she knelt quietly before the little open door of the low shed.

She looked in, then looked up at Brennan. "What the hell?" Davis whispered softly. "What are the cats doing in there? Clyde's cat and the Greenlaws' Kit. Why would they . . . ? How did they . . . ? Come out of there, Joe Grey.

I never saw such a cat to turn up at a crime scene! What do you do, scout for trouble?" But then she turned her attention to the child.

"Come on, honey, it's all right. Were the cats keeping you warm? They are warm, aren't they? This is Joe Grey, he's a friend of mine," she said gently. "And the dark fluffy one is Kit. I'm glad they found you, to keep you company and to keep you warm, it's getting really cold.

"Joe Grey lives nearby. He's a good cat. I guess he likes to roam among the gardens." At Davis's gentle voice, the child began to relax and listen, and to unclench her tight little fists—but now Joe was all the more uneasy. It was bad enough to stir Brennan's suspicions, but now they had Juana Davis wondering. Beside Joe, Kit was frozen rigid with nerves, she looked as if she was about to bolt past Juana and vanish, leave Joe to face the law alone.

Juana continued talking softly to the child, then she reached in quietly and closed her hand over the little girl's small, cold hand. "It's all right," Juana repeated. "I have children of my own. I'm a police officer, I won't hurt you. I know how to make gingerbread, and hot cocoa, too." With her other hand she reached to stroke Joe and Kit. "You like kitties? I do, too. Sometimes," she said, rubbing Joe's ears, "sometimes these two come down to the police station and sit on my desk, and beg for some of my lunch. And"—she laughed—"I always give them what they like to eat.

"Maybe," Juana said, "if you wanted to ride in a real police car with a police radio, I could make us some hot cocoa, and I have some gingerbread. I'd love to have a nice hot cup of cocoa, with a marshmallow in it, it's so cold out here tonight."

The child looked at Juana questioningly, some of the glaze of fear and loss leaving her dark eyes. She drew Kit closer into her arms, as she would hug a teddy bear. She spoke no word, made not the slightest sound. For a long time, as Juana talked to her, she stayed still, hugging Kit, squeezing so hard that the tortoiseshell cat had to swallow back a yowl of distress; Kit was not a cat who liked hugging. She had not grown up being hugged by humans. As much as she wanted human companionship and loving, too much hugging always felt like a threat, like she was trapped. If this had been a grown-up, the claws would have come out—sometimes, with too much closeness, a cat who has grown up wild just can't help but lash out, even at the most friendly hand; the need came over one like a jolt of lightning, Kit would react before she could think not to hurt a friend. But now, with this child, despite the sense of panic that descended on her, she tried desperately to remain gentle, tried with every ounce of feline discipline she could summon to keep her claws sheathed, and her paws still—and slowly, slowly the terrified child was relaxing, responding to Juana's words.

"Will you come out," Juana repeated, "will you come with me where it's warm and safe? I promise I won't leave you alone, I won't leave you to be afraid or alone."

Brennan had backed away; he turned and left, removing one seeming barrier to gaining the child's trust, but even with all Juana Davis's calm patience, it took her over half an hour before the little girl decided to trust her, and loosened her grip on Kit and crawled out and warily let Juana pick her up. Even then, as the child looked back over Juana's shoulder, the cats could see her lingering fear.

They watched Juana carry the little girl out of the plaza's

side entrance avoiding the ambulance and the crowd of men and police cars—avoiding the scene of the murder. They watched Juana head for her squad car, parked along the quieter side street. Crouched in the bushes, they watched her lift the child into the backseat, tuck a blanket around her, and fasten the seat belt, then slip into the driver's seat. Through the white Chevy's open window they listened to Juana call Detective Garza, tell him that she was headed for the hospital, for the children's wing, and that she would stay with her then take her home to her apartment.

"Why the hospital?" Kit said worriedly as Davis started the engine. "Why would she . . ."

"They'll need to see if she's hurt," Joe said. "See if there are any marks on her." He looked intently at Kit. "See if she's been abused."

"Oh," Kit said, shocked. "Oh, not that little girl."

"Maybe Juana can get her to talk," Joe said. "Get her to describe the killer and tell what happened."

"She didn't speak at all," Kit said doubtfully. "Not a word, not a sound. And she's such a little girl. Not like an adult witness."

But as the two cats whispered in the bushes, and Juana Davis headed for the hospital, not even the cats saw the dark figure in the building across the street, watching from the black window of the vacant store; they did not catch his scent among the sharp smells of tar paper and new lumber, were not aware of the lone man watching Juana Davis, listening as Davis told Detective Garza where she was headed, for the hospital and then her own condo.

• • •

JAMES KUDA WATCHED the woman cop come out carrying the kid, all hugs and soft words, and his hand tightened on the automatic—but hell, he couldn't shoot her in a cop's arms; he'd never get away. Well, now he knew where she'd be. When the cop drove away, Kuda turned back into the black interior of the bare store, moving so silently that even the cats across the street didn't hear him, nor did they glimpse a shifting shadow or change of light within the dark interior—an omission that, if they'd known of it, would have embarrassed both felines.

After the white patrol car sped off toward the hospital, Kuda waited. He waited a long time, until the coast was clear, until most of the cops finished up and left, then he retrieved the bike he'd stashed behind the lumber, wheeled it out through the back door, and vanished into the night; rode fast and silently, thinking about his moves from the moment he'd slipped up on his victim—but then thinking uneasily about that faint sound on the roof, just after the shooting. Raccoon, probably. Except that didn't explain who'd called the cops.

He'd just made it, before the sirens blasted, had dragged the body into the car, keeping to the walk so as not to step in the soft garden dirt. Pulling the heavy man along, sweating from nerves. But he'd made it, got the body out of there. And now, a little while longer and he'd have disposed of it. Then to take care of the girl. Not likely she'd ever ID him, kid that age and all, but even so it might be better not to push his luck.

6

THE SCREAM OF sirens had awakened Joe Grey's tabby lady; Dulcie slipped out from beneath the flowered comforter and sat up in bed beside her human housemate and lifted one dark striped paw, listening to the high *woo woo* of an ambulance followed by the urgent wail of the police units. Lashing her tail, her sharp ears forward, she was as alert as any ambulance-chasing lawyer. Though her intentions were less greedy, she was just as hot for the excitement of the hunt. The screaming stopped somewhere on Ocean at the north end of the village. Somewhere, she thought, near Joe Grey's house. Shaking free of the quilt, trying not to disturb Wilma, she was off the bed and up the hall, a dark tabby streak heading for the kitchen and her cat door, when she heard Wilma stir behind her, heard the mattress give as she sat up in bed.

"You don't have to chase every ambulance and cop car that leaves the station, Dulcie." Wilma's voice was hoarse from sleep, but alert enough to give her hell. Her annoyance brought Dulcie padding dutifully back to the bedroom, her ears back, tail lashing.

Her housemate sat clutching the quilt around her. The woodstove's cozy fire was long dead, and their bright bedroom was bone-chillingly cold.

"I just . . ." Dulcie began. "It sounds like it's near Clyde and Joe's house. I have to go and see," she said reasonably.

"Feline hearing is amazing. There are dozens and dozens of houses and shops near Clyde's house. Can you tell me the exact address?"

"You don't need to be sarcastic," Dulcie hissed. "You're getting as testy as Clyde."

Wilma smiled. "I'm sorry. I guess that was rude."

"I guess."

Wilma's long silver hair hung loose from its usual ponytail, flowing down over her flowered flannel nightgown. She looked a long time at Dulcie. "Guess I still have a case of nerves, after the kidnapping."

"I know," Dulcie said gently, jumping up on the bed to rub against her. When Wilma had been kidnapped a few months earlier, it had seemed the end of the world to Dulcie. The dark-striped tabby stared into Wilma's face. "Why don't you buy another police scanner? That was the only thing missing, when Cage Jones broke in here. If we had one now, we wouldn't have these arguments. We'd know what's happening on the street!"

"What difference would it make? You'd go anyway. You know Max seemed suspicious when I bought that one. As if, why did I really want it? You know that's why . . ."

But before Wilma finished, Dulcie had escaped, racing

away up the hall and through the kitchen, and plunging out her cat door.

Behind her, Wilma sighed and lay down, pulling the quilt close around her. No point in trying to stop the hardheaded tabby; Dulcie would have her way, and they both knew it.

Fleeing across the yard through Wilma's lush winter flowers, Dulcie sped across the empty street and up a pine tree to the rooftops, then ran like a streak for the village, hitting little more than the high spots. She guessed she couldn't fault Wilma for worrying. Wilma, as a retired probation officer, could not be fooled about the dangers the cats faced when snooping into police matters—she understood very well the compulsion that drew the three cats to the scene of a crime and also drew them, with stubborn commitment, to track the thief or killer, to join with law enforcement using their own special talents of scent detection and anonymity. Wilma understood but that didn't keep her from worrying.

Leaping up a steep, shingled peak and down into a gust of cold wind, Dulcie had no doubt that Joe Grey and the kit were already at the scene, summoned by the siren's wails— she had no notion that it was Kit who had started the action when she called 911, but she wouldn't have been surprised. She just prayed the problem was not at Joe's house.

She came down from the roofs at the divided expanse of Ocean Avenue, raced across behind three parked police units making sure there was no approaching vehicle, and up a bottlebrush tree to the roof of the plaza. There, crouched on the cold, rounded tiles, she looked down on the whirling red lights. Cop cars all over the place, and the rescue vehicle was backed up onto the little walk that led between the first shops, two of its wheels in a flower bed crushing the bright cyclamens, its siren silent now, its rear door open.

Trotting across the roof of the one-story wing at the front, to where she could look down into the gardens, she was below the top of the village Christmas tree; its colored lights mingled now with the whirling red emergency lights. Directly below her, the paramedics and officers stood well back from the Christmas tree as Detective Dallas Garza photographed the scene. She saw and smelled blood, smelled death, but there was no body. She peered down into the emergency vehicle, and found it empty, and she flicked her ears, puzzled. No one would move a body until the coroner and detectives were finished with it.

Hunched at the edge of the roof, she could see no damage to the surrounding shops, as from vandalism; no shop window broken, no benches or small tables overturned. The Christmas tree didn't seem to have been damaged. The oversize wooden toys were disarranged, but nothing looked broken or missing. Yet the stink of human death rose up to her sharply, making her flehmen and shiver. No clearer message was needed of what had come down here. But, where was the body?

And where were Joe Grey and Kit? They couldn't have missed hearing sirens.

She watched Detective Garza taking pictures, moving carefully around the tree and then the surrounding area. As he stepped aside from where he'd been blocking her view, Dulcie studied the blood on the blue drop cloth. Bloodstains on the toys, too, on the rocking horse and on an oversize baby doll. Flehming at the stink, she listened to the cops' shorthand remarks until, piece by piece, she put together some idea of what had happened here.

A disappearing dead man? And a live, frightened child who had also vanished? And then on the roof tiles she found the scent of Joe and Kit, where they had leaped into a tree, heading down into the gardens. They'd be down there now, the tabby thought, searching for the child just as were half a dozen officers, the beams of their flashlights swinging in and out among the shrubbery and tall flowers as the officers themselves kept carefully to the brick walks so as not to leave footprints or destroy evidence.

Peering over the edge of the roof, she watched Detective Garza begin to bag fibers and bits of bloody leaves. The bloody rocking horse was bagged along with the two bloodied, oversize toys and locked in a squad car. Dallas had already photographed half a dozen partial shoe prints and a clear tire mark in the dirt of the garden, and now he nodded to Eleanor Sand, to begin pouring plaster casts of these. There were three sets of footprints in the earth, and all appeared to be men's shoes. So far, no prints of a child.

"If there really was a child," Sand was saying, looking up at Garza from where she knelt, preparing a cast.

"This better not be a hoax," Garza said. "If that analysis comes back as animal blood . . ."

"Was it the same informant?" Sand said.

Dallas nodded.

Sand just looked at him. "She wouldn't do that, she wouldn't lie to us. You know she wouldn't."

Dallas nodded and turned away. But he was still scowling, his square, Latino face drawn with anger, surely thinking of the cost of such a hoax, cost to the city for trained personnel coming out on such a call, to say nothing of the diversion of Molena Point's police and rescue units from some other crime or serious incident. On this stormy December night, a diversion of their forces could, at the very worst, prove life threatening.

But that wasn't the case, Dulcie knew. *Kit placed the call,* she thought, her predatory fires stirring. *Where is Kit? Where's Joe?* She peered down again into the dark gardens.

Apparently the body had been taken away in the vehicle that had left its tire tracks in the garden. If that was so, it hadn't been very smart. Didn't the killer know the kind of evidence he was leaving? Or maybe he thought he'd gotten away clean. Dulcie was crouched to slip down into the gardens and sniff at the edges of the crime scene, see what kind of scent she could pick out, when Garza's radio came to life: Officer Brennan's voice. She paused, listening.

"I have the little girl. She seems all right. Hiding in that little pump house behind the dog fountain . . . I don't want to drag her out, she's scared as hell . . . You got a woman out there?"

Garza glanced at Eleanor, who was busy with pouring casts, then looked up toward the street, where Detective Davis was just coming around the corner. "Juana's on her way," he said shortly.

"Get a blanket," the detective told Juana, nodding toward the rescue unit, which was closer than her squad car, "and hike on back to the fountain—the pump house—we've got a scared little girl hiding back there, apparently a witness."

An EMT handed Juana a folded blanket; she tucked it under her arm and headed swiftly back between the plaza gardens. The square, dark-haired detective was in uniform, unlike Dallas, who was dressed in jeans and a wrinkled sweatshirt. Dulcie was crouched to race after her when, out front, a Chevy pickup pulled up and Chief Harper swung out, and again Dulcie waited, listening.

Max Harper was long and lean and hard-muscled, his thin leathery face sun-lined, his brown eyes watchful now, a cop's eyes—but eyes that could laugh and look loving, particularly when he looked at his redheaded bride. He and Charlie had married when Charlie was in her thirties, Max the other side of forty. Charlie was Wilma Getz's niece, and was just about the only family Wilma had left.

"Call to dispatch came from our snitch, from the woman," Dallas told Max. "How the hell do they do that? This stuff gives me the creeps. How is one or the other always on the scene?"

Max said nothing. Dulcie knew their calls upset and worried the chief, whether from Joe or from her or Kit. And despite the fact that she often felt guilty for deceiving him, Dulcie had to smile at their delicious deception. The mystique for which cats were most admired was, for them, a fine and satisfying source of entertainment.

As far as the cats knew, Dulcie and Kit's telephone voices were enough alike so that Harper and his two detectives, and the dispatchers, thought there was only one female snitch, along with the one male—but Joe Grey's gravelly telephone voice was well known to a good many in the department, and Dulcie wondered sometimes if Joe's harsh meow didn't match the tomcat's human words too closely.

Still, no cop seemed ever to have caught on. To believe

in a talking cat would be just too far out for a fact-oriented law enforcement officer—unless they spoke directly with the cat, unless they confronted in-your-face proof.

Harper and Dallas had moved up the walk beyond the Christmas tree, Dallas filling him in on what had gone down, when Davis's voice came on the radio. She had the little girl, and was on her way to the hospital.

"She seems fine," Juana said. "Cold and scared, but she doesn't seem hurt. She hasn't said a word. I'll go straight to the children's wing, and stay with her. She doesn't need to be left with strangers. If she's okay, how about I take her home with me for the night? She is so scared, Max."

"Do it," Max said. "Make sure the dispatcher knows. Tell Mabel to double the officers on the patrol around your condo." Juana's apartment was directly across the street from the station, which would contribute somewhat to the child's security. Juana had bought the condo just last year, a small one-bedroom unit with a view of the village, and a deck large enough for a chaise, a comfortable wicker chair, and a few pots of flowers, and from which Juana could see the station.

Now, as the radio went silent, Dulcie leaped across the roof to where she could look down on the side street, where Juana's police unit was pulling away from the plaza. Peering over, she saw Joe and Kit just below, half hidden in the bushes. They looked up at her, and scrambled up a bottlebrush tree to the roof. They smelled of little girl. All three cats, in an unaccustomed breach of vigilance, had missed the movement of the dark shadow in the shop across the street.

On the roof they settled down near the Christmas tree, their paws in the leafy gutter, watching Garza finish bagging evidence. And now with the bloodied toys removed, he retrieved his camera for some close-ups of the disturbance in the blue plastic dropcloth where it was rumpled and stained.

When he finished photographing, he began to lift additional particles from the plastic, tilting them into a clear bag, sealing that in an evidence bag and dropping it into the deep pocket of his sweatshirt with the bags of fiber and hair samples. The cats, looking beyond Garza, watched uniformed officers cordoning off the plaza with yellow crime-scene tape; and they looked at one another with a sudden sense of amazement.

It was daunting to see the officers of Molena Point PD doing a full crime-scene investigation without a victim, doing it on their word alone, on the word of a tortoiseshell cat.

But the evidence *was* there, and the blood was on its way to the lab. And now they had found the child who, if she would speak, was surely further proof of the snitch's veracity.

When Garza had finished with the immediate scene, he and tall blond Eleanor Sand moved on into the gardens looking for footprints among the flower beds and bushes. The cats watched him photograph the child's small footprints that led to the pump house, then photograph that refuge inside and out. Then Eleanor, who was slimmer, pushed as far as she could through the little door, to collect samples from where the child had hidden.

"We could collect samples for them," Dulcie said wistfully, "if we had opposing thumbs." The tabby imagined, not for the first time, the endless possibilities available when one had clever human hands.

"At least," Joe said, "if they lift cat hairs in there, they're legit." The cats worried, often, about cat hairs at a crime scene where none should be found; cat hairs duly bagged could royally confuse a police investigation. Dulcie sometimes had nightmares of Max Harper confronting her, shaking a handful of tabby hairs in her face, demanding that she explain. She would wake mewling and clawing at the quilt, waking Wilma, who would hug her tight and tell her not to worry—but Wilma, herself, could offer no solution to the problem. She could only repeat that no cop would ever believe such a wild phenomenon as talking cats. Telephone-literate cat snitches. Cats addicted to the same adrenaline-high challenge of law enforcement that the cops themselves experienced.

When Eleanor backed out of the pump house, placing several small bags of evidence in her pocket, the two officers walked the length of the dark plaza using their lights to examine windows and doors, moving slowly along beside the small shops though Dallas had already walked the scene. The cats watched Garza post guards around the plaza and send the few remaining men back to their patrols, watched him leave in his own unit, heading for the department. When chief Harper left, the cats, with the scene cleared of human disturbance, spent more than an hour prowling the gardens, walking the scene themselves, in their own way, sorting through hundreds of scents—trying to identify them all, and to isolate the one fresh scent they didn't recognize, trying against heavy odds to sort out the smell of the killer.

They found nothing definitive. They isolated a scent that might be the killer, but there was no way to be sure. With the smell of death around the Christmas tree, they had no sure point of reference. At last, their heads full of questions, the three cats called it a night and headed home, tired and hungry.

Kit's Lucinda and Pedric Greenlaw, being early risers, would soon be out of bed to make her a nice breakfast. Dulcie was thinking of a quick little snack in the kitchen, without rousing her housemate, and then crawling back under the warm comforter beside Wilma—of not waking Wilma, unleashing a barrage of questions and receiving another lecture. But Joe Grey, racing home along the plaza wall, was too hungry to wait for Clyde's alarm to go off. He meant to wake Clyde at once and demand a good hot breakfast. Eggs, bacon, cheese, and anchovies—the works.

7

CLYDE DAMEN LAY prone on the bed, trying to get his breath despite the twenty-pound weight solidly planted on his chest. "What the hell, Joe! What are you doing? I can't breathe. Your feet are as hard as pile drivers." He lifted his head enough to stare eye to eye with the gray tomcat. "It's the middle of the night! What the hell do you want?"

Joe Grey narrowed his eyes, and tried to keep from smiling.

"This is the third time this week, Joe! Third time you've jumped on me in the middle of the night, nearly cracking a rib. What the hell's with you?" Despite the hindrance of the heavy tomcat pressing down on his solar plexus, and despite Joe Grey's yellow-eyed smirk, Clyde managed to struggle up on one elbow.

He looked, heavy-eyed, at the bedside clock. "Four thirty-five." He lay down again, sighing. When the tomcat smiled and began to purr, Clyde raised a threatening hand.

"You wouldn't," Joe said complacently.

"Nothing in this world, Joe, could be so important as to warrant your behavior. Your rude and thoughtless behavior. You're not a lightweight kitten anymore. You weigh in about the same as a Peterbilt eighteen-wheeler loaded with concrete."

"Muscle," Joe said in a rough tomcat voice. "How could I be heavy? I'm only a little cat, not a German shepherd. Whatever infinitesimal weight I might possess is pure muscle. If you were in better shape, if *your* stomach muscles weren't so flabby, you wouldn't even feel my delicate feather ounces."

"Might I point out that it is still pitch-dark. That it is not yet dawn, that it is not even five o'clock, and that I—"

"It's winter," the tomcat said. "December. This time of year, it stays dark until—"

"Can it, Joe! Shut up and get the hell off my stomach and let me go back to sleep! You know damn well I have to go to work in the morning to support your prodigious appetite. If you had one ounce of consideration, you . . ."

But now Joe's expression changed as if by magic, from amused and mildly sadistic to bewildered hurt. Clyde's eyes widened as the tomcat turned his back, dropped cringing off the bed, and fled to the far corner of the bedroom, where he curled up on the cold hardwood floor, his back to Clyde, his white nose tucked under and his eyes closed, breathing out a soft sigh of wounded resignation.

Staring at the tomcat, Clyde swung out of bed. Shivering in bare skin and Jockey shorts, he padded across the room and knelt beside the gray tomcat.

"I'm sorry, Joe. What's wrong? Tell me what's wrong," he said softly. With Joe curled into a miserable ball, Clyde couldn't see the cat's expression, couldn't see Joe's sly grin, his yellow eyes slitted in amusement. When, gently, Clyde turned Joe's sleek silver face toward him and looked into his eyes, there was, again, only a pitiful look, an expression so wan and lost, so filled with desperate hurt, that Clyde could think only of the starving, fevered stray kitten Joe had once been, when Clyde found him abandoned in that San Francisco gutter.

Clyde had rescued Joe then, gently picking up the sick kitten and taking him home to his small apartment, where he fed him rare steak and milk, and then took him to a vet—who treated Joe for a broken and infected tail, and duly removed most of that appendage. Clyde had nursed Joe back to health, and they had never been parted since. Now, studying the suffering look on the tomcat's gray-and-white face, Clyde was overwhelmed once more with pity. "Do you hurt somewhere? What happened?"

The tomcat rolled his eyes.

"Do you feel sick? Are you feverish? Is your stomach upset?"

Silence.

"Or could it be," Clyde offered, "that you are weak and faint from hunger?"

Joe Grey smiled.

Clyde uttered another long-suffering sigh and, dispensing with shower and shave, pulled on his pants and headed downstairs to get breakfast.

The kitchen was cold and silent. No shuffling doggy sounds getting out of bed, no clicking of doggy toenails on the cold linoleum, no glad panting. The room was hollow with an emptiness that neither Clyde nor the tomcat could get used to. Even when Clyde threw on the light and turned on the radio and spoke to the three sleeping cats in the adjacent laundry, the silence pressed in. No glad huffing, no doggy yawn and whine, no doggy mumbles of greeting. Old Rube was gone. Buried out at the back of the patio, with a little flat headstone marking his grave, right next to Barney's marker.

How long would it take, Joe wondered, until he and Clyde learned to live more equitably with the death of the old black Lab? It had taken a long time of grieving after golden Barney died, and he knew that the aftermath of Rube's death would be no different. He peered into the laundry at the three household cats who, despite Clyde's greeting, still slept, the two older cats twined together in the top bunk among their blankets, Fluffy's head resting on Scrappy's flank—Scrappy, through several name changes, had finally settled in with the name that had fit him best when he was young. Now that he was in his later years, that name didn't seem to fit very well, either.

Only Snowball, the younger, white cat, slept on the bottom bunk. In Rube's old bed. Grieving. Snowball had mourned deeply since Rube died.

She looked out at them, now, with only a sad expression, then curled tighter and squeezed her eyes shut.

Joe spent a long time licking and grooming her, but she didn't respond much. Even when the smell of frying sausage and then scrambled eggs began to fill the room, Snowball remained in bed. As did Scrappy and Fluffy—the older cats letting Clyde know that it was too early, and too cold and dark, to get up. They would come yawning down later, stretching, and then hopefully Snowball would follow.

The aromas of sausage and eggs sent Joe Grey up onto

the kitchen table, where he stretched out on his own side, impatiently waiting. Clyde set a place for himself, then went to get the paper, which they'd just heard hit the step. The time was 5:10. Clyde got up at six anyway, Joe thought unsympathetically. This would give him more time to read the paper.

Returning, Clyde shook open the paper and stood at the stove with his back to the tomcat, making toast as he read the headlines and sipped his coffee. Joe hated when Clyde hogged the front page. Rearing up on his hind paws, on the table, he could just see over Clyde's shoulder, the headline above the fold.

So there *had* been a reporter on the scene last night, slipping around, keeping out of the way, quietly pumping an officer or two for information. The guy had had to hustle, to get his article in this morning's paper. Joe wondered what "important" story they'd pulled off the front page at the last minute, to make room for the more sensational headline:

COPS CONVERGE ON PLAZA CHRISTMAS TREE
POSSIBLE MURDER? NO BODY FOUND

Clyde put their plates on the table and sat down, continuing to read, leisurely finishing the article—payback for the early wake-up call. Watching Clyde fork in scrambled eggs, Joe wolfed a few bites of his own breakfast. It tasted bland. "Do we have any kippers? Or a can of those imported sardines that you so carefully hid behind the canned beans?"

"You're getting fat. No one eats sardines with sausage and eggs."

"I do. You know perfectly well that I like a little fish

condiment with my breakfast, it makes the eggs go down."

"I didn't know you had trouble making anything edible go down." But Clyde rose, reached deep into the back of the cupboard, and withdrew a can of sardines. "I'm just lucky I have a strong stomach." He twisted the little key to open the lid. "No one wants to smell sardines with their eggs at five in the morning."

Dishing sardines onto Joe's plate, he looked intently at the tomcat. "So *that* was what last night was about! When Kit came barging in and woke me up and then made that phone call. She reported a dead body that wasn't there! I swear, Joe . . ."

"Woke you? How could we wake you? You never stopped snoring."

Clyde looked hard at Joe. "The department got a phone tip, caller reports a dead man. Cops arrive, nothing. No body. A little blood—they don't know, yet, if it was human blood." He studied Joe. "What are you cats trying to pull? Cops search the plaza and find nothing. Nothing, Joe!" He laid aside the paper. "You want to explain this?"

"What's it say about the child?"

"What child? There wasn't any child. The paper doesn't mention a child." Trying to curb his temper, Clyde scanned the last column more carefully, then shook his head, still looking hard at Joe. "What did you tell the cops, you and Kit? What are you cats up to? What have you done now?"

Joe just looked at him.

Clyde laid down his fork. "You didn't . . . Oh, hell! You didn't mess with a crime scene? You didn't lure away some witness? Some kid who saw a murder? Why, Joe? Why would you do that?"

"Do you suppose," Joe said patiently, "that the law didn't give the reporter the whole story? That they found something last night that they decided to keep quiet and didn't share with that reporter? Is it possible for you to imagine, in that hidebound brain, that that child could be a holdback? A witness they don't want the public to know about? That maybe they're trying to protect her?"

Clyde concentrated on finishing his last bite of sausage. Then, "Was there a body? And who's the kid? Why is a kid so important? You want to tell me what happened?"

Joe licked sardine oil from his whiskers. "Maybe Harper figures the kid's safer if he keeps her under wraps, if the killer doesn't know where to find her."

"Will you start from the beginning? *What* child? Who is she? And," he said, fixing Joe with a keen stare, "if there *was* a body, where is it?"

"Strange, though," Joe mused. "Strange the guy didn't kill her when he had the chance. She had to be a witness, she was right there in the dead man's arms when Kit found her. Except, maybe the shooter didn't have time, maybe he heard something, and hurried away dragging that heavy body—maybe he plans to go after her later." The tomcat sat thinking about that, then returned to his eggs and the bright little sardines, which, along with the sausage, certainly did enhance the eggs' bland flavor.

Only when he had finished his breakfast and licked his plate and cleaned his whiskers and methodically washed his front paws, a procedure that took some time and left Clyde fidgeting impatiently, did Joe fill Clyde in on the events of the previous night, on as much of the story as Joe himself knew. He described the body that only Kit had seen, and then the little girl they had found. Who the child was, and who the dead man was, and where the body was now, no one yet knew. The fingerprint reports might help. Or not, Joe thought. The killer could have no previous record, though that didn't seem likely.

"So what happens," Joe said, curling down on the want-ad section, which neither one of them read, "the way I see it, the killer knocks this guy off. Shoots him right there under the Christmas tree, maybe even while he's holding the kid. He's about to get rid of the body when something startles him, some noise or maybe some late passerby, maybe a car slowing out in front of the plaza. Noise scares him, and he runs.

"I'm guessing he hides somewhere close by. At about that time, Kit comes along over the roofs, smells blood and death, looks down, and there's the body and the kid. Who knows, the guy might even have heard Kit herself scrambling up to the roof, maybe that's what scared him off. Anyway, Kit sees the dead man and the kid, and takes off to get help.

"Now," Joe said, "the plaza is quiet again, and the guy returns. Maybe he means to knock off the kid so she can't ID him, but meantime, the kid has run. Vanished. Found a place to hide. Have to give her credit that she got the hell out of there, she's only five or six. Kid took care of herself the minute she could, and she had to be scared witless, still scared when we found her. Some kids would just fall apart screaming."

Joe took a last lick at his plate, then had to wash his whiskers again. "With the kid gone, the guy starts to get nervous. Maybe he looks for her, maybe not. He's in a hurry to get the body out of there. Maybe figures she's too little to give the law a coherent description. Figures if he gets the dead man away, maybe no one will ever know there was a body. Fat chance of that. Anyway, he . . ."

Clyde was fidgeting again. "This is really . . ."

"I'm not totally guessing here," Joe said. "Dallas found tire marks coming into the plaza, up over the flower bed, along the sidewalk, and out again where someone had backed down over the curb. Eleanor made a dozen casts where tires went over the flowers and dirt, and she made casts of a man's footprints, someone besides the corpse.

"Guy brings his car around, drives into the plaza, loads up the body, and takes off—while Kit is racing to our house and waking me and calling the dispatcher, and then we're scorching back there. Then the sirens, and that had to scare him and make him hustle.

"We get back, the cops are on the scene, but no body and no kid. Blood. Footprints. Tire marks. The samples and fibers and stuff that Dallas collected for the lab." Joe scratched his ear with his hind claws, looking across at Clyde. "So, except for the little girl, Kit was the only one to see the victim."

"This is making my head ache." Clyde glanced at his watch and rose. Stacked their dishes in the sink and started to rinse them. "Does it occur to you, Joe, that if that child—"

"Kit and I found her," Joe interrupted, "in the pump house behind the dog fountain. Little shed the size of a doghouse. We were in there with the kid, trying to calm her, when Brennan found her—and found us."

Clyde spun around, glaring at him. "Oh, that's great.

58

That's just the kind of caper I like to hear about. That's the very kind of stupid move I keep warning you cats about. What the hell did Brennan think?"

"How do I know what he thought? You think I'm clairvoyant?"

Clyde shrugged. "How the hell do I know? You're everything else unnatural."

Joe let that pass. "She wouldn't come out for Brennan, so he called for a woman." He smiled. "The kid came out for Davis, nice as you please. Scared as hell, but she snuggled right up to Davis. She wouldn't say a word, though. Not a sound. Davis took her to the hospital for a look-over, told Harper she'd take the kid home with her, that she didn't want to leave her among strangers. God knows what happened to her," Joe said darkly, not wanting to think about the possibilities.

But Joe's sudden sick look of concern so touched Clyde that Clyde came around the table and, in a rare show of gentle affection, picked Joe up and cradled him against his shoulder, much as Detective Davis had cradled the little, silent girl. Moving to the window, Clyde stood holding the tomcat, the two of them looking out to where the sky was still dark. It would be several hours yet until dawn, and even then they wouldn't be able to see the rising sun, for the high wall that defined the back of their patio and ran on behind their neighbors—but they would be able to watch a brightening streak of light finger up along the top of the wall, heralding the coming of dawn, and they had learned to live with that.

But while Clyde stood holding Joe, feeling ashamed of doubting the tomcat, Joe's mind was on the vanished murder victim and on the little girl. Wondering where the man and child had come from. Strange to have such a young child out in the middle of the night—unless they had just arrived in the village.

"So the department was able to lift prints?" Clyde said.

"Prints from the decorations and toys," Joe said. "It'll take a while to get everyone who worked on decorating the tree into the station for sample prints—take time to check for missing children statewide and then national, check the airlines, go through the missing adult lists . . ."

"No description," Clyde said. "And no one saw the car. They're asking in the paper for witnesses."

"There was no one on the street to *see* a car. Not a soul, Kit said. With the storm, the whole town was deserted, except for patrol cars."

"And the victim and his killer."

"It all takes time," Joe said. "That's what makes you want to claw and yowl, the damn waiting. Dulcie and Kit and I *know* the blood was human, but the department has no proof until the coroner's lab tests it. The cops only know what Kit told them. Though I have to say, they didn't hesitate. Moved right in, on her word—on the word of a tortoiseshell cat," he said, smiling. "But the blood . . . Depends on how backed up the lab is, how soon the coroner gets to it."

"Maybe the child will tell them something when she recovers a little from the shock."

"If she can talk at all," Joe said. "She didn't say a word last night, but maybe she'll open up for Davis. Maybe . . ." He twisted around on Clyde's shoulder, his whiskers tickling Clyde's cheek. "It would be pretty neat if the kid did ID that bastard. To shoot a man like that while he's holding a little child. That experience will sour Christmas for that little girl for all the rest of her life. I hope that little girl nails him good," Joe hissed. "I want to see that guy burn." The tomcat's yellow eyes blazed at Clyde—and this was one time when Clyde Damen and Joe Grey were in perfect agreement. If they had their way, that killer would burn slowly and forever, with unthinkable agony and pain.

8

Having backed the car into the small garage, Kuda hid the two duffel bags in a storage cupboard, but left the pillows and blanket in the car.

He tore up the car rental agreement and registration, stripped off the rental stickers, tore all of it into confetti and stuffed it, a few pieces at a time, into the drain of the laundry sink, running all the pieces on down with a lengthy cascade of water.

With tools he'd found days earlier in the garage, he removed the license plates, then, taking off his shoes, he stood atop the car in his stocking feet, shoved the plates up into the attic through the crawl hole, and pushed them under the soft blanket of fiberglass insulation, smoothing it back over them. He was still wearing white cotton gloves. Last thing, he put the bike in the trunk of the car and tied the lid closed over the protruding rear wheel.

He waited a long time, his ear to the crack in the garage door, listening for the soft sounds of cop cars moving outside on the narrow streets, and trying to be patient. Had to make sure the cops had given up looking—given up, depending on what that witness had told them. Where the hell had that unseen witness been? What had they seen? *Someone* had called the law. He knew he'd been careful. He was certain the cruising patrol hadn't seen him. And he sure as hell hadn't seen anyone on the streets or standing in the shadows. Hadn't heard anyone—until that sound of running, almost like it was overhead, a sound so soft. Most likely some animal. Or could have been some kid on the street, the echo playing tricks? Some kid slipping out at night to see the Christmas tree?

Time to get moving, everything quiet out there. The cops would still have a guard at the plaza, but he'd use the back or side entrance. He looked around the garage to make sure he'd tidied up. No, nothing there but the two small duffel bags in the cupboard, under a bunch of old rags, and they wouldn't be there long. Silently he stepped out the side door to see if the street was clear, before opening the garage door.

WHILE CLYDE DAMEN stood in the kitchen holding Joe, staring out at the predawn dark, and while James Kuda prepared to dispose of the body, across the village in her condo apartment Juana Davis was tucking the little girl into a hastily made bed on the wide velvet love seat. She had placed the child so she would not face the Christmas tree. She thought of covering it or moving it to another room, after the trauma the child had suffered.

But there were Christmas trees and decorations everywhere, all over the village, no matter where they went. She would be taking the child to the station in the morning, and dispatcher Mabel Farthy had a small, beautifully decorated tree on the counter beside the in-box.

Juana thought sometimes it was a lot of fuss and extra work for a person living alone to buy and decorate a Christmas tree—but she always did, always had a fresh, live tree, and she guessed she always would.

Though it would soon be dawn, Juana had slipped into a pair of warm, comfortable pajamas, over which she had rebuckled her shoulder holster with her automatic. She had lit a fire on the hearth, only gas logs but real enough to be cozy, and had brought out an extra blanket and pillow from the bedroom so she could sleep lightly in the upholstered chair near the sliding-glass door to the balcony with a view of the street below.

Davis's one-bedroom condo rose just across the street from the courthouse complex—with her husband long dead and her two sons gone from the nest, she had sold her house up in the Molena Point hills and rented an apartment while she waited, it seemed forever, for the right condo to come on the market. When this one became available diagonally across the street from the station, it was hard to make a low offer and chance losing it. Hard not to snap it up. But as both the real estate agent and the seller well knew, the market for a condo where two women had been murdered was somewhat limited—this was a small town, and no one had missed the details of that brutal killing.

The fact that this had been the scene of a double murder last summer didn't bother Juana. The one-bedroom unit had been listed for less than a week when her low offer was accepted. She had worked the case, so she knew the apartment well, and she had no complaints about it except for a leaky bathroom faucet and the noisy refrigerator; she was not a person to worry about lingering ghosts. All traces of blood had been cleaned away and the walls freshly painted in a pleasing off-white; she had installed new, off-white carpeting—and she took a quiet pleasure in being so near to work.

From the wide balcony she could see down onto the block-long courthouse building and its surround of old twisted oak trees and bright gardens, and the wide parking lot on its far side. She had a clear view of the end of the two-story complex and the single-story wing that housed Molena Point PD. She could see the department's back door and smaller police parking area and the small jail, all enclosed within a woven wire fence. She could see, beneath the gnarled branches of an ancient oak that hung over the red tile roof of the building, the small bared window that was cut into a raised clerestory, allowing light and ventilation for the department's one small holding cell that opened off the front entry. Now, at just before six on this cold winter morning, beyond her drawn draperies, Juana's balcony was black and chill, a light dew clinging to the teak chair and love seat and the three potted camellias that were in full bloom. But here within the bright, firelit living room, she and the child were cozy. This was nice, the cheerful blaze on the grate, the little girl curled down, her tummy full of cocoa and a cookie, hopefully falling into welcome sleep.

Since her own two boys had grown and left the nest, Juana had seldom held a small child in her arms. Maybe someday there'd be grandchildren, but not for a while.

Both her boys were cops, neither one married yet. When that time came, she wondered what kind of grandmother she'd make. Well, she wasn't holding her breath. At this point both her sons were married to their work, Randy as a detective with the Tacoma Sheriff's Department, and Jed with California Highway Patrol.

Guess I'm married to my own work, she thought, amused. Still, as a widow and an empty nester, she found it surprisingly satisfying to shelter this little girl, to hold her and to put her to bed, tucking her safe under the quilt. The child was such a fragile little thing, thin as a baby bird. Shoulder-length hair as black as a raven's wing, and skin as pale and clear as milk. Long black lashes, and when she was awake, those huge black eyes staring up at you, so sad, filled with such hopelessness.

In the hospital, and then in the car coming home, the child hadn't spoken. She had made not a sound even when the woman doctor examined her, an examination that had to be frightening. Juana had called ahead and asked for a woman, and found that Terry Wayne was on duty. Juana's white-haired, cheerful friend had been waiting for them at the emergency-room desk, and Juana, not knowing what the child had been through, was relieved not to have to deal with a male doctor.

Terry hadn't kept the child long. The little girl was so frightened, and so tired and cold. Just long enough to wrap her in warm blankets, and then gently examine her to determine that she had not been molested and had no physical wound that Terry could find. Nor could Terry find any malformation of the throat or mouth that would account for the child's silence.

Last night was not the time to run complicated hearing or speech tests, even if they had been available, at that hour. Terry thought the speech problem was simply trauma. Whether the child had been so traumatized by the murder that she'd stopped speaking, or whether this was an older condition, they couldn't guess. They only knew that the child was still very afraid, and cold and clinging, and jumpy at any loud sound. The two other doctors on emergency duty had wanted to keep her in the hospital, but Terry wouldn't hear of that. Even with a private room and a guard at the door, a hospital setting made Juana uneasy. She could make the child more comfortable in her apartment, make her feel that maybe someone cared what happened to her; and both she and Max felt that the child was safer with an armed officer, and with extra patrol around the building.

Max would be setting up a round-the-clock schedule for the few woman officers in the department to take shifts staying here with the child. That would be hard on the officers, taking double shifts, even if they could get some sleep while they babysat, and it would be hard on the department's budget, which was always tight—but at the moment there was no viable alternative. No one in the department wanted to dump this child into the gaping jaws of the state bureaucracy. Watching the sleeping child, one hand curled now in a more relaxed gesture, not clenched rigidly, and her black lashes thick and soft on her pale cheeks, Juana told herself again that the child's silence was indeed caused by trauma and that with rest and love and quiet, she would speak again—and, thinking like a cop, *and then maybe we'll have a witness.*

A frail, frightened little witness. How much would a six-year-old remember as it had really happened? How much would she be able to make clear to an adult? To a judge or jury?

How much of the testimony of a six-year-old child would grown-ups believe?

All night the child had clung to her, at first hadn't wanted anyone else to touch her, her dark eyes huge with dread, her ivory skin clammy and damp. Was it her father who had been shot? Shot as they stood looking up at the wonderful Christmas tree?

For the rest of this child's life, what would her Christmases be like? Chestnuts and blood. Bright lights and rocking horses heralding death.

But Juana had known one thing from the first moment she saw the little girl. She wasn't taking her to Children's Services. Not now, not in the morning that was fast approaching. Neither she nor the chief nor Dallas liked the lax security at Children's Services, even in the Protective Division. Although some of the caseworkers were conscientious and understanding, too many were hard-nosed paper pushers, political climbers, or just plain incompetent. As if the children in their care were so many packages to be sorted, held in will-call, and delivered when required.

Some ugly stories about Children's Services had reached the department, and then when young Lori Reed was found last year hiding in the library basement, and had refused to have anything more to do with the caseworkers, and after Juana and the chief had talked with Lori and looked into the handling of the child, they felt even more strongly that the County Department of Children's Services would benefit from a good housecleaning. Nine vanished children who had never been found and whose cases were still open. A boy in foster care for five years when all Children's Services had to do was pick up the phone and check information, in order to to locate the child's relatives in Seattle. And too many "accident" cases among the foster homes, logged in to hospital emergency. Children with old scars, and with new bruises that could not be accounted for.

Lori Reed, after spending nearly a year on the East Coast, in the custody of Children's Services and a number of foster homes, before being returned to her father, had told Juana other ugly stories that enraged her.

Lori had run away from a seriously depressed father who, in his secret and unrevealed fear for Lori, had inadvertently terrified her. He had boarded up their windows, padlocked the doors, and had forbidden her to leave the house even to go to school. With Lori's mother dead of cancer, with no one to explain to her the real cause of her father's distress, and with her fear of being sent to another foster home, the twelve-year-old had taken matters into her own hands—had packed a blanket and some food, and found a very clever and safe place to hide.

But Lori Reed was twelve, not six years old, and had been far more skilled and resourceful in solving the problems that were dumped on her. This child was hardly more than a baby.

And the fact that she might be the only witness to a murder was more than sufficient reason not to turn her over to a lax bureaucracy where anyone could get at her.

Without opening the draperies, Juana stepped behind them and looked out through the slider to the balcony; standing in the shadows, in the predawn silence, looking down at the village, she considered other options than keeping the child too long in her apartment, where the coming and going of officers might be noted.

She thought of the Patty Rose Orphans' Home, a very caring private facility. But, though the child could lose herself among the other children, the home didn't have sufficient security. The Patty Rose Home was not a jail, the kids were not locked in, and, conversely, visitors were not locked out or rigidly screened. Even with an officer assigned to guard her, the Patty Rose Home was not a good choice.

She thought about Cora Lee French and her housemates, with whom Lori Reed lived until her father would be released from prison. Lori was an understanding little girl, and might be good for the younger child. It was a big house, up in the hills away from the village, with plenty of room for the child and an overnight officer, and Juana wondered if the senior ladies would be interested.

Maybe a rotation, from one private residence to another, always with a guard. This little girl was too precious to be hurt again. Juana had to remind herself that this was police business, that besides her personal fear for the child, the little girl was their only witness to a crime.

Hoping they got something positive on the blood samples or the prints, hoping they could find the body, nail the killer, and wrap this up quickly, she listened to the crash of the Pacific ten blocks away. The waves sounded violent, and would be black and churning—with the extremely high tide just after midnight, the Pacific all along the coast would be dangerous. That meant emergency calls, and another strain on the department. Every year some fool, most often an uninformed and overly trusting tourist, went too near the sea during a storm and had to be rescued—rescued if they were lucky. And either way, needlessly putting lifeguards and law enforcement in danger. The rule was, never turn your back on the sea. Even in calm weather. That bright, seductive monster was always hungry, waiting for the foolish and unwary.

Turning back inside, she locked the slider, feeling secure within her own space. Cheerful fire on the hearth, her old familiar Christmas ornaments on the tall, fragrant tree, her grandmother's Creech on the mantel, the hand-carved Creech she'd had since she was a child in Ventura in their close Mexican family—a childhood of safety and warmth, in sharp contrast to what this sleeping child might have known.

Moving to the kitchenette, she started a pot of coffee, then went to take a shower. Stripping off her holster and pajamas and stepping into the pelting hot water, Juana had no notion that the storm that now battered the shore was about to claim another victim. No notion that the black water crashing up the cliffs was already licking at its prey, hungry to receive the sacrifice offered. No idea, as she soaped and rinsed off and wrapped her towel around her body and moved into the bedroom to put on clean clothes, that the eager sea was already doing its best to swallow what murder evidence might remain.

9

THE GRAY TOMCAT strolled into Molena Point PD yawning, and full of breakfast, still licking sardine oil from his whiskers. He had, crossing the roof of the courthouse complex heading for the station, seen Juana Davis leave her condo building, hurrying in the same direction.

Scorching down an oak tree and racing across the parking lot, he'd moved inside behind her through the bulletproof glass door, receiving only an amused glance from the detective. Slipping into the shadows of the empty holding cell that faced the reception area, he tried to hold his breath against the faint odor of old urine and the stronger nose-twitching stink of disinfectant. Tried to breathe in only the fresh, forest smell of Mabel's little Christmas tree on her dispatcher's counter.

The child wasn't with Juana. He hoped to hell she hadn't taken the kid to Children's Services. He didn't think Juana would do that. From his shadowed retreat beneath the single bunk, he watched Juana move away down the hall to the back of the building, watched as she checked the overhead surveillance camera that showed the officers' fenced parking area, then opened the steel back door a few inches to look out. He heard a car pull up, caught a glimpse of a white patrol car close outside the door. Watched Juana step aside as Officer McFarland entered, his black trench coat bulging so severely one would think Jimmie McFarland was pregnant with twins.

Behind McFarland, four officers crowded in, effectively shielding him from anyone standing outside the fence or looking down from one of the second-story windows across the street. When the door had safely closed, McFarland removed the black coat.

The little girl clung to him, her arms around his neck, and didn't want to get down. As Joe heard the car take off again and move away out the gate, he came out of the cell, crossed the reception area, and padded toward them down the hall—just Damen's tomcat come to freeload, to cadge his morning handout of doughnuts or coffee cake.

Juana took the child from McFarland, cradling her against her shoulder—but as the child looked over Juana's shoulder, her big dark eyes looked straight down the hall and into Joe Grey's eyes. She opened her mouth as if she would speak; but then she closed her eyes and turned away, her face pressed against Juana, quiet and unresisting. As if she didn't care what happened to her. Juana came up the hall carrying her and talking softly to her, and turned in at Max Harper's office, where a light burned, and where Joe could hear the chief and Detective Garza talking.

As Davis's voice joined the men's, Joe wandered in behind her and lay down beneath the credenza, with another wide yawn. Juana was tucking the child up on the couch with a lap blanket around her.

"They gave her a little sedative last night," she said. "She drank some cocoa when we got home, and had a cookie. Didn't want anything this morning but a few bites of oatmeal."

"No disturbance during the night?" Dallas asked.

"Nothing. Did the coroner identify the blood?"

"Human," Dallas said. "All of it. He called about an hour ago. Blood on the toys, all the samples—same blood type as from the child's clothes." Joe knew it would take several days, at best, to get results on the DNA that might, with great good luck, help identify the victim.

"Question now is . . ." Juana said, glancing at the child on the couch and then at the chief, where he sat behind his desk.

Max was silent for a moment, then, "If I talk with the director of Children's Services, maybe—"

"No," Juana said. "They don't know what security means. You could take her up the coast and lock her in juvenile hall, she'd be safer."

Max just looked at her.

"She's better off in my apartment," Juana said, "with guards on all watches. I know it's a big-budget item, but there's no way around a guard, wherever she is, sure not in Children's Services. Not until we lock up the shooter."

Max glanced at the sleeping child, and his thin lined face softened. "We don't know what she saw. Don't know what the killer thinks she saw. I don't like keeping her in your apartment long enough for someone to notice activity there."

Joe had been watching the child, wondering if she was really asleep. Now suddenly she stirred, looking up at Davis and Harper and Garza—and then straight across the room into the shadows beneath the credenza, staring again straight into Joe Grey's eyes.

Why did she do that? Joe wondered. *Don't do that! Look away from me!* She was way too interested in him. Above him, the discussion had ceased, the three officers were all watching her. Then Juana rose and knelt before the credenza, and gently hauled Joe out. He hung limp, didn't complain as she carried him to the couch and knelt, holding him up to the child and gently stroking him. Joe cut Juana a look. But the child reached out to him, her dark eyes needy. And of course, ham that he was, he slipped into her arms and snuggled against her—and found himself purring like a steam train.

Dallas and Max chuckled, which made Joe scowl. But the child stroked him and buried her face against his shoulder, and when he looked up at the officers again, they looked only pleased. They looked, in fact, almost admiring—as if Joe's role in calming the kid was not at all to be laughed at.

But they looked puzzled, too, and Joe could almost hear the questions churning—questions he didn't want to think about. Juana said, "She was like that with the cats last night, when we found her. Cuddled up to Joe and that tortoiseshell cat. Maybe," she said, "she only feels safe around animals."

Both officers, being dog men and horsemen, could relate to that. Max said, "We have dogs at the ranch, she might do well up there—isolation could be to our advantage. Or not," he said, concerned about the lack of security among the open hills and woods and pastures.

"What about the seniors?" Dallas said. "Those two big dogs are pretty protective, a good early-warning system. Their place would be easier to patrol."

"Cora Lee's good with kids," Juana said. "Our little girl could hang out with Lori and Dillon while they work on their playhouse for the contest. With a couple of guards . . ." She looked down at the child snuggled with Joe. "It's a beautiful big playhouse, big enough for you to really play house in, two stories, a slide, a ladder . . . And the dogs . . . A big brown poodle who'll lick you all over, I bet. And a spotted, firehouse dog . . ."

The child looked up at her trustingly with, Joe thought, a spark of anticipation—but a spark that was quickly gone again, drowned by sadness.

This was a hard call, Joe knew, to adequately protect their small, frightened witness, and yet put her in a friendly and comforting environment where she'd loosen up enough to talk, to tell them what she'd seen. With a six-year-old child, time was of the essence—before the event morphed, in a child's naturally imaginative mind, into any number of dark and twisted fantasies only loosely based on the facts.

Max said, "Maybe a couple of hours up there, to be with the other girls and play with the dogs. I'm not sure about overnight. See what the senior ladies say. We can't jeopardize anyone, nor put the older girls in danger.

"Take McFarland with you," he told Juana. "The young lady seems to like him." Max smiled. "When Cora Lee sees this little girl, she won't be able to resist." He buzzed the dispatcher, asked her to get Jimmie McFarland on the radio.

"I'll call Cora Lee," Juana said. "She . . ." She paused

when the dispatcher buzzed through, and Max switched on the phone speaker.

It wasn't McFarland, but Officer Sand on the line.

"I'm bringing in a homeless man, he was asleep in the alley behind Green's Antiques, an empty billfold shoved under the newspapers he was sleeping on. His shoes are way big for him, look like they could fit my casts, and there appears to be blood on one. Old jogging shoes," she said with excitement, "waffle soles. Looks like a speck of garden dirt—and some shiny red flecks.

"Says he lifted them from a Dumpster out on the highway, early this morning, that his own shoes were worn-out and sopping wet. He seems more than usually nervous, looked all around when I cuffed him and put him in the car."

"Get him in here," Max said.

"Holding cell?"

"Let's call him a person of interest. See if you can get any identification, then bring him on back to my office, tell him we just want to talk." Max clicked off the phone. He was smiling.

Davis glanced at the child. "You want us out of here?"

Max shook his head. "First reaction's worth a lot—her reaction, and his."

The child was still stroking Joe. She smelled nice, the cat thought, a sweet little-girl scent. Snuggled up with her, Joe Grey began to feel protective—so protective that he began to wonder if the prisoner would try to hurt her, and he felt his claws tense.

But what could some old tramp do with four cops guarding the little girl? Still he waited, nervous and alert, until, ten minutes later, Eleanor Sand escorted the ragged, smelly old man into Max's office.

The old fellow entered hesitantly, Eleanor walking behind him. He smelled so ripe and looked so rough that Joe wanted to rise up defensively in front of the child. Instead he slipped off the couch, sensibly out of the way. These officers wanted the little girl's reaction, not that of a cat; and they wanted the tramp's first reaction to her, without distraction. And Joe sat down quietly beside the couch, unobtrusive but ready to leap and defend her.

From the floor beside Dallas's chair, Joe studied the old guy. He sure as hell could use a bath. His wrinkled old clothes were worn-out and dirty, his long gray hair tied in a ponytail, his head bald on top and sunburned. Wrinkled cheeks with an inch of stubble. And the smell of unwashed body and clothes was overlaid with the acrid stink of wood smoke as if from innumerable campfires.

On any cold morning Joe could see, from the treetops and highest roofs of the village, smoke rising down along the Molena River where homeless men slept, building up their campfires to get warm and to make coffee.

Well, the old guy had his coffee this morning. He was carrying a full Styrofoam cup that Eleanor must have picked up in the squad room.

He wore no shoes. They would be in the sealed bag that Eleanor had probably dropped off in the evidence room. Padding onto the Persian rug in bare feet, he looked warily at Dallas and the chief and then his eyes widened in surprise at the child on the couch. Everyone was still, watching the two of them.

The child looked at him without interest. Not frightened, not at all alarmed. Her only reaction was a wrinkled nose, from the smell of the old man. He looked at her, caught sight of Joe, and scowled around at the four officers.

"Didn't expect to see no kid in a police station. Sure didn't expect cops to keep no cat—well, hell, didn't expect to see no Christmas tree neither, out there in the entry."

"You know the girl?" Eleanor said softly.

He shook his head. "Never seen her." He looked at Eleanor with the beginnings of alarm, and backed away a step. "How would I know her? Why would I know her? I ain't done nothing, I never laid eyes on the kid."

"Just asking," Eleanor said quietly. "Where did you get the shoes?"

"Told you. Dumpster, couple miles out, on the highway. By that tourist café out there."

"That's what you told me. What else did you take from the Dumpster?"

Joe expected, knowing Eleanor, that she had already sent an officer back to search the Dumpster for anything suspicious, anything with visible blood.

"That empty billfold is all else I found," the old man said testily. "Don't know what good a billfold does me, ain't got nothing to put in it. I thought maybe to sell it."

Dallas rose, pushed Joe Grey gently aside, and motioned the old guy to sit down. He filled up the old man's coffee cup from the pot on the credenza, and then settled on the couch so the child was between him and Davis. Sand stood leaning in the doorway. Joe, anticipating an informative interrogation, slipped back under the credenza.

The old man, very likely imbuing the leather chair with

a permanent stink, looked at Dallas and Eleanor, and raised a bushy eyebrow. "You worried about that kid?"

No one answered.

"I might know something about kids—not her, exactly. Other kids—guess she might be one of 'em."

The officers waited, silently alert.

"Something that might be . . . of interest, as you like to say."

"Go on," Max said.

"Mighty cold morning," the old fellow said. "Long time since I've had a good hot breakfast." He watched without expression as Dallas slipped a twenty from his pocket, added a ten, and handed it over. The old guy sighed. "Might be pretty valuable information."

Dallas fished out another ten and passed it across. "That's it. Let's hear it."

"That orphans' school up toward the hills? That one that movie star owned?"

"The Patty Rose School," Dallas said.

"Big tan mansion with these brown timbers crisscrossing the walls?"

"We know the place," Max said.

"Guy watching them kids up there, I seen him twice standing in the woods peeking out. I, ah . . . got me a little shelter place up there. Place I can go sometimes, out of the storm. Rain coming bad, I go up there."

"Why weren't you there last night?" Dallas said.

"Came up the highway last night, headed right into the village to get me something to eat. I don't go there much, they watch that place. All locked up, but they watch it. Last night, found me a bit of overhang to sleep under." He looked hard at Dallas. "I wouldn't want to lose my good shelter, up there. Winter ain't over yet. That wind and rain, fellow could die of pneumonia."

"That stone building?" Max said.

The old man nodded.

"We'll see no one runs you off, at least for a while—if the school finds nothing wrong. No fires inside there. Understand?" Again, the old man nodded. "Can you describe this man?" Max said. "Tell us when and where you saw him?"

"Up at the school, like I said. Across the street in them woods, watching the front. And then the other time at the side, near the old stone house. Watching the play yard. Kids outside both times. Watching them orphan kids."

"What did he look like?" Eleanor prompted.

"Couldn't see much, him turned away. Skinny. Skinny head. Big ears. Short hair and them big ears sticking out."

"And he was watching the children?" Dallas said. "For how long? What did he do while he was watching them?"

"Long time, maybe half an hour or better. First time, just stood there looking and done nothing much. Stood kinda limp, hands down on his crotch. Next time, he had a camera, taking pictures. Long thing on the front of the camera like a telescope, taking pictures of them kids."

"When was this?" Max said.

"Maybe . . . over a week. Maybe two weeks. Just after one of them bad storms—the storm before last, I think. Cold. Sure looked nice and warm in that big school, firelight through the windows and all them colored lights on that big Christmas tree, and the smells . . . Smell of baking, of gingerbread and spices," the old man said longingly.

Joe watched the old fellow for a moment with a keen

sense of camaraderie. *Homeless men,* the tomcat thought uneasily, *like homeless cats, out in the storm without shelter.* He might hassle Clyde unmercifully over the quality of his meals and his own shelter, but in truth Joe was mighty thankful for his home. His kittenhood, trying to survive alone in San Francisco's alleys, had been no picnic—he still didn't like the garbage stink of Dumpsters.

Joe remained at the PD until the old man ran out of things to tell the officers, until Eleanor put the old fellow back in her squad car, to drop him at the hole-in-the-wall café where he wanted to have breakfast.

She told Max she'd pay the restaurant bill for him before she left. Joe thought the old man wasn't a drinker, at least he hadn't smelled of booze, but Max wanted to be sure he ate, and didn't slip out again to buy wine. Strange old man, Joe thought. Somehow a cut above most homeless, some of whom would kill a man just for the thrill.

Joe watched Juana gather up the child to take her to the seniors' house, where McFarland would meet them; and the tomcat left the station wondering where Dulcie had gotten to and thinking about a little snack in the alley behind Jolly's Deli—a gourmet experience that was, always, a far cry from anything remotely connected to Dumpsters.

10

CORA LEE FRENCH had been up since well before daylight on this cold winter morning. She had always been an early riser; her housemates teased her that she wanted the newspaper on the doorstep when her bare feet first swung out of bed. But this morning, even after she'd showered and dressed and put her breakfast on the table, the paper still wasn't at the front door.

Over a solitary breakfast of instant oatmeal, and then three Christmas cookies with her last cup of coffee, she had, out of desperation, read yesterday's classified section. Breakfast didn't taste right without something to read, and by the time she'd finished eating, she knew more than she wanted about how hard it was to get skilled help, how high real-estate prices and rents were climbing, and how many small animals were coldly given away to strangers, via the want ads, as casually as one would donate one's unwanted clothes. She left the house wondering what had happened to the sober responsibility that had infused the training of her own generation.

Getting old, she thought, amused at herself. *Old and cranky.*

The interior of her car was bone-chilling cold, the wet windshield soon fogged over. Waiting, with the wipers swinging, for the engine to warm the interior and clear the glass, she glanced at her shopping list, which included half a dozen last-minute Christmas errands she'd put off in deference to choir rehearsals; then she headed down the hill to the village, the oaks and pines dripping, the dropping street and the rooftops below her shining from the rain.

The grocery would be open, but she'd have to wait for the shops, even with their earlier holiday schedules. *Banker's* hours, she thought, and laughed at herself again because she wanted all the stores to open up at dawn—she couldn't help it if she was a morning person.

Though when she was doing a play or concert, like the upcoming Christmas pageant, she would be a night person, too, for a while, enjoying afternoon naps when necessary to provide sufficient sleep. You can sleep when you're dead, Cora Lee believed. That was one of Donnie's favorite sayings. Even when they were kids, he'd said that, quoting his own father. Now, with Donnie's reemergence into her life, Cora Lee was interested to note that they both still used that expression.

Happy-go-lucky Donnie French. He'd been the closest thing to a brother she'd had. Inseparable playmates when they were small, blue-eyed, golden-haired Donnie, and her own dusky, black-haired coloring caused folks, even on New Orleans's streets, to turn and stare at them. Donnie, suddenly back in her life. What a wonderful Christmas present for them both.

As she left her car, heading into the market, the air was filled with the scent of pine from the cut trees stacked outside the door. Red and green decorations hung within, festooning the tops of the shelves beneath gold garlands. The store was filled with popular Christmas tunes and with the spicy smells from the bakery. This time of year she missed having family and children of her own. Her husband dead for so many years, and they'd never had children. But now she had family again, real family, besides her housemates and her close friends.

She and Donnie had been a pair when they were kids, Cora Lee the dusky tomboy, Donnie the sweetly smiling blond charmer—but Donnie was always the bolder and more adventurous, the wilder troublemaker. A pair of scoundrels. Well, they'd never gotten into serious trouble, just pranks and dares, and foolish acts of poor judgment. And Donnie, despite his sometimes wild and defiant ways, had been in some respects the more even-tempered.

He had been the methodical planner when he set his mind to it, when they had something to gain. While she had swung crazily with her overwhelming moods, between soaring joy often generated by the jazz music that surrounded them on New Orleans's streets and a deep sadness generated by her mother's own sadness—at their poverty and then at her father's senseless death from stray gunfire.

Even as a child, Cora Lee had known instinctively that she would have to make her own happiness as she grew older, that she would have to learn how to lift herself out of the kind of sad days that her mother experienced. She hadn't known, then, the word "bipolar" or the other fancy terms. But she had understood her mother as best a child can, and she had vowed never to fall into the kind of mourning to which her mother had succumbed.

She had vowed that *she* would be strong enough to lift herself out of sadness. And always, she had refused to call those dark moods depression. She still hated that overused, catchall word that was used to describe so many different situations.

As a child, she'd only known that she would be on her own far too soon, and that no one else would, or could, teach her the survival skills and resiliency she'd need. That only she could teach herself how to cope. How to solve life's problems. Maybe she'd learned by watching her inept mother—learned that you always had a choice of solutions to a problem. You did, she had known even then, if your thinking was open enough and creative enough to ask all the right questions, and to choose the best answers. It made Cora Lee incredibly sad that her mother had never learned how to do that.

Now, as she finished her shopping and left the market, wheeling her loaded cart, she paused beside the newsstand, the headline of the Molena Point *Gazette* catching her eye. So that was what the sirens were about, last night.

COPS CONVERGE ON PLAZA CHRISTMAS TREE
POSSIBLE MURDER? NO BODY FOUND

She scanned as much of the article as she could see above the fold. She was damned if she'd buy a paper; they paid for newspaper delivery. It was terrible to think of a murder at Christmastime. The circumstances sickened her—to kill or wound a man beneath a Christmas tree. She frowned, reading the strange details. Blood, but no body. Maybe the victim had been injured, but had gotten away. Except, the paper said, there had been a witness; someone had seen a body.

But could that be a hoax? A false report? Maybe the blood wasn't that of a person at all. Animal blood? That thought didn't comfort her.

The police wouldn't have had any lab information last night, when the paper went to press. Maybe . . . A hundred conjectures ran through Cora Lee's mind, and with them, the coldness. Hoax or not, this was ugly. Death, violence, the defiling of Christmas. Ugly, when there should be only love.

She was loading her groceries in the trunk when a squad car pulled into the parking slot next to her, and Juana Davis gave her a yawning "good morning."

"You've been up all night," Cora Lee said.

Juana nodded. "Most of it."

Cora Lee looked at the little girl huddled in a blanket, in the front seat next to the detective, crowded up next to the complicated console, as close to Juana as she could get. A little girl with eyes darker even than Juana's eyes, black as obsidian in such a thin, white little face. Long, ebony hair framing her milk-white skin. And such a sad expression that Cora Lee longed to pick her up and hold and comfort her. The child's eyes were filled with fear, as she pushed closer to the detective—eyes as wary as those of a wild creature.

"There was an incident last night in the plaza," Juana said, scanning the half-empty parking lot.

"I saw the paper."

"The paper doesn't mention this little girl, but she was part of it. We found her hiding in the plaza, pretty scared.

Blood on her clothes. The call came in from an unidentified informant who saw the child at the scene with the body. Max kept that out of the paper."

Cora Lee nodded. The child had said no word, she only watched Juana. Juana's eyes told Cora Lee that the officer hated talking about the little girl in front of her, as if she weren't there, told her it couldn't be helped.

Cora Lee wondered if the child did not speak English. Or if, perhaps, she couldn't speak at all.

"We have no identification, no idea who the man was, or who this young lady is. She came home with me last night." Juana waited a moment, watching Cora Lee. "We don't want to take her to Children's Services."

"Of course you don't." Cora Lee had heard plenty about situations with various child welfare departments from Lori Reed. She looked at Juana's dark eyes, the detective's sternness gone now. "You need somewhere for her to stay."

"We're not sure, yet." Juana held the child's small white hand. "Maybe for a few hours. There'd be an officer with her."

"We have plenty of room for both of them to stay. Susan's in San Francisco for the holidays. Mavity and Gabrielle and Lori and I are just rattling around, and my cousin Donnie is downstairs. We'd love to have any officer you send, two if you like. We'd really love to have another child for the holidays."

"Overnight might not be safe, for any of you. But for a few hours, so she could spend some time with Lori and Dillon, and play with the dogs. She loves animals—cats, at least. When we found her last night she was snuggled right up to Clyde's cat and the Greenlaw cat."

"The dogs would be thrilled to have someone to play with. Lori and Dillon have been so busy on their contest entry they've had no time to roughhouse with them. And of course the girls would love to have her." Leaning down, Cora Lee looked in at the child. "I think our guest might be the first one to test out the new playhouse." She smiled. "Would you like that?" Then, to Juana, "Would you like to come on up now? I'm headed home."

"On my way," Juana said. "If you're sure you're comfortable with this."

"I'm sure," Cora Lee said. "Our dogs are good protection, they can be fierce, when someone threatens." She looked at the child again. "And yesterday evening, Mavity baked pumpkin pies."

Juana laughed. "You know *my* weakness. I won't follow you, I'll take another route."

Cora Lee, swinging into her car and heading up the hills, glanced in her rearview mirror to see Juana's white Chevy leave the parking lot, turning in the opposite direction. But when she pulled into her drive, the squad car was already there. Down the street two neighbors were out in their yards, looking, making Cora Lee smile. Every time a squad car showed up at their house, she'd see a neighbor or two peering out, and that highly amused Cora Lee and her housemates—though most of the neighbors knew of their friendships within the department, there had been one time that was serious police business, and some folks preferred to remember the unpleasantness. That case, Cora Lee thought uneasily, had also involved children.

But nothing would happen to this little girl, not with police protection, and two big dogs on guard. Parking in the drive, she made two trips into the house loaded down with grocery bags while Juana sat in the squad car talking in a one-sided conversation with the little girl, until at last the child seemed willing to get out. Across the yard, Donnie was at work on the garden wall he was building along the side of the property.

It seemed a very cold day to be mixing mortar, but maybe that didn't matter. As Juana helped the child out of the car, Donnie turned away, heading for his truck. Cora Lee went on into the kitchen to put away her groceries, leaving the door unlocked behind her.

Soon Juana and the little girl came into the kitchen hand in hand, Juana letting the child take her time. Cora Lee thought the dogs were in their fenced yard, in the back, but when the big poodle and the Dalmatian heard a strange voice, they came racing through the house. The child shrank against Juana, and Juana lifted her up, to make her feel more secure. Cora Lee grabbed the dogs' collars, telling them to sit and stay.

It had taken several months for Susan Brittain's three housemates to learn to handle the dogs properly and insist they respond to commands, but the training sessions had paid off. As the dogs sat obediently, avidly watching the child, the little girl looked down at them, big-eyed—and the next minute she struggled out of Juana's arms, straight to them; Lamb, the big chocolate poodle, surged forward, and then the child and dogs were all over one another, the dogs licking and whining, the frail, silent little girl hugging and hugging them.

Juana stood close over her for a moment, in case of trouble, but then she looked up at Cora Lee, grinning, and backed off—and the women watched with wonder the child's transformation from a terrified and shrinking little being to a vibrant and lively creature. Still silent, but very much more alive.

"She needs animals, all right," Cora Lee said.

"She only trusts the animals."

The two women sat at the kitchen table with coffee and pumpkin pie. There was milk and pie for the child, but the little girl wouldn't sit down, she wanted only to play with the dogs.

"That was your cousin who just pulled out?"

"Donnie, yes. He's been working on the garden, building plastered garden walls, the way we've planned for so long. He laid the new stone walks, too."

"It's looking great, Cora Lee. You've all worked hard on this house—you've made a new, beautiful home from a place too long neglected. And the Christmas decorations, your huge tree, and the red bells and wreathes . . ."

"Donnie helped a lot—we'd never have dared such a big tree without him. It's been a boon for us, to suddenly have him here, he's done so much to the house. I didn't know he had those skills. He's been doing some jobs around the village, too, and people have already started to seek him out. He just finished a renovation for Sicily Aronson's gallery."

Davis nodded. "Opening it up to the café and bookstore. Makes all three more inviting."

"I wanted to pay him for our work, but he refused. Said if we wouldn't let him pay rent and board, he'd work for his keep." Cora Lee smiled. "He said, 'If you ladies keep feeding me so elegantly, I have to do something or you'll be rolling me down the driveway.'"

"Sounds like a nice guy. I saw him in the village the other day; Dallas pointed him out. He was talking with a middle-aged couple—tall, dark-haired woman, strangers. He'll have all the work he wants, as difficult as it is to get skilled craftsmen."

"What did happen last night, Juana? You're pretty concerned about the little girl, if Max didn't tell the reporters about her."

"I'd already gotten her away from the scene when the reporters showed up." Juana described the events of the previous night. And the anonymous phone call, like tips they had received in so many other cases, this one telling them about the child.

"The caller said she was clinging to the dead man," Juana said. "When Brennan found her, she was huddled in that little pump house behind the dog fountain, and those two cats were with her, Clyde's big tomcat, and the Greenlaw's cat cuddled right up to her."

"I guess even that macho tomcat might have a soft spot," Cora Lee said, smiling.

"She was afraid of Brennan, shrinking away from him. That's when he called for a woman. She likes Jimmie McFarland, though, maybe because he's quieter. She didn't shy away from the chief and Dallas, either. I think it was just last night, so soon after the shooting, and Brennan's voice is loud and gruff."

"Can't she *stay* here with us?" Cora Lee said. "We're all women in the house, except for Donnie, and he's a gentle soul. She and the guard could sleep in my room, with the dogs in there, and in the daytime she could hang out with Lori and Dillon while they work on the playhouse."

Though there was two years' difference in age between Lori Reed and Dillon Thurwell, the girls were fast friends, in part because both rode together, both keeping their horses up at Chief Harper's ranch. Lori Reed, though she was the younger, had helped Dillon in school. Lori was intently committed to "real history," as she called it, and to English, and her eagerness had rubbed off on Dillon, an interest that had changed Dillon a great deal.

Juana looked out to the living room, where the big poodle and Dalmatian and the little girl had curled up in a tangle among the floor cushions, the dogs panting.

"There's no name tag on her clothes?" Cora Lee said. "No labels you can trace?"

"Kmart labels, could have come from anywhere. I bathed her last night, bagged her clothes for evidence, put her in one of my T-shirts. This morning Officer Kane brought me some clothes, his boy's about the same size."

"There've been no California missing reports," Juana said, "for an adult or for a child of her description. Nothing so far on the West Coast, and nothing yet in the national reports. Taking the word of our informant that there was a dead man, we're guessing he was a tourist."

"You think she was kidnapped?"

"It seems unlikely if, as the caller said, the child was snuggled up to him. It's possible that an estranged father could have taken her, and run, against a court order. We have no report to that effect, yet, where the child fits that description."

Cora Lee shivered. The two women looked at each other, both touched by the horror that the child must have experienced, if she was in that man's arms when he was shot.

Though the child seemed busy with the dogs, they kept their voices low. She might not speak, but it was obvious that her hearing was just fine, turning when a dog huffed, glancing up at the women if they laughed. When they finished their pie and coffee, Cora Lee called the dogs, Juana wrapped up the child's pie for later, and they headed out the front door, across the front deck, and down the four steps to the big garage, where Lori and Dillon were building their contest entry.

11

PASSING THE WIDE garage doors, Cora Lee and Juana stopped to wait as Jimmie McFarland pulled in, then the three adults moved, with the child between them, around the side to the pedestrian door accompanied by the two gamboling dogs. They could hear, from within, the buzz of the electric screwdriver and the rhythmic pounding of a hammer, and the two girls bantering and laughing. Pushing the door open, Cora Lee turned, looking across the yard for Donnie, but his truck was still gone. His wheelbarrow and bags of cement and tools were scattered where he'd been working, which wasn't usual for him. But he'd been at work since dawn, and was obviously coming right back—he must have run out of something unexpectedly.

When she and her housemates had bought the house, the yard was a mass of weeds. But once they'd moved into the neglected dwelling, most of their work had at first gone into the interior, painting and repairing, decorating the communal living area in a way to bring their divergent pieces of furniture and tastes together. Each of them had designed her own room as she pleased. Blond Gabrielle, who wasn't much for yard work and who didn't like to get her hands dirty, was a fine seamstress and had made all the curtains and draperies. That, in Cora Lee's opinion, took far more patience and skill than wielding a garden trowel or a paintbrush. Holding the child's hand, she led her inside. "You have an audience," she called, "a special visitor."

Along the walls of the three-car garage, Cora Lee and the girls had constructed a sturdy cutting table and a paint table out of sawhorses and plywood. The permanent workbench offered ample room for hardware, nails and hinges, and the small power tools. Ordinarily the garage was Cora Lee's furniture studio, and she had orders nearly three years ahead. But until later this week, when the girls would deliver the playhouse to the contest grounds, this space belonged to them. The playhouse nearly filled it.

There were twenty-three entries, most of them produced by adult teams and professional builders. Once the winner was chosen, all the other entries would be auctioned off. Given the popularity of custom playhouses along the coast, Cora Lee had no doubt they'd all sell at a profit—in her mind, it was a win/win situation; but the girls were set on getting the first prize.

Above them, Dillon Thurwell was perched atop a six-foot-high platform of joists, the red-haired fourteen-year-old carefully balancing as she screwed lightweight cedar boards onto the raised deck—the playhouse, which was nearly finished, could be taken apart in three sections to be transported by truck. If the girls' dream came true, their entry would win twenty thousand dollars to be split between them, to add to their college funds.

Dillon's parents had started her college fund long ago,

and added to it regularly; but Dillon's mother was a real estate agent, and her father a college professor. Lori, on the other hand, with her father in prison and her mother dead, had little more than odd jobs and her own ingenuity with which to amass the huge sum she would need for her education. And Lori Reed was dead set on college, no matter what it took. Lori had lived with the four women since her father was sent to San Quentin to serve a sentence for second-degree murder, a crime that everyone who knew him felt they might have committed themselves, considering that the man he killed had brutally murdered innocent and very bright children, and had intended to kill Lori.

The little child beside Cora Lee stared up round-eyed at the bright, multicolored playhouse; it was a confection of brilliant colors, of closed and open spaces and ascending levels, and of wild cutouts for air and light, and all the surfaces were painted in amazing patterns. There were three ways to climb to the top—a knotted rope, a ladder, and a vertical bar with protruding rungs. Standing on the tumbling mats that were scattered underneath, to make the low work easier, the little girl stared up at the wonderful confection, her eyes wide, her mouth curving in the tiniest hint of a smile.

"Paint dry?" Cora Lee asked, keeping the dogs back, worrying that they would smear Lori's careful work.

"It's dry," Lori said. Kneeling beside the front of the playhouse, she was nailing on freshly painted, bright persimmon trim. The younger girl had long, straight brown hair, light brown eyes that could look achingly hurt and needy— or could look as secretive and feisty as could Dillon's impish glance. But Lori's attention was on the little girl, clearly seeing the child's shy fear. Lori put out her hand.

The little girl came to her slowly at first, but then with trust. This was not an adult bid for contact, this was child to child, as nonthreatening as the earlier, guileless greetings of Joe Grey and Kit, and then of the two dogs. Above them, Dillon remained still, her red hair catching a shaft of light through the garage windows, her cropped, flyaway locks gleaming like flame.

At the sound of a car pausing on the street, Davis stepped to the door, but then it moved on by, and she returned to watch the child explore the bottom part of the playhouse then scramble up the ladder. Forgetting the adults, the little girl disappeared into the three rooms and out again in a little dance across the various decks, so losing herself to wonder that Davis and Cora Lee beamed at each other—and Davis dared to think, now, that the child might find her voice, and be able to speak to her.

So THIS WAS where they meant to hide the kid, at least part of the time. This, and that detective's condo. What a laugh—those women had no clue that he knew all about this place. Kuda watched the woman cop lift the kid out of the car, and he smiled. The kid was a sitting duck.

He waited warily but with patience while they were in the house. Watched the second, lone uniform pull in. So the kid had two guards. Oh, this was too good. This was security?

And still he waited.

Kid hadn't said a word, so far, he could bet on that. Hadn't, or the cops wouldn't be so relaxed. They were just normally watchful, but not sweating it. No, the kid hadn't told anything she saw, and he didn't think she would—and how much could they believe, from a kid? Kid was no kind of witness.

So why mess up a good thing? Kill her, and they'd be after him for sure. No, for now, let sleeping dogs lie. So far he was home free. Keep it that way. Body disposed of, and only some passing witness's word there ever was a body. How far would the cops go to investigate hearsay? This was Christmas, the stores had to be full of enough shoplifters and petty thieves to keep the street patrol plenty busy.

No, he thought, leave the kid for now. Leave her, and he'd be able to slide right out of this berg, once he got what he came for. Disappear so the law would never find him.

He'd disposed of the clothes and duffels pretty well, scattering them in several places. He hadn't wanted to leave stuff in the car that might be traced, even though he'd checked the labels. All were generic. Kmart. Penney's. Wal-Mart.

He'd dumped the empty billfold, after wiping it down, in a bin out on the highway at the edge of the state park as he pedaled back toward the village in the predawn dark. Had left his own shoes there, too. Waffle soles, that had been foolish. Was afraid they'd left prints. Best place to dump them was the highway, where some homeless man walking that stretch might pick through, might put them on. And then, who'd ever find them?

He'd worried about the two duffels, even empty. Hadn't wanted to leave them in the garage, and for some reason didn't want to leave them in the car. He'd decided to bring them with him, tied on the back of the bike, riding along like a homeless person, himself.

He'd emptied some of the pants and shirts down into the bottom of the highway Dumpster, too, and pulled debris over them. Rolled the bigger, emptied duffel in mud and stuffed it down in there. But the kid's stuff had worried him. Pretty little girl's clothes, too new to throw away. That'd attract attention.

Coming into the village, he'd cruised the streets, passing three charity shops, all closed, of course, then circled back when he saw a car stop before one of them. And luck had smiled on him, big-time.

Woman got out, hauled out four big black plastic garbage bags, tucked them up against the shop's door with a note pinned on. Got back in her car, all dressed up for work, sleek black suit and high heels, and took off.

It had taken him only a minute to tuck the kid's clothes down inside. He used three of the bags, a few garments in each, the small cloth duffel rolled up and stuffed in, too, and that ragged doll—had to get rid of the doll. Sealed them up again with the twisties, swung on his bike, and took off, wanting to hide the bike or get rid of it. Thinking again that the cops weren't going to spend a lot of time digging through charity shops—not this time of year, not with organized crime working the shoplifting rackets so they were more than just random events. How thin could that small department spread its uniforms? They only had two detectives, only two that he'd seen.

Going over his routine of last night, he watched the tall house, watched the kid come out with the two women, heading around the garage. He watched the lone uniform pull up and join them, and then he turned away, and headed on down into the village.

12

THE THREE CATS crouched shivering on the roof of the Molena Point Little Theater, able only to listen to the music of *The Nutcracker*; on this cold night they could not enjoy the dancing and costumes and sets. Ordinarily, they would have slipped inside at the last minute behind the crowding audience, but with the icy wind blowing in through the open doors, those doors had been closed too quickly.

But even though they were shut out in the cold, the music filled their heads, dancing up through the roof. Kit's fluffy tail twitched in delighted rhythm to the lilting cadences, to visions of Marie and Clara and the Nutcracker and the King of the Mice, to all the convoluted and interwoven scenes of the tale so sharply brought to life in the bright music. And now, as the theater let out, they peered down at the happy, departing crowd, looking for their friends.

Charlie Harper and Dorothy Street were the first of their party to emerge, presumably leaving their companions in the lobby lost in scattered conversations. As the two women headed up the street, the cats followed, padding across the icy roofs and across slippery oak branches and more roofs, making straight for the Patio Café. There the cats paused on the clay tiles looking down to the restaurant's outdoor terrace as Charlie and Dorothy were seated. In the center of the terrace, a fire burned in the round brick fire pit, sending up welcome heat to warm their fur and paws and their cold noses. The patio, decorated with red swags along the eaves and huge pots of poinsettias, was crowded with late, cheerful diners, most of them talking about the ballet.

"Charlie had a ticket for Max," Joe said. "I don't think he's into ballet, he opted out. Said because of the murder."

"If not for the murder, he'd have gone," Dulcie said shortly. "He'd go almost anywhere, to enjoy an evening out with Charlie." She looked hard at Joe. "You like *The Nutcracker*, you just don't want to admit it." But then she turned her attention to Charlie and Dorothy.

The two women had been seated at a big round table beside the fire pit; though they were almost directly beneath the cats, their low conversation was hard to hear among the rising tangle of voices. Only Charlie was aware of them on the roof above. She glanced up once as they basked in the warmth from the blaze; she watched them sniffing at the heady scents of broiled shrimp and lobster, and she raised an eyebrow, then looked away again, hiding her smile.

The brick patio was enclosed on two sides by the restaurant itself, the other two by a two-foot-high wall topped with the pots of poinsettias and bright red winter cyclamens separating the café from the sidewalk. The street beyond was busy with tourists and locals coming from the theater or enjoying last-minute, late-evening Christmas shopping. The whole village was festive tonight, the shop doors hung with wreaths, the overhanging oaks and pines strung with colored lights—and their friends looked festive, too. The cats seldom saw Charlie in anything but jeans. Tonight she wore a soft, metallic-gold tunic over slim black pants, her untamable, kinky red hair bound back with a heavy gold clip, and a thick, golden stole over her shoulders. Dorothy Street was sharply tailored, very handsome with her sleek, dark hair, and her winter tan from running the beach, her clean beauty set off by a black silk blazer over crisp white pants and white boots. She had let her dark hair grow long, and was wearing it in a braid wrapped smoothly around her head—a more serious, finished look than the short, wind-blown mop she'd sported when she worked for Patty Rose as the retired actress's assistant, an efficient young secretary who often went to work in jeans and sweatshirt and smelling of the sea. Now, as Patty's heir and new owner of the inn, and as trustee for the Patty Rose Home and School, she presented a far more businesslike demeanor. The cats weren't sure they liked her new look; but they supposed that status-conscious humans were impressed, and that that was good for business.

Dorothy was talking about a break-in at the Home, speaking so softly that over the noise of the other diners, the cats had to crouch low across the roof gutter to hear at all.

"Nothing was taken," Dorothy was saying. "There's nothing in there to take. Why would someone break into that old, empty studio? Not a stick of furniture, you can see through the windows that it's empty. But the front door was jimmied last night, fresh scars in the molding. Last week, after we found the back door open, we changed the locks. But the next morning, two of the boys came to tell me they'd found a window open, banging in the wind.

"I went over, found the lock broken, and called the department again. It's embarrassing to have to call them out for such a small thing, but . . . Whatever this is about, we need to find the cause before Ryan starts work. She'll have material and power tools stored in there."

Above, on the roof, the cats glanced at one another, wondering if that had been the work of the old tramp. On these cold nights, that old stone studio would be dry, all right, just as he'd said, a welcome retreat from rain and wind.

Charlie pushed back an escaped strand of red hair and gave the waiter a long, annoyed look where he lingered just beyond their table, coffeepot in hand. Charlie liked good service, but she didn't like overt attention.

"The old window locks were easy enough to break," Dorothy said. "Ryan says they were the original ones. That studio is nearly a hundred years old. She sent a carpenter over to replace them."

Dorothy sipped her coffee. "That, combined with whatever happened in the plaza last night, is giving me the fidgets. I keep thinking about our Christmas bazaar, in a just few days, about how vulnerable we are up there, how vulnerable the children could be.

"I've hired six more guards," she said softly, "besides the regular three."

"You really do expect trouble? But . . ."

"I don't know what to expect."

Charlie frowned. "You think there's some connection between the plaza murder and the break-ins?"

"I don't know, Charlie. But the two things at once . . . If we'd had only a simple break-in . . . But three times, without anything to steal. That's so strange."

"No possessions of Anna Stanhope's left forgotten? Maybe tucked away in a closet?"

"Nothing. The few paintings that were left locked up in there, all those years after she died, and a few books and papers, we'd already removed and stored safely. Her son had long ago sent most of her remaining work up to her gallery in the city."

"I understand that Anna was rather secretive, inclined to stash things away."

Dorothy smiled. "I really don't think there was anything left hidden. There's nowhere *to* hide anything in that studio. I think that's one of those stories that gets started—maybe John Stanhope started it, to boost the price of the studio when he sold it. I wouldn't put it past him."

John Stanhope, Anna's son, had built the big, newer mansion on the property some years after Anna died. The mansion badly dwarfed the small, stone studio where Anna had lived and worked. Later he'd sold the studio as a separate dwelling, but had retained most of the estate grounds with the new mansion. When actress Patty Rose bought the mansion, wanting to convert it to a children's home, the smaller house was not available. Then last year, after Patty died, the studio came on the market again, and Dorothy, representing the Patty Rose Trust, quickly bought it, thus reuniting the property. She meant to turn the historic studio into additional classrooms for the children, and she badly wanted to get started with the work right after the holidays.

"These break-ins made me feel so . . . not just vulnerable," Dorothy said, "but as if I've let Anna Stanhope down. She loved that old studio, she would not have liked this invasion. Her journal is full of entries about how happy she was there, and now I feel responsible that this has happened.

"But most of all, I'm worried for the children. I don't want . . . It's almost like a personal attack on the children themselves, that someone would break into the Home, where we've tried to make everything safe for them. Those kids . . ."

"Those orphan kids are like your own babies," Charlie said. "But—you don't think the intruder was some jealous village child, playing pranks?"

"That's possible, I suppose. Certainly none of our children would do that." Dorothy smoothed her dark hair. "Why do I keep trying to tie the break-ins to the murder in the plaza? Assuming there was a murder. How *could* there be a connection? Why do I keep thinking of that?"

Charlie couldn't answer.

"I don't mean to talk about things you aren't free to discuss."

"There isn't much to discuss—not until Max knows more about what happened there. Dorothy, I just don't have any answers."

"It isn't my nature to fly apart," Dorothy said. "I guess, after Patty was murdered last year, and the things that happened to her daughter and grandchild, that I'm overly nervous about our kids."

"You have a right to be anxious. But you have extra

guards in place, and you use an excellent agency. Have you talked with Max about . . ."

They looked up as Lucinda and Pedric Greenlaw along with Cora Lee French came in, crossing the terrace to join them. Cora Lee's cousin, Donnie, and her housemate, Gabrielle Row, came in behind them, holding hands like youngsters, the two so wrapped up in each other that the cats had to smile. *A Christmas romance*, Dulcie thought, purring. It pleased her when older people found that kind of happiness. She looked at Donnie's blond and white hair, and at Gabrielle's blond dyed hair that was very likely graying, too, under that elegant color. The two were so attentive to each other that they hardly seemed to know anyone else was present.

The Greenlaws sat down next to Charlie. Lucinda had pulled a warm cashmere stole close around her shoulders, over her silver-toned wool suit. The elderly Greenlaw couple was the tortoiseshell kit's human family, a tall pair of octogenarian newlyweds as spry and adventurous as folks half their age. Pedric looked handsome tonight in a pale cashmere sport coat, white shirt, and camel-toned tie and black slacks. The new arrivals had, as they entered the patio, also been talking about the Stanhope house, the subject having been brought to their attention by a large display in the theater lobby showing old photographs of Anna Stanhope's studio and giving some of Anna's background, as promotion for the Home's bazaar and auction on Sunday.

"Over eighty years ago," Cora Lee said, sitting down across from Charlie. "The village was really bohemian, then. So many famous names— Jack London, John Steinbeck, and a lot of lesser folk, all a close-knit group with

Anna Stanhope. She worked for years in that small stone studio, hidden back in the woods." Cora Lee's dusky Creole beauty was set off by a simple cream velvet suit. Blond, bejeweled Gabrielle was overdressed as usual in a long blue satin gown, too much bright jewelry, and a pale real fox wrap. Donnie looked handsome indeed in a cream-colored cashmere suit, pale blue shirt, and tie—perhaps a bit overdressed or citified for the village, but a man whom all the women on the terrace were glancing at with thinly concealed interest.

"Where's Lori?" Charlie asked Cora Lee. "She didn't want to come?"

"We left her and Dillon holed up with that . . ." Gabrielle began; she went quiet at Charlie's annoyed look and the faint shake of her head. Gabrielle looked surprised. Donnie hugged her closer, looking back at Charlie with sour disapproval, as if his ladylove could do or say no wrong.

". . . busy with their playhouse," Gabrielle finished, almost simpering. "I never saw two children work so long at anything. It's really quite unusual."

Everyone at the table knew that Gabrielle thought the playhouse was silly, that young girls should not undertake that kind of challenge against adult contenders. That two young girls could never complete such demanding carpentry work, that there was no way they could produce an acceptable construction, let alone win the huge prize they were hoping for. Gabrielle's criticism was a sharp bone of contention between her and Cora Lee, one that Cora Lee tried her best to hide in deference to Donnie's infatuation with her housemate.

Obviously, Charlie thought, Gabrielle had not bothered

to look at the nearly finished playhouse, had not wanted to see how wonderful it was, and how well constructed. Nor had she considered that Dillon had trained for some time as a carpenter's apprentice to Ryan Flannery. As Donnie tried to cheer Gabrielle, cajoling and flattering her, Charlie noticed her ring.

Reaching across the table, Charlie gently took Gabrielle's hand, holding it up so the large diamond on her third finger gleamed in the firelight. Everyone at their table stopped talking, then all talked at once congratulating them as Gabrielle and Donnie beamed. Gabrielle managed to blush, and Donnie's blue eyes were as bright and excited as the eyes of a boy. Across the table, Cora Lee smiled upon the happy couple like a proud parent.

"When did this happen?" Lucinda said. "When did you become officially engaged?"

"This afternoon," Gabrielle said softly. "Donnie . . . I . . . It was a surprise. I . . . I'm still shaken. And it looks like we might move up to the city, too."

"A job offer," Donnie said. "They called this afternoon. A large company. If it pans out, looks like I might work myself into a managerial position within a year."

They were still exclaiming and congratulating when the waiter brought additional menus and took drink orders, then turned away to linger, again, inside the door to the kitchen, keeping an eye on the tables. He returned with two additional menus as Clyde Damen and Ryan Flannery crossed the patio to join them.

Ryan looked beautiful tonight, her short dark hair windblown, her green eyes set off by a green velvet pullover, topping a slim black skirt, a green velvet shawl around her shoulders. The cats liked seeing their human friends dressed up; they were used to seeing Ryan and Charlie in comfortable jeans and work boots, Ryan because she was a builder, Charlie because she and Max kept horses up at their small ranch among the Molena Point hills.

And Clyde, who favored old worn jeans and ragged T-shirts, had made an effort, too. Joe Grey's housemate was turned out in a tan suede sport coat, a black turtleneck, and cream slacks, was newly shaved, and his dark hair freshly cut. As he held Ryan's chair, Dorothy looked up at Ryan questioningly.

"Nothing yet," Ryan said, sitting down. "We could be in our graves before we get this permit." As the project's contractor, Ryan was out of patience waiting for city and county permits and the final okay from the historical society. "The planning commission knows you want to have the classrooms ready by spring semester, they know you have four new teachers coming."

Dorothy nodded. "Without the new space, we'll be really crowded. Well, we'll make do—crowded doesn't really matter, if the kids are excited about what they're learning. Give them an intellectual challenge, show them how to run with it, and they're happy.

"They're looking forward to the new quarters, and to having a real fireplace in the big classroom, but they understand about the Historical Society—they know the old stone house is the only real monument left to Anna Stanhope."

Lucinda said, "Her studio in the woods must have been lovely then, before her son cut down so many trees and built that big ostentatious mansion—though in the long run, that turned into a blessing, as if it was always meant to be a children's home."

"Strange to think," Charlie said, "about the wild parties and unleashed sex and drugs that went on, when those things were far less common. And now the Stanhope house is a children's refuge from just that kind of ugliness."

"Those artists did more partying than work," Gabrielle said, fluffing her fur wrap. "They just played at being artists and writers."

"Not all of them," Cora Lee said. "Not Anna Stanhope, she was a serious painter. She must have managed, somehow, to protect her privacy and working time. She was very dedicated, and very fine. She left a huge legacy of work." Anna Stanhope's paintings appeared in many fine collections and were included in many art histories, the landscapes jewel rich in color, the essence of scenes they saw around them every day in the shifting California light.

"Haven't you ever wondered," Gabrielle said, "why her son boarded up the house all those years? I'm surprised the city let him."

"It was his property," Dorothy said. "He paid the taxes. He wasn't breaking any law if he wanted to close it up. And he did come down from San Francisco sometimes, to check on its condition."

"To clear out her paintings," Gabrielle said. "Sold them a few at a time, in that gallery in the city."

"Maybe he didn't want to flood the market," Cora Lee suggested. "They've increased so much in value." Cora Lee's own background as an artist lent her a quiet authority that silenced her housemate. Donnie, caught between his cousin and his fiancée, kept out of it, silently sipping his drink. Dulcie was watching him, frowning, when her own housemate appeared hurrying up the street to join them.

Earlier in the evening, Dulcie had lain on the bed as Wilma dressed, and the tabby had pawed through Wilma's jewelry box helping to choose which barrette Wilma would wear. They had agreed on an onyx-and-silver creation to clip back Wilma's long silver hair and to complement her soft red jacket and long paisley skirt. Wilma Getz might be in her early sixties, but her tall figure was as slim as a girl's. She walked several miles a day, and since she'd been kidnapped last summer, she worked out more often at the village gym, intending to be in far better shape if another of her old ex-parolees surprised her.

Dulcie watched her swing in through the patio's little iron gate, cross between the crowded tables, and pull out the last chair at the big round table, sneaking a look underneath to see if the cats were there waiting for a bit of supper. Not seeing them, she glanced up to the roof, and hid a little smile.

When the waiter came for their orders, Wilma chose a shrimp bisque and, for dessert, a rich crème brûlé. Both were among Dulcie's favorites. When Wilma ordered two of each, one meal for herself and one to go, Dulcie, above on the roof, hungrily licked her whiskers.

As Wilma sipped her coffee, Ryan looked across the table to the Greenlaws. "When do you want to go over plans for your remodel? I can come by any day, but better if it rains. We're just starting a new house, so it's all outside work, and rain will give me some free time. We've finished both the current remodels—both couples wanted to be settled back in by Christmas." She grinned. "They'll have to hustle. We did the best we could, but Christmas is almost on us."

"What about now, tonight?" Lucinda said eagerly, glancing at Pedric.

The old man nodded. "Sooner the better. But if you're starting a new job . . ."

"Just for a look?" Lucinda said. "A general idea, maybe enough to give us a rough estimate?"

"Enough," Ryan said, "so I can draw a rough plan of the space and some tentative sketches, and can suggest some materials you could look at. The only thing that will hold me up is when we get the permit for the children's home. Then it will be all-out, until it's finished."

"I still say," Gabrielle said darkly, "it's the public-school children who were allowed to transfer up there that has the city so riled and reluctant to issue the permit. I don't see why those children did that."

"Because the school is better," Wilma said shortly. "Because those kids were bored out of their minds in public school."

Gabrielle huffed impatiently, as if Wilma knew nothing about children or about learning.

The small exodus of students from public school up to Patty Rose had created a deep anger among some of the village teachers. Both Lori and Dillon had transferred, both girls rebelling when Lori was told by her principal that she was not allowed to attend the school of her choice. Lori Reed did not take well to being told that she could not do what she longed to do—not without a logical reason, not by strangers, certainly not by a county bureaucracy. "What do they mean, I *can't*?" Lori had ranted. "When did this country turn into a slave state!" The girls said that a few teachers were so dull, they put everyone to sleep, that they weren't learning anything, that all they did was follow workbooks like robots, so why shouldn't they turn to a school that challenged them? Dillon's parents and Cora Lee had fought the school officials for months to make that happen.

"Our remodel," Lucinda was telling Ryan, "is pretty straightforward, if we can turn the half bath into a small kitchen. And it's all inside work, so maybe you could work on rainy days when you can't be on the new job."

"The way the weather's been," Ryan said, "an inside job for rainy days will be a big help, if you can live with the delays. It could be a very long delay, for the Orphans' Home, and that could be frustrating for you." That was the biggest complaint Ryan heard about contractors, that they would juggle several jobs at once, pull men back and forth, and prolong all the work. Some clients were demanding penalty agreements from contractors, a hundred dollars a day off the bill, for not meeting the finish date.

"We don't mind delays," Pedric said. "One thing, though. First day you have free, could you take a look at the plumbing? There seems to be a leak somewhere. Sometimes for short periods we hear water running, but then it stops. We've checked inside and out, but we can find nothing."

"Could you come tonight?" Lucinda said again, eagerly.

Ryan glanced at her watch. "It isn't too late for you?"

"Ordinarily, it might be," Lucinda said, laughing. "I think, tonight, we're too energized, our heads too full of the ballet, to go right to bed, even to read. And too full of ideas for the apartment."

Ryan nodded, glancing at Clyde. "We'll meet you up at your place, then."

Above them on the roof, the kit moved nervously. She wanted to be home before Ryan got there and they all went downstairs to those empty rooms.

Kit, too, had puzzled over the strange behavior of the water pipes. And prowling the backyard, she'd thought she caught the scent of a stranger. Though sometimes the neighbors crossed there, coming down from the street above rather than going around the block, so she couldn't be sure—but now suddenly as she thought about her old folks and Ryan and Clyde entering those dark rooms, a shock of unease gripped the tortoiseshell cat. And her fear sent her spinning away toward home, racing across the rooftops, wanting to have a look before her humans entered that empty downstairs apartment.

13

Racing home over night-dark rooftops, Kit crossed high above the many-colored Christmas lights of the shop-lined streets, leaping from peak to peak and then spanning above the shadowed streets on spreading oak limbs. At last on her own block she scrambled down a pine trunk into a dense cover of dry needles, and raced through a tangle of gardens toward home, stopping only when her own house towered high over her, its plaster walls pale in the night, its two stories of decks looking down over the village. From the front, the Greenlaw house faced the end of a quiet cul-de-sac, and appeared to be one story. But here at the back, on the downhill side, the windows and decks of the main floor and the daylight basement looked out over the lower street to the far, tree-shaded cottages and shops of the village.

Lucinda and Pedric had bought the house for its view of the village and the open green hills beyond. The real-estate ads had said it provided, as well, "a glimpse of the sea," but Pedric said you'd throw your neck out trying to see the ocean from that vantage. Their plan was to convert the downstairs rooms to a separate apartment so that at some future time they could have a live-in, personal caretaker. But one of the biggest selling points was not a part of the house at all.

On the west side of the house stood five old twisted oak trees, and tucked among their highest branches, half hidden, was a sturdy tree house. It had been built for the previous owner's children—and it was now Kit's own. A private retreat that Kit considered nearly as elegant as Joe Grey's rooftop tower, a shingled aerie that she could reach from the dining-room window across a thick oak branch or, of course, up the trunk from the garden below. The day they moved in, Pedric had installed a cat door in the bottom of the dining-room window.

Tonight the old couple had left lights on in the dining and living rooms, and Kit, approaching the warmth and smells of home, began to purr a happy rumble—but suddenly she froze, listening.

That sound. The pipes again. Water running in the house. And this time, in the night's silence, without competing neighborhood noises, she knew that it came from the downstairs bath.

Slipping in among the bushes beside the lower floor, she could hear someone there, all right, in the unoccupied downstairs bathroom. Someone moving softly about, an intruder where no human should be. She approached the lower deck stealthily, and across it to the sliding-glass door that served as the outside entry.

The downstairs was dark. She could see down the hall, but no light burned, not even a flashlight. Crouching on the little entry deck, she was peering through the glass doors into the black interior of the empty family room when, inside, someone coughed. Kit backed away into the shadows.

She waited for some time, but hearing nothing more, she slipped closer and reared up against the glass. A cold wind nipped at her backside, ruffling her fur and tugging at her tail, carrying with it the smell of a new storm, smell of rain approaching, smell of ozone. Pressing her nose to the cold surface, she tried to see in.

She could discern no one inside, no movement down the dark central hall. Examining the lock, she didn't think it had been broken or tampered with, she could see no scars or scratches on it, nothing bent, no screws removed. And no one could have come down from upstairs. Months before, one of Ryan's carpenters had sealed off the inner stairway with timbers and plywood, so there was no access. The only way in was here, through this six-foot glass door, which was reached from the upper level by the outside stairs to this deck.

Quickly she circled the lower floor, slipping along among the bushes and flowers close to the wall, moving back and looking up at each window to see if it might have been jimmied. In the dark, she could see no damage, they all looked securely locked. No fresh scratches, no tool marks. Coming around to the narrower, front deck, she hopped up there and reared tall to examine the front windows.

Here, along the front, there were no sliding-glass doors, as one would expect to open onto a deck, only windows. Below her, as she padded along, the lights of the village sparkled and shifted between the deck's rails. Overhead the stars were fast disappearing as storm clouds gathered, carrying the serious smell of rain—then suddenly she caught a human smell, the smell of a woman.

The fact that the intruder was a woman made little difference, a woman could be just as violent as a man, just as cruel to a small cat. Pausing beneath the window where the scent came strongest, she could see tool marks there, all right. Scars on the molding and a tiny slit where the lower half of the double-hung window had been left open a crack. The woman's scent was strong—cheap bath powder, cheaper hair spray, and female perspiration.

On silent paws Kit leaped to the sill. Pushed up the glass and slipped under, into the long dark family room.

Padding across the big, empty room to the dark hallway, she looked down its length, considering the open doors. On her left were two small bedrooms that she knew had a bath between. On the right, a half bath next to the family room, and behind it the blocked-off stair leading up to the main level. At the back, the original laundry room. Lucinda had installed a new washer and dryer upstairs. There was no sound now. The woman's scent led up the hall.

Was she waiting there in the dark for Lucinda and Pedric to get home? But why wait down here, if she meant to rob them? Had she thought, breaking in, that she could get up to the main level from inside and burglarize the house while they were out? When she found the stair blocked off, she would have had to change her plans.

So, what did she mean to do now?

But Clyde and Ryan were with the old couple, and those two hot-tempered, younger folk would handle the house-breaker.

Except, what if she had a gun? Neither Clyde nor Ryan, out on a date, was likely to be armed, Kit thought, amused.

How dangerous was this person? Or was she only some homeless woman taking shelter from the winter cold? Kit imagined her luxuriating in a hot shower, to get warm. Would there be, in one of the two small bedrooms, a thin, dusty bedroll or a pad of old newspapers or maybe old discarded clothes and food wrappers? Moving silently, tensed to spring away, Kit had started up the dark hall when she heard the Greenlaw car, on the street above, turn in to the drive. And behind her, light bloomed through the glass door as the outdoor security lights came on. Ahead, down the hall, there was no sound. She heard the garage door rise up on its metal track, heard the car pull in—she heard movement near her again as the woman slipped softly across the front bedroom. Above Kit, the car doors opened and slammed, then the garage door rumbled closed.

At the end of the hall, a figure appeared, a dark silhouette. The woman stood looking, and then started toward Kit.

I am only a shadow, Kit told herself. *A smudge of darkness, black on black to human eyes.* She heard, above her, the door open from the garage into the kitchen. She heard Lucinda and Pedric cross the kitchen to the living room—and out on the street, two more car doors slammed. The woman had paused again, as if listening. More light bloomed through the glass sliders as additional yard lights went on. She heard the upstairs front door open, then Ryan's voice, then Clyde. Someone closed the front door and locked it, she heard the dead bolt slide home, then multiple footsteps came along the stone walk above, and down the wooden stairs. The woman had vanished into the far bedroom, stirring about in a flurry. *She's going to run*, Kit thought, ducking into a corner. *This way, down the hall? Or out a front window?* But the narrow deck along the front was a full story above the ground.

She's trapped, Kit thought. And like any trapped creature, this could make her more dangerous. Kit had to warn her old couple. She spun around, racing back down the hall. Beyond the glass, Clyde and Pedric were talking as Lucinda fit her key into the lock. As the lock clicked open and Pedric slid the door back, Kit flew at them, streaking through the open door, leaping at Lucinda, mewling and crying in Lucinda's arms, her tail lashing, her claws going in, in a way she never did, and desperately flinging herself at Lucinda's ear, whispering—she'd hardly gotten a word out when footsteps pounded down the hall and the woman bolted straight at them.

From Lucinda's shoulder, Kit leaped desperately into the intruder's face. The woman screamed and grabbed Kit and flung her violently aside and bolted past Lucinda, nearly knocking her down.

Pedric and Ryan caught Lucinda between them as Clyde dove at the dark-clad woman. She tripped him and was past him and out the open glass door, racing down the lower stairs to the backyard, her dark coat flapping, Clyde hard on her heels, and Ryan close behind, as she crashed away though the woods; she was thin, very fast.

Lucinda picked up Kit and held her, burying her face in Kit's fur. "Are you hurt? Did she hurt you?"

"No," Kit whispered.

Pedric, when he saw that Lucinda and Kit were all right, followed Clyde and Ryan, running after the woman.

Alone with Lucinda, Kit nuzzled her face. "I heard the water running down here and then I smelled her and I came in to see and then you got home and I couldn't shout out to you because Ryan would hear, and I let that woman . . . Oh, she could have killed you. Oh, Lucinda . . ."

"It's all right, Kit. You did warn me. Hush now, hush."

"I saw her face in the light for an instant," Kit whispered. "Thin. Bony, like a starving stray. Big nose. Thin legs in tight black jeans, and that dark, floppy coat. Dark hair. And I smelled her."

Kit would not forget the woman's scent, she would retain that precise identification as unerringly as the AFIS retained the record of a perp's fingerprints, or as the lab would record the DNA of a felon or of some unfortunate victim.

14

IN THE COLD night, Ryan and Clyde and Pedric returned from chasing the burglar, panting and ashamed to have lost the fast and elusive woman. "Disappeared in the heavy woods like a running deer," Pedric grumbled. "All overgrown, tangles of blackberries back in there, catching and slowing us."

"We were halfway through," Clyde said, "could hear her crashing, then silence, and in a minute a car started, maybe a block away. Went roaring off without lights—we couldn't see the plates."

Pedric leaned against the wall, the thin old man getting his breath. Ryan put her arm around Lucinda. "Are you all right?" She looked at the kit. "This little cat tried to warn you. I've never seen such a thing, the way she leaped at you . . . And then she leaped at that woman, scratching and raking . . ." She reached to stroke Kit's ears. "No dog could have done better. She's a real watch cat, Lucinda. But how did she . . . Did she come in on our heels? She must have, and then she heard something we didn't. What a fine cat you are, Kit! I wouldn't have believed a cat would turn so fierce to protect her human family . . . Even Rock, who was a trained guard dog, couldn't have done better!" Kit purred and smiled. Such praise, from Ryan Flannery, was, indeed, a grand compliment.

Holding Kit close, Lucinda smiled shyly at Ryan. "I guess cats are more complicated than people imagine. They're strange little beings, and often, when they think there's a need, they're very creative little souls."

"She was creative tonight," Ryan said with admiration.

Kit purred for Ryan, watching her with interest. Ryan Flannery, Kit thought generously, had simply never been around cats. Ryan had never, she decided smugly, had the opportunity to deal with the amazing feline mystique.

Behind Ryan, Clyde and Pedric were looking exceedingly uneasy. Lucinda, not wanting Ryan to become too interested in the abilities of certain cats, said almost cloyingly, "She sure did hear something, poor little thing. But to be fair, maybe she wasn't warning me at all. Maybe she ran to me for protection. I think," she said, "that we often misread our animals."

"Maybe," Ryan said doubtfully—she might not know cats, but she knew animal body language, and Kit's behavior had been a sharp warning, not a panicky bid for help.

In the dark and empty family room, Pedric switched on the lights and he and Clyde examined the windows, quickly finding the jimmied panel. Moving on down the hall, they turned on the lights in each empty room. Ryan and Lucinda followed them, Lucinda still cuddling Kit—they found nothing until they reached the back bedroom.

There, in the far corner, propped against the wall, stood

a black canvas backpack. There were marks on the window-sill near it, where the thin coat of dust had been disturbed, as if something small had lain there. And Ryan found, half hidden behind one closed venetian blind, an empty film cartridge, carelessly abandoned or forgotten.

Using a tissue, she picked up the little plastic cylinder, wrapped it, and tucked it in her pocket. "Thirty-five-millimeter. Strange thing for a burglar to leave in a house. Unless . . ." She looked at Pedric. "Did you have a camera down here? Any camera equipment?"

"Nothing," Pedric said. "There was nothing at all to take, these rooms were all just as you see them, bare as old bones." Taking a clean linen handkerchief from his pocket, he covered his hand, knelt a bit stiffly, and opened the backpack. Touching the items within as little as possible, he lifted them out one by one and lined them up on the floor. Binoculars. A thin plastic grocery bag that contained candy bars and a dry cheese sandwich, two unopened boxes of film, and an expensive-looking camera with a telephoto lens.

Clyde and Ryan moved to the window together, looking away down the hill between the Greenlaws' oak trees to where the next house loomed, surrounded by woods. Three windows were faintly lighted behind drawn shades.

"Not much to take pictures of," Ryan said.

"That's a rental," Lucinda said. "New neighbors, they just moved in."

Pedric was examining the film. He handed it to Clyde. "Regular thirty-five-millimeter. Fast, four hundred speed."

Behind Ryan, Lucinda looked down at Kit, questioning. The tortoiseshell, forced to remain silent, twitched her ears and flicked her tail in a clear gesture: *I don't know any more than you do, Lucinda!* Kit had hardly noticed the new neighbors, and that embarrassed her. *She* was supposed to be the spy in the family, and now she knew no more about those tenants than she knew about the black-clad, sour-faced woman who had invaded their home. All this going on unheeded, right in plain sight, right under her suppos-edly sleuthing paws.

"I remember," Clyde said, "seeing a moving truck over there, a week or two ago."

"Two men and a woman," Lucinda said. "A big woman, tall, not fat. Sturdy-looking. Shoulder-length dark hair. There wasn't much in the moving truck that I could see, some cardboard boxes, only a few pieces of furniture, old and tacky. I think that house rented furnished."

Ryan cut a look at her, and laughed, and Lucinda grinned at her. "Nosy neighbor—nosy old woman."

"Not old. And not nosy," Ryan said, putting her arm around Lucinda. "Just observant. But I couldn't resist." They stood a moment, Lucinda counting back the days.

"It was about a week before they moved in that I saw a Pine Tree Rental Agency car over there, saw an agent go in and out a couple of times."

Outside, the wind was coming stronger, rattling the old windows and driving the scent of rain in around the glass. Again Pedric examined the marks on the sill. "Looks like she balanced the camera here. What's so important that she would break in, with the purpose of taking pictures of that house or of its occupants?"

Clyde said, "You haven't met the neighbors, don't know anything about them?"

Pedric shook his head.

Ryan, kneeling over the camera, studied its cumbersome telephoto attachment, then carefully searched the nearly empty backpack, slipping her tissue-covered hand into its inner pockets.

The last pocket yielded a large manila envelope and a smaller yellow envelope that bore the Kodak emblem, the kind one would pick up at the drugstore photo counter. She glanced into the brown envelope, then slid both inside her jacket. "Let's get out of here. We can look at these upstairs, and call the department." Replacing the camera and binoculars and plastic bag in the backpack, Ryan did not see Lucinda's look of hesitation at the mention of calling the dispatcher.

They took the backpack with them. They left the jimmied front window ajar, as they'd found it, and locked the sliding doors behind them. Lucinda carried Kit, talking softly to her, though Kit wasn't free to answer.

"You scared that woman bad," Lucinda said, stroking Kit. "I wish I could make you understand how wonderful you were."

Kit purred and snuggled against her.

"When you leaped and screamed like that, you very likely saved me from a far more violent attack, Kit." Lucinda scratched Kit's ears. "You're way smarter than any watchdog, my dear!" Lucinda gave her a wink that no one saw, and Kit didn't dare even smile. She hid her face against Lucinda's shoulder to keep from giggling. Clyde cut them a half-warning and half-amused look, and turned away. Pedric had moved on ahead; if he was smiling, no one saw. Everyone but Ryan knew the truth about Kit, it was only Ryan Flannery who didn't have a clue.

Kit wouldn't mind Ryan knowing her secret—hers and Joe's and Dulcie's secret. Ryan was a good person, and certainly the cats trusted her. But so many people knew already that it really wasn't smart to tell anyone else. Despite the best intentions, important secrets had a way of escaping as quickly as mice slipping from a cracked barrel.

Charlie had figured it out, as had Lucinda and Pedric. As had more than one of the criminals who the cats had helped send to prison—and that was more than enough people knowing. Ryan, being Detective Garza's niece, might find it very hard indeed not to let their secret slip—look how hard it was for Charlie.

Kit knew, too well, that Charlie was sometimes sorry she knew. Such knowledge had to be awkward for a police chief's wife, when the cats in question were the chief's prime informants—and when they spent so much time on Max Harper's desk pretending to be simple little freeloaders. The worst of it was, the cats had no idea how long they could keep up their charade before even that hard-nosed cop guessed the truth.

Everyone moved upstairs into the big, raftered living room, and Lucinda lit a fire and turned on the Christmas-tree lights. The house smelled of ginger and vanilla and that sweetly scorched smell of cookies that had browned around the edges. While Clyde and Pedric walked through the rooms to be sure the woman hadn't gotten in there, too, Ryan, sitting down at the dining table, put on a pair of Lucinda's cotton gloves and shook out the contents of the two envelopes. Lucinda fetched her own take-out container of shrimp bisque and warmed it, and set Kit's late-supper snack on the dining-room windowsill. Kit, wolfing down her good supper, watched Ryan examine the photos from the yellow Kodak folder.

"A roll of twelve," Ryan said, "processed through the Village Drugstore." She shook her head. "Under the name Jane Jones." She looked up at Lucinda. "Are you going to call the station?"

"I'd like to wait a bit. Let's have a look at these, first. The woman's long gone, by now."

Ryan looked at her, frowning, but said nothing. Lucinda sat down beside the younger woman, studying the individual photos as Ryan laid them out. All twelve shots were of the neighbor's house, all with the same distorted perspective produced by the telephoto lens, the house and figures sharp enough, but the trees in the foreground looking flat and out of focus. Two pictures showed a man inside at a window. Three showed a woman at another window. Six showed two different men outside the house, two of those with the woman as well. The last shot was of a car coming down the drive, the woman at the wheel. When Clyde and Pedric joined them, Pedric picked up Kit from the windowsill and held her in his arms as he sat down so she could see better. It was the nine-by-twelve pages from the larger envelope that made them all uneasy.

Ryan lined them up. Each sheet of slick white paper was printed with four color photographs. The twenty pictures were all of a different location. Lucinda's hand trembled as she reached out for the nearest page. Ryan stopped her, taking her hand, and offered the older woman the package of cotton gloves.

"Those are pictures of the Patty Rose Home," Lucinda

said, pulling on the gloves, so upset she'd forgotten about fingerprints. She brought the sheet closer. "What does she want with pictures of the Anna Stanhope estate—pictures of the children?" And already, within herself, Lucinda feared the answer.

Two of the twenty pictures were of the Stanhope mansion with its appealing Tudor design, its dark timbers incising their strong patterns across the pale plaster walls. Three pictures were of different angles of the artist's small home and studio, a simple stone building constructed in the early part of the previous century. The other fifteen photos showed the buildings at more distance, with the children in the foreground running and playing in the tree-shaded garden and on the playground. Five of those were close-ups of individual little girls, all distorted by the telephoto lens, which flattened the perspective and made the pictures seem even more immediate and threatening. All five little girls had pale skin and black hair, and it was this detail that brought Kit sharply alert and made her shiver. All five little girls resembled, in coloring, the child she'd seen huddled against the dead man.

"Max needs to see these," Ryan said. "Now, tonight. And you need to report the break-in to him, before that woman comes back."

Lucinda looked at her uncertainly.

"When she finds the pictures and camera missing," Ryan said, "she'll do one of two things. Either she'll run, or she'll come up here to take these back. Possibly take them back, armed."

"I . . . If she were armed," Lucinda said, "she would have drawn on us downstairs."

"You don't know that. We don't know what she'll do. She might have a gun hidden somewhere else, in a car maybe. Bring it back with her." Ryan looked hard at her. "Call the station, Lucinda. Or I will." And she glanced through to the kitchen, to the phone that stood on the counter.

Pedric put his arm around Lucinda. "Ryan's right."

Lucinda nodded, rose, and headed reluctantly for the phone. Kit watched her, puzzled, and didn't understand what held Lucinda back. This was not like her. As Lucinda talked with the dispatcher, Ryan looked at Clyde. He was scowling, and silent.

"What?" she said, laying her hand over his.

He shrugged. "I guess . . . Just that we don't need this stuff at Christmas."

But Clyde was thinking far more: Joe Grey and Dulcie and Kit were already in stalking mode, drawn into last night's murder. And whatever the cats were into made huge waves in the lives of their three families and Charlie. Now here was another involvement, which, no matter how valuable the cats' contribution might turn out to be, would keep their human friends totally uptight for the rest of the Christmas season, keep everyone on edge waiting for unseen complications—or for disaster. Would increase everyone's stress level at a time that should be restful, restorative, and filled only with Christmas joy.

For some reason, Clyde thought, laughing at himself, he had innocently imagined a quiet Christmas this year. Low-key suppers and relaxed parties with close friends. He and Ryan snuggled before the fire on Christmas Eve sipping eggnog and opening small, personal gifts while the tomcat dozed idly beside the hearth, content with the season and with his own Christmas eggnog.

Well, hell, Clyde thought. Living with Joe Grey, he should know that kind of holiday was not to be.

But then, when he glanced at the kit, expecting to see the wild flame of challenge that crime always generated blazing in her yellow eyes, he saw, instead, only a puzzled frown. Kit's full and suspicious attention was keenly on Lucinda. And when Clyde looked into the kitchen where Lucinda was talking with the dispatcher at Molena Point PD, it was Lucinda's eyes that burned with challenge—Lucinda Greenlaw looked as excited, and as sly and secretive, as the tortoiseshell kit ever had.

15

Joe Grey didn't learn about the Greenlaws' intruder until Clyde got home late that night. When Clyde's car pulled in, the tomcat was asleep in his tower, among the cushions, lying on his back with his four paws in the air. The reflection of moving car lights flashing across the tower's conical ceiling woke him. He blinked and flipped over among the pillows, his nose to the glass, looking down to the drive to make sure that it was really Clyde pulling in.

Joe's private, cat-size tower, rising four feet above the roof of the second floor, with its unique hexagonal shape and operable, full-length windows, was a masterpiece of luxury and, Dulcie said, ostentation. Joe disagreed about that—the tower was, in his mind, simply a utilitarian source of comfort, unimpeded view, weather control, and fast and easy access to the rooftops. To hell with ostentation.

As he listened to the purr of Clyde's antique roadster, wild barking erupted from the back patio, where Ryan's big Weimaraner had spent the evening. Joe rose and stretched, then lay down again, listening as Clyde and Ryan let Rock in the house, laughing and greeting him. He listened to kitchen noises as they made coffee and fixed a snack, and soon the smell of coffee rose up to him. Outside his tower, the night wind increased, fitfully shaking the glass and hustling the oaks and pines against the shingles, and smelling sharply of rain. He didn't head downstairs—as lonely as he felt at that moment and as fond as he was of Ryan, he could not talk in front of her. If he went down, as out of sorts as he was, the enforced silence would leave him even more irritable.

He'd gone to sleep thinking about the little frightened child, so alone and terrified at Christmastime. He'd chided himself for growing sentimental, but he'd waked hurting for her, and badly needing company. Now, irritated by his own shaky and sentimental mood, he wondered if he was sickening for something.

He listened to the buzz of conversation from below, waiting and dozing until he heard Ryan's truck pull away and he could go on down and talk freely. Could dump some of his misery on Clyde.

Slipping quickly through his cat door onto the rafter above Clyde's desk, he dropped down onto a mess of paperwork, most likely orders for engine parts, and then to the floor. He was crouched to race downstairs when he heard Clyde slamming things into the refrigerator and rattling ice: quick, angry noises that clearly telegraphed a fight, or at best a lovers' quarrel. *Oh, hell. Not a fight with Ryan, not at Christmas!* The two seldom argued, even mildly, though they unmercifully teased each other. Trotting reluctantly down the stairs, knowing that Clyde might need a sympathetic friend, too, he pushed in through the kitchen door, leaped to the table, and silently watched his housemate irritably mixing a bourbon and water.

Clyde turned, his scowl deep, his dark eyes worried. "What the hell do you want?"

"Milk and gingerbread?" Joe asked meekly.

"I suppose you want it warmed!"

"Yes, please." Joe studied his housemate's dark scowl as Clyde poured a bowl of milk, broke a thick slice of gingerbread into it, and put the bowl in the microwave. In a moment Clyde set the warm bowl, and his own drink, on the table. The tomcat looked sternly at him. "You and Ryan had a fight?"

"We didn't fight. We were having a discussion. We had a very nice evening. I don't need you to spoil it."

"Then why all the slamming around? Why the scowl?" Joe's yellow eyes burned at Clyde. "What happened up at the Greenlaws'?"

Clyde glared, and didn't answer.

"What?" Joe said.

"Just for tonight, Joe, could you just eat and come to bed, like a normal, ordinary house cat?"

"What? What happened, up there?"

Wind buffeted the kitchen windows, then eased off. From the living room the fresh pine scent of the Christmas tree drifted through the house, mingling with the smell of the gingerbread that Clyde had made as part of an early dinner before he and Ryan headed for the ballet.

Ordinarily, Clyde would have taken Ryan out to dinner, but neither one had been in the mood for the incredibly crowded restaurants on a theater night. Instead, he'd fixed a simple supper that they'd eaten in the living room before the fire, enjoying the Christmas tree that they'd decorated together. *I am*, Clyde thought, amused, *getting to be a regular homebody.*

This Christmas, in fact, he found himself entertaining thoughts of marriage; the theme played so repeatedly that he was glad the gray tomcat couldn't read his mind. Joe couldn't keep one damned opinion to himself, he'd have way too much to say on the matter.

"So, what happened?" Joe said, patiently licking milk from his whiskers.

Clyde sighed. He really had no choice. The damned cat would just keep on pushing, as nosy as a case-hardened cop. No one who'd ever lived with Joe Grey, when the tomcat felt left out of the loop, would deliberately withhold information and incur his verbal abuse, as sharp as his threatening claws.

Refreshing his drink, then settling again at the kitchen table, reluctantly Clyde filled Joe in on the Greenlaws' female intruder, the backpack and camera, and the two envelopes of pictures. He'd barely finished when Joe's ears twitched toward the living room, and he crouched ready to spring away through his cat door. Clyde rose fast, shut the kitchen door, and stood in front of it. Like a flash Joe leaped for the big doggy door that led out to the back patio, not looking carefully in his haste.

He hit the locked plywood cover, bouncing back, as off balance as a flailing cartoon cat.

Clyde restrained a belly laugh. He had set the cover in place after Ryan and Rock left. He had, in fact, locked the dog door every night since old Rube died, since the black

Lab was no longer sleeping right there, near the two-foot-high opening, to ward off potential burglars. Even Clyde himself, in an emergency, could squeeze through that dog door. Though it was unlikely an intruder would take the trouble to breach their patio walls, in these days of weird crimes, who knew what a thief might do.

With Joe trapped unceremoniously in the kitchen, Clyde picked him up. Joe growled and bared his teeth. Clyde set him down on the table again, and held him by the nape of his neck in a way that enraged the tomcat.

"Just listen, Joe. Just listen for one minute. Then, if you insist on heading for the Greenlaws', okay."

Joe glanced toward the closed kitchen door. Clyde squeezed the fold of skin more firmly. "Harper's up there. Lucinda was calling him when we left. By this time, he's going through the apartment, maybe with Dallas, maybe the two of them already fingerprinting and taking photographs. Don't you think it would seem strange if you came waltzing in, quite by accident, in the middle of the night? How many times in the past have you appeared precipitously at a crime scene and made Max Harper wonder? How many times has Dallas Garza looked at you strangely? How many times have those guys watched you so closely you began to squirm?"

"Don't squeeze so hard. That hurts!"

"How many times, before even those hard-nosed cops are *forced* to guess the truth?" Clyde leaned down, his face inches from Joe's face. "Max Harper isn't stupid. Dallas Garza isn't stupid. Neither would *want* to believe in talking cats. But you keep pushing it, Joe, and they may no longer be able to avoid the truth."

Joe sighed.

"Do you really want to hasten the arrival of that cataclysmic day?"

Joe just looked at him.

"You don't think Harper gets uneasy, with you three cats showing up every time they're working a case? You don't think he wonders about all the times evidence has appeared 'mysteriously' at the back door of the station? You don't think he gets goose bumps every time an anonymous snitch calls in a new tip—and that tip brings in the goods? You don't think that makes a cop edgy?"

Clyde let go of his neck and propped a chair against the kitchen door. "Have you thought about would happen if Max Harper ever takes the time to really think about this! To put aside all his more immediate concerns, put aside his natural skepticism, and really examine this phenomenon?"

"Of course I've thought about it. How could I not think about it? Don't be such a nag!" Joe had thought about the matter more than he wanted to admit—and about the possible repercussions.

From a purely selfish aspect, if he and Dulcie and Kit blew their cover with the law, life would change dramatically for them. But their human families would suffer far more. Clyde, Wilma, and the Greenlaws—and Charlie Harper, the chief's own wife—would be the ones in the hot seat. Their silence would render them far more guilty, in Max's eyes, than the cats themselves.

There was no way, if Max ever did suspect the truth, that Charlie could convince him of her own ignorance. Not when, in her forthcoming book, both her drawings and her story revealed such a keen knowledge of feline nature that

Max marveled at her perception, at her amazing intimacy with feline secrets. Max was already impressed to the point where he sometimes looked at Charlie in the same way that he studied the cats, puzzled and just a bit uncomfortable.

The bottom line was, instead of heading for the Greenlaws' and making Harper wonder, Joe padded docilely up the stairs beside Clyde and crawled into bed—making sure to hog both pillows. Drifting off, he thought he'd catch just a few winks and then, in the small hours after Harper had left the Greenlaws', he'd slip on up there and get the scoop from Kit.

Maybe they'd toss the downstairs rooms, too, to see what the law might have missed. Then they'd go get Dulcie, and hit the station—innocent, hungry, freeloading little cats. Get a look at Harper's report and at the photos. And the tomcat fell asleep wondering about those pictures of the children.

But when he was deep under, his dreams of the orphan children and the break-ins at the school and at the Greenlaws', and of the body under the Christmas tree and that little girl huddled in the pump house all tangled together in confusion badly frightening him.

He woke worn-out, hissing and angry. He felt better only when, trotting downstairs to the kitchen, he found Clyde in a cheerful mood again, an omelet already waiting for him on his side of the breakfast table and the morning paper opened neatly beside it. He did not, tucking in to his breakfast, question the change in Clyde's demeanor, from grouchy to sunny. Clyde seemed almost as if he'd settled some personal quandary, made some decision. But maybe it was only that he had finally decided, at the last minute, what to get Ryan for Christmas.

16

WHILE JOE GREY twitched through fitful dreams of threatened children and secret photographs and jimmied windows, the tortoiseshell kit took the investigation into her own paws. She woke several hours after Max Harper left her house. The sky outside the bedroom window was black. The lighted dial of the bedside clock said 5 A.M. The cold winter wind huffed at the windows, sending a chill over the top of the blankets. Lying tucked warmly between Pedric and Lucinda, she woke so filled with questions that she couldn't help but wriggle and scratch at nonexistent fleas, was so fitful that after a few minutes Pedric turned over, irritably glaring at her, stared at the bedside clock, and glared again at Kit.

Ashamed of waking him, Kit dropped off the bed and raced away through the house to the dining room. Leaping to the window and out her cat door, and across the oak branch to her tree house, she looked down to the rental house—not a sign of Christmas cheer down there, no bright tree or colored lights, though the other neighbors' Christmas lights, even at this hour, were cheerily burning. No smells of Christmas from that rental, just the smell of mud and rotting leaves surrounding the old neglected dwelling, sad and depressing and somehow coldly foreboding.

But someone was awake down there, already stirring. A light was on in the kitchen and she could see movement behind the shade.

Twice last week she'd seen the woman leave very early. Now, backing down the thick oak trunk, dislodging bits of bark with her claws, she hit the ground running. It crossed her mind that she might be foolish to prowl there alone and try to get inside, among strangers, that she really should wait for Joe and Dulcie, for a little backup, an additional arsenal of tooth and claw.

But Kit didn't often heed the wiser choice, it wasn't her nature to wait for the safer moment. Right now she felt far too impatient. Belting down the hill through the oak woods, she paused in their leafy shadows, her paws sinking deep in masses of wet leaves, looking up at the old, dusty windows.

They were all closed and covered with cheap brown window shades hanging slightly askew. As she circled, looking up at the flaking tan walls and studying each window, her paws were soon soaking. If there had ever been a lawn, generations of leaves had long since eaten it away. All she needed was one window left open, and she could be up and through in an instant.

She didn't know, at this point, who was on the right side of the law, these three strangers or the woman who had spied on them. Or maybe they were all on the wrong side. Crooks against crooks?

She ignored the fact that there had as yet been no crime

committed by these three, that the only criminal act was that of the woman breaking into Kit's own home. She ignored the possibility that the woman's spying might be the result of a domestic crisis, perhaps a cheating husband, a situation in which the Molena Point police wouldn't have the slightest interest unless it turned violent. At that moment, the tortoiseshell kit wanted only to know why that woman had been spying, to know what she found so compelling.

There was no garden walk leading around the house, just the deep layer of wet oak leaves beneath the dripping trees. Soon not only her paws were soaked, but her legs and belly and tail, her long, fluffy fur sodden with icy water. Circling the house, she could see no windows open. The light had gone off in the kitchen; now that room, too, was dark. Three times she crouched to leap up to a first-floor windowsill, hoping to force an ancient lock, but each time, a frightened chill made her drop down again and sent her hurrying on around, not really knowing what had scared her.

She could hear no movement within, but at the back of the house, when she paused beneath the higher windows of an upstairs bedroom, she could hear the soft, slow breathing of someone asleep; and at the next bedroom window she heard the same. Trotting around the far side and up onto the driveway, she left dark, wet paw prints on the pale concrete. The car that stood in the drive was cold and dripping with dew, its tires and wheels cold, the air around the hood reflecting back to her only the night's chill. She wondered why they didn't use the garage.

How could it be full? It was a double garage, and she hadn't noticed another car down here; and when they moved in she hadn't seen very many boxes. That day, as the movers unloaded, as she and Lucinda watched through the dining-room window, Pedric had teased them about being nosy, and he had disdained to spy on the new neighbors— but later they saw him secretly looking, and they'd grinned at each other.

The garage protruded out beyond the skinny front porch. Padding along beside it, Kit approached the three concrete steps leading up to the front door. Above her in the garage wall were three high little windows, so small they'd be a tight squeeze for a human. Might one of those have been left unlocked? But when she reared up to look closer, they appeared to be covered from the inside with plywood or cardboard.

She considered the thin trellis beside the porch, where a dead vine clung. From its top rung she could easily leap to the first sill and try to get in. If that *was* only cardboard, wouldn't it be taped or tacked to the window frame? If she could fight the window open, maybe the covering would go with it.

Silently she padded across the porch between a dozen empty clay pots, some tilted over, spilling dried clods of earth and dried-up ferns, brown and brittle, maybe abandoned by some previous renter. Crouching, ready to leap and scale the trellis, she heard footsteps within the house and before she could run, the porch light blazed on and the front door flew open. Kit froze, hunched among the pots, hoping her dark mottled fur looked like just another dry fern.

She could smell sleep on the woman who stepped out. A tall woman, her dark hair hanging lank and dry. She was fully dressed, but hurriedly so, her blouse only half buttoned over dark jeans, and over that, a heavy black peacoat. She didn't notice Kit; she shut the door behind her and the lock clicked. But then, fumbling with her car keys, she glanced down—and caught her breath, staring straight at Kit, and backed away from her with a look of fear that quickly flared to anger.

Phobic, Kit thought. *I'm in luck, she's scared of me, she . . .* The woman dove at Kit, striking out at her. Kit yowled and clawed her hand, and ran; as she hit the drive she glanced back, ducked as a clay pot came flying. It crashed on the concrete inches from her, flinging shards in her face; she leaped away, terrified, through the deep leaves and up an oak tree, climbing and not stopping until she was so high among the tangled leaves that the woman couldn't see her.

There she crouched, shivering and licking sweat from her paws and wanting suddenly to be home, wanting to be held and comforted, wanting to be home with Lucinda and Pedric. She had done some wild break-and-enters, but never where someone threw things at her, threw great, hard pots at a poor little cat.

If that pot had hit her, it could have done her in. She imagined her lifeless body sprawled on the drive as flat as highway kill, imagined her two old folks finding her there and kneeling over her, weeping. Imagined her little cat spirit wandering alone and lost in some mysterious otherworldly realm as she tried to find her way into cat heaven. And she wanted to be gently held and comforted.

But she couldn't go barging into the bedroom soaking wet and covered with rotting leaves, reduced to nothing but a heap of trembling fear. Nor did she want to explain to Lucinda and Pedric where she'd been, after they'd warned her not to go snooping around that place.

No one had ever thrown things at her like a stray mutt, not since she was a starving kitten and a man in an alley had thrown a shoe at her. That had frightened her very much, had enraged and shamed her because she was so small and alone that she could not fight back.

That shame filled her now, and she was not ready to go home.

Leaping through the oak branches to the next tree and the next, she headed away across the roofs for Dulcie's house. Dulcie would understand. Both Dulcie and Wilma might scold her for being reckless, but she would not be embarrassed to confess to them, as she would with Lucinda and Pedric. Through the dark predawn she ran, the sky above her streaking with paler gray, the sea wind fingering cold into her wet fur.

Wilma's garden flowers were wet, too, when she plowed through; she was soaked when she plunged in through Dulcie's cat door, the plastic flap slapping her backside like a powerful hand chastising her.

She stood in Wilma's kitchen dripping onto the blue linoleum, sniffing the lingering scents of crème brûlé and chowder from last night, of Dulcie's late-evening snack that Wilma had brought home, and of the Christmas tree from the living room. And the aroma of freshly brewed coffee, too, which she followed through the familiar house; crossing the dining room toward the hall and Wilma's bedroom, she paused, dripping water on the Oriental rug, to look in at the Christmas tree; it shone bright and festive with its white and silver and red decorations gleaming among the deep green needles. She looked with interest at the richly wrapped gifts, then moved on, following the smell of fresh coffee.

Dulcie's housemate so loved coffee in bed that when she woke up she would pad barefoot out to the kitchen, switch on the coffeepot, wait patiently in the cold dark dawn, then carry a full mug back to bed, where she'd tuck up again beneath the warm, flowered quilt. Kit found her so now, sitting up in bed cradling a steaming mug, a warm fire lit in the woodstove, and Dulcie curled by her side looking up sleepily as Kit entered.

"What?" Wilma said, putting out her hand, seeing clearly Kit's distress; and Dulcie leaped down to sniff her face and her wet fur.

"Where have you been?" Dulcie said. "Oh, what happened?"

"Come up, Kit," Wilma said, patting the covers. "Come up and get warm, I don't care if you're wet."

Leaping up onto the quilt, Kit snuggled down between them. She was silent for a long time, getting warm, licking at her wet fur, and wondering where to begin. She remained silent until Wilma lifted her chin and looked into her face.

"What, Kit? What upset you?"

Sensibly, Kit started from the beginning, from the moment last night when she'd left Dulcie and Joe on the roof of the Patio Café. Carefully she told everything that had happened since, every little detail. If she didn't tell it all, Clyde or the Greenlaws would—and if Kit told it first, she could tell it her way.

17

As Wilma Getz sipped her coffee in bed, and Kit snuggled down between her and Dulcie telling all about the Greenlaws' break-in, up in the hills at the Harper ranch, Charlie Harper hurried to do her morning chores, feeding the horses and dogs, turning them out into the pasture and cleaning the stalls. The sky was barely light, the time not quite seven. Max had left for the station some time ago, warmed by a breakfast of buckwheat pancakes and thick sliced bacon. Charlie, seeing him off, had stood in the stable yard watching his truck move away up their long, gravel road, worrying because he never got enough sleep. At the far end of the road, as he turned onto the highway, Max had blinked his lights once and then he was gone over the rise, heading down to the village.

He'd been up late the night before with the Greenlaw break-in, and the night before that he'd gotten to bed later still because of the missing body. Max wasn't the kind of chief to stay in bed and leave his men to do all the legwork;

but it was hard sometimes to rein herself in and not fuss at him that he needed rest.

Last night's late rain had left the ranch yard muddy and squishing under her boots. As she entered the barn, dawn was beginning to brighten the sky. The air was as cold and fresh as springwater. Soon, as the sun rose, the pasture grass would gleam emerald bright—this time of year the four horses were wild to get out of their stalls, hungry to get at the new sweet grass. Besides Max's big buckskin gelding and her own sorrel mare, they were boarding the kids' horses now, a dun mustang that young Dillon Thurwell's parents had bought for her, and a small, borrowed mare called Parsnip, named for her color, who had been a fine teaching pony for younger Lori Reed.

Lori was experienced enough now for a bigger and more challenging mount, but she so loved Parsnip that Max and Charlie had hesitated to return the little mare to her owners. As Charlie fed the horses and the two big dogs and then turned them all out to the pasture, her thoughts moved from the disappearing body to the Greenlaws' mysterious intruder, her head filled with a tangle of questions. The department would come up with the answers, given time—but how much time was there for that scared little girl?

And was there a connection between the child and the break-in at the Patty Rose Home? It seemed to Charlie there had to be, if someone was secretly taking pictures of the orphan children.

As late as it had been last night when Max got home from the Greenlaws', he'd described the break-in and the photographs; he had been royally irritated that Lucinda had refused to press charges. Without charges they couldn't arrest the woman, nor could they officially do much to investigate the incident. Max said Pedric had tried to reason with Lucinda, but Lucinda wouldn't give, and that wasn't like her at all. She'd said she wanted a few days to see what the woman was up to, and had promised not to put herself in danger. But why did Lucinda care about a woman who'd broken into their home?

When Max pointed out that there could be a connection between this woman, the neighbors, and the break-in at the school, Lucinda had shrugged it off. That, too, was not like sensible Lucinda Greenlaw. Lucinda knew the woman could be violent, but she wouldn't listen.

It wasn't as if the older lady didn't believe bad things could happen; Lucinda's first husband had turned out to be a thief and philanderer. After he'd deceived her for years, Lucinda had grown far more wary.

She'd been so lucky to meet and marry Pedric; he had helped her through that time, and was a dear. But then, while the two were on their extended honeymoon trip in their RV, they had been kidnapped and nearly killed. Pedric's cleverness, and the toughness of both old folks, had saved them.

That was when they changed their minds about building their new home up on the crest of isolated Hellhag Hill, and decided to settle instead in the village, closer to law enforcement and to medical facilities. The Greenlaws weren't cowards, far from it, but at eighty-some, it can be nice to have certain support services near at hand. Their biggest consideration, however, had been the fact that Kit would be closer to Joe and Dulcie, that the little cat wouldn't have that long and sometimes dangerous race up and down the hills to the village. *So,* Charlie thought, *when Lucinda is usually so levelheaded and sensible, why is she suddenly so protective of this housebreaker? Well, maybe I can talk to her.*

JAMES KUDA THOUGHT again about the moves he had made, about the car and the body. Not likely they'd be found for a while—not until he was long gone, had put the West Coast behind him.

Having left the garage of the empty house, driving at a normal rate through the dark village streets, he'd headed south down Highway One, the waves thundering high and violent below the dropping cliffs—big, hungry waves. To his left, though he hadn't been able to see much in the dark, were the rolling hills dotted with small, scattered ranches; he'd glimpsed only a couple of lights up there, at that pre-dawn hour. With his window open he'd enjoyed the cold wind and the roar of the crashing sea, the smell of salt and iodine—had relished the sound of the extra-high tide. He always read the tide schedules, as well as the society page that offered up a nice working bible, a regular menu of lucrative possibilities, more than one man could ever make use of. Driving slowly, he'd watched the cliff carefully for the turnoff, which was nearly invisible in the dark.

He supposed he could have dumped the body some-where up there beyond those ranches where the land turned wild, dumped and buried it. Days before, he'd driven all around up there, and looked. Had spotted that cop's ranch, too—saw the chief's truck and a couple of squad cars parked there, saw lights blazing in the house and heard music and laughter. Wouldn't that be a joke, if he buried it on that police chief's land?

Yeah, it would. Tantamount to teasing a maddened rattlesnake. And what was the point? No, that Max Harper would come after him with a vengeance.

He'd left no ID on the body or in the car, no prints but the victim's own and the kid's. Anyway, his own prints weren't on record; he'd always been careful about that.

Making his turn in the pitch-dark, and dimming his lights to park, he'd eased along the edge of the cliff, pulled up where it dropped smoothly down. Setting the hand brake, he'd sat there a moment thinking, then swung out of the car, on the highway side. Found a long heavy rock just the right shape, careful to walk only on the bare stone outcroppings where the cliff had been cut to build the highway.

Pulling the body over into the driver's seat, he'd retrieved the bike from the trunk and set it upright on the asphalt. Then, returning to the car, he'd set the rock ready, reached in and started the engine again, and in one practiced motion had shoved the rock in place against the gas pedal, slammed it in gear, released the brake and dove away fast, clearing the door as the car shot over the side.

He'd stood listening to tons of metal thudding and dropping against the rocks, the scrape of metal on rock, the sudden explosive crash into the sea—listening to the altered rhythm of the breakers suddenly as the vehicle sank, the sucking sound, and then the rising waves returning again to their own cadence, breaking only against the cliff.

Still stepping carefully only on the stone outcroppings, he'd returned to the highway, swung onto the bike, and headed back toward the village, the sky still dark, heavy with cloud. He'd almost cheered aloud when he felt a few drops of water on his face, and heard the rain start to pelt behind him—a good rain to wash away the tire marks. The way the weather had been, nothing was sure, but he'd lucked out, this time. Nothing in life was sure, he thought, smiling. You took it the best way you could.

18

Having finished her stable work, Charlie loaded the big portfolio of her newest etchings and drawings into her Blazer, changed her muddy boots for cleaner ones, hastily brushed her hair and clipped the red mass back out the way. Making sure the house was locked, she headed down the hills to deliver the last pieces of work to the framer, driving slowly, drinking in the morning, enjoying the emerald-bright pastures dropping ahead of her. The sky was a clear azure above the dark blue sea, the tide high and wild. Where the hills rose darker with scattered pines and brush, a long white streak of fog trailed across their brightening crests, a veil as thin and delicate as a chiffon scarf. It was on such a dawn as this that she imagined flying in that clear air, that she wished she could see all the earth at once reeling below her, the next emerald hill and the next, on forever. No wonder some wild souls couldn't stay out of the sky, sacrificing all luxuries and many necessities for a way of life that counted for far more. But, horse-poor or airplane-poor, such folks were content and happy.

She arrived at the framer's so filled with the morning's beauty that she didn't want to make small talk; she was glad Jim Barker wasn't a big talker, that this slight, graying man understood silence. He spoke only to promise he'd have the eight pieces of work ready by Friday, when the gallery would be hanging her show. "With Sicily Aronson," the thin, balding man said gently, "one has no choice but to be on time."

Driving the few blocks from Barker's to the gallery, enjoying the festive shop windows with their holly and wreaths and beautiful wares, she parked two car lengths behind her own blue Chevy cleaning van. She guessed the girls were cleaning up the gallery after the last of the remodeling. Hurrying in, she stopped to talk with Mavity Flowers, who was mopping the Mexican tile floor. She could hear the water running in the powder room, where one of the girls would be cleaning the fixtures and tile. Little wrinkled Mavity Flowers was sixty-some but she liked to work, and she liked the work she did, liked making things bright and clean; and she was certainly healthy and strong. As one of Cora Lee's housemates, she did much of the cleaning at home, too, while Cora Lee and Susan took care of the shopping and garden.

But this morning, Mavity seemed distracted. Setting aside her mop, she looked up at Charlie. "You're not going to sell the van?"

"Of course not. What made you think that? Not after Clyde rebuilt the engine and we fitted it all out for the cleaning and repairs. Why . . . What did you hear?"

"Susan *said* that was silly. I was going to tell you about it, but then decided it was nothing. I was leaving the Johnson house, Monday a week ago. There was a man looking at the van, walking round and round it. I stepped back inside, I don't think he saw me. He looked and looked, wrote down something on a pad of paper, and then he left. He was walking, he had no car that I saw. I wish I'd asked him what he was doing."

"It's all right. What did he look like?"

"Thin face, short haircut that made his big ears look even bigger. A real narrow face, and black, bushy eyebrows."

"Maybe a tourist," Charlie said. "If you see him around the van again, let me know. Or call Mabel, have her send a patrol car around. Whatever he wants, that should put a stop to it. Where's Sicily?"

Mavity nodded in the direction of the new archway that had been cut into the adjoining café. "This is real nice, the way she cut through."

Charlie smiled. "I like it, too." She gave Mavity a little hug, and went on through to the restaurant to join Sicily. The gallery owner sat at a back table where a wall of windows looked out on the patio, each window decorated now with a border of holly. Though the gallery had been left plain and stark, to show off Charlie's work, the restaurant was all done up for Christmas, red swags from the rafters, a decorated tree in the far corner, and, of course, the scent of Christmas baking. Sicily, at her table, looked sleek and elegant, as usual, in black tights, a camel tunic, and half a dozen handmade necklaces—making Charlie wish, as she clumped on back in her jeans and boots, that she'd taken time to change her clothes.

"Coffee?" Sicily said, indicating a silver pot. "Have a cinnamon twist." She pushed the plate toward Charlie. "It's their new recipe, and it's wonderful."

The little café had opened only a month ago, when a dress shop moved out, to larger quarters. Sicily and the new owner had decided to join forces, and had been joined, as well, by the bookstore next door, which now opened to the café on the opposite side, through a second archway. The three owners had named their enterprise the Hub, and though the gallery had been there for years and was one of the busiest in the village, the new joint venture was an exciting addition. All three businesses opened to the back garden, where additional small tables welcomed patrons.

Some sour-minded people said a gallery and café and bookstore wouldn't mix, that none of them would do well. But the complex was indeed becoming a hub, as the owners had anticipated. Sicily's had already been popular; and the new bookstore was well stocked and cozy, with a warm, attentive staff who really knew books, who were eager to do special orders, and who paid a singular attention to all the local writers. Charlie, glancing from their table through to the bookstore, could see copies of her new book stacked high on a front table before a poster of the book jacket, awaiting Saturday's signing. Charlie's drawing on the jacket showed a startled, big-eyed Kit, one tortoiseshell paw lifted, whether in alarm or surprise, Charlie had left to the imagination.

"They already have a long reserve list," Sicily said. "Customers wanting signed copies." She sat observing Charlie. "You haven't said a word. Aren't you excited?"

"Excited? I'm ecstatic! My second one-man show, and my first book signing—and one of your wonderful parties." She took in Sicily's costume, delighted as always by her friend's choice of clothes. Her jewelry today was silver, wooden beads and small, handmade clay medallions, her tunic nipped in by a wood-and-silver belt, her dark hair piled high and held by silver clips.

"You've finished the gallery work," Charlie said, looking back through the archway at the new, movable walls all freshly painted—all waiting for Charlie's drawings and prints, most of which were stored in the back.

"Cora Lee's cousin Donnie did the remodel," Sicily said. "The arches, everything. Didn't he do a nice job? When I found I'd have to wait weeks for Ryan, that she'd be able to start only about now, Donnie stepped right in. He's good, Charlie. Someone's going to snatch him up for full-time work. Maybe Ryan herself, when she sees this. Look at the detail, and the molding."

"He's cute, too," Charlie said, watching Sicily.

Sicily grinned. "Those big blue eyes and that nice crew cut. I love blond hair with a touch of gray—when it's set off by a good build and a nice tan."

Charlie laughed. "Donnie French has to be pushing sixty, he grew up with Cora Lee. He *is* cute, but . . . I hate to tell you, but Gabrielle is wearing his engagement ring. As of yesterday, I think."

Sicily shrugged. "Well, cute is cute. And maybe I still have a chance. From what I hear he's a shameless flirt, comes on to every attractive woman he meets. Maybe Gabrielle won't tolerate that for long."

"And would you?" Charlie said, teasing. "How long would that last, with you?"

"Not long," Sicily said, laughing. "I just said he was cute, not that I have my sights set on him. Although . . ." They both laughed. But Sicily Aronson wasn't a fool over a good-looking man; she was a keen businesswoman, clever and skilled and no pushover for just any cute guy.

"He has done nice work," Charlie said, considering the beautiful plastering job around the archway and the smoothly installed, curved molding. The gallery was done in off-white, the tall white exhibit panels reaching, on one side, to within a few feet of the balcony where smaller paintings and drawings were hung. "He seems skilled at so many things. You're right, I don't know why Ryan hasn't hired him. She's always complaining about having more work than she has reliable men."

"Maybe Donnie doesn't want to tie himself down," Sicily said. "He was in, this morning, for a minute, to pick up some tools he'd left, said he was headed for the city on a job interview. He said something about a child, that Detective Davis had stopped by their place with a little girl in tow. What was that about?"

Charlie looked blankly at Sicily. "I don't think Davis has any grandchildren, but I could be wrong." She shrugged. "Some of the other officers have little kids. Maybe Davis is babysitting. On company time," she said, laughing.

She had no idea why Juana Davis or Cora Lee hadn't warned Donnie not to talk about the child, when Max wanted the little girl protected. "Well," she said, trying not to telegraph her unease, "Donnie French *is* attractive, and he's just as kind and friendly as he can be." She didn't know what it was about Donnie French that bothered her. Probably some pointless association that had no basis. Inwardly shrugging, she busied herself with her cinnamon twist.

"And what was that about, in the paper this morning?" Sicily said. "A body someone thought they saw, under the village tree? That's pretty bizarre. Some prankster call, I bet. I heard the sirens—what a pity, to bring out practically the whole department for nothing, on a stormy night."

"Max left so early, and I had the horses to feed—we didn't talk much this morning. I was hoping that, during Christmas, Max and the men might have some time off."

"It would be nice if you and Max could have a little vacation. If you don't even have time to talk to each other . . . You're not . . . Having problems?"

Charlie laughed. "We're fine, Sicily."

"You *were* cheated out of your honeymoon." Sicily picked up the empty pot and signaled the waitress for more coffee. Then, more gently, "Maybe you'll have time, now, to get away. With the book long finished and this exhibit put together—and already three great reviews on the book— you do need a breather. When you leave here, go on over to the station, Charlie, see if you can entice Max away for an early lunch. He can't be that busy."

"It's a thought," Charlie said. She was used to Sicily's managing ways, they didn't usually annoy her. And she would like to stop by the station to see if anything more had turned up on the Greenlaws' break-in. She couldn't get her mind off the danger the two older folks might have been in last night, couldn't shake her sense of unease for them.

She didn't mention the incident to Sicily. That, too, was not yet public knowledge. She would talk to no one about it except those who already knew—including three nosy cats, she thought uneasily. Probably the cats were at the station right now, slyly absorbing newly arrived electronic intelligence—fingerprint information, DMV records . . . She was more than a little curious, herself.

"Why the grin?"

"Thinking about the show," Charlie lied. "About Saturday night, about these rooms crowded with people, about the wonderful parties you always throw." But then suddenly a wave of panic struck her. "What if . . . Sicily, what if no one . . . ?"

Sicily laughed. "Have you ever been to one of my openings that wasn't packed, and with the most elegant and influential people?"

"Never," Charlie said, smiling in return. "I just . . ."

"Nerves," Sicily said, patting Charlie's hand like a solicitous mother. "Go have lunch with Max. Go shopping, spend some money, buy something frivolous, that'll brighten your day."

But Charlie wasn't in a mood for shopping. Leaving the gallery, she headed straight for Molena Point PD. Maybe Max could tear himself away, if not for lunch, then for a late-morning coffee break—and maybe she'd see Juana, and the little girl. She wanted to tell Davis and Max that Donnie French was talking indiscreetly about the child.

The morning after the Christmas-tree incident, Max had looked distressed and angry when he told her about the three cats snuggled up with the little girl, and she could do nothing but brush it off. "Clyde lives right behind the plaza, Max. I imagine his cat does roam in those gardens, that's safer for a cat than the street."

"And the other cats? Wilma's cat? Greenlaws' cat? Why would . . . ?"

"They hang out together," she'd said with a shrug. "You know how cats are."

"No, Charlie, I don't know how cats are. I know dogs

hang out together. I know horses hang out together. I've always believed that cats were loners."

"No." She'd laughed. "Cats are just as social. They're simply quieter about it. You've never been around cats very much. Look how Clyde's cat hangs around the station. That's about as social as a cat can get."

"That's because Mabel feeds him."

She shook her head. "Joe *is* a very sociable cat. I've watched him, and I think he likes you and Dallas. Cats are fascinating, Max. They're all so different from one another."

Max had to take her word for it. Charlie, having studied cats for her drawings and for her new book, had gained a reputation with him as an unchallengeable authority on the subject. *And that*, Charlie thought, *is just the way I want it.* As long as Max considered her an authority, she might be able to sidetrack his doubts.

But maybe I am an authority, she thought, hiding a laugh, *considering what I know about the talents of certain felines.*

19

THE CHILL, SUNNY morning had warmed considerably as Charlie left her car, walking between the pale stucco courthouse, the broad parking area, and the courthouse gardens that were bright with red and pink camellias and cyclamen. Moving into the station through the heavy glass door, she stopped at the dispatcher's desk to chat with blond, middle-aged Mabel Farthy. She admired Mabel's countertop Christmas tree, and handed Mabel the bakery box that she'd bought from Jolly's Deli, picking it up on her way from the gallery.

"Not homemade," she told Mabel. "The spirit's willing, but I can't seem to find the time. They're good, though," she said, opening the box of Christmas cookies. "I sampled a couple, at the deli, just to make sure."

They gossiped idly until Mabel's radios demanded attention, then Charlie moved on down the hall to Max's office. There she paused, swallowing back a laugh.

Max sat at his desk, deep into a stack of paperwork. When he looked up and saw her, his lean face broke into a grin.

Across the room, Dallas sat on the leather couch behind a messy stack of files spread out before him on the coffee table. But it was the other three occupants who made her smile: from beneath the credenza, Dulcie's green eyes and Kit's yellow gaze met hers, as wide and innocent as kittens'. And from the book shelves behind Max, between volumes of the California Penal Code, Joe Grey looked boldly back at her.

Max's closed, cop's look had vanished at the sight of her, his brown eyes lighting with pleasure. "Come join us. Get yourself some coffee, we were just going over the Greenlaws' break-in, you can help us brainstorm."

Flattered, Charlie poured a mug of coffee and sat down in the leather chair from where she could catch glimpses of Dulcie and Kit. Max's office was welcoming and comfortable, nothing like the old, noisy corner of the open squad room, before he'd bullied the city into remodeling the department—nice oak desk, leather chair and couch just nicely worn, the deep-colored Persian rug that Charlie had contributed, and three walls hung with her drawings of Max's other love, his buckskin gelding.

Settling down into the leather chair, balancing her coffee, she thought how handsome Max looked, leathery and lean—and all hers, she thought, suppressing a grin. "What did you get on the prints?"

"Nothing," he said. "Nothing on the woman who broke into Greenlaws'. Nothing on the prints from the Christmas-tree scene."

"You mean they haven't come back yet? They must be backed up."

"No, I mean both sets came back negative. National, and regional."

"I can't believe that."

"It happens. Guy doesn't have a record, never been in the military, has never applied for a government or sensitive job."

Behind Max, Joe Grey looked royally annoyed. But at Garza's glance, he busied himself washing his paws. Max and Dallas were used to Joe prowling their offices, but this intense scrutiny wasn't needed. Charlie knew both men enjoyed the tomcat's company, though they wouldn't admit it. Maybe a friendly, visiting animal is as therapeutic for a cop as it is for a hospital patient. A little purr to break the tension. Therapy cats for cops, the latest medical breakthrough—soothing feline intervention for overstressed law enforcement. If she didn't stop, she was going to giggle.

But as Max laid out what they did have on the Greenlaws' burglar, the cats were not in a nurturing mood. Watching the three little beasts, Charlie could see clearly their sharp annoyance at the lack of information.

There was nothing the three cats valued so highly as the nationwide electronic data available within the department—that intelligence, plus their access to the officers' private discussions, all provided needed answers and filled in empty spaces. Without these visits, their clandestine assistance to Molena Point PD would be much less helpful; every investigation in which the cats took part was, unknown to the officers, a cooperative effort between feline and cop, reinforced by nationwide electronic resources.

"Possibly we have the make on the woman's car," Max said. "Car's been parked for several days on different streets near the Greenlaws'. Four neighborhood complaints. Brennan was about to have it hauled off. It's registered to Evina

Woods. Eugene, Oregon, address that turned out to be a vacant lot. Cameron is lifting prints—but there's not much else we can do, unless the Greenlaws file charges."

"I thought," Charlie said, "that by this morning Lucinda might have changed her mind."

Max shook his head. "I've never known Lucinda to be so indecisive. Or hardheaded. She knows a break-and-enter can turn ugly. Says she wants a couple of days to watch the woman, see what she does."

"That just isn't like Lucinda," Charlie said. "What if this *is* connected to the break-ins at the school? Or to the murder or whatever happened in the plaza?"

"We don't know that," Max said.

"You said yourself you don't believe in coincidences."

"I don't believe in jumping to conclusions, either. But," he said, his voice softening, "we do know that the little girl wasn't molested, and that's good news."

"Has she told Davis anything?"

"She still hasn't spoken. Maybe she *can't* speak, though the doctors could find no physical cause."

Dallas said, "The bloodstains on her clothes and around the Christmas tree were human, all type O positive, that's pretty common. Looks like the body was dragged into the car that was backed up into the plaza."

"And still no witnesses?" Charlie said. "No one came forward after the newspaper article?"

"Not yet," Max said. "If we had a make on the vehicle, something besides the tire casts . . ."

"They don't match the car around the Greenlaws' house?"

Max shook his head. "We've found no connection."

"But what if there were? What if that woman turned out to be the killer, hiding at the Greenlaws'? Is Lucinda thinking of that?"

"That's all conjecture, Charlie. We can't force Lucinda to file."

"But Pedric . . ."

"Pedric is standing back, this time. If we had anything to put that woman at the plaza—"

"Not her prints?"

"No. Nothing." Max rose to fill his coffee cup. "Half my mind says Lucinda's being foolish. The other half says listen to her, let her run with it."

Charlie looked at him. "That's why she talked you into leaving the camera and backpack there. Into printing the pictures, copying them, then putting them back in the empty apartment."

Max nodded, his thin, lined face expressionless.

"Anything on the people this woman's watching?" Charlie said.

Dallas said, "The names they gave the rental agent are Betty and Ralph Wicken, Eugene, Oregon. No record under those names on the West Coast. We're waiting for the national report. There's another man with them. He's not on the rental agreement.

"The Kodak envelope was marked Jane Jones." Dallas shook his head. "Really original. I talked with the photo clerk at the drugstore this morning, he remembers a woman, same description as Greenlaws' burglar, bringing in an envelope of photos she claimed was given to her by mistake. She said both inner envelopes got into the one outer envelope, into the one with her own name on it. She may match the description of a customer who did some machine copies at Mail Boxes."

"The woman," Max said, "could be spying on a strayed husband, maybe he and his girlfriend moved into that rental. In that case, without a complaint from the Greenlaws that she broke in, we have nothing."

"Unless," Dallas said, "we feel she or the Wickens present a threat to the school. With those pictures . . ."

"I'm on my way up to talk with Dorothy Street," Max said, "to show her the photographs." He looked at Charlie. "We ran half a dozen sets last night, and some enlargements, before I took them back to the Greenlaws'. And we're increasing patrols around the school. We can't let this lie, with children involved. If we had the Wickens' fingerprints and could come up with an old warrant, something to bring them in for questioning . . . I don't . . ."

Charlie's attention was snapped away by a flurry of movement beneath the credenza. Pretending to choke on her coffee, she leaned down—staring straight into Kit's blazing yellow eyes.

The tortoiseshell was so tense and excited suddenly that Charlie was afraid she'd speak. Dulcie must have feared the same, the way she was pawing at Kit. *Oh, Kit!* Charlie thought as she mopped up her coffee. *Be still, Kit! Please be quiet!* What had Max said that so electrified the little cat? What did Kit know? Or suddenly remember?

20

THE CATS VANISHED from Max's office like smoke, one instant there, the next instant slipping out the door: three swift shadows, quickly gone. Charlie left close behind them, muttering something about shopping. Max said, "Come back around noon, I'll try to get away for lunch." He'd patted her on the backside and sent her out the door.

She'd wanted to follow the cats, but by the time she pushed through the glass door to the street, they were gone. She stood scanning the gardens and then moved to her car, stood looking back at the roof to catch a glimpse of them.

She saw only a flock of pigeons fluttering down as if returning to their strutting ground after being rudely rousted, and imagined the cats flushing them up in a panic as they sped away across the tiles. Sighing, she got in her car, and with no cats to follow, she went shopping.

· · ·

KIT TOLD JOE and Dulcie on the way, running full out, as wild as bees in a windstorm. "When I went down there," she said, leaping a narrow span between peaks, "that woman came out of the house and threw a clay flowerpot at me." She went silent as they raced across an oak branch above the Christmas traffic.

"So?" Dulcie said. "So what's the excitement? You're lucky she didn't . . ."

But Joe Grey was grinning from ear to ear; and he and Kit raced ahead like Thoroughbreds sprinting for the finish line.

Kit looked back at Dulcie once, with impatience. "Come *on*. Hurry! Before she throws it away!"

Dulcie hurried, puzzled and irritated. Kit ran so fast she couldn't talk anymore; not until they were in sight of Kit's own house did she stop again, long enough to blurt, "Fingerprints! Dallas and Harper want fingerprints, and that woman . . ."

"Threw the pot," Dulcie interrupted, getting the picture at last, and they were off again, streaking for Kit's house.

Above them the sky was deep blue, the clouds white and towering where last night's storm had given way to a bright and dramatic morning. Kit was crouched to scorch up the oak to her dining-room window when she saw Lucinda looking out—the moment Lucinda saw her, the old lady drew back out of sight.

She doesn't want me to see her? Kit thought, surprised. *Why ever not? That's fine with me, she doesn't need to see us around that rental, after she told me to stay away. Maybe she's wrapping a present and doesn't want me to see, maybe that's why she ducked . . .*

Climbing, the three cats waited hidden among the densest leaves of the oak until Lucinda left the room, then Kit leaped to the window and slipped in through her cat door, making not a sound. Racing for the kitchen and pawing open a cupboard, she was out again almost at once, carrying in her mouth an empty plastic bag. She bolted out her cat door as Lucinda came out of the bedroom and they were gone, racing downhill, lunging awkwardly through the sodden leaves toward the old rental.

As THE CATS paused in the neighbors' driveway, Kit dangling her white plastic bag, across the village in a small café, James Kuda sat at a table in the far corner among the shadows, though very likely he had no need to hide. He was annoyed at himself for feeling edgy. The place was self-service, there was only the cashier, back behind the counter. Kuda sat mulling over what he'd seen.

A weird twist of fate—or maybe providence—that he'd spotted that homeless guy in the village wearing what looked like his cast-away shoes. The shoes that he'd left in the highway Dumpster. Grizzled old tramp. Well, he'd left them there thinking a homeless man might fish them out. Better than some cop finding them. By the time the guy had walked the highway from that Dumpster into the village, there'd be nothing left clinging in the soles, no trace from the plaza. And what police department would have the time and personnel to check every pair of shoes walking around town, when there wasn't even a body to investigate? When all they had was a scared kid who probably wouldn't talk, a little blood, and apparently some phone call that could be the work of some prankster or drunk?

Not likely they had a bullet, he was pretty sure that hollow-point .22 had stayed in the skull where he'd put it. Rising to fill his cup again, he thought about that kid. Still not sure what to do about her.

It would take some kind of miracle for her to tell what she'd seen. He had to laugh, the cops hauling her around from one place to another trying to protect her. Some kind of security. He'd have no trouble at all if he decided to kill her, if he decided she was a threat. That cop taking her up to those four helpless women, that was a laugh. And that old cracker-box house—might as well hide her in a paper bag.

It might come to that, he thought, he might have to go after the kid, if there was some unexpected turn. Or, worst case, he might have to get out faster than he'd planned—and he wasn't ready, he wasn't finished, yet, with his business.

Well, he wasn't going to panic now, and run, turn his back on half a million or maybe twice that. No, he'd be all right. He'd always slipped through slick and fast, and no one to follow him. It would be the same this time, he just had to keep his nerve. Play it cool, keep an eye on the kid, the unknown element, and he'd be just fine.

THE CAR WAS still gone from the driveway, the shards still lying there on the cement, the shattered pieces of clay scattered among dry earth and dead fern fronds. As the cats hit the drive, the fading scent of the woman hung above them, mixed with the last remnant of exhaust fumes.

Glancing up at the rental and seeing no one at the windows, they began to pick up the sharp fragments of the red clay pot between their teeth and lay them in the plastic bag. They tried not to drool and smear the evidence, could only hope they weren't obliterating the woman's prints. Little bits of dry earth dropped off into their mouths, and Kit got the sneezes. Just as Joe placed the last shard in the bag, they heard a car coming. Snatching the heavy bag between them, they dragged it awkwardly away through the wet leaves into the bushes; and there they crouched over the white plastic to hide it, waiting for the car to pull in.

The car didn't pause, it went on by, speeding away up the hill. The cats had risen to move on when Kit glanced toward home and saw Lucinda's silhouette in the window of the downstairs apartment—exactly where she had promised Max and Pedric she wouldn't go. She was standing at the laundry window, looking out; and she was not alone. Behind her, turned away, stood the shorter, dark-clad woman.

"What's she doing?" Kit hissed.

"Come on," Dulcie said, peering out from the heavy juniper foliage. "Come on, Kit, we'll leave the bag here and come back for it."

"That woman might have been looking out, too," Kit said. "She might have seen, and what would she think, cats putting something in a plastic bag and dragging it away?"

"Lucinda might have seen," Dulcie said. "But she would never let a stranger see such a thing. Lucinda's quick, Kit. She wouldn't . . . Don't be nervous, it's all right. We'll just leave it here and—"

"We can't leave it. What if someone—"

"No one," Joe said irritably, "would have reason to look under here. If someone did, who would care about a broken flowerpot?" But even so, before they raced away, Joe pawed damp leaves over the bag with deft swipes, effectively burying it until not a trace of white plastic shone through. Then they raced away through woods—*To catch Lucinda in the act*, Kit thought with a flash of unaccustomed anger at her housemate.

Approaching the downstairs window at the front of the house, they found it wide open. Crouching to leap to the sill, they heard voices inside, and footsteps coming down the hall.

"I will," Lucinda was saying, "but you'll have to trust *me*, Evina." The soft scuff of their steps passed by the window, approaching the sliding-glass door. "I'll do what I can, but in return you have to give me your word."

There was a pause, another scuff, as if Lucinda had turned to face the woman.

"It will do your niece no good," Lucinda said, "if you do something foolish and end up in prison. How would that help her?"

Evina's voice was low and slightly raspy, with a soft Southern accent. "If you pull the law into this, old woman, I swear you're the one to regret it."

"I told you I would not. If it can be avoided. That's the best promise I can make."

"The law did nothing to help me. Nothing to help find Marlie. That sheriff's thick with Leroy's family, he'd do nothing against them. Cops. They're all the same, don't tell me about cops."

"They're not all the same. Our police aren't like that."
Silence.

"Our law enforcement folks couldn't be more caring. And they are friends of mine. If I have to go to them, I promise they'll help you."

There was another shuffle, as if Evina had moved fast. Kit sprang to the sill, growling, meaning to leap in at her. But then the glass door slid open, and Kit dropped down again and raced around the side of the house as Lucinda came out, crossed the little deck, and started up the stairs. Dulcie and Joe held back as the slider closed again, and the woman's soft steps turned away into the empty rooms. They were about to leap to the sill and inside, when they heard her approaching the window.

As they drew back into the shelter of the mock-orange bushes, the small, dark-clad woman swung a leg over the low sill, ducked under the upper glass, eased herself out and dropped to the ground. She was still dressed in jeans and a navy sweater, and was carrying black canvas backpack. Moving past the bushes where the cats crouched, stepping close enough so they could have slashed her ankles, she headed fast down across the yard to the street below and then along the narrow sidewalk.

Silent and quick, Joe and Dulcie were behind her. Trotting along through the neighborhood gardens, taking what cover they could, they tried to look like wandering neighborhood kitties as they followed Evina Woods. Twice she turned to look behind her. The first time, they leaped after a nonexistent bird that seemed intent on escaping them. Evina was so small and fine-boned that from the back she looked like a girl; only when they saw her face did they see the lines from sun and weather, and the large, prominent nose. Her black hair was short and scraggly, with a reddish gleam where the sun hit it. She made no friendly gesture toward the wandering kitties, as many folk would do; she was not, apparently, a cat lover. The cats, drawing more deeply into the shadows, followed her for two blocks, ducking into the bushes, watching as she got into a big, tan, rusted-out Chevy so old it had tail fins, a dinosaur of a car.

"A '51 Chevy," Joe said, well schooled in matters automotive from living with Clyde. "I don't remember the name of that model." They memorized the Oregon license number, though very likely this was the car on which Harper had already run the plates. They watched it head downhill toward the village, its dented top rust red where the tan paint was worn away to the primer. When they could no longer see it, they headed back for Kit's house.

"You can bet Lucinda went down there without telling Pedric," Joe said. He turned to look at Dulcie. "What's she up to?" They had never known Lucinda to keep secrets from Pedric; the old couple were completely devoted to each other. They rounded the house through Lucinda's camellias and ferns, scrambled up the oak and across the horizontal branch to the dining-room window. There they paused, listening.

Kit and Lucinda were arguing, a heated family disagreement that made Joe and Dulcie back away. The two seldom argued, not with this kind of anger. And now Pedric joined in, snapping at Lucinda. Through the cat door came the lovely smells of Christmas, pine scent from the Christmas tree and the lingering aromas of baking—all spoiled by the angry voices. The two cats listened, shocked, Joe's ears back and his yellow eyes narrowed. But then as the argument raged, he sat down on the sill and began with great concentration to wash his front paws. He cleaned all four feet and then his silver-gray coat—while Dulcie responded to her friends' quarrel by nervously biting her claws, removing the outer sheaths to sharpen each curved rapier.

Both cats felt they shouldn't be listening to this private family scuffle. Except that this was not strictly a family disagreement, this might soon be a matter for the police, Lucinda's safety was at stake here. And, anyway, who ever said cats weren't nosy?

21

"I TOLD EVINA," LUCINDA was saying, "that the police had already been here and we didn't file charges. I said before we did that, we wanted to know what this is about."

"That's not what *I* want," Pedric grumbled. "I want her out of here, pronto. I want her in jail, Lucinda, before she hurts you." Pedric was no longer standing back. The thin old man was worried, and furious. Dulcie and Joe had never seen him so angry. They looked at each other, half amused, half frightened.

"She hasn't harmed anything," Lucinda said evenly.

"She scared the hell out of all of us, and she could have hurt you, bad. And damage? We don't *know* what damage she might have done taking those pictures and spying. Do you want to be a party to some kind of blackmail?"

Lucinda looked surprised, as if she hadn't thought of that—but Kit leaped to the arm of her chair, hissing at both of them. "When you questioned her," Kit asked impatiently, "what did she say, Lucinda?"

"She gave me a wild tale," Lucinda admitted. "And yet . . . She was so upset. She sounded . . . Well," Lucinda said with embarrassment, "I'm really inclined to believe her."

Pedric snorted. Kit didn't reply. Joe and Dulcie, unable to remain uninvolved, slipped in through the cat door and dropped from the windowsill to the dining-room rug, beneath the table.

Looking into the living room, which Lucinda had turned into a forest of evergreen boughs dominated by the Christmas tree in the far corner, they were very still. The room smelled of pine and nutmeg, and a fire burned on the hearth. The cats could see only the back of Pedric's head where he sat, rigid and angry. Kit sat on the rug, between their two chairs, looking intently at the thin old woman. "Tell us, Lucinda. Tell us what she said." The fire's pleasant crackling was the only comforting sound in the tense room.

"She told me she followed those three down from Eugene," Lucinda said. "She thinks—is convinced that one of them killed her niece, after the girl testified against him."

"This was in Oregon?" Pedric said.

"No, that was in southern Arkansas, some little backwoods town. She told me that when the killer ran, she thought he would head to Oregon to his girlfriend, and—"

"Then why is she here?"

"Let me finish. She said that he'd been phoning the girlfriend, that she'd found portions of his phone bills in his trash." Lucinda gave Pedric a wrinkled smile. "She broke into his cabin and tossed it. She said she couldn't go to their sheriff with her suspicions, that he would have done nothing."

"Lucinda," Pedric said, "that's—"

"She said the killer was thick with the law in their town, and that the sheriff was so corrupt she had no faith he'd ever arrest the man."

"Lucinda, this sounds . . ." But at her look, Pedric went silent.

"You grew up in the South," she said. "You know what some of those little country towns are like that. Good-old-boy buddies, looking out for their own."

Pedric wouldn't argue. "Start from the beginning," he said. "Try to make sense of what you're saying."

Lucinda looked beyond Pedric to the dining room. "Come in by the fire, you two, and get warm."

Quietly, Dulcie and Joe padded in, settling on the thick rug by Pedric's feet, and Lucinda continued. "Her name is Evina Woods. She followed Leroy Huffman, the man she thinks killed her niece, from Arkansas to Eugene, then down here."

"From the beginning," Pedric repeated.

Lucinda sighed. "Huffman had been dating a friend of her sister, Neola Black. Evina said he milked Neola for everything, including ten acres of land that he got her to deed to him. Evina's sister couldn't talk sense to Neola, not even when there was nothing left but the woman's house. Only when he tried to get her to mortgage that, after he hadn't paid back any of the money she'd loaned him, did Neola come to her senses.

"Evina said that when Neola refused to mortgage her house, Huffman killed her. Maybe to avoid her filing a complaint with the county attorney, or simply in a fit of rage—Evina said he was known for his violent temper.

"Evina's seventeen-year-old niece, Marlie, saw him kill Neola; she was the only witness. She saw them in the woods behind Neola's house, saw him stab her . . . saw them fighting, saw Neola twist and fall and lie still. Marlie ran home to her mother, she didn't think Huffman saw her. When Marlie and her mother went to the sheriff, he laughed at them.

"He sent someone out for Neola's body, all right. But he made fun of Marlie and her mother, said he knew for a fact that Huffman had left town two days earlier, that the sister's death had been a simple accident, that she'd fallen on her own butcher knife.

"Marlie asked why she'd have a butcher knife in the woods, and the sheriff said he'd heard she collected herbs sometimes, and that she liked to gather mushrooms.

"Now, mind," Lucinda said, "this is what Evina told me. She and her sister went to the county attorney, and he took action. Finally this Leroy Huffman was arrested and charged with murder.

"Marlie testified at the trial, but according to Evina, even the county attorney wasn't too clean. She said Huffman got only six months, for accidental manslaughter, that the jury apparently believed, or was bullied into saying, that's all it was."

"Sounds," Pedric said, "like something she took off a TV movie."

Lucinda shook her head. "She sounded . . . It was hard for her to tell this. The poor thing kept . . . Either she's a mighty good actress, or her story's true. She seems really shaken over this."

"But how does that put her here?" Kit said. "What was she doing in our house, taking pictures?"

"She said that the same week Leroy Huffman got out of prison, Marlie, who had testified against him, disappeared. That she hadn't told her mother she was going anywhere, and she wasn't the kind of girl to just take off. And then, a few days later, Huffman was gone. Apparently there was nothing legal to stop him, he'd done all his time.

"Marlie was popular, and the sheriff said she probably ran away with some guy, or that if she hadn't run away, then maybe she felt ashamed after she'd testified against Huffman. Evina says Marlie wouldn't go away like that and worry her mother.

"She was so sure that Huffman had either killed Marlie or had her prisoner, that she broke into Huffman's house, dreading what she'd find." Lucinda stroked Kit, and sipped her cold coffee. "She didn't find any trace that Marlie had been there. But she found letters from Huffman's girlfriend in Oregon, and the torn-up phone bills in the trash showing several recent calls to Eugene. She traced the phone number, and it was the girlfriend's number, all right.

"Now she had the woman's address, and with no other clue to where Huffman might have gone, and still thinking he might have Marlie with him, she headed for Eugene, caught a red-eye flight. In Eugene she bought an old car so she'd be able to follow him.

"She watched the girlfriend's house until she saw Huffman, he was staying there with the girlfriend and another man that Evina thought was her brother. For several days she spied on the house. She saw no sign of her niece, and was beginning to think he'd killed her. She waited until all three were out, and then broke in there, too. But again, no niece."

"Quite the skilled little housebreaker," Pedric said, and Dulcie cut an amused look at Joe. Pedric Greenlaw was the gentlest of people, though he was far from weak or innocent. He had committed his own share of petty crimes in the distant past.

Maybe that was why he was angry now, was more distressed by Evina than was Lucinda, more willing to see through Evina's story.

"But in the house in Eugene," Lucinda said, "Evina found her niece's locket and watch.

"There were several duffel bags packed and sitting by the door, and in the garage a stack of packed boxes. On a desk, she found some clippings and papers that made her think they meant to head down the coast, that they had some business in California.

"She left Marlie's jewelry there, but took pictures of it in that setting. She watched the house, and when they left Eugene, she followed them." Lucinda paused when Kit rose to stand on the arm of her chair, looking her squarely in the face.

"This is too much, Lucinda. That woman is putting you on."

"Just listen, Kit. Just, for once, be still and listen."

"I *have* been listening," Kit said crossly, exchanging an exasperated look with Pedric before she turned her face away from her beloved Lucinda.

"Please, Kit." Lucinda looked shaken at being pitted against both Pedric and Kit, the two she loved best in all the world. She stroked Kit, trying to make up, but Kit remained aloof, her tail lashing.

"Let me finish," Lucinda said more sharply. "From

the clippings she found, Evina thought that in coming to Molena Point, they were after some kind of artwork, something from the last century.

"I asked her if they seemed the kind of people to know about art. She said the woman's letters to Huffman mentioned several Seattle galleries where she'd worked. Evina said the letters were vague, didn't spell out exactly what they might be planning, but said that if he wanted to come out to the coast and help them, they might make a real haul. That's how the letters put it.

"She said the letters also mentioned Betty Wicken's brother, Ralph, that she had to keep him with her, after what had happened, that he was a real worry. That if she left him on his own he'd be in trouble again, and be back in prison."

Lucinda shook her head. "Evina said she cares only about what happened to her niece. That when she found out more, she'd go to the police, and get an attorney. That she took those pictures of the Wickens so she would have some identification to give the police. The Xerox copies, she said, are from a roll of film that Betty Wicken's brother took into the drugstore.

"She said she saw him by accident, she was back by the cosmetics aisle when he took the film in. Curious about him and what crimes he'd committed that Betty was so worried about, she returned early on the day the pictures were to be ready, picked them up, Xeroxed them, and then returned the envelope saying it was given her by mistake, said the clerk didn't question that."

Lucinda looked hard at Pedric, and at Kit. "Evina came all this way to find out what happened to her niece. She planned well enough to bring a piece of Marlie's laundry, for DNA testing. She means to get into that house down there and look for Marlie or for some further evidence."

Pedric remained silent. Joe and Dulcie couldn't see his face. The whole story sounded so strange and unlikely—yet the cats had never known Lucinda to be such a soft touch for a hard-luck story.

"This Leroy Huffman," Pedric said, "did she tell you anything else about him?"

"She said he'd lived all his life in their little town, and had always been in trouble, but his family had always been tight with those who ran the town, that the present sheriff and Leroy's father were second cousins, and that Leroy and his two brothers could get away with anything."

"But how do the pictures fit in?" Kit said. "The ones of the Home and the children?"

"In the house in Eugene, she had found one old, yellowed clipping about the brother, Ralph, and a child abduction. She tried to check on him, to see if he was a registered sex offender, thinking the information might help in some way, but molesters living in Oregon aren't required to register." She said no more, but they were all thinking of the dead man and the little child in the plaza. Could Ralph Wicken have tried to kidnap her, and the man fought him off, and Wicken killed him?

"Did she see if he was registered here?" Pedric asked.

"She tried on that Web list," Lucinda said. "For California, and then the national one, but he wasn't listed in either."

The kit began to fidget, thinking about Betty Wicken's fingerprints on the broken pot shards, and what those prints might show. Did Betty Wicken have a record? And was Wicken their real name, or an alias? Was that why Ralph didn't show as a registered sex offender?

But now, with Betty's fingerprints, could the department identify her? And if she had a record, would it show information about her brother? *So much to learn*, Kit thought nervously, *all based on the fingerprints lying unguarded among the bushes, hidden only by a few rotting leaves.* She looked intently at Lucinda.

"What?" Lucinda said uneasily.

"We have Betty Wicken's fingerprints," Kit said with a twinge of guilt.

Lucinda was very still. "You promised me, Kit, not to go down there."

Kit looked at Lucinda, as wide-eyed and innocent as a kitten.

"Where are the fingerprints?" the thin older woman said patiently.

Silence.

Lucinda sighed. "Down in that house?"

"Not exactly."

"You are not to go down there again, for any reason. Particularly now that we know more about those three. Is that clear, Kit?" It was. Kit dropped her gaze in consternation.

But Pedric looked at Kit slyly and rose from his chair, and hiding the first smile the cats had seen all morning, the old man put on his outdoor shoes and his jacket, questioned Kit further, and then went down the hill himself.

Despite his somewhat shady past, Pedric Greenlaw was a tall, erect, white-haired man as dignified-looking as a federal judge. No one who saw him wandering the oak woods would suspect him of prying into the lives of others—even when he knelt to dig among the wet leaves and lift out the white plastic bag, slipping it swiftly under his coat. Pedric had been raised from childhood to the skills of a pickpocket and shoplifter, talents of which he was no longer proud but that could sometimes be put to good use.

22

FELINE PROMISES ARE not, from a cat's view-
point, really meant to be kept. Except, of course,
when the cat is closely watched and can do little
else. Five minutes after Pedric returned up the
hill with the evidence hidden in his coat, while he was busy
in the kitchen and Lucinda was on the phone to Max Harper,
the cats slipped out and headed for the rental house, reas-
sured that the pot shards were on their way to the police.

Even as they raced down through the wet woods, they
heard the Greenlaws' garage door open, heard the car start.
They ducked when they glimpsed Lucinda backing out.
Then, in a moment, her car came around and down the
hill on the street below, heading for the village with the
plastic bag, delivering, hopefully, a vital key to the identity
of the strange neighbors—certainly Lucinda might notice
her neighbor drop a flowerpot and, already curious and
entangled in the mystery of who these people were, would
of course hike on down at the first opportunity, and fetch
the possible evidence.

Perfectly logical, Pedric said. No need for the snitch to be hanging around the kit's house, to "accidentally" see that evidence, no need to invite unnecessary connections regarding the cats. They had already been in the cops' faces this week, during the murder investigation at the plaza, and during the search for the little girl, why encourage unnecessary speculation and awkward questions?

But now, with neither Lucinda nor Pedric watching, the cats approached the rental house studying the blind-covered windows above them. Didn't anyone in there ever want to look out at the daylight, or ever long for a breath of fresh air?

The driveway was still empty, the car still gone, and so, presumably, was Betty Wicken. There was no sound from within the house, the morning was quiet except for the scratching of a fat gray dove, in the bushes. Were the two men gone? If they, too, had left the house, the empty rooms were prime for a quick break-and-enter. If Evina's niece might be held prisoner in there, this was the moment to find her.

Or were Leroy Huffman and Betty's brother, Ralph, still sleeping? Crouching beside the front door, the cats listened. The house seemed taller than it was wide, just the garage at the front, the entry, and one small window. The kitchen and living room were at the back, with a view downhill to the village. Upstairs there seemed to be three bedrooms and a bath—a classic circa-1940s house that hadn't received much attention since it was built, some seventy years ago. Circling, they paused below the kitchen, where the dinette window jutted out—the kind of shallow bay window that one would decorate with potted plants. The Wickens' decor ran to newspapers and tattered paperback books stacked on the wide sill, ragged garish books such as one might pick up for a quarter in a used bookstore. They could hear the footsteps of two men, and could hear them talking, then the rattle of a cup against a saucer and the rustle of papers. The coffee smelled like it had been cooking for hours.

"If they stay in the kitchen," Kit said, "we can be in and out, and they'll never know."

They thought the windows, with their dry, cracked frames, would be a snap for the three of them together to jimmy, but by the time they'd leaped up, trying half a dozen double-hung panes, working at the old locks with impatient claws, they decided these round, brass closures were stronger than they looked. All the windows were locked tight or perhaps stuck tight with the ancient paint. Sealed for eternity, as far as they were concerned.

The garage might have proven easier, except that its three small high windows were covered, inside, with plywood. They sniffed beneath the electric garage door and smelled a miasma of grease, mildew, new paint, and gas vapors.

At the far side of the garage, a small door opened to the backyard. Leaping up, Joe swung on the knob. It turned freely, but kick as he might against the molding, the door wouldn't open. "Feels like it's bolted from inside."

Beside the little door stood an overflowing garbage can amid a half-dozen sodden cardboard boxes filled with empty bottles and wet, wadded newspapers. Very high above were three small, mesh-covered ceiling vents. Maybe big enough for a cat, maybe not. Leaping from the top of the garbage can, Joe managed to snag the mesh of one—and got his claws hung in it. He couldn't get loose. Panicked, fighting the screen, he tore it enough to free himself. He dropped down, his ears back, swearing angry hisses.

"Mesh is nailed or stapled on, and sealed with old paint."

"Come on," Dulcie said. "We—"

"The car's coming," Kit said. Ducking into the bushes, they watched the old green Dodge turn in to the drive, parking before the front door. Betty Wicken stepped out, her long, dry-dull black hair tangled on the collar of her black peacoat. Moving quickly up the steps, she was just stepping in through the front door when the cats, with swift timing, shot in behind her. They made not a sound, did not once brush her ankles as they passed her and ducked under the hall table. The whole house shook when Betty slammed the front door.

The table had a low shelf just above them, which helped to hide them—a shelf thick with dust. Didn't people know how to use a duster? It seemed to Dulcie that they had spent half their lives crouched in mite-ridden household dust beneath someone's unkempt furniture—and household dust was not at all the same as good clean garden dirt or beach sand, was nothing like the fresh earth on the wild, far hills.

When Kit tried to stifle a sneeze and couldn't, Dulcie and Joe threw their bodies against her, muffling the sound. Above them, Betty had pulled off her coat, tossed down her keys, and moved away down the hall toward the kitchen. They breathed easier when she'd gone.

The entry was dim and small. To their right, a flight of stairs led up to the bedrooms; the living room was beyond it, looking out to the back. Shoddy furniture, early Salvation Army, that made Dulcie wonder what kind of rent they were paying.

Down the hall near the kitchen was a door that breathed out the same garage smells of gas, motor oil, and paint. Joe thought the paint smelled like automotive enamel, with which he was familiar from Clyde's classic-car restorations. In the kitchen Betty poured herself a cup of scorched-smelling coffee and sat down at the breakfast table.

"They fit?" Leroy asked, lifting his big-boned hand to scratch his shaggy brown hair.

Betty nodded. "They haven't changed the locks, the garage, or the house." She jingled two keys on a ring and dropped them back into her pocket. Using her fingers as a comb, she shook out her black hair, its tangled mass so dry one imagined dandruff drifting into her coffee. With the three tenants thus occupied, Joe Grey peered with predatory interest up the narrow stairs.

Before Dulcie could speak, he was on the first step. "Stay and watch them," he hissed. "Distract them if they start up there. I won't be a minute." And he disappeared up the worn carpet treads to the top floor. Dulcie hoped no one else was there—except maybe the kidnapped girl. If she *had* been kidnapped, if Huffman had brought her all this way. That seemed so strange. Why would he? As some kind of hostage protection?

"Supposed to rain again tonight," Betty was saying. "Maybe hail."

Leroy smiled, easing his muscled bulk in the small dinette chair. "That hail the other night . . . Could of fired off a canon, no one'd of heard."

Ralph Wicken grinned. He was a small man, thin head with short crew-cut hair, ears sticking out as if he might take off in frightened flight.

"Gets dark about seven," Betty said. "They tuck the kiddies up at eight. Lights go on upstairs, off again around eight-thirty."

Huffman said, "They've hired more guards, they're all over the place at night. Middle of the day would be better. The day they do that judging, place'll be crawling with people, trucks, power tools, carpenters hammering away. That should be enough diversion."

"What time do the day-school kids leave?" Ralph said. His eyes were muddy brown, like Betty's, but his brows were thick and black.

"You'll keep away from the kids," Betty told him. "You mess around this time and blow it, I swear I'll turn you in, Ralph. Leave you in prison for the rest of your stupid life."

Ralph smiled. Betty seemed pale and nervous. "I mean it. I won't have one of your mindless escapades mess this up."

Ralph's face flushed red and he lowered his glance. Betty watched him with distaste, then glared at Leroy. "Why the hell did you let him have the camera? I told you—"

"I didn't let him have it, he took it. Middle of the night, sneaked in our room, took it off the dresser. *You* didn't wake up! Well, hell, neither of us missed the damn thing."

"I don't see what difference," Ralph whined. "How come you can do what you want, but you're always on my case?"

Betty fixed her gaze again on her brother. "You stay away from that school. There's a hell of a difference."

"We better take him with us," Leroy said. "Keep an eye on him."

Ralph's thin face twisted into a toddlerlike sulk. "No one knows me here. Why do you always have to . . . ?"

"This isn't Oregon," Betty snapped. "California, these new laws, they find you're not registered, you're as good as locked up anyway. Serve you right," she said coldly.

The kit, sitting silently beside Dulcie, watched Betty Wicken, puzzled. "Maybe I've seen her in the village," she whispered softly.

"Where, Kit?"

"A long time ago. I can't remember where, I've been trying."

Whispering, both cats glanced toward the kitchen, but no one had heard. No human had a cat's range of hearing. Mankind was, in many ways, an inferior and handicapped specimen. *God's work left unfinished*, Dulcie thought, *at least in the areas of auditory skills and night vision.*

But now Kit's own skills seemed to have faltered. For the first time Dulcie could remember, the tortoiseshell didn't have total recall. The more she studied Betty Wicken, the more shadowy was the memory Kit tried to bring forth of where she had seen the woman. Where and when? Under what circumstances?

Betty drained her coffee and picked up a stack of papers from the kitchen table, flipping through them. They seemed to be magazine articles. The cats could see colored pages torn from slick publications, some stapled together, some with pictures of houses. Was that the Stanhope mansion? Both cats swallowed back mewls of recognition as Betty sat looking at the page. But then Betty flung down the pictures and rose, giving Ralph another glare—a look of distaste and of long-standing resignation.

"Let's get to work." She headed for the door to the garage, and Leroy got to his feet. Ralph remained at the table, his expression one of stubborn secrecy. Dulcie glanced up the stairs, wishing Joe would hurry; she was crouched to leap up after him when he appeared at the top.

Silently he trotted down to them, a gray shadow with only his white marks to attract any sudden attention. And as Betty and Leroy moved into the garage, the three cats were behind them, diving through on their heels, another bold gamble that left their paws sweating; and they melted among a stack of cardboard boxes standing beside the door.

"What did you find?" Dulcie whispered, edging close to Joe.

Joe Grey pawed cobwebs from his whiskers. "No sign of anyone else, no scent but theirs. I don't think that girl was ever here." He reared up between the boxes until he could see Betty and Leroy standing at a workbench along the opposite wall—and could see the vehicle parked less than two feet from his nose. His stifled growl made Dulcie and Kit rear up, staring.

As the Wickens stood selecting tools from a cardboard box on the workbench, assembling sledgehammers and handsaws and an electric drill, the cats could only gape with shock. In the dim and crowded garage, parked between a row of storage cupboards and a large tan SUV, stood Charlie Harper's blue van. Charlie's "Fix-It, Clean-It" van, its logo lettered clearly on the side. Charlie's blue Chevy van that she had bought when she started her home maintenance business and had used ever since, the van that should be parked either at a cleaning job, or up at the seniors' house for Mavity's convenience.

"What's it doing here?" Dulcie hissed. "Charlie's crew sure isn't cleaning this house! And why inside the garage?"

"Did they steal it?" Kit said. "But when? Charlie didn't say a word last night. How . . . ?"

"Shhh," Joe hissed. "Keep your voice down."

"That Betty doesn't work for her?" Kit whispered. "That woman hasn't gone to work for Charlie?" But Charlie *was* hiring, the business was expanding, and they all knew that it was hard to find competent help.

"Of course she doesn't work for her," Dulcie said shakily. "I know everyone she's hired. You saw the record checks that Davis ran on the applicants—every one of Charlie's employees has signed a release so the department could check for a record." The police chief's wife could not afford, for the safety of Max and his men and for the reputation of the department, to hire anyone who had the least potential of turning dangerous or stealing from her clients.

"But how . . ." Dulcie began, then, "Where's Charlie? Oh, they haven't . . . This can't be another kidnapping!"

"It's Mavity who drives it the most," Joe pointed out, staring up at the van's windows, half expecting to see someone looking back at them trying to get their attention. All three cats were thinking of last summer, when both Dulcie's housemate and Charlie Harper had been brutally kidnapped and their lives in danger. But then, "Look," Joe hissed, rearing up taller. "Take a closer look."

23

IT WAS JUST noon when Ryan Flannery left her construction job in the village and walked the three blocks to Clyde's house. A cozy lunch, just the two of them in the sunny patio, should take the edge off her grouchy mood. Glancing in the front window, she paused a moment to admire the tree they had decorated, and the garland wreath Clyde had hung on the door, then she headed around to the back. She was greeted by wild happy barks and loud banging as Rock leaped at the gate; and, when she opened the gate, by a dervish of excited hound. Rock danced around her, but never touched her, testimony to the improvement in his behavior. She took his outstretched front paws in her hands, let them rest on her arm as she talked baby talk to him.

A year ago, when the big, stray Weimaraner had adopted her, he would have nearly knocked her over leaping on her and clawing her arms for attention, a lovable clown with no idea of manners. Kneeling, she hugged Rock and scratched his sleek, sun-warmed back. He grinned, and slurped her ear—though the big, silver purebred had mastered the basics of obedience training, he was still a clown, and a challenge.

No one, she thought, unless they were dedicated athletes with plenty of time to devote, should even think of owning a Weimaraner, a breed meant for action and hard work. Without both, the dogs were miserable, and so were their owners.

Rising, she moved into the patio with Rock at her side, and closed the gate behind them. The walled retreat was almost balmy on this bright winter day; and she was inordinately pleased with the small, private world she'd designed and built for Clyde. Clyde had swept away the last of the fallen maple leaves, and the chair cushions were clean and dried of their morning dew. The long, plastered planters were bright with cyclamens and begonias, and a pot of poinsettias stood on the picnic table. The cushion on the chaise still bore the impression of the big silver hound, where Rock had been napping. On the table beside the poinsettias were a cooler, picnic plates and napkins, and a tray laid out with packets of sandwich makings and plastic containers of salad—this, too, attested to Rock's improved manners, that he could now be left alone with a table full of food, she thought smugly. But then she looked up through the kitchen window and saw that Clyde was on guard. He grinned, and waved at her.

Fetching a bottle of nonalcoholic Buckler's from the cooler, she popped the lid and stretched out on the chaise, rubbing Rock's ears as he came to lean against her, and watching Clyde through the window as he filled the coffeepot. It was nice that, since she'd started the nearby job, she could run over for lunch. Slowly, now, the tension of the morning began to ease.

She'd been so hoping for a quiet holiday season, for lovely, peaceful evenings with Clyde before the fire, admiring their joint-effort Christmas tree, Rock and Joe and Snowball and the two older cats sprawled around them. No serious worries, no violent police matters to prod her with fear for her uncle Dallas and Max and their friends.

Certainly Max and Dallas had enjoyed very little about the Christmas season, with the department looking for a killer and for a vanished body, and trying to identity a silent little girl who was too scared and traumatized to say a word—and now the Greenlaws' strange break-in that seemed to hint at an uglier scenario. And to top it off, there was Charlie's strange preoccupation and her unwillingness to share her problem.

Charlie should be turning handsprings right now, should be ecstatic with her upcoming exhibit and book signing, but instead she was grim one minute, and drawn away the next as if to another world.

In fact, when Ryan thought about it, Charlie was that way with every major crime. Whenever Max and the department faced more than the usual danger, Charlie turned moody and secretive—and that thought saddened Ryan. A cop's wife couldn't live like that. Charlie knew that. They'd talked about it at some length, and she'd thought Charlie was finally committed to living each day to the fullest and not fretting about tomorrow. Committed to living the only way a cop's family could live, and still survive. Charlie *said* she lived like that and thought like that. But if that was true, then what was this preoccupation?

Was worry over Max *not* the only cause of her stress? And a sudden realization startled Ryan: It wasn't only Charlie who seemed to experience these worried, preoccupied spells. Clyde did, too. And Wilma Getz. And even the older, levelheaded Greenlaws. During every increase in crime that stressed the department and kept the men extra busy, Ryan's friends seemed to turn moody and withdrawn, and, sometimes, inexplicably secretive.

She had never before realized this. Or maybe she hadn't wanted to see it. Maybe, she thought, she didn't want to think about it. Didn't want to understand what this was about.

Clyde came out carrying a plate of freshly sliced bread still warm from the bakery, its scent filling the patio. He set it on the table, opened a beer, leaned down to give Ryan a long kiss, then sprawled in a lounge chair, taking a good look at her. "You're wound tight."

"I'll be better when we can start on the Stanhope house. The damned city—these delays make me want to pound someone.

"But," she said more cheerfully, "this present job, Clyde . . . a few more days, we'll wrap it up. The house is charming, if I do say so. I can't wait for you to see it all finished."

"All your work is charming. It's what you're known for. Look at this house—from a shabby bachelor's pad to a designer's gem." He grinned at Ryan. "Not only beautiful and intelligent, but incredibly talented."

"That kind of flattery will get you a long way, with this lady. Meantime," she said, rising, "I'm starved. I feel like Rock, ready to dive into lunch with all four paws." Rock, though he had his own bowl of kibble, had been eyeing the picnic table with ears up and nose twitching. He knew better than to grab, but this degree of restraint wasn't easy on the energetic young dog. Ryan was putting her sandwich together when her phone rang.

"Maybe Scotty," she said, glancing at her watch. "He stopped in to see Jim Holden again at the building department." She fished her phone from its holster, listened expectantly—and her hopeful look exploded into a dark scowl.

"They *did* all that. The research! The hearings! The historic look *won't* be changed! We aren't *doing* anything to the outside. What the hell do they . . ." Ryan's face was flushed, her green eyes burned with anger. Clyde opened another Buckler's and handed it to her.

"We're not *changing* the outside," Ryan shouted into the phone. "Can't they understand simple English! Can't they read a simple damned blueprint! What kind of . . ." She listened; then, "I know it's nearly eighty years old! We've been through all that, Scotty!"

Scott Flannery was Ryan's uncle, and her construction foreman. He was her father's brother, a big, burly, redheaded Scotch-Irishman. He and Dallas Garza, her mother's brother, had both moved in with Ryan's dad when her mother died, and had helped to raise Ryan and her two sisters, staggering their work hours and sharing the household chores. Scotty was largely responsible for Ryan's interest in the building trades, while Dallas had honed the girls' interest in fine bird dogs and hunting, and in safe firearms training.

"The Historical Society is totally out of line," Ryan snapped at Scotty. "They can't have the gall to . . ."

But they could, Clyde thought, watching her. Everyone

knew that the city historical committee could be incredibly high-handed and officious. When Ryan hung up at last, Rock pressed quietly against her, looking up at her with concern, his pale yellow eyes almost human. The big silver hound might be rowdy, and an aggressive protector of those he loved, but he was supersensitive and highly responsive to Ryan's moods.

"Maybe," Clyde said, "the two public school teachers who pitched such a fit when children began to transfer to the Patty Rose School, maybe they're responsible for this."

"If they are," Ryan said, kneeling down to hug Rock, "that's even more maddening—a personal vendetta. Small-minded personal rage, aimed at hurting the school and hurting those children.

"But," she said, looking up at him, "it isn't the teachers that make the public school so dull and ineffective—not all the teachers. It's the policies, the administration, the red tape and constrictions and their morass of stupid rules."

"And whose fault is that?" Clyde said.

"Ours." Rising, Ryan moved to the table and finished slapping her sandwich together. "The city, the state. The voters," she said, sighing with frustration.

Clyde, watching her, knew that that kind of bureaucratic control upset Ryan perhaps even more than most people. When Ryan moved down from San Francisco about a year ago, a big change in her life, it was to end the cold patronization of an emotionally brutal marriage. He put his arm around her.

"Slow down," he said softly. She was almost crying, and Ryan never cried. He took her sandwich plate from her, set it down, and held her tight. She had worked so hard on this redesign for the old Stanhope studio, so intent on retaining its historic character while creating the needed classrooms. She had endured endless meetings, endless bureaucratic rejections, each of which sent her back yet again to the drawing board. She had put up with senseless arguments that had little to do with the quality and integrity of the designs and a lot to do with people's desire to control.

She looked up at him, swiping at a tear. "I didn't come down here to fight another bunch of small-minded, short-sighted, selfish . . . I thought I got away from all that." She pressed her face against him. "I'm so tired of this damned squabbling, I don't even want to do the renovation."

Clyde held her away. "You'd let the city win? Let the city make you back down, and beat you?"

"Screw them," she snapped. "I don't *care*."

"Lori and Dillon didn't back down. They fought the city and won. Two little girls . . ."

"Two little girls and three adults. And I *said*, Clyde, I don't care!"

Clyde hugged Ryan harder, knowing that she would rally. But he had to wonder about the reason for the harassment. Was it only the small-minded teachers? Or was there something else, besides the petty backbiting and power struggles? And that thought stirred his own cold and protective anger.

24

LUCINDA GREENLAW, leaving the house earlier that morning with the pottery shards safe in her pocket, smiled again thinking of Pedric wandering down the hill like some distinguished-looking mushroom hunter, kneeling among the neighbors' wet leaves and digging out the plastic bag of broken shards; as soon as he returned, she'd called Chief Harper. Her call had just caught him, he'd just come in and was about to leave again. She'd hurried down to the station, parking hastily among the courthouse gardens. As she headed in through the heavy glass door of the police wing, Mabel Farthy looked up from her realm of electronic communications.

"Lucinda!" Mabel swung out through the little gate to give her a hug, the pudgy blonde laughing, her dark uniform a bit tighter around the middle, Lucinda thought, not unkindly. "It's been a long time." Mabel sniffed at the white plastic bag that Lucinda had laid on the counter. "What did you bring? Some of your good Christmas cookies?"

Lucinda laughed. "Not this time. This is . . ." She did her best to look embarrassed. "I think it might be evidence. Well, fingerprints," she said hesitantly. "This is so . . . so busybody of me, Mabel. I . . ."

Max came up the hall as they were talking, took the bag she offered, and led her back to his office. The tall lean chief poured her a cup of coffee and made her comfortable on the couch, sitting down beside her. She opened the plastic bag, still trying to appear embarrassed when, in fact, she wasn't at all, she was having a fine time. But her story required a certain shy reluctance, she was not in the habit of bringing in evidence, and she had to make this look good.

Well, she thought, amused at herself, she'd always wanted to do a little acting. As she laid out her story, she knew she was letting the three cats off the hook—Joe Grey was right, the timing would have been way too pat if the snitch had called about this evidence: The cats are in the office, the chief says he'd give a lot for Betty Wicken's fingerprints, and not an hour later the snitch calls, telling him where to find those prints. "With that scenario," Joe had said, "everything would hit the fan."

"I know it's meddling," Lucinda said now, looking at Max shyly. "But that woman in the rental, the woman our housebreaker was spying on? You said last night, if you could get information on her . . . Well, I was afraid if I didn't slip right over there when I saw her break this flowerpot, if I didn't snatch up the pieces before she threw them away . . . I don't even know if a flowerpot can hold fingerprints, but . . . Am I making any sense . . . ?"

Max looked into the bag, didn't touch the broken shards.

"When she dropped it on the drive . . . She looked in such a hurry . . . It shattered and she just left it there, got in her car and drove off. Can you take fingerprints from this? Will that help find out about her?"

Max was silent for so long that Lucinda began to get nervous. She looked at him uncertainly, and sipped the coffee he'd poured for her. "Those photographs of the children, Max. I worried about that all night, I find that really frightening."

"As do we," Max said. He watched Lucinda so intently that she grew increasingly uneasy. She knew she was gushing, and that wasn't like her. Max put his arm around her as if, she thought, he meant to humor her, to tell her kindly that what she had done was very clever of her, and then send her away.

But instead, he had beeen interested in what she told him about Evina Woods.

"If we can lift some prints," he said, "and if we can get anything from AFIS on them, if the woman turns out to have a record, we'll have something to work with."

Max rose to refill their coffee cups. "So far, on those three tenants, we have false names, false IDs, falsified car registration. That in itself might give us reason to bring them in for questioning, but it leaves a lot of holes." He picked up the plastic bag. "We have a call in to Arkansas, to check on Evina Woods's story. I'll take this back to Dallas, see if he can lift clear prints. If not, we'll send it along to the lab, where they have more sophisticated equipment."

"I feel so sure," Lucinda said, "that Evina was telling the truth."

Max took her hand, helping her up. "You were bold to go down there and talk with her, Lucinda—I won't say foolish."

"She didn't threaten me, Max, she seemed really scared. When she saw I wasn't going to call the police, she calmed down. I know that could all have been an act, but . . . Call it a gut feeling. I think she's telling the truth."

She looked intently at him. "I'm not a soft touch, but once in a while, you have to take a chance on someone. This is one of the times . . . If I'm wrong, I expect I'll pay for it. This gamble," she said, "is one I choose to take."

IN THE DIM garage, as Betty Wicken and Leroy Huffman sorted tools at the workbench, packing them into a canvas bag, Joe approached the blue Chevy van. Slipping up onto a stack of cardboard boxes piled between the van and the wall, he balanced with a forepaw against the van's window, peering into the dim interior, his nostrils filled with the stink of automotive paint, from the amateurish blue paint job.

Pressing against the tinted glass, he saw not the pristine interior of Charlie Harper's van, no neatly built-in cupboards, no polished worktable running down one side. Only bare metal bracing and raw composition walls. This ancient, neglected interior had never had any care; it was stripped and ragged, only an empty hulk.

Dropping down to the garage floor, he studied the lettering painted on the van's side—the hasty, unprofessional logo, an amateurish copy of the more finely spaced CHARLIE'S FIX-IT, CLEAN-IT.

Somewhere, the Wickens had found another old Chevy van and had treated it to a home paint job on a par with what any active five-year-old kid could accomplish.

"Not Charlie's van," Kit whispered, narrowing her eyes and lashing her tail.

But Dulcie smiled with relief. "Charlie's safe, and Mavity's safe. But why would anyone copy Charlie's van? What do they mean to do?" Her green eyes flashed. "Setting Charlie up," she hissed, "But for what? For some burglary?" she said softly. "Or . . . could this be the missing vehicle that hauled away the dead man?" Her eyes widened. "Did you smell death in there?"

Joe slipped under the van, Dulcie and Kit beside him, and they reared up, sniffing among the axles and brakes. Trying, over the stink of grease and hydraulic and brake fluids, to detect the faintest scent of death; but there was nothing else, no foreign smell.

Dropping down again, they fled among the boxes as Leroy opened the side door of the van and tossed in two bags of tools, some cans of paint, and then ladders, drop cloths, everything one would need to renovate a house, or repair it.

"Are they horning in on Charlie's customers?" Dulcie whispered. "Pretending to work for her?"

"That doesn't make sense," Joe said softly. "And there's no cleaning equipment, just the repair stuff." The tomcat frowned. "Doesn't make sense, unless . . . Unless they've staked out Charlie's wealthy regulars, meaning to rob them—that would set Charlie up, big-time."

They looked at one another, feeling sick. Law enforcement families were prime marks for any scam to embarrass or compromise them, to put them on the wrong side of the law. The cats remembered too painfully when Captain Harper had been framed for a double murder.

"That won't happen again," Joe said.

But Kit shivered, pushing closer to Dulcie.

"Nothing has happened yet," Dulcie said. "We won't let that happen!"

25

HURRYING BY THE station, loaded down with shopping bags, hoping Max was free for lunch, Charlie found him gone. "He had to meet with the judge," Mabel said. "He went straight there from the Patty Rose School, from talking with Dorothy Street."

"Another rain check," Charlie said, laughing. It was well past noon, and she was starved.

"That's what you get when you marry a cop," Mabel said good-naturedly. "Lucinda Greenlaw brought in some kind of evidence. They talked for a while, then he headed over to meet Dorothy. Leave your packages here if you want to get a bite."

Charlie nodded. She didn't like to leave packages in her SUV, with no locked trunk. Not this time of year, when bright store packages containing free Christmas booty were all too tempting.

Tucking her packages out of the way in Max's office, she stood a moment wondering what kind of evidence Lucinda discovered. She was headed out of the station, meaning to stop for a quick bowl of soup, when she saw Dorothy Street and Ryan coming out of the courthouse. Ryan was in jeans, work boots, and a red sweatshirt, Dorothy elegant in a soft gray suit, sheer hose, and Italian flats—succeeding very well in her new, businesslike mode. They waved, and Charlie went to join them. Ryan looked mad enough to explode. Meeting them on the steps, Charlie didn't ask what they'd been doing. This had to be about the permit for the children's home. "Have you had lunch? I'm starved."

"I ate with Clyde," Ryan said. "Scotty called me in the middle of lunch. They've denied the permit again. If I die young, of a coronary, you can blame that bunch of bigots!" She glanced at her watch. "I need to get back, meet the landscaper," and with a wave she headed across the parking lot to her big red Chevy pickup.

Dorothy looked after her, shaking her head with sympathy. Then, "I guess Max stood you up. I rode over with him to pick up some papers. Come on, I'm hungry, too. Want to go back to the inn, have lunch in my office, where we can talk?"

When Charlie nodded, Dorothy flipped open her cell phone, hitting the code for the inn's kitchen. "The shrimp melt okay?"

Charlie nodded enthusiastically. "And hot tea?"

Dorothy gave her chef the order, and as they strode out together past the courthouse gardens, Dorothy glanced at her. "Those people taking pictures of our children . . . That really scares me. Max called me last night after the Greenlaws' break-in, and then, just now, he showed me the pictures—the copies he made—to see if I could add anything.

"I feel better knowing he's doubled his patrol around the school. But to take pictures of the children . . . In my book, that means only one thing," Dorothy said with disgust. "I'm glad they have the woman's fingerprints—the tenant in that house where the pictures came from. Max said he was hoping to get an immediate hit on them, something about having to get an expert to examine them, and he didn't know how long it would take."

Charlie hadn't known about the prints. Was that what Lucinda had brought in? But how had Lucinda gotten the woman's prints? Why had she . . . ? *Oh,* Charlie thought, *maybe it wasn't Lucinda who retrieved that evidence.* And the scene in Max's office, earlier that morning, played back to her: The officers' mention of the prints. Kit's sudden excitement, the little cat hardly able to contain herself, she was so wild to race away. *This time,* Charlie thought, *this time, those cats sent Lucinda Greenlaw as their courier.*

But to Dorothy she said, "It's great when AFIS can get back with an immediate reply, but if the prints aren't clear, someone does have to do a visual exam. And if the prints are close to a lot of others on file, finding a match can take some time." She studied Dorothy. "Have you talked with the children, about those people?"

"Oh yes. As soon as we knew about the pictures. We don't like to keep things from the children. We all get together after breakfast in the central hall, before classes, talk over anything that needs discussing."

She looked seriously at Charlie. "We told them about the pictures, and we described the two men and the woman as well as we could from the photos that the intruder shot. Described the car in their driveway, the old green Dodge.

Told them not to play alone, anywhere in the school yard. Not to leave the grounds without one of us, for any reason. It's hard to get the message across to the little ones, and not give them nightmares. Takes a lot of hugging and reassurance.

"But our kids are pretty wise," Dorothy said. "They all know what to do if they're approached. That's part of the survival course Patty designed—self-protection, managing their money, good health practices, making positive choices in life—and, of course, values."

Dorothy laughed. "We've had several teachers apply for jobs who said they wouldn't be caught dead teaching values to the children."

"And? What did you do?"

"We sent them packing," Dorothy said. "Values are a part of survival, and that was important to Patty, after her little grandson was so brutally murdered. She told me the main reason she left Hollywood was the brutality and glitz and false values, the way the entertainment industry changed, over the years she was a star."

Turning in through the inn's wrought-iron gate, they crossed through the patio gardens. The sprawling, Spanish-style building, with its pale stucco walls, red tile roof, and generous inner patio, looked as if it might have stood during the days of the Spanish ranches and the first missions. It had, in fact, been built in the late years of the nineteenth century and had served as an inn since its beginnings, under half a dozen owners. Patty Rose had bought it when she retired from Hollywood and moved to a quieter environment. Having always loved Molena Point, she soon became a comfortable part of the village family.

They went in through the tearoom that wouldn't open until midafternoon, when formal tea would be served. The cheerful, chintz-curtained room was chilly, with no fire burning on the hearth to warm the little round tables and the Mexican tile floor. Dorothy led her on through, to her office.

Nothing had changed in Patty's office. Dorothy liked it just as Patty had designed it, the wicker-and-silk sofa, the big leather chair facing the desk, the hand-carved desk and bookshelves that had been made by a Mexican craftsman Patty had known during her Hollywood days. The carved screen behind the desk that, Charlie knew from talking with Joe Grey, concealed a wall safe where each day's receipts were held.

"Ryan and I have an appointment with the mayor at three," Dorothy said. "His secretary said he was at a meeting up the coast. I think that was an excuse, to give him time to talk with the building inspector and get their ducks lined up. Against us, of course. I did my best to—"

There was a knock at the door, and a tall young waiter wheeled in a cart bearing two covered plates of the inn's famous shrimp melt, a pot of hot tea, and a selection of small, rich desserts. Reaching deftly past Charlie, he pulled out the sliding tray at the back of the desk and set her place with a linen mat and napkin and heavy silver flatware, then he set Dorothy's place on her side of the desk. Charlie found it interesting to see Dorothy in this new light, all spiffed up and so businesslike, and yet so comfortable in her new role. Patty had trained her protégée well.

When the waiter had gone, Dorothy said, "Even though Max has more men patrolling, I'm hiring more guards. I find it incredible that someone, planning to abduct a child, would have the nerve to come here in daylight and take pictures. Incredible that none of us saw him, that none of the children did." She shivered. "But those telephoto shots of our little girls. You can tell just about where the photographer stood, behind the cypress trees across the street. Max said that Dallas photographed the area and made casts of some shoe prints." She looked at Charlie. "Does everyone get this much attention? Is it because we're friends? Or because this involves children?"

"It's the children," Charlie said. "The whole department is on the watch, they hate this kind of predator. I wish . . . This is just so sick. And now, at Christmastime, when little kids should be happy . . . When innocence should be a good thing, and not a safety problem."

"We try our best to keep the kids informed, but not to scare them unduly. The little ones are tender, and kids dramatize everything. But they have to be alert, Charlie. We've stressed that they're better equipped than most children, if they use common sense and stay together. We have to trust what we've taught them. We're hoping, too, that the excitement of the Christmas pageant and the playhouse contest will give them a heightened sense of community, of being together."

Dorothy was quiet for a moment; then, "It's less than a year since Patty's vindictive murder, and I keep wondering if someone wants to take out that same hatred on the school . . ."

They had all been at the theater that night, at a retrospective of Patty Rose's old movies. It was the one night that Patty herself hadn't attended. They returned from the theater to find her dead, lying in blood on the exterior stairs that led down to the parking garage. It was Kit who had found her. It was the kit who, all alone, had tracked and found her killer—and had subsequently been locked in the house with him, trapped and terrified.

Charlie finished her lemon tart and sipped her tea, puzzling over her feeling of almost knowing something, something she wasn't seeing. She looked at Dorothy. "This is such a strange set of events. I keep wondering, Are we all missing something? Something right in front of us, that we all should recognize? Something I can't bring clear."

Dorothy thought about that. "Did your cleaning girls mention anything unusual, when they were up here?" Ever since Dorothy lost three of her cleaning staff, in September, Charlie's crew had done most of the work while Dorothy interviewed for new hires.

"That's been a week ago," Charlie said. "They cleaned up here the end of last week. Mavity didn't mention anything, but I'll ask."

"They came back yesterday. I thought you'd changed the schedule. I'd just pulled in through the gate when I saw the van pull away from the curb, down by the studio. I wondered why they didn't park on the grounds as they usually do."

Charlie frowned, puzzled. Maybe Mavity's crew had cleaned one of their accounts near the school, though she didn't remember anyone up there changing their standing appointments. And why would Mavity park down at the end of the school?

Charlie seldom went out on the work crews anymore, but she kept the schedules, paid the girls' salaries and benefits, and handled the paperwork. Her cleaning teams were booked months in advance, and she could use more help, but it was hard to find competent new hires. Dorothy was proof of that, as hard a time as she was having finding acceptable people.

"I thought I saw one of the school's old cleaning women in the village, a few days ago," Dorothy said. "She drove off before I could hail her. I wish she'd come back—though I wasn't sure it was the same woman. Her hair was black instead of mouse brown. Same tall, awkward look. She was a good worker. A rather sour sort, but she didn't mind heavy, dirty work. She did most of the cleanup when we bought the old studio, got rid of some trash and an invasion of mice. Good thing the paintings had all been moved out, long before. Those mice would have done hundreds of thousands of dollars' worth of damage."

They parted after their delicious lunch, and Charlie, walking back through the village to her car, thought about the old stone studio. It was easy to imagine the lovely isolation Anna Stanhope had enjoyed, living and working in that charming retreat.

She had to wonder about Anna's studio appearing, at different angles, in the background of several of the intruder's telephoto copies. Well, but the studio was *there*, she told herself. Of course it appeared; a photographer could hardly mask it out.

26

From among the boxes behind the blue van, the cats watched Betty and Leroy finish loading their tools in through its side door, then vanish back into the house. The door to the kitchen clicked shut and the dead bolt slid home, seating itself with a solid thunk—and there was no way to open the dead bolt on the garage side, except with a key.

They hadn't wanted to barge back in the house behind those two, to be shut in again with Betty and Ralph Wicken and Leroy. Getting into the house originally, on Betty's heels, and then slipping into the garage so close to her, had already stretched their luck. It would take only one faint rub against a pant leg, and those three would be on them like hawks on a rabbit.

And, while Betty Wicken was admittedly a brutal woman to throw a clay pot at a little cat, her brother, Ralph, stirred a deeper fear. Ralph gave all three cats the chills. His thin face and close-cropped hair and big meaty ears made him seem almost like a predatory animal they might meet on the wild hills—but it was Ralph's smell, of unhealthy, nervous sweat, that made their fur really bristle.

Even if, to most humans, they were only cats and presented no imminent threat, they did not trust what Ralph or Betty Wicken might think to do to them.

But now, locked in the Wickens' garage like mice in a cage, the cats grew uneasy. To someone small, with only claws and teeth, the solidly built garage seemed nearly impregnable.

The other pedestrian door, which led to the backyard, was secured high above the knob, near the top, with a fastening that they might, or might not, be able to manipulate. And the plywood over the three small, high windows looked to be securely nailed.

And of course the electric garage door, if they leaped up to push the button, would cause a racket that would bring all three residents storming out—to glimpse them racing away, to realize it must have been cats who had opened that door, and to grow unreasonably alarmed and hostile. Dulcie licked her sweaty paws. Kit bit at a nonexistent flea, and Joe Grey paced, staring up to the ceiling, at the screened air vents high above them between the rafters.

But first he approached the small side door leading out to the garbage cans, the door they hadn't been able to open from outside. There was a thin line of light on the left, where the door fit unevenly into its frame. The dead bolt had an interior knob, but while it might be possible to turn that, the hasp and loop high above, installed nearly at the top of the door, made the tomcat lay back his ears in consternation.

There was no padlock through the loop; instead the householders had shoved a heavy stick of wood through. Interesting that they were so security conscious. He wondered if he could climb on the stacked boxes and make a wild leap at the stick—wondered how much noise that would create inside the house as he thudded against the door. Behind him, Kit and Dulcie fidgeted. Joe leaped at last, not at the door but to the top of the van and from the van to the rafters.

Crouched on a rafter, he considered the three tiny, mesh-covered vents. They were so small that he wondered, even if he could claw the screen off, whether a cat could squeeze through. There looked to be less than three inches of clearance, and Joe wasn't sure he could get his head through.

But behind him, Dulcie wasn't waiting. Leaping to the van's roof and to the rafter beside him, she stood up on her hind legs and attacked the screen, wildly clawing.

Off balance, she tore a rip down the nearest mesh grid, and slipped and nearly fell. Joe snatched at her, and braced her with his shoulder. The grid was tightly in place, stapled to the wooden molding and sealed with old paint. Kit leaped up beside them and reared up, too.

Frantically clawing and joggling each other, the two females at last loosened one corner, blood spattering from their paws. Then Joe took a turn, and with teeth and claws the three cats together managed to pull a corner of the screen free—they pulled until the whole screen came flying, flinging Dulcie off the rafter. She hung clinging, Joe's teeth gripping her neck like a mama cat holding a kitten.

He pulled her up until she got a purchase and, scrambling, righted herself. Her paws were bleeding, and her lip was cut—but Kit had squeezed though the vent and was gone, tufts of her dark, bushy tail left behind on the torn screen. They heard her hit the garbage can.

Dulcie went next, fighting through the rough opening, pulling out hanks of her own fur and raking her tender flesh. Joe heard a second thud as she dropped onto the metal lid.

Gingerly, the tomcat reared tall and poked his head into the little space. He was bigger than Dulcie and Kit, and he'd hate like hell to get hung up. If he could get his head through, though, then the rest of him could follow. He fought, clawing and wriggling. Rusty wire ripped along his shoulder, and something jabbed down his leg. A nail? But suddenly he was free, and falling.

He hit the garbage can and thumped to the ground—and they ran, scorching around the side of the house and across the drive, smelling their own blood and leaving bloody paw prints, and into the shadows of the woods, where they crouched together, Dulcie and Kit shivering and Joe Grey tense and angry. Well, at least he'd memorized the license plates of both vehicles, though that seemed, at the moment, small reward.

"Whatever the Wickens are up to," Dulcie said, licking her paw, "Harper needs to know about the van."

Joe looked back at her. "I'm not sure that's smart."

"Why ever not? We—"

"If the Wickens go up there during the playhouse competition, we'll *see* the van. Whatever they mean to steal, we'll see them in the act, and then we'll call the department."

"What if they kidnap a child?"

"They're not *after* a child. You heard Betty Wicken,

she told Ralph to lay off the kids, to stay away from the school."

But Dulcie laid back her ears. "What if we're wrong? What if we missed something, and they do take a child? I'm going home, to call Harper."

Kit said, "My house . . ."

Dulcie shook her head. "Lucinda and Pedric have had enough involvement. Let's don't make more waves." And she crouched to leap away.

Joe stopped her, pushing belligerently in front of her. "Just listen. They're not going to steal a child. This isn't about kidnapping, you heard them. I think they're after something in the old studio." He looked at her intently. "If Max puts a tail on them, if they spot a cop before they make their move, maybe no one will ever know what they're after."

"You don't give Harper much credit."

"The department is working a murder case, Dulcie. They're looking for a vanished body, and trying to keep on top of shoplifting and increased holiday thefts. And Harper has officers on double shift to protect the little girl. Plus three officers off for the holidays, and extra patrols around the school. If he sends a uniform up to tail the Wickens, it may have to be a rookie. And if the Wickens make the rookie, they'll dump the van and take off—maybe never be found."

Dulcie quieted. Joe looked intently at her. "The department only stretches so far. And think about this. If the snitch tells Harper that the van was hidden in the Wickens' garage—and where else would they hide it?—that puts the Greenlaws right on the spot again.

"Don't you think," Joe said, "that Lucinda has been involved enough, for the moment? She brings Harper the pot shards with, presumably, fingerprints on them. She leaves. Then, in a little while, Harper gets an anonymous call that there just happens to be a blue van like Charlie's, right there below Lucinda's house? Where," he asked, "does that leave Lucinda?"

"With egg on her face," Dulcie said contritely. "With *snitch* written all over her."

"Is that what you want?"

The kit looked from one to the other. "Joe's right, I don't want to drag Lucinda in again. We just need to be up there when the Wickens get there with the van, we just need to watch them. Meantime," she said, "Lori and Dillon are going to load up the playhouse and I'm going to watch." And Kit took off for the seniors' house, meaning, this once, to keep her mouth shut and not tell the law what she knew.

Dulcie watched her go flying through the leaves, and then turned quietly for home. She knew that Joe was right. Or, she hoped he was.

Joe Grey watched them both, twitching an ear, then he laid back his own ears, spun around, and headed fast for the department—to see what he could learn, what new information might have come in. And to put to rest the niggling and edgy voice that said, *Is this the right decision? You sure you want to withhold that information from the chief?*

27

A SQUAD CAR STOOD in the seniors' drive, its wheels and hood radiating a gentle warmth. *As if it had arrived maybe half an hour earlier,* Kit thought. The big white Chevy was parked just to the left of the garage, at an angle that left the closed garage doors clear—and that provided, unknown to the cop who had parked it, swift feline access to the hood, to the top of the car, and onto the garage roof. Three leaps, and Kit looked down from the flat, tarred roof at her own paw prints embossed delicately into the squad car's thin coating of dust—then she padded across the warm tar paper to peer in through Cora Lee's windows, into her friend's sunny, bright bedroom.

The little girl was there, with Officer Eleanor Sand. Kit, twitching her tail with interest, studied the child curled up on the rug before the tall bookcases among a pile of cushions. Cora Lee sat on the floor beside her, an open book in her lap. Eleanor Sand sat on the window seat—looking directly out the window at Kit. The tall, lovely blonde showed surprise for only an instant, and then amusement, at the sight of a cat on the roof. Kit looked back at her uncertainly—then the two big dogs were leaping to the window seat beside Sand, wagging their tails and pressing their noses to the pane inches from Kit's nose. Everyone was staring at Kit; she didn't know whether to be embarrassed at being caught snooping or to play it up and let herself strut a little. Because she was certainly, at the moment, onstage.

But then Cora Lee, laughing, rose and opened the window. Kit stepped in, and the dogs were all over her, slurping and soaking her fur. Cora Lee settled them down, so they backed off, only wagging and grinning. She closed the window and sat down on the floor again, as lithe as a dancer. But the child reached from the cushions, wanting Kit. Her black hair was rumpled, her dark eyes huge. Dodging the dogs, Kit leaped down into the pillows and stepped into her arms, and together they snuggled down in the warm nest.

Gently Cora Lee pulled a lap blanket over the two of them, took up the book again, and, in a dialect that Kit had never heard from her Creole friend, continued the Christmas story. The bright jacket said *Ole Saint Nick*.

Cuz dere on de by-you [Cora Lee read],
W'en I stretch ma' neck stiff
Dere's eight alligator
A pullin' de skiff.

The pictures, when Cora Lee held them for the little girl to see, showed not winter snow, but a sultry river among swampy trees; not reindeer and sled and Santa in a red coat, but the alligators hitched to a little square boat that was filled with bags of gifts. Santa was dressed in brown, but he had a real white, bushy Santa Claus beard; and the child seemed quite comfortable with the change from reindeer to alligators. Halfway through, Cora Lee paused to look up at Eleanor.

"Our family told a similar Christmas story in Cajun dialect when Donnie and I were little. This book wasn't published then, but we loved our family version, we heard it several times every Christmas. I was around twenty when this book came out, and I wrote to the author for this signed first edition."

"It's charming," Sand said. "I've never heard it, but the Cajun way of telling makes me feel happy. Interesting," she added, "that our young friend picked it from among all your picture books."

Cora Lee, being an artist, had a handsome collection of picture books, and she could hardly resist buying the most beautiful ones that came out each year. She had followed with excitement the progress of Charlie's book; though it was not a picture book, it had many illustrations, and Cora Lee had predicted after seeing the first sketches and reading the first rough draft that it would have deep appeal to readers of all ages.

Kit hoped so. Charlie's book was *her* story, it was based on her own kittenhood, on that frightened and lonely time when she had no one to love her, no one to care if she lived or died.

When Cora Lee had finished reading the rhythmic Cajun phrases, the child reached up for the book. Hugging it to her possessively, she tucked it beneath the blanket beside Kit, and held both the book and Kit close. *This little girl might be mute*, Kit thought, *but she surely made her feelings known.*

"I wish Donnie were here to share it," Cora Lee said. "When we were kids, he always read aloud with such pleasure." Automatically she glanced toward the window, though she could not have seen his car from upstairs. Kit had not seen it when she arrived; there was only Cora Lee's car at the other side of the drive, and the squad car—though when she'd crossed the drive she'd padded over a cold patch of concrete that the thin winter sun hadn't yet warmed, where a car or maybe Donnie's old pickup had recently stood.

There was no blue van parked in the drive today, so Mavity must be off in the real van, on a cleaning job. Kit had seen Mavity's ancient VW parked around the side of the garage where Mavity kept it—so as not to offend the neighbors, she said. She said her old car looked like a rusting hulk up on blocks in the yard of some backcountry shack.

The VW didn't look that bad to Kit, but probably Gabrielle encouraged Mavity to hide it—it was not a sleek new Mercedes, such as Gabrielle herself drove.

"You said your cousin Donnie's family was killed in the hurricane?" Eleanor was saying.

Cora Lee nodded. "His children, yes. There are a lot of questions about those failed levees, about the shoddy way they were reinforced, and where the federal money went, that was given to the state to do that work. Questions," Cora Lee said, "that in my view ought to lead to some serious charges. But I guess . . . I guess I'm getting old and crotchety."

Eleanor laughed. "You don't look like you'll ever get

old. But a bit judgmental? Why not? My daddy told me, 'If you are not brave enough to make judgments about life, you'll end up with a head full of porridge.' My daddy wasn't big on shady politicians, either, and on the folk who allow and encourage them."

Cora Lee smiled. "There's plenty of that, in New Orleans. Even as a child, I was aware of the ugly stories about the good-old-boy politics." She stood up when they heard a truck pull in, and moved to the window. Kit could hear a tractor or some kind of heavy equipment, and already the big chocolate poodle and the Dalmatian had charged out of the room and down the stairs, barking and threatening.

Kit wanted to see, too, but that would appear too strange. Racing to the window must be traditionally left to the rowdy and protective canines. Instead, she yawned and stretched, and made a show of slowly extricating herself from the little girl and from the quilt and pillows. She gave the child a nose touch, then languidly jumped to the sill beside Cora Lee, rubbing up against her as if for a pet, glancing out only slyly, as if she didn't give a whit what was out there. Behind her, Eleanor Sand knelt to gather up the little girl, perhaps uneasy at the activity below. "I think we'll move on," she said quietly.

"I didn't know they'd be here so early," Cora Lee said, picking up Kit and holding her, watching a flatbed truck as it backed carefully up the far side of the drive. It parked well away from Eleanor's squad car. The forklift ambled between them, to the garage door; and when the two women and the child headed downstairs, Eleanor holding the little girl's hand, Kit padded down behind them and out the front door.

She paused on the front porch, watching Eleanor's squad car pull away, and Cora Lee and the truck driver disappear into the garage. The driver was a big, bald, sad-faced man who resembled a grieving bloodhound.

In a moment the garage door rumbled open to reveal the bright, many-colored playhouse that nearly filled the interior. Lori and Dillon stood talking with the driver, both girls gesturing and looking as anxious, Kit thought, as two mother cats protecting their kittens.

But soon, under the girls' hands-on direction, the truck driver and the skinny, wrinkled forklift driver showed that they could be gentle and careful as they helped the girls separate the house into its three parts. Lori and Dillon insisted on removing all the bolts themselves, but they allowed the two men, under their nervous instruction, to separate and slide each section onto a heavy-duty dolly, and roll it out the door to where the forklift could raise it onto the truck bed.

Kit watched, hiding a smile, as Lori and Dillon shepherded every move, Dillon's short red hair rumpled every which way, her old blue T-shirt torn and stained. Lori's long dark ponytail had come loose from its ribbon and hung in a tangle, and her own T-shirt was stained with red and green paint.

The girls might look scruffy, Kit thought, but their finished creation shone perfectly groomed and impressive. They were so excited about the contest, and so afraid some accident would mar their work, that they gripped each other's hands, white-knuckled as each piece was loaded onto the flatbed. Kit could see, inside Cora Lee's car, where the bright turquoise and blue and red floor pads waited, along with the rope ladder neatly piled on top.

The two men were tying padding around the three sec-tions when Donnie's old truck pulled in, the truck he had bought used in the village when he'd arrived by plane from Texas. The tall, slim, graying blond man swung out, grin-ning. "Looks like you're all set to go."

"We're going to have some pie and milk first," Cora Lee said. "The girls need fuel before they get to work putting the house back together." She put her arm around Donnie. "Come join us."

She looked at Lori, who was fidgeting to get started. "We'll be up there, Lori, by the time the truck is in place. The men will have to wait in line at the gate and be directed in, and there'll be a mob waiting."

"We'll be in, in a minute," Lori said, "as soon as they're finished tying down."

"Sometimes," Cora Lee said as she and Donnie headed up the steps, "watching the girls, I feel like I'm a child again, too. The way we used to be," she said, heading for the kitchen. She turned to look at Donnie. "Fifty years. We're totally different people, now. And yet . . ."

"And yet," he said, "we're the same people. We're the same two kids we were. Only the packaging is different."

Cora Lee laughed. "A bit frayed around the edges?"

Kit padded into the kitchen behind them, watching Cora Lee set out the pie and begin to cut it, while Donnie started the coffee.

"You're proud of the girls," he said.

"They've worked hard on this project, and with such excitement. They did a huge amount of library research

229

into architectural styles, surveyed every kind of structure and style from French Country to African huts to those Dutch-influenced hex-sign details from the Caribbean— and put it all together in their own way."

"Including the hex signs," he said. "I like that." The hex signs were no more than big, primary shapes—triangles, circles, rectangles—painted on the shutters and walls in bright, contrasting colors.

"I so hope the girls will win," Cora Lee said. "But whether they win or not, they should realize a nice profit. That money would give Lori a leg up for college, with her father in prison. And Dillon . . . her folks can pay for college, but she wants to contribute as much as she can. Dillon has come a long way since the bad time she had when her parents nearly divorced."

"I understand a lot of credit goes to the police chief?"

Cora Lee nodded as she dished up the pie. "Teaching her to ride and handle horses, to be responsible for an animal, that has steadied her. As has Ryan's training."

"Ryan Flannery?"

"Ryan hired Dillon as a carpenter's gofer and then helper. She had to get special permission from the school. Between the two experiences, Dillon's a different person now, much more sure of herself and what she can do. Much more responsible." She changed the subject when they heard the girls coming.

"We read the *Cajun Night Before Christmas*, today," she told him. "Do you know the book? We were grown, when it came out. But it was so like the Christmas stories that your dad used to tell."

Donnie gave her a faltering glance, as if he wasn't

tracking. Then, "You read it to Lori and Dillon? A picture book?"

Cora Lee laughed. "No, to the little girl who was found in the plaza. Where the murder was reported. An officer brought her up to visit—they just left. I'm sorry you weren't here, you'd love her. She's so solemn, and so hurt, Donnie. I wish you could have read some of the book to her; I used to love to hear you read.

"But maybe later. I'm sure one of the officers will bring her back." She looked up when Lori and Dillon came in, and asked Lori to give Kit some milk and a few crumbs of gingerbread.

"Those were happy times," she said to Donnie, "those hot summers when we'd play in the walled garden after supper and lie on the grass, and you'd tell a story or read a book to me."

Donnie was quiet, turned away to see to the coffee. When the phone rang, Cora Lee picked up. "Yes, he's here. Just a moment." She handed him the phone.

He answered, listened; then, "I'll take it in Gabrielle's study," he said. "Would you hang up for me? The connection seems faint."

Gabrielle's bedroom and sewing room/study were just across the hall from the kitchen. Cora Lee waited until she heard him pick up. When she heard his voice, she reached to hang up. Donnie was saying, "Fine, she's just fine." Cora Lee didn't know what made her pause. She wanted to hear more; she listened for only a moment, then hung up guiltily. Who would be fine? Was he talking about Gabrielle? But there was nothing wrong with Gabrielle.

Or maybe he was talking about *her*, because she had

rehearsals and then the concert. But who would he be talking to, about her? She wished she'd had the nerve to listen to the rest of the conversation—if the girls hadn't been there, she might have. Something in Donnie's voice, as well as his words, left her puzzled.

But then, seeing the girls' impatience, and that they'd hastily finished their milk and pie, she called to Donnie that they were leaving, and headed for the car.

Opening the front door, she was startled at the brush of fur across her ankle, but then she smiled as the tortoiseshell kit raced past her and up a pine tree. As the girls headed for the car, Cora Lee stood a moment watching the kit vanish across the rooftops, delighting in the cat's bright and eager nature, and wondering where she was headed. *She's such a strange little cat,* Cora Lee thought. *So inquisitive and so wildly impulsive.*

28

Sauntering into Molena Point PD behind tall bony Officer Crowley and little Officer Bean, Joe Grey endured the two officers' usual joking remarks about freeloading cats, and leaped up onto the dispatcher's counter, where he lingered for a session of Mabel's skilled ear scratching. Mabel Farthy had cats of her own, she knew what a cat liked.

"You *are* a freeloader," she said softly. "But what would the world be without a few bums—charming bums," she said, seeing his sudden glance. "Sometimes, Joe Grey, I could swear you understand me."

And sometimes, Joe thought, *I need to be more careful, not telegraph my thoughts just because I like someone!* Mabel turned away when three calls came in on a fender bender. And Joe, thankful for the diversion, dropped off the counter again, leaving Mabel to her phones and radios.

Strolling on down the hall to where Harper's office lights were burning, he could hear Max and Dallas talking. The room smelled of leather and gun oil. Behind his desk, Harper looked up when Joe entered, a twisted smile starting at the corner of his mouth—a smile he reserved for cryptic jokes and nosy tomcats.

Leaping to the desk, Joe gave Harper a preoccupied but friendly look, then stepped boldly past the chief's shoulder into the bookcase as if this office were his space, as if he, Joe Grey, ran the show here.

Harper turned to look at him, the wrinkle in his cheek deepening, then he continued with what he'd been saying. Joe looked at Harper, and down at Dallas, with bored annoyance, as if hoping they'd shut up and allow him to have a nap. Harper was saying, ". . . came in to bring me a set of prints." He explained to Dallas how Lucinda had gotten the clay shards, that she had seen the woman drop the pot, and when the woman left, she'd retrieved it. "Wearing clean gardening gloves," Max said, grinning. "I got a positive from AFIS right away."

"Well, that's a first."

"Prints belong to a Betty Wicken. One conviction for attacking a police officer with a butcher knife as he arrested her brother. This was in Eugene. Ralph Wicken was arrested for attempted kidnapping of a nine-year-old girl. Kid snatched his car keys, slashed him in the face with them, and ran. Dropped the keys in a storm drain."

Dallas smiled with appreciation.

"Ralph got a year," Max said with disgust. "A year earlier he'd kidnapped a ten-year-old girl. She was rescued within hours, and wasn't molested. Parents dropped the changes."

The officers looked at each other and shook their heads, that silent, disgusted look that Joe knew well. Of all the crimes on the books, the molesting of a child was the most heinous;

and when people withdrew charges or tried to protect such a criminal, they joined in the guilt and cruelty.

"Ralph has a dozen arrests for trespassing and loitering around school yards," Max said, "but no convictions. One arrest for enticement on the Web, that never went to trial. Reports say the guy isn't too bright. Apparently the sister intercedes wherever she can, tries every way to keep him out of jail, keep him from getting in trouble."

Max rose to refill his coffee cup, and returned to his chair. "Greenlaws' intruder was back in the house, this morning. Lucinda went down and talked with her."

"She didn't," Dallas said, shaking his head.

Max laid out the tale that Evina Woods had told Lucinda, the events in Arkansas, Evina watching the Eugene rental then following the Wickens to California. Evina's stubborn belief that Leroy Huffman had either abducted or killed her niece.

"We have only Evina Woods's story," Max said. "I called the sheriff in Arkansas. When I finally got him on the phone, he was less than friendly, pretty noncommittal. Said the niece, Marlie James, disappeared, but a body had never been found. He didn't say they looked for her. Said she was eighteen, of legal age, which seems to be stretching it a bit. Said the story around town was she'd run off with some guy. He said she was pretty loose.

"That's not how Lucinda told the story, not how she said Evina described the girl. Evina said a missing report was filed with the sheriff and then with the D.A. I have a call in for the D.A." Max leaned back in his chair. "So we have no warrant on Leroy Huffman. And no outstanding warrant for Betty Wicken, and nothing outstanding on her brother."

"Not enough to arrest him as an unregistered molester?" Dallas said.

Max shook his head. "We have enough, with those photographs of the Home and children, to bring him in on suspicion."

"Where's our Jane Doe?" Dallas said.

"Sand and McFarland took her up to the seniors'. McFarland is watching the place, keeping out of sight. There's no connection yet between Ralph Wicken and the little girl, but this makes me uneasy."

Dallas nodded. "You want me to talk with Evina Woods? See if I can turn up anything more?"

"I think . . ." Max began, when the dispatcher buzzed him.

"Captain, there's a call on your line you'll want to take," Mabel said. Harper pressed the speaker button. When a woman's voice came on, Joe went rigid, thinking that Dulcie, after all, was calling Harper about the blue van. But then, listening, the tomcat hid a smile.

Evina Woods wanted to come in. She told Harper she'd only take a few minutes, maybe half an hour, but really needed to talk with him. Joe didn't know what had changed her mind, but he eased deeper into the bookshelf, intending to hear it all. Max told Evina to come on ahead, and it wasn't five minutes later that he rose from his desk and went up to the front to meet her.

He escorted her back to his office, walking behind her, asked her to take a seat, and offered her coffee. She refused the coffee, sat rigidly on the edge of the leather chair, laying her purse on a small table near her right hand. Both officers watched the purse and watched her movements. Joe, sharing their wariness, leaped down and wandered around the table, taking a good sniff at the handbag.

He smelled lipstick, orange Life Savers, old leather that was the purse itself. No gun oil. Nothing that smelled to him threatening. Strolling under the credenza, he lay down, well aware of Dallas Garza's puzzled glance. Rolling over on his back and rumbling a purr, he dangled all four paws in the air—a pose of amusing and beguiling charm that the tomcat had learned from Kit and that, for some reason, always made humans smile. Eyes closed, he could feel the officers study him for a moment before they turned back to Evina.

"This is about the break-and-enter?" Max said.

"The Greenlaws . . ." Evina gave the chief a direct look. "They've given me permission to stay there for a few days. Lucinda . . . both of them, they're really nice people, more than nice. Lucinda loaned me some towels and a cot, and told me to turn the heat up so I'd be comfortable."

"Lucinda came in, this morning," Max said. "She told us what you told her, about the Wickens, and Leroy Huffman."

Evina nodded. "I came in, now, because I just talked to my sister. Beryl called my cell phone, about half an hour ago. So strange," she said, "here I am way out here on the opposite coast, and we don't call long distance. It's all local."

She looked at Max and then at Dallas, and her voice went quiet. "They found . . . Arkansas Bureau of Investigation found my niece last night. Found her body."

She was silent a moment, swallowing. "An ABI agent found Marlie in the woods, five miles north of town. She . . ." She had to stop again, to get control.

Max said, "The sheriff didn't call us, as I asked him to. I'm waiting for a call from the D.A."

"The sheriff *wouldn't* call. But the D.A. . . . ." She went silent as Mabel appeared in the doorway. The comfortably built blonde stepped in just far enough to hand Max a sheet of paper. Joe could smell the scent of the fax machine. Max looked up at Evina, nodding. "Your county D.A."

"Does he tell you how she was . . . That she was buried under . . ." She couldn't talk for a few minutes. She said at last, "Buried under the remains of a dead deer?" She looked forlornly at the officers. "So . . . Maybe so dogs wouldn't track her scent?"

When Evina reached for her purse, both men came alert. Seeing their concern, she unzipped the bag and handed it to Dallas. "There's a plastic bag in there, with a pair of Marlie's panties. I . . . brought it with me for the DNA. In case . . . I thought . . . if her body was found here, that might prove that Leroy . . ." She was trying hard not to cry.

Dallas withdrew the clear plastic freezer bag. "If this matches up with anything on Leroy's clothes . . ." He glanced at Harper.

Max nodded. "Go pick him up, Dallas. Bring him in as a person of interest."

Joe, seeing the pitiful little cotton panties and Evina's distress, felt his claws digging hard into the rug. Evina smiled at Max, as if she was grateful someone in law enforcement seemed to want to help, seemed to be straight with her. Then suddenly she burst into hard, wrenching sobs. Dallas sat down beside her and put his arm around her.

She looked up at him at last, gulping. "For the first time," she choked. "Some . . . someone . . . who listens.

CAT DECK THE HALLS

Well, Mrs. Greenlaw did, but . . . A cop who listens, and cares. Thank you," she whispered.

It took Joe Grey a while, after everyone left the office and turned out the light, to stop feeling teary, himself. Evina's reaction to simple decency nearly undid the tomcat. He had just slipped out from under the credenza when Dulcie and Kit appeared in the doorway looking hot and harried.

"Come on," Dulcie said. "They're moving the playhouse earlier than Cora Lee thought. The truck's headed for the school, and so are Cora Lee and the girls. Kit was at the seniors', and—"

"And the little girl was there," Kit said, "with Officer Sand, and Cora Lee was reading her a picture book about Christmas with alligators and then they loaded the playhouse on a truck and had milk and pie and when the truck and car left I came over the roofs to get Dulcie and then we . . . The Wickens will be there by now with the blue van. Come *on*, Joe." And she spun away, Joe and Dulcie following her out of the darkened office and down the hall, Joe yowling at Mabel to let them out.

Mabel scolded him for his impatience as she hurried to open the front door, looking puzzled that they were in such a swivet. The cats galloped through, scorched up the overhanging oak to the roof, and took off for the Patty Rose Orphans' Home, not really caring, at that moment, what Mabel might be thinking.

239

29

Slowing her car and turning in to the drive of the Patty Rose Orphans' Home behind the forklift and loaded truck, Cora Lee sat a moment waiting to be admitted by the gate guard and admiring the huge Christmas tree that gleamed out through the hall's two-story windows. Patty had loved to decorate the Home for Christmas, she believed that the children needed, and thrived on, such joyous rituals in their lives. Cora Lee thought about the old-fashioned name that Patty had insisted on for the Home. Though most people called it the childrens' home, Patty had been adamant that there was no shame in the word "orphan"—that word always put Cora Lee in mind of the New Orleans street children, when she was a little girl.

Maybe ten children living in one room, often with no father in residence, and their mother trying to provide for them. And some children had nowhere to live but the streets, children with no education and little hope for the future. The churches had saved many, giving them hot meals and a place to sleep and trying to find adoptive homes for them. But the children at the Patty Rose Home were so lucky—these kids had more than many children who still had both parents.

Pulling on through the gardens behind the truck to the rear parking lot, Cora Lee hid a smile as Lori and Dillon, crowded on the seat beside her, tried to see everything at once and to assess every playhouse, even though most of them were still in their separate parts. The mansion's usually tranquil lawns were crowded with people and trucks, and playhouses being unloaded and set into place amid a confusion of workers. Who knew there were that many forklifts in the county? The small houses being bolted together had begun to form a small city of Lilliputian dwellings, some as bright as crocuses, some rustic, some Mediterranean, all with decks and ladders, all fascinating. The girls were wriggling to get out. Cora Lee could hardly wait, herself, for a closer look.

The gate attendant had taken the girls' names when they came through, and checked them off on his list. Now they followed their own truck to the south side of the Tudor mansion, not far from Anna Stanhope's studio. Most of that smaller building was hidden by huge rhododendron bushes that would flaunt a riot of reds and pinks in the early spring. A spot of sun glinted off the slanted skylights that transformed the stone interior into a bright though secluded work space. The artist had spent the last thirty years of her life painting there. When she died, her rich coastal landscapes had been stacked in every room and in the small garage, though most of her work had already sold through several prestigious California galleries. The girls exploded out the door before Cora Lee quite had the car parked.

She watched them swing up onto the truck to help the two drivers release the ropes. Watched the forklift get to work as Lori and Dillon and the truck driver guided the first portion of the little house into place. There was so much noise from the other trucks and from hammering and power tools that Cora Lee could feel a headache beginning to wrap around her temples.

The judging would be the next day, after all entries had been inspected for soundness by a local architect and builder. When, over the noise of the drills and hammering, Cora Lee heard the delighted cries of a flock of children, she looked up toward the mansion.

The two-story Tudor's dark half timbers shone in rich contrast to its pale plaster walls. In the low winter sun, the steep, shingled roofs cast angled shadows down onto the wide, second-floor deck that roofed the downstairs dining room. The children stood crowded on the deck, leaning over the rail, shouting and pointing as the little houses took shape.

Cora Lee watched as the third portion of Lori and Dillon's house was set in place, watched the girls bolt the parts together while the drivers held them steady. But when she saw that they had everything in hand, she turned away and headed home.

The girls wouldn't leave until late this evening, until they'd seen every playhouse that was entered and had rated them all, in their own minds, against their own construction. Then they'd come walking tiredly home. Tired, and . . . what? Satisfied with what they'd created? Or discouraged? How could they be discouraged? Their house was wonderful. But no matter what their assessment, they'd be a jumble of nerves, not fit to live with until the judging was over.

WATCHING FROM THE bushes as Cora Lee pulled out of the school yard, the cats moved on in behind her car, trotting between beds of poinsettias and nearly deafened by the banging of hammers and buzz of electric tools and the roars of trucks and tractors. Above them at the mansion, kids were crowded on the roof deck talking and pointing, longing to get inside those small houses where only a child would fit, where a child could step into any adventure he chose. Circling the front of the estate, they slipped in among the tall rhododendron bushes that sheltered the Stanhope studio.

They drew back at once, hissing, crouching down beneath the heavy leaves.

The sagging garage stood open, and the fake blue van stood half inside, the front end sticking out, the rear door open. And from within the house, partially masked by the noise of builders and trucks, came the pounding of other hammers. Then the dry-harsh noise of ripping wallboard, and the ragged, tooth-jarring screeches of old, rusted nails being pulled.

Padding closer to peer into the dark, small garage, the cats saw no way through that cramped space into the house itself, no inner door. Circling the studio then moving around to the front, they looked for an open window, but they were all closed, probably locked, as Dorothy had left them.

In the side yard a giant cypress tree stood shading the mossy roof. Storming partway up, they tried to see in. Sounded like the Wickens were taking the whole house apart.

They could see little through the old dirty glass; the small panes reflected more of the tree and of themselves than they revealed of the room within.

"Maybe," Dulcie said, leaping to a higher branch, "maybe we can see through the skylights, maybe the rain has washed them clean." Scrambling up, she sailed to the mossy shingles and looked down through the nearest slanted pane.

The glass was embedded with chicken wire. Joe and Kit nudged up close to her, their noses pressed to the cold surface. Directly below them stood Leroy Huffman, his dark thick hair so close to them that, if not for the glass, they could have dropped onto his head. He was prying at the wall with a small crowbar, carefully removing soft pieces of composition wallboard. The scarred pine floor beneath his jogging shoes was covered with scraps of the dry, flaking board. Across the room, Ralph Wicken sat on the floor, his back to a narrow strip of wall between two doors. He was doing nothing, he sat sullenly watching. At an adjoining wall Betty Wicken was gently chipping away plaster, revealing the chicken wire beneath.

"Why," Dulcie said, "would one wall be covered with wallboard, but the other one with plaster?"

Joe Grey shrugged. Who knew, with these old buildings? They watched Betty shake back her dark hair, concentrating on her careful work as if not wanting to damage whatever might lie beneath. The cats couldn't see that her efforts had gleaned anything of interest, only plaster chips.

Leroy's wall was another matter. The next piece of tan wallboard that he removed revealed, beneath, something that made him step back, his voice rising.

"Got it," he said, almost shouting.

"Shhh." Betty hurried to stand beside him. The cats could see nothing more than a rusted screw. No, three screws, lined up one above the other, some six inches apart, holding in place a thin strip of polished wood.

The strip seemed to frame a smooth portion of wall beneath the outer wall, a very white wall, as if plastered, but as Leroy moved aside, they could see it was painted in patches, too. Patches of gray, green, blue shone out, and quickly Betty ripped away more wallboard.

The screwed-on strips and the board they framed ran from floor to ceiling. The cats, their faces pressed against the skylight, watched Betty move along, tearing off more wallboard to reveal the treasure beneath.

After a quarter hour, they had uncovered a four-foot-wide, floor-to-ceiling painting. "A mural," Dulcie said. "Part of a mural." For now the two were stripping away the cardboardlike covering of successive panels of painted landscape. With every panel, the green hills shone more vividly, so filled with light and space that the cats might have been looking through the wall itself to the green winter hills that rose above the village: hills that were emerald bright with new grass beneath a wild and stormy gray sky so sharply reminiscent of these last winter weeks. This painting *was* Molena Point, the work so rich and real that the cats could almost hear the wind blowing, feel its cold fingers in their fur. Crouching over the skylight, their noses to the glass, they watched Leroy and Betty slowly remove the remaining covering to unveil the entire work; while on the floor in the corner, Ralph still sat, sulking.

"Poor Ralph," Dulcie said, watching him. "He can't be too smart. No wonder she watches over him. A man like that, in prison, wouldn't stand a chance. He'd be victim of every prison brutality in the book."

"If he *is* a child molester," Joe said, "that's exactly what he deserves."

Six panels formed the mural, each maybe eight feet tall by four feet wide, each edged by a strip of hardwood to hold it in place and keep it from warping without marring the work itself with screws or nails. The Molena Point hills ran for twenty-four feet of rolling green that slowly turned to summer brown, in a panorama of the central coast seasons—the stormy winter of the present to the sun-golden burn of summer and then back again.

The sense of space and distance made Dulcie think of C. S. Lewis's words that she so loved, of spaces larger, and mountains higher and farther away, than a living human had ever experienced. The painting filled Kit with the old wild longing she had known as a kitten and that often still returned to her, a hunger of the spirit that made the young cat tremble. The hills that Anna Stanhope had rendered so magnificently made all three cats want to leap away forever into far and unobtainable distances.

Betty Wicken, working with a much gentler hand than she'd displayed when she threw that flowerpot, undid the screws from the stripping and gingerly removed the first panel. This operation showed another side of the woman, showed her art-gallery background in dealing with valuable wares. She had set the first panel aside, leaning it against the wall, when a heavy vehicle pulled up the gravel drive. She spun around, as did Leroy, staring at the door.

"It's Ryan," Joe hissed, looking down over the edge of the roof. "Ryan's truck." And before Dulcie or Kit could move or speak, Joe's gray rump and short tail disappeared over the edge and down the cypress trunk. They leaped after him, scrambling into the bushes, and stood watching.

The truck door slammed, and Ryan headed for the cottage. "Mavity?" she called. "Charlie? Who's here?"

Trying to think what to do, the cats could only crowd through the door behind her.

When Ryan saw strangers, and saw the painting, she stopped cold, her hand flying to her pocket. "What are you doing?" Raised by cops, she wasn't slow to react, she saw clearly what they were up to. "Get back! Now! Stand against the wall, now!" The bulge in her pocket might be a gun, or might be a wrench or a screwdriver. "Move against the wall *now*! Face the wall *now*! *Do it now!*" She moved quickly, and her split-second reaction was second nature.

Little Ralph Wicken immediately did as he was told; he stood up to face the far wall, and he stood still. Leroy stood still, watching Ryan, undecided about her resolve or whether she was armed. The cats knew she didn't have a gun, that she wouldn't come onto the grounds of the children's home armed. As Leroy made a move toward her, Betty dove at her, swinging a hammer and hitting her a glancing bow; Ryan sidestepped and tripped her. At the same instant the cats leaped and landed on Betty's back, biting and clawing. Ryan grabbed the end of Betty's hammer, bending Betty's wrist back and jamming the hammer into her ribs. Catching her breath, Betty fell. As Leroy lunged at Ryan, Joe Grey leaped in his face, raking with strong hind claws. Beside him, Kit, too, clung to the man, biting and clawing. But Leroy, despite their attack, swung his hammer a glancing blow at Ryan hitting her hard on the side of the head. She staggered, dropped, and lay still.

Betty spun away, ripped a panel from the wall, and passed it to Leroy. "In the van. Hurry up. Put the blankets between." She snatched another panel, spattering it with her blood. The cats wanted to go to Ryan.

"They'll be gone in a minute," Joe whispered, "be still."

"I can't be *still*," Dulcie hissed. "She needs help."

30

"HOLD THE DAMN door, Ralph! Get out of the way!" Betty stepped over Ryan where she lay unconscious, bleeding onto the stone floor. Quickly she and the two men loaded the panels, piled into the van, and took off with a squeal of tires, leaving the garage door banging.

Leaping to Ryan, the cats crouched over her, nosing and pawing at her, trying to rouse her. "Her cell phone!" Dulcie said, pawing at her jacket pockets and then at her belt, trying to find the little holster. "Where . . . ?"

"The truck!" Kit mewed, and fled for Ryan's truck. Leaping and scrambling in through the open window, she vanished, her tail waving and then gone.

She appeared again almost at once, her mouth gaping around Ryan's cell phone. Dropping out the window and bolting into the studio, she laid it at Joe's feet.

Joe knew how to operate Clyde's phone, and he'd used Wilma's. But every phone was different, and it took them precious minutes to understand this one. Finally, with a prayer and a fast paw, he reached the dispatcher—one ring, two, and a familiar voice.

"Thank God it's Mabel," he blurted to Dulcie. "Stanhope mansion," he shouted. "Thieves, struck Ryan with a hammer, she's out cold, maybe concussion . . . The old studio . . ." He heard Mabel speaking to the medics on another line and in a second they heard the siren whoop, half a mile away. *Whoop, whoop,* coming fast, straight for the school. Joe described the blue van look-alike, gave Mabel the plate number and the number of the tan Suburban with which, he thought, the van might rendezvous. They wouldn't get far in that conspicuous blue van, they'd have to shift the paintings somewhere. As Joe talked with Mabel, Kit and Dulcie pawed at Ryan and licked her face, trying to wake her.

TWO MILES SOUTH of the village, below the black cliffs, a lone hiker descended to the shore. The tide was unusually low, the sea sucking back into the far distance, leaving a long slope of wet and gleaming sand bejeweled with tiny, sea-washed treasures. Wandering slowly, the woman left a single line of footprints pressed into the silver skein, each indentation quickly filling again with seawater; the cold smells of salt and iodine were strong enough to taste.

Although it was against coastal rules, she bent down now and then to collect a rounded stone or a shell of particular beauty, or a small bit of sea-smoothed driftwood, placing each carefully in the lightweight backpack that she carried over her shoulder. She was twenty-two, with lank brown hair, a lean and tanned young woman who seldom wore makeup. The wind was at her back, pressing her along as she moved north from where she'd left her small, two-door Civic on the cliff above, parked in a pullout, its bumper against the log barrier at the edge of the cliff stairs. Her stride was long and swinging, her delight complete at finding the beach empty on this bright, cold afternoon. Buoyed and excited by her isolation, relishing the perfection of the day that nothing could spoil, she stopped suddenly.

Startled.

Stood very still, sniffing the air, frightened by the unnatural smell.

She stood at a bend in the cliff. She could taste the cloying, sweet smell, it nearly made her retch. She stood staring, then she started forward again, hesitantly, her hand over her mouth and nose to block the smell. Above her the cliff rose some thirty feet, sheer and wet, and black as obsidian.

Just ahead, beyond the stone outcropping, something gleamed. She approached until she glimpsed it, dark and curved, sleek as a beached whale, half hidden beyond the turn in the cliff; whatever it was did not belong there.

Oh, not a baby whale, she thought, recoiling with pity and dread. Donna Reese loved the eerie songs of the whales; she played her wildlife tapes over and over through earphones at night in her college dorm, to help her sleep.

But no, this was not a smooth, water-sleek animal. This was metal. Dark, wet metal. At a change of the wind that drove the stink at her, she gagged, the wind's shifting gust slapping the sick-sweet stink right in her face, making her stomach twist.

But in a moment she approached, her hand tighter over her nose and mouth.

She saw the fender first, and then the whole car. Water dripped from the metal, water left when the tide had receded. The vehicle was turned up on its nose, badly dented, wedged beneath a hollow of cliff that was being slowly cut by the sea into a shallow cave.

How long had the wreck been here? Through how many changes of tide? Ignoring the need to heave, she cupped her hands to the cracked passenger window, peering in.

She stood a moment looking at the dead man, then looked up at the sheer black cliff and the narrow highway some hundred feet above. Down the side of the cliff she could see fresh scrape marks where the car had gone over.

At the base of the cliff lay jagged humps of broken black rock protruding from the wet sand. Once, millions of years before, this whole coast had lain on the sea bottom. She didn't know what that had to do with the dead man, she just thought it. The thought sent a thrill of fear through her that made her glance warily behind her at the endless sea, made her think about the frailty of human life.

Moving away from the body and the wreck, she threw up.

When she had emptied her stomach, probably of all her meals for the last week, she thought, her mouth tasting vile both from throwing up and from the permeating stink, she dug into her pack for her cell phone.

Donna Reese, at twenty-two, might be adventuresome and independent and prefer to hike alone without talkative companions, but she carried water, candy bars, and a cell phone. She was generally levelheaded, but now she stood trying to gather her wits, trying to put out of her mind the swollen, ugly body, the transformation that death had bestowed upon what had once been a living man.

And then she dialed 911.

One ring, and a woman dispatcher picked up. Carefully Donna gave her location, told the woman that she'd seen only one person in the car. Yes, he was definitely dead. Swollen. Far beyond need for the paramedics. As she spoke, she longed suddenly to be home, if only back in the dorm, back in her own familiar place in the world, where she'd be safe; and for a moment, she wondered if she had the nerve, now, to drive back toward the village along that narrow and precarious two-lane highway.

As Max Harper moved out with a dozen other police officers, their silent units seeking the blue van and the tan Suburban, Dallas Garza headed for the hospital on the tail of the EMTs, cursing the medic's slow, careful driving even with its siren blasting, wanting to jam his foot on the gas. He was going to get his hands on Betty Wicken, on all three of those bastards, and he wasn't sure what he'd do to them. If violent retribution lost him his job, so be it. Swinging a sharp U into the emergency parking beside the rescue van, he moved beside Ryan's stretcher as they hurried her in through the emergency entrance. She hadn't moved. She didn't move now.

In the ER, he hovered over her while Dr. Hamry took a look, cleaned up the wound, and then had her moved to a bed where he could watch her. Ray Hamry was young, maybe forty. A tall, thin, athletic man with short brown hair and blue eyes, tanned from tennis and swimming. He was a man Dallas had known a long time, and respected—but

SHIRLEY ROUSSEAU MURPHY

even Hamry could not have all the answers to her condition until he'd examined Ryan further, and run the X-rays and scans. Hamry tried to ease Dallas's fear and rage, knowing that wouldn't do much good, that Dallas was going to fuss and pace until he had answers.

THE THREE CATS couldn't very well hitch a ride in the rescue vehicle with Ryan or in Dallas's squad car. Beating it to the station across the rooftops, they were on the dispatcher's counter waiting for word about Ryan when the call came in about the body, Dulcie and Kit curled up beside Mabel's in-box, Joe Grey sprawled across a stack of outgoing reports. Mabel had the phone speaker on, leaving her hands free for a copying job. The caller was a woman.

She sounded young, and shaken. "There . . . there's a dead man. Below the cliff. In a wrecked car. It went over the side, you can see the marks. He's been dead for a long time. Swollen." She sounded like she was trying not to retch.

"Where?" Mabel said. "Can you tell me exactly where you are?"

"I . . . just below the state park. My car's at the top by the stairs. About two miles south of the village, I think. I was walking the beach, and . . . the wrecked car's all sand and mud, and dripping water."

"How many people in it, besides the driver? Can you see anyone else inside?"

The girl didn't answer.

"Stay on the line. *Please* stay on the line," Mabel shouted, turning to the radio to send two cars on their way. Then, "Are you still there?"

"Yes, I'm here."

"What kind of car are you driving?"

"White, two-door Civic." The girl gave Mabel the license-plate number.

"Stay on the line, I'm putting you on hold." Punching another line, Mabel called the coroner, and then tried to reach the captain and Detective Garza. The cats heard the back door slam as officers headed out to their units. They heard two cars start and race away, and then Dallas came on the line.

"I'm at the hospital."

"How is she?" Mabel said.

"Concussion, but stable. They don't know any more, yet."

"We have a body in a wrecked car, bottom of the cliff, two miles south of the village. Caller says it's been dead awhile. Two cars dispatched." Mabel gave him the location, near the cliffside stairs. "Caller's car's parked there, a white Civic."

"I'm on my way," Dallas said. Mabel kept trying to reach the chief, but couldn't raise him. It wasn't like Captain Harper not to answer, either on his radio or his cell phone, and Mabel began to fidget. Joe wanted to tell her that Max was chasing the Wickens and maybe was too mad or too involved to pick up the call, but he could only lie there, mute, edgy, and frustrated.

Ten minutes later, Mabel reached Harper's cell phone. She was relaying the information about the body when the radio came alive. Four officers were at the scene. Brennan said, "Looks like we might have the Christmas-tree body."

Three sets of ears pricked with interest, three small bodies tensed.

"There's a teddy bear in the car," Brennan said, "and a little girl's sweater about the right size. Pillows and a blanket, like maybe they'd traveled a ways. No kid, no luggage, no other clothes. Car's a gray 1997 Toyota Camry. No plates. Nothing in the glove compartment. McFarland's checking for . . . Hang on."

There was a lapse of some minutes. Mabel and the cats could hear background voices and bouts of disturbance that sounded like gusts of wind. Brennan said, "VIN number's been filed off. No ID on the body. Coroner's here. See if you can pick up a stolen report on that make of car."

As Mabel typed the information into the computer, Joe Grey grew increasingly restive. He wanted to be at the scene; Mabel's electronic command post was good, but it was second best. Mabel was talking with Dallas again when they heard Detective Davis coming up the hall.

Mabel filled her in, and Davis spoke with Garza, and because the victim might have been traveling but no luggage was found, they decided to pull a couple of guys off their beat to check the motels. See if they could find a man registered with a little girl, someone who hadn't been seen for a couple of days.

Now that they had a body, there was an outside chance they might get an identification through the DNA. At least they'd have DNA to compare with the blood around the Christmas tree.

"Lucky," Mabel said, "that the lab has two new technicians."

"Lucky if they stay," Davis said. "With the cost of living in the area, it isn't likely." For over a year the lab had been understaffed, with two desks vacant. And the county was making little effort to raise the salaries for those urgent positions. Cases had been backed up, with resulting complications, and many minor cases let walk or ignored because the arresting officers couldn't get the latents processed or get the lab work needed to get these cases into court.

"With pillows and a blanket in the car," Mabel said, "does that sound like the dead man kidnapped her?" She looked around. "Where *is* your young charge?"

"She's with Sand. Eleanor took her up to the seniors' for a while. No, I don't buy kidnapping. Informant said she was huddled up to the guy. If you can believe her. Why would . . ."

Mabel nodded. "Why would she lie? That informant has never led us wrong. I know her voice, I've taken her calls enough times."

"And this call from down the coast? That wasn't the same?"

"Not at all," Mabel said. "But the call when Ryan was hurt . . . No doubt about that one. I'd know *his* voice anywhere."

The two women were quiet, looking at each other. The cats were quiet, and seemed to be dozing. "How do they do that?" Mabel said softly. "How can those snitches always be at the scene?" She stroked Dulcie nervously. "I think about that too much, Juana. Sometimes it gives me the shivers."

Under Mabel's stroking hand, Dulcie was getting shivers. On the counter beside her, Joe Grey felt his skin twitch, his nerves so jumpy his whiskers quivered. Kit was very still, as if wishing she could vanish—like a rabbit gone to ground hoping to disappear in the tall grass.

Dallas came back on. "If the motels don't turn up their luggage, maybe the killer dumped it so we couldn't ID the victim."

Davis said, "What about I pull the two rookies, let them do some Dumpster diving?"

Dallas chuckled. "And what about the charity shops?"

"I'll do that, and take the kid," Davis said. "She seems to like pretty clothes, as much as you can tell what the silent little thing likes. She might recognize something of her own, a favorite little dress, and go for it."

"Good idea," Dallas said. "Gotta go, I've got Max on . . ."

As Davis turned back toward her office, Joe Grey yawned and rose. Davis's idea, to try to pick up the little girl's clothes, hoping to find trace material from the victim, was fine. The kid might go for her own clothes. But to find the dead man's clothes, mixed with all the others on the rack, would be harder. Davis would have to find out when recently donated clothes of the right size had been brought in, if the volunteer on duty even knew. And once she'd narrowed the search to the right size and time frame, she'd still be working in the dark.

While all a cat had to do was walk along the rack, sniffing.

Joe looked at Kit. She was the only one who had been near the dead man, who would know his scent. He twitched an ear. Dulcie and Kit came fully alert, and the three cats leaped down mewling at Mabel until she opened the heavy glass door.

"You cats come to visit, just get settled, and you're gone again—fickle as all cats, no sense of loyalty to old friends," she said, smiling.

But even as Mabel turned back to her phones and radio, up on the roof above her head, the tortoiseshell kit looked at Joe, wide-eyed and uncertain. "What?" she said. "Why are you . . . What did I do?"

"You're going to find the dead man's clothes. If we hit the charity shops before Davis . . ."

"But . . ." Dulcie said.

"I . . . The only scent I caught from the roof," Kit said, "was death. Nothing else, Joe. How could I smell anything else, over that stink?"

"He'd only just died," Joe said stubbornly. "Try to remember, Kit. Or maybe the scent of the killer is on those clothes, too."

"The dead man will be hard enough. But I was trying to track the little girl among the geranium smells and all the cops' scents. I didn't have time to sort out the killer's scent. I wouldn't know the smell of the killer if I stumbled over him."

Kit smoothed her long fur with a rough tongue. "The child's scent, yes. I could pick out her clothes from the racks of castoffs, but . . . *Oh!*" she said, lashing her tail with excitement. "Of course I can find the victim's clothes! *His* scent will be on the little girl's clothes—and her scent will be on his. She was in his arms, she was hugging him." And Kit's yellow eyes blazed with challenge. "I can do that, Joe. I can find both scents!"

31

THE WOODS BEHIND the high school were dense, not much used except by students skipping class or crowding in at night to party. The narrow road that wound between the scraggly pines was littered with empty drink cans and debris of a less appealing nature. The old tramp wouldn't ordinarily camp up here, but now, wanting to avoid the village, and never liking the homeless camps down by the river where things could get dicey, he found the woods inviting. After the cops picked him up yesterday, he'd slept in here last night, moving deep in behind a bushy stand of poison ivy where no one would see him, and high school kids weren't likely to invade. Poison ivy didn't bother him, he could roll in the stuff and never itch. He was sipping coffee, thinking to open a can of beans for his supper, and congratulating himself on not having encountered a living soul, when he heard a car coming. Breaking branches and crunching rocks.

Beyond the bushes, he watched a van pull in, heading toward him along the narrow dirt road, brushing overhanging limbs and side branches, a blue Chevy van. And a big tan SUV right behind it. Well, hell. Person didn't have no privacy, nowhere.

Real fast, he scraped dirt over his little fire and rolled up his blanket, did up his kit preparing to move out. But then he hunkered down again, watching the Suburban as it backed around on the narrow road with a lot of hustle and fuss, until it was heading out. He knew he ought to get out of there, but he was too interested.

The Suburban parked with its tail just a few feet from the rear of the van. A tall woman swung out of the van and moved around to open the rear doors at the same time as a muscular guy stepped out of the Suburban and opened the tailgate. Then a smaller man slid down out of the Suburban and, at the woman's direction, walked back a ways up the dirt road and stood as she told him, watching the street beyond the high school for cop cars.

When the big man and the woman began to transfer the van's load into the SUV, pulling out panels that stood upright in the van but, going into the Suburban, had to lay flat, the old man was way too curious to leave, too interested in what they had there.

The big panels were pictures—blue, green, glimpses of a stormy sky. The woman was cranky and bad-tempered, the exact same scowling kind of female he'd never cared for. Like the women in his own family when he was a kid, loud and bossy and you couldn't never trust 'em. She snapped at her partner the whole time as they lifted the panels. She'd pause between loading each, though, to stuff blankets between. Like they was real valuable.

When they closed the doors of both vehicles, real quiet,

and got in and headed back the way they'd come, he decided he wouldn't have to move along after all. It sure didn't look like they meant to come back. The woman handled the van real nifty among the dense trees. She stopped by their look-out, the little guy. She stepped out, got in the SUV, left the little guy to drive the van.

Smiling, the old man unrolled his blanket again, and sat down. He listened as the two vehicles moved away to Highway One, sounded like they turned right, up the coast. Scraping the dirt off the hot ashes, he fed in a few twigs, hoping to get a blaze going again. The wind was up; he shivered, and sat thinking.

This was the kind of switch, back out of sight, that the cops sure would like to know about. If a fella liked cops well enough to tell 'em.

Them cops here in the village were okay. He'd rather deal with cops, sometimes, than some of the scum he met up with. Them cops yesterday, they'd taken him right on into the chief's office, give him a cup of coffee. Keeping his shoes for evidence of some kind, they'd hustled up a fine pair to replace them. Fit him real good. And afterward that blond cop that picked him up, she'd bought him a real nice deli lunch before she sent him on his way. A real looker, that one. He wondered why she'd wanted to be a cop.

Getting the little fire going and wrapping his blanket around him, he thought about that body that was supposed to have been in the plaza, the stiff they'd lost and wanted the evidence for, wanted his shoes for—and wondered if this switch he'd just seen could have something to do with that.

He didn't see how. But who knew? He wasn't no cop.

Wondering, he covered the little fire again that he'd just got started, but didn't shoulder his pack. He buried it among the poison ivy. Then, thinking about the cold supper he'd have when he got back, he left the woods. The sky above him was gray and dull, the winter evening cold. Shrugging down into his jacket, he headed for the center of the village wondering if that tall blond cop was still on duty. Wondering, if she was there at the station, she might buy him something hot from the deli, for his supper.

THERE WERE FIVE charity shops in the village, all providing good used clothing, often with impressive labels, to the astute shopper, and offering, as well, an occasional antique treasure that would turn out to be worth considerably more than the buyer paid for it. The senior ladies hit these shops regularly and then sold their finds on eBay, always making a nice profit.

The treasure that Kit was after had nothing to do with monetary gain—and everything to do with nailing a killer. It was late afternoon when she left Molena Point PD heading for the small SPCA resale shop just a few blocks away. She would have maybe half an hour until the stores closed.

As she raced across the roofs and down to the sidewalk, her mind was half on finding the killer's scent, and half worrying about Ryan lying unconscious in the hospital—seeing over and over again that woman and then Leroy hitting Ryan, seeing Ryan fall, seeing blood start from the wound across Ryan's forehead.

Kit crossed the last street close on the heels of a pair of

gossiping young women who were hurrying back to work in the library. When she heard someone behind her gush, "Oh, look at the cute kitty," she ran full out, never eager to consort with tourists, certainly not anxious to endure strangers' too-personal stroking and petting—she could leave that familiarity to the canine crowd. Dogs loved that smarmy attention. Dogs loved the admiration of people they'd never seen before and would never see again. Baby talk from strangers. That stuff sent a dog right to the moon, inanely wagging and wriggling.

Leaping up three steps to the brick alley where half a dozen shops were tucked away, Kit skirted around a planter of red poinsettias, approaching the open door of the SPCA resale shop. She would have to get in and out before Davis and the child did, or the little girl's new scent would be all over everything. Fresh and old scents all mixed up, and she'd be able to find nothing.

Slipping inside, she melted behind a rack of men's sport coats, keeping low until she could spot the clerk. Charity shops weren't heavy on personnel, most of whom were volunteers. Rearing up, she saw a woman behind a far counter, and she could hear a radio playing softly in the back room, as if maybe someone was back there sorting donations. Padding along the racks, and past a display of luggage and tired-looking tennis rackets, she spotted the children's dresses.

Quickly she sniffed along the little hems, keeping out of sight, forgetting as she often did that she was only a cat, that it wouldn't matter if the clerk saw her—most shops didn't mind a cat wandering in. Reaching the end of the rack of little dresses and shirts and pants, she'd found no scent of the child.

She could see no more children's clothes, and she moved to the men's racks, again rearing up and sniffing. But, again, nothing.

She left the SPCA empty-pawed, racing for the next shop, four blocks away. She had maybe twenty minutes before the stores closed. Was Ryan still unconscious? Had she come to? What was happening to her?

Had she, upon awakening, remembered cats talking close to her face, remembered Joe Grey using her cell phone? Oh, my. Kit hoped not.

But concussions could cause visions, and a kind of dementia, Kit thought. She didn't wish Ryan bad luck, she wanted her to be whole and well again. But if those were possible symptoms, then surely Ryan would blame such wild ideas as talking cats on the terrible wound in her head.

At Millie's Treasures, two clerks were in attendance, two elderly ladies with purple-tinted hairdos. Lurking in the shadows, Kit went through the same drill, padding along beneath tables of old books–world globes–antique radios–flowerpots–hiking boots–handbags–suitcases–rag dolls–you name it, to the rack of little girls' used clothes—almost at once, she caught the child's scent.

It was just a whiff, but enough! She was so excited she almost yowled. The child's scent right there on a little blue dress. Yes! Quickly she moved along the rack, rearing up, searching for more of that little girl's clothes.

She found two more dresses, and some folded jeans and T-shirts atop a table that smelled of the child. She was almost at the end of a second rack when she heard a familiar voice and she rose up to look, balancing with a forepaw against the end of the rack.

Juana Davis stood in the doorway, holding the little girl's hand. She looked frustrated, and the child looked tired, worn-out, so pale and docile that Kit wanted to pat her face with a soft paw—that little girl was like a sick little kitten.

Kit knew Juana had to put her through this, and knew the detective would make it as easy as she could. But the little girl looked so ill. *Well, if she saw her* father *die, that night,* Kit thought, *then of course she's sick. Sick deep inside herself.* Watching the pale little girl, Kit let out a tremulous sigh. *And now,* she thought, *that man's body has been found, and the department will be working all out to ID him. So strange,* she thought, *that there was no record of the prints that Dallas Garza lifted at the plaza and on the evidence they retrieved. Where in the world did that man, and the killer, come from, that there are no prints on file?*

Maybe there *were* a lot of people in the world, as Joe Grey said, who had never applied for a sensitive job or a federal job, who had never been arrested, and who had never been printed in school as a child to help find them if they were lost. Maybe after all, she thought, the human world was still a bit uncontrolled, not all cataloged and accounted for. And that pleased her, that thought satisfied the independent nature of the young cat.

Kit did not like to see everything organized and made docile, she wanted to sense *some* stubborn independence among her fellow creatures.

Davis headed on into the shop, walking slowly, talking gently to the child. *Bring her here,* Kit thought. *Right here! Bring her right here! These are her clothes! These!* Besides the two dresses and the jeans, she had found two little pairs of corduroy pants, another T-shirt, and a pair of pajamas, all smelling of that particular child. And here they came, Juana heading for the children's rack, while the little girl's attention wandered around the store—and suddenly the child came alert.

She stopped, and tried to pull her hand from Juana's, but Juana didn't let her go. The child's eyes were wide, and the hint of a smile touched her pale lips—and with sudden strength she jerked her hand free and ran across the shop straight at Kit.

Drawing back, Kit slipped under the chair. But it wasn't Kit she was after, it was the heap of stuffed animals and dolls in the far corner. The child passed Kit, never seeing her, and plunged into the little mountain of toys, reaching high among them.

At the very top sat a faded cloth doll with ragged, floppy angel wings, a handmade doll with long and tangled pale hair, a doll with a long white dress, torn and dirty, and with a dark stain on the front, like blood. One little white shoe was missing. The child, climbing to the top of the heap, tumbling animals and dolls all around her, grabbed the angel, hugging it to her, and clambered down again. Stood clutching the dingy creature tight, tears running down her face.

As Juana knelt beside the little girl, Kit drew close behind her, close enough to get a whiff of the doll—she knew a cop's awareness is as sharp as a cat's, that a cop misses very little; but Kit was quick. She inhaled one deep scent of the doll then she melted out of sight, vanishing behind a stack of baskets—and thinking hard about the additional scent that clung to the faded angel.

The scent of a man. A scent that left the tortoiseshell kit crouched shivering in the shadows, amazed, hardly able to believe what she had smelled. Not wanting to believe it.

But unable not to believe it.

D ALLAS GARZA SWUNG a U-turn on Molena Valley Road and headed back fast for Highway One, turning north up the coast without sirens, where Mabel had cars moving in—two units up the hill ahead, a third coming fast and silent out of the village, its lights flashing. Two more cars coming down out of the westerly hills, no lights or siren. They'd all be visible from the highway, but there were no side roads where the perps could turn off. They had the van and Suburban in a pincer that would soon close tight. It was hard not to floorboard his unit and run down the bastards, tooling along there with the traffic in the fast lane.

The detective's usual quiet, laid-back approach was out the window. This was Ryan they'd messed with. This was his niece. Ryan was like his own daughter, and he was damn well going to nail their asses. Weaving in and out, wishing he could use his siren, he cursed the drivers who weren't watching behind or who, seeing a cop car in a hurry, didn't have the courtesy or the sense to get over.

Damn civilians probably thought he was headed for an early dinner. The blue van sure did look like Charlie's van, from a distance. It was following the tan Suburban with five cars between. Swinging into the right lane and then the bike path, he overtook seven cars on his left, swerved in at the van, and motioned the driver onto the median. He had two units behind him now, Wendell and Hendricks. Using his speaker, he told the van's driver to stay put, that he was blocked in. Told him to get out of the van and stand in front of it, hands on his head. He took off as Wendell and Hendricks pulled up. He swung into the left lane and hit the gas, giving it the lights and siren, speeding after the Suburban. There was no nearby off-ramp. The five cars ahead, all in the left lane, slowed reluctantly and pulled over, and the Suburban took off like it had been standing still, straight into the pincer between two units.

Dallas pulled in behind as they forced the Suburban onto the median. He heard three shots—and saw the blue van in his mirror, careening at him from behind. The explosion of two shots from that driver's window jerked him to attention. He hit the brakes to avoid ramming the two units, but as he turned to fire behind him, another shot exploded. He spun the wheel, wondering if he'd been hit. A jam of cars ahead. The two units and the Suburban filled the median. Two more units coming fast on the other side, pulling over to divert traffic. His shoulder wasn't working right.

He could smell his own blood. Damn it to hell. He didn't have time for this. Where the hell were Wendell and Hendricks? Then his radio squawked, "Officer down. Officer down," and he knew one or both had been hit. Blood was seeping through his jacket. When he turned to look behind him, the blue van was gone. In a second he heard the siren of the EMT.

He swung out of the unit swearing as McFarland jerked the female driver out of the Suburban, and Officer Bean, standing on tiptoe, rammed the burly passenger against the vehicle, hands on the roof, Bean's weapon jammed in the small of the guy's back.

McFarland was cuffing the woman as she fought and screamed. She had dropped her gun, and McFarland had it safe. More sirens as two more units arrived and another EMT. Dallas's shoulder was beginning to hurt, he couldn't make his right hand work. Heading for the dark-haired woman as she twisted and swore, fighting her cuffs, he had to forcefully keep himself from touching her, from pounding the hell out of her. They'd damn near killed Ryan and he wanted to see them hurt, see them dead.

32

RYAN WOKE HEARING voices far away, but she couldn't see anyone. Fuzzy voices. She was dizzy, so dizzy. Pale walls around her swimming into darkness and tilting back again. Something swung at her from nowhere, a hammer, she tried to duck, caught her breath with pain. A woman swinging a hammer, big woman, darkly clad, her voice blasting loud but then faint. Dizzy. The woman was gone. A man's voice, blurred. "Mabel . . . it's Mabel Mabel Mabel . . ." She was so cold, cold deep in her bones. "Stanhope studio studio studio studio . . . Ryan Ryan Ryan Ryan . . ." Ringing in her ears like diving deep underwater. Fuzzy voices all throbbing and she was falling, falling . . .

Then men's voices, coming clearer. She reached up to touch them, but she couldn't find anyone, her hand met cold metal. Metal bars . . .

A cell? A prison cell? Why would she be in a cell? No, it was a bed, she was under blankets in a bed. She hit out at the bars, but someone pushed her back. She tried to fight but was pushed down hard against the mattress, strong hands but gentle, easing her down. She had no strength . . .

She woke to a light burning, a metal lamp, and wondered why she'd been asleep when all she'd wanted was to sit up. A figure leaned over her, making her cringe.

But it was Clyde. It was all right, it was Clyde. As he smoothed her sheet and blanket, she remembered being lifted and carried. White paramedic uniforms. Everything after that seemed far away, car doors slamming, men's urgent voices, a truck engine, lying on a cot or something, bumping along. Blackness and then bright cruel light in her eyes like a knife, and voices leaping so her head throbbed. It was still throbbing, she tried to pull away from the pain, and couldn't.

"Be still, Ryan." Clyde leaning over her again, his reassuring voice. "Lie still." Again she tried to sit up, but again he held her back. "Lie *still*, Ryan," he said in a no-nonsense voice. "You're in the hospital. You're going to be fine. You have a concussion, and you have to be still. Someone hit you with a hammer. The doctor wants you to lie still. Do you understand?"

She knew there'd been a hammer, she could hear the shattering sound when it hit her and she felt her belly twist sickly. When she moved, her head hurt bad, she guessed she'd do what Clyde told her, she really didn't want to move. She tried to remember what had happened.

There had been trucks all around, and forklifts. And parts of little houses cut apart . . . the playhouses, the contest. But then she was in an empty house. How could there be green hills inside a house? Huge green hills in her face, stormy sky . . . Then strangers. Two men, and the tall woman. Their startled scowls at her, the woman hissing something . . .

swinging the hammer, then another hammer came at her, the crushing *thunk* that sent her reeling. She remembered falling, hitting the stone floor. . . She looked up at Clyde. He leaned down over the bars and kissed her. "There were cats," she said.

"Cats?"

She tried again to sit up, but he wouldn't let her. "There were cats. I was lying on a stone floor. Cold. Cats were looking down at me. Your cat, Clyde. Joe Grey. But they . . ." She swallowed, her mouth dry.

He lifted her head enough to guide a bent straw to her lips. She drank, then reached her hand to feel the tightness across her forehead, to feel the thick bandage. "They were talking, Clyde. *Talking.*"

"Who was talking? The medics? They—"

"The cats. The cats were talking."

Clyde smiled. "You do have a concussion."

"I could see light in the roof. Skylights. There were huge green hills inside the room. But then when the cats came, the hills were gone. It was all stone walls. Cold. Cold stone floor, cold under me.

"I was in the Stanhope studio," she said, looking at him more clearly. "And the three cats *were* there. Your cat. Wilma's cat. The Greenlaws' cat. Standing over me. Talking about me."

His mouth twisted. "You had a concussion. Dr. Hamry says—"

"Talking, Clyde. I swear." And in her head, the voices repeated themselves, *Mabel Mabel Mabel Mabel . . . Ryan Ryan Ryan Ryan . . .* She looked intently at him. "I swear. Cats. I heard cats talking. Something about my cell phone, and then *Mabel Mabel Mabel . . .*"

Clyde grinned. "That'll be the day, when a *cat* talks. I wouldn't want to be around to see that. I'm surprised you didn't think Rock was there, giving the medics directions."

"But Rock's here," she said, feeling the weight on her legs. "He always sleeps on my bed." Reaching gingerly down so as not to make her head throb any worse, she felt across the covers for the big hound.

But now the weight was gone. She could feel the warm place, but no one was there. And, had that weight been heavy enough to be Rock? Was that warm patch of blanket under her hand big enough to accommodate an eighty-pound Weimaraner? She looked up at Clyde. It hurt to move her eyes. "Where's Rock?"

"Will you lie still?" Clyde eased her back. "You're hurting yourself. It's dangerous to thrash around like that. The blood . . ."

"Where is Rock?" she whispered. Under her hand, the warm spot was already cooling.

"Rock's at my house. He's fine, Ryan. Feisty, and missing you." Leaning over, he smoothed her covers again. She felt herself drifting, drifting into sleep . . .

SHE WAS TRYING to climb out of a dark pit, trying to open her eyes and come awake. A voice beside her said, "Ryan?" She wanted to be helped up, to be pulled up out of the darkness.

"Ryan?"

She opened her eyes, and a harsh light reflected on the pale wall, a stark metal lamp so bright it made her head hurt. This wasn't her studio apartment, she wasn't in her own bed, she didn't know this place. But beside this bed, Clyde sat in a chair, watching her. "You've been asleep."

She was in a strange bed, in a strange room, her head hurt like hell. Gingerly she fingered the bandage. "Why am I . . . What happened to me? I heard Charlie's voice, and Hanni. Why is everything so muddled?"

"Someone hit you. You have a concussion. Leave your bandage alone, don't pick at it. Don't try to sit up, and don't wriggle around. You had a blow on the head and if you . . ."

She turned just a little, to look at him, and her head throbbed. She remembered the stone room, Betty Wicken swinging a hammer and a man with a hammer . . .

"It's going to hurt for a while. Everyone's been here. Scotty; your sister, Hanni; Charlie; Wilma; the seniors; Lori and Dillon . . . Slipping in, holding your hand for a minute, and then leaving. The doctor pitched a fit. But they were here, touching you for a moment like some kind of blessing."

"How long have I been here? You didn't say Dallas was here. Where's Dallas?" She sat upright, jarring a pain through her head that made her sick to her stomach. *"Clyde, where's Dallas?"*

"Chasing the bad guys," Clyde said easily. "Chasing the people who hit you. He's fine, Ryan."

She tried to relax, tried to think clearly. "Charlie was here? I'm missing her book signing, her opening . . ."

He glanced at his watch. "It's nearly six, she'll be there now, for the children—the adult party starts at seven."

She tried to look sideways toward the windows to see

if it was still daylight, but that hurt. "And the contest? The girls . . . ?"

"Their house is all in place. The judging is tomorrow."

"Clyde, I can't miss Charlie's opening. I could just . . . ?"

"You're not supposed to talk so much. You need to rest, and mend." He kissed her on the cheek and rose. "The doctor will be in around six. He'll have the CAT scan and X-rays. He'll want me out of here, he's not happy about so many visitors."

He picked up a gym bag that he'd set on the floor beside his chair. "There's a guard outside. When Dr. Hamry leaves, go to sleep. They're bringing a cot in for Hanni, for the night. She'll be along later, after the opening, in case you need anything extra. I imagine she'll bring you some party food." He kissed her again, tenderly. "I'll be back in the morning." He turned away and was gone, disappearing into the hall with his heavy gym bag. Why would he bring a gym bag to the hospital, he didn't work out in the evenings. As he swung the door halfway closed, she glimpsed a uniformed officer sitting on a straight-backed chair, just outside.

What had she done to deserve a police guard? Or, what had she seen? That she did not remember?

She guessed she slept, because the next thing she knew, more lights burned, the room was bright, and Dr. Hamry stood beside her bed, touching her shoulder. His voice was very soft and caring for such a clumsy-looking big man. She had dreamed about cats. Cats talking. She imagined she could still feel warm fur against her neck and cheek.

• • •

Not until he was back in his yellow roadster did Clyde open the gym bag. "I hope you didn't leave cat hairs on the bed."

The tomcat stuck his head out, sniffing the cold wind, then stepped out onto the creamy leather seat, stretching luxuriously. "That's better. I thought I'd smother in there. Did you have to *zip* the damned thing?"

"It has air vents. What do you think that screen is? That's why I used the gym bag, so you could breathe."

"This is your *gym bag*, Clyde. You put your sweaty clothes in here. The damn thing smells like a jockstrap."

Clyde glared, and started the engine. Joe, as they headed for Ocean and home, was still wondering how that bogus, look-alike blue van had been slipped into the school and successfully hidden back in the trees behind the Stanhope house with not one of Harper's patrol guys seeing it. He looked up when Clyde started to laugh. "What?"

"She thought you were Rock. On the bed."

"Watch the road. You don't have to look at me to talk. What's so funny about that? Rock isn't some scroungy mongrel, I don't see being mistaken for Rock as an insult. Anyway, the woman's half out of it."

"You have a lot of sympathy. I should have left you in the car."

Joe looked a long time at Clyde. "You think she'll be all right?"

"If she lies still and does what she's told." Clyde glanced at Joe. "She kept talking about cats. You heard her. About *talking* cats, Joe."

"She was out cold, after Betty hit her. Well, we thought she was."

Clyde turned to glare at him.

"When she's better, how much will she remember?" Joe said diffidently. Then, "*You* heard her, her thoughts are all mixed up."

"Let's hope," Clyde said.

"She thinks too much like a cop to believe that stuff," Joe said. "Talking cats? No way."

"Charlie figured it out."

"Charlie's an artist and a writer. Charlie encourages her imagination, it's part of her work. With someone like Ryan, who's all facts and reality, something that far out would never wash. Not for a minute."

"Ryan *isn't* all facts and reality. That's really unfair. Don't you think it takes imagination to create the houses she designs?"

Joe looked at Clyde, and shut up. For once, Clyde was right. "Just for the record," Joe said, "you were so shaken over Ryan that you damned near asked her to marry you."

"I didn't do any such thing. Now whose imagination has gone wild?" Turning into their drive and killing the engine, Clyde reached to stroke Joe. "That would screw up our lives. You could never utter another word in your own home."

"Sometimes even a cat has to make sacrifices."

Clyde looked surprised. "Not you."

Joe gave him a long yellow-eyed gaze.

"You'd do that for me?"

"Would I have a choice? If things got too uncomfortable, I could move in with Dulcie and Wilma."

"I wouldn't ask her to marry me without settling it with you. We're family, Joe."

"Maybe," Joe said, "it's time you got married. You're not getting any younger. You *would* be acquiring a live-in carpenter, electrician, and plumber. And Rock is a very nice dog, as dogs go."

Clyde swung out and headed for the front door. Unlocked it, flipped on the lights, and scowled down at Joe. "I'm not marrying anyone for her talents at home maintenance."

Joe leaped to the couch. "You're not marrying her at all, yet. You haven't asked her properly. She won't remember that half-assed hint at marriage when she was just coming to. Talk about a coward's proposal." Leaping up onto the mantle, he looked hard at Clyde. "The problem is, you're not sure Ryan wants to get married. And you're scared to find out."

Clyde sat down on the couch. Confirmed bachelor and tomcat looked at each other. It was Clyde who glanced away, and rose again, and headed for the kitchen.

And his bachelor mind was indeed full of questions. There were a lot of reasons why Ryan might not want to get married, at least in the near future. She was still recovering from a bad marriage. She wanted some peace and independence. She was a self-sufficient woman, busy building her own design/construction business. She rented a nice big studio apartment with the room and solitude to work uninterrupted on her blueprints and architectural drawings. Did she really need, or want, to be jammed into the same house with him, on a full-time basis?

He had talked with Wilma about this. Wilma was as close to an older sister as he'd ever have, he'd known her since he was eight and she was twenty-some, and he'd sought her opinions on many matters. Wilma's judgment was clearly thought out, and sensible.

But in the matter of Ryan Flannery, Wilma had said only "I don't know, Clyde. Just ask her. If she says no, don't trash what you two have. Just swallow your pride and go on as you are. Stay the distance, and see where it leads. I like Ryan. Don't blow your future chances."

Wondering for the hundredth time what the hell that really meant, Clyde pulled a Mexican dinner from the freezer, stood staring at it, then realized how late it was getting and put it back—Sicily would have sumptuous party food. And anyway, frozen Mexican was reserved only for moments of extreme desperation, when the real thing was inaccessible. As he headed upstairs to change clothes, Joe trotted up past him, hit the desk, leaped to the rafter, and was gone through his cat door. Clyde could hear him galloping across the roof, double-timing for the gallery, the little freeloader.

33

An hour before Clyde and Joe Grey left Ryan's hospital room, the tortoiseshell cat sat alert behind a fuchsia vine just outside the SPCA resale shop. The time was nearly five, and the shop would be closing soon. Kit sat quietly listening to Juana Davis speak on her cell phone with the chief. The alley smelled of bayberry from the candle shop across the way. Juana and the little girl sat close together on a hand-carved bench, a small fat duffel bag at Juana's feet, the child clutching her angel doll tight in her arms, its ragged wings flopping against her.

"Clerk says the doll and clothes, and a small duffel bag the child recognized, were in plastic garbage bags," Juana said. "Four black bags that were left at the front door before they opened. She remembers because of the doll and the duffel.

"There were men's clothes in all four bags, but of several sizes. Now they're mixed in with everything else on the racks. They have a sign on the door asking people not to leave things before they open, but no one pays any attention."

Kit knew about that. Sometimes, during her predawn prowls, she would sit among the shadows watching a car pull to the curb, watch someone hurry into the alley loaded down with boxes or bags or perhaps a small piece of furniture. Leaving their discards at the locked door, they would hurry away again as if late for work. Once, someone left a nice baby crib complete with mattress, and Kit had enjoyed a little nap before the shop opened.

But this early-morning donation had not been because someone was late for work. Hastily depositing the evidence concealed among other donations might, in the killer's view, be far more efficient than hiding the clothes in a Dumpster.

But not so, Kit thought smugly. *Not this time, my friend! This time you didn't count on a little kid and her favorite doll.*

Nor did you, Kit thought, smiling, *nor did you count on the power of a cat's nose*—but the information Kit had uncovered, however, had left her indeed very frightened.

Earlier, in the shop, the child, clutching the doll to her, had gone along the rack carefully picking out her own clothes, pulling each little dress off a hanger and handing it to Juana, looking up at her with trust. From the shadows Kit had watched, impatiently shifting from paw to paw, her whole being filled with the secret she had discovered, with the scent of the man who had handled the doll, the same scent that was on the child's discarded dresses. Shocked and distressed by what she knew, she was hardly able *not* to blurt it right out to Juana Davis. How she longed for a phone, longed to make just one urgent phone call of her own.

But, afraid she might miss something, she was unwilling to leave Juana. The detective was saying, "They go over them, put aside those that need mending or washing. Clerk said the doll was too fragile to wash, that they'd thought of throwing it away. Said it was too pitiful, too appealing. Clerk wiped it off, put it in the sunshine for a few hours, then laid it on the stack."

Juana listened; then, softly, "Not a word. But she cried, Max. Silent tears. Cried and clung to the doll." She listened again; then, "You think that's smart? She *does* seem stronger, but . . ."

Kit could hear the indecipherable murmur of the captain's voice, then Juana said, "Okay, we'll give it a try. Sicily's 'little snack for the kids' should be a sumptuous supper, so maybe that will appeal. She hardly touched her lunch."

Silence; then, "That should be safe enough. We'll stop by the apartment, give her a little rest and clean up, then we're on our way."

As Juana hugged the little girl close, and the child in turn hugged her doll, they rose and headed for Juana's squad car. Kit watched Davis buckle her into the backseat and tuck a blanket over her knees, then swing in behind the wheel. She spoke on her radio and drove off, turning right at the next corner in the direction of her apartment.

Behind Juana's car, Kit crossed the briefly empty side street and scorched up an oak tree to the roofs. And she ran, her whole being fixed on what she had learned, and on telling Max Harper, on calling the department. She was crouched to leap a narrow alley, heading for home and a phone, when she stopped so abruptly she almost fell. Clinging at the edge of the shingles, she watched the man on the sidewalk below.

He had stepped from the shadows as Davis's patrol unit disappeared up the street. Now he was jogging quickly after her, keeping to the late-afternoon shadows along the buildings, his gaze never leaving the patrol car.

Forgetting the phone, Kit followed him, her tortoiseshell coat a dark smear racing across the windy rooftops. As evening drew down and darker clouds moved in over the village, bringing the storm that had threatened all day, and as Joe Grey slipped in through Dulcie's cat door to escort her as formally as any human paramour to Charlie's book signing, Kit alone followed the killer. Racing over the roofs, she followed the man who, moving fast along the shadowed street, trailed Detective Davis and the little girl. The man who, Kit was certain, the child could pick out of any lineup.

WHILE KIT FOLLOWED the killer, and Charlie's human friends spiffed up for the party, Charlie hurried home from the hospital to get dressed. Her visit to Ryan had been brief, and worrisome. Dr. Hamry would know more in the morning.

She hadn't wanted to leave the hospital, had wanted to call Sicily and say that they'd have to have the opening without her, that to please tell Jennifer Page, the gracious owner of the bookstore, that she'd sign books later for those who bought them, would mail them or deliver them in person.

But Clyde, sitting by Ryan's bed, said she was being foolish. And on the phone, Sicily scolded her and told her to go home at once, get herself dressed, and get her tail over there, that children were already lining up for the signing and that she'd better not show up smelling like horse and wearing boots and jeans. Clyde, gripping Ryan's cold hand, said that if Ryan had her wits about her *she'd* tell Charlie more than that, and that she'd better get moving. She'd left the hospital with the sick, illogical feeling that if she left Ryan alone and she got worse . . .

"What could you do if you stayed?" Clyde had said. "You're a doctor, now? A healer? Ryan couldn't have better care. Even if she took a worse turn, which she won't, you'd only be in the way."

"But I'd be here."

"Go," Clyde had repeated. "I'm here."

Sighing, she had left. Had hurried home feeling shaken and vulnerable. She'd quickly fed the horses and dogs and put them up, a chore that could never be neglected; but she hadn't taken time for a shower. She'd made a quick phone call, then had dusted on some talc, praying she didn't smell too much like horses, or that the children liked that sweet aroma. Had hurriedly pulled on the lovely gold lamé gown her aunt Wilma had given her. She'd meant to take a nice hot shower, put on fresh new silk lingerie, spend time on a fancy hairdo. Instead she pulled on the gown, quickly bound up her hair with the gold clip, put on a little lipstick, and she was out the door again—until she'd remembered the necklace Wilma had given her, and she raced back to slip it on, too.

Now in the car heading back down the hill, hoping

she'd locked the door when she left, Charlie was still cursing the Wickens for nearly killing Ryan—if Ryan didn't mend quickly, Charlie wouldn't be responsible for what she did to those people. And she was cursing them, too, for making Max miss this special evening. This was the one night that he'd promised to leave work early, get spiffed up in civilian clothes, and escort her to the opening in style—hand her out of her car at the door, offer his arm as they entered, bring her champagne. Promised to forget the department for a few hours. How unrealistic was that? He'd even promised to make nice to people he didn't much like.

With the window down and cold air streaming in, she scanned the village below, wondering if the chase was still on for the blue van and the tan Suburban. It enraged her that they'd copied her van. She could hear no sirens from below, could see no whirling red lights moving through the village on the dusky streets or above on the hills. Had Max's officers already cornered them? The last she'd talked with Mabel—she'd called when she first got home, from the secure line—the department had a tip that the mural panels had been transferred to the SUV. It was against department regulations to communicate information on a chase, but Mabel was careful. She knew, from the way Charlie spoke, that she was on the secure line. She said Max wasn't part of the chase, that he was down the coast where wreckers were pulling a car and body up the cliff. Was that the body from the plaza? And was that another part of whatever convoluted crime these Wicken people had set in motion?

• • •

CHARLIE WOULD NOT learn that Dallas had been shot until she arrived at the gallery and Sicily told her that the detective was, in Sicily's words, "Just slightly hurt. He may be delayed, they're taking out the bullet. Just a flesh wound."

Flesh wound or not, the news sickened Charlie, made her wish someone had shot both the Wickens and that good-for-nothing Leroy Huffman. She spent the evening smiling and trying to be charming and answering hundreds of questions, while inside her worries about Dallas and about Ryan were eating her up, and she wanted only to be at the hospital with them.

So, THAT WOMAN detective found the kid's doll and the duffel. Must have found the clothes, too, the way the duffel bag was stuffed full. Standing in the shadows of a doorway half a block up, on the other side of the street, he'd watched her coming out of that used shop, heading for her police unit. That angered him, that she'd found the clothes, he thought he'd disposed of that stuff pretty well. Damn cops.

In a Dumpster, the kid's pretty clothes would have stood right out. He'd figured they'd dive the Dumpsters. But what made them bring the kid to search the used shops? Sure as hell, no one else but her could spot that stuff, mixed in like it was with all the castoff pants and shirts—he really hadn't thought they'd drag her around the shops, as puny and sick-looking as she was.

But what the hell? So they had her clothes. What were

they going to find? Penney's and Kmart labels. *He* hadn't handled the clothes, except with gloves. This was just cops' busywork and amounted to nothing.

Worse luck that she'd found that old doll—but why let the doll bother him? So it was handmade, so it might be traced. By the time they'd ID'd the body, if they ever did, or by the time anyone at the other end thought to look for father and child, he'd be long gone where they'd never find him.

Looked like that detective was headed back to her condo with the kid, just as he'd hoped she'd do when the day was done. Earlier in the day, he'd parked his vehicle two blocks from her place, had walked down around the PD and waited a while, hoping to spot her and the kid—then saw them coming out of the charity store. Now, moving fast to keep up with the squad car as she drove through the crowded streets, he paused in the gathering shadows of a doorway as she swung into the parking garage beneath her condo.

Standing under an overgrown lilac vine that climbed around the door of the closed shop, he could see across the street straight into the garage. She had pulled into her regular slot, near the entrance. He watched her help the kid out and head around to the front stairs.

Once she was inside, she wouldn't be able to see him from her balcony or windows, not here beneath the thick vine. But he'd be able to see two sides of the condo, looking up between the lilac leaves. Behind him in the shop window was a fancy collection of women's lingerie, some in pink, printed with purple rabbits, that he found particularly amusing.

He watched her draw the living-room draperies, and a light went on behind them, throwing a muted glow onto the terrace. Another light came on behind the bedroom shades. He couldn't see the kitchen window, which was at the back. He wondered if they were in for the evening. It was plenty early, but kids went to bed early. He'd tried earlier to get into the apartment when they were out, but that cop had it buttoned up tight with double dead bolts and special window locks. He'd seen no alarm system, but with the PD just across the way, who knew what they'd worked out? Too easy to blow his cover on a clumsy break-in, give the whole thing away. Finding no easy access, and deciding it was too risky, he'd left, feeling frustrated. And even now, waiting to see what that cop would do next, he was still undecided about the kid.

He waited maybe forty-five minutes, and then both lights went out. Waited another ten minutes, and place remained dark. They didn't come down the front stairs, didn't appear in the parking garage.

The narrow back stair let into a fenced area of garbage cans, with a noisy gate, and he hadn't heard the gate squawk and rattle, though he'd been listening hard in case she slipped out that way. Now, as he watched the condo, a dark cat appeared on the sidewalk, dropping down from some high perch; it stared at him for a minute, damned night prowler, then moved on out of sight. As early as it was, it looked to him like the cop had tucked up for the night. Maybe she was scheduled to double back for late watch. She was no spring chicken, she'd want her rest. And that frail kid, she'd drop off to sleep early.

But even when he was satisfied that they weren't coming out, still Kuda waited awhile longer, to make sure. This was one night that, as long as that cop had the kid with her, he wanted the two of them tucked away safely asleep. This was probably the last time he'd have to worry about it, and he sure didn't want to blow it.

HALF A BLOCK in front of the killer, the tortoiseshell kit had dropped to the sidewalk and stood looking at him, sick at what she was seeing. Then she slipped behind a potted fern and into an alley. There she paused, still watching him, wondering what to do now.

He was just a smear of black there in the dark under the vine. A dark figure, still and waiting. She had to tell someone, tell them he was there watching the condo, tell someone quick. But she didn't want to leave and lose sight of him. Not when he was so close to the little girl, not when he was watching for her to come out. Not now, when he might have decided to make sure she was silenced. Silenced before she could point him out, as clearly as she had found her doll.

She had to warn Juana, tell her the killer was just outside, tell her who he was. *Had* to tell her who he was. Had to find a phone, before Juana and the child left the condo or before he tried to break in.

Leaping up into a potted tree, she made a wild leap for the roof, heard the branch crack behind her. Scrambling up, nearly falling, she ran. Dulcie's house was the closest. Fleeing across shingles and tiles, flying from peak to peak, she nearly outran the wind that scudded behind her. She reached Wilma's panting and her heart pounding, scrambled backward down the nearest oak, and fled in through Dulcie's cat door. The house was dark, as if Wilma had already left for Charlie's party. She bolted through kitchen and dining room straight for the living-room phone. Pausing with one black-and-brown paw lifted, and then with the perfect recall that Joe Grey and Dulcie so admired, she punched in the number for Detective Davis's cell phone.

34

In the softly lit café, a fire blazed on the hearth, its reflections dancing across the Christmas wreaths at the café windows and across the deep red poinsettias on the tables; firelight glanced through the archway into the bookstore, too, onto stacks of Charlie's books, onto the bookstore's Christmas tree, and onto enticing Christmas books that also stood waiting for small hands.

On the other side of the Hub, in the gallery, the white walls shone pristine, showing off only Charlie's black-and-white drawings and etchings.

This was the children's time, before the grown-ups arrived, and as Sicily welcomed the first visitors, Dorothy Street shepherded them on inside. None of them saw, behind their feet, the tortoiseshell kit slipping in, too.

Kit paused behind a sculpture stand, and then, seeing that no one had noticed her, she flew up the stairs that led to the gallery's balcony. Having used Wilma's phone to call Detective Davis, she'd left the darkened cottage again, racing away to the party. As she sailed over the roofs, the wind's icy fingers had pushed down into her fur, chilling her through—even her paws felt frozen. Now, pausing halfway up the stairs, she turned to look down at the gallery and to bask in the delicious warmth that rose and spread from the blazing logs in the café's fireplace.

Below her, the gallery's white walls and panels handsomely set off Charlie's drawings and prints, and Kit listened to a slim, dark-haired teacher telling the children about the animals—the wild animals that Charlie saw among the Molena Point hills, and the dogs and cats and horses, some of whom lived on Charlie's ranch. As she explained which were drawings and which were etchings, Kit padded on up the stairs to the balcony and, warmer now, settled between two potted ferns to look down between the rails.

Fresh holly decorated the two archways; the windows of the raftered café were not only hung with wreaths but framed with evergreen branches, and in the garden beyond, five little trees wore fairy lights. Delicious smells rose from three long buffet tables in the center of the room, where hot entrées and salads and desserts waited, all arranged around a big bowl of Christmas eggnog. Soon, as the children finished up in the gallery, they'd be heading boisterously for the fine buffet.

Sicily Aronson had to be patient, caring person, Kit thought, *to have invited that wriggly, busy, happy mob of kids before the elegant grown-up party began.* Licking her whiskers, Kit tasted the delicious supper smells of turkey tetrazzini, lasagna, tamale pie; and only reluctantly did she remember Lucinda's cautionary lecture.

"You must not," Lucinda had said earlier that afternoon, "*must not* go begging among the gallery viewers, Kit, *or* among the children."

"Oh," Kit had said, "I would never . . ."

"And you must not," Pedric had added prophetically, "panhandle the waiters and waitresses, in the kitchen."

"Oh, I wouldn't . . ." Kit had looked back at her dear old couple with well-practiced innocence. And now, as the children swarmed into the café and around the buffet tables, she remained obediently on the balcony, doing just as Lucinda and Pedric expected of her. So far. *But*, Kit thought sweetly, *the night is still so young.*

Dorothy Street and Sicily stood in the gallery archway below her, watching the children heap their plates, find tables, and tuck hungrily into the delicious fare.

"As if we never feed them," Dorothy said.

Sicily laughed. "Those kids eat better than most of the village."

Kit studied the two women. Dorothy, so tailored in black velvet pants and a creamy V-neck tunic, a simple silver belt, and her dark hair plain and sleek. Sicily was dressed, tonight, in a red gauze caftan over a white silk sheath printed with red poinsettias, her long hair twisted up high and held with glittering red clips. Pizzazz, Charlie called it fondly. *Maybe*, Kit thought. *But Sicily Aronson wears exactly the clothes that make her feel good.*

Detective Davis and the little girl had not arrived, and that worried Kit. When she'd placed the call in Wilma's empty house, Davis had thanked her and had promised she'd be careful. That had to mean that, despite the man following her, the detective was still headed for the party. Davis's implied information was a lot for a cop to tell a snitch; that sharing made Kit feel warm and pleased, that Davis trusted her—that the detective trusted her unknown informant.

Or was Davis jiving her, leading her on because she didn't trust her, because she thought . . . Oh, Kit hoped not. That would be too bad.

She hoped, even more, that something would prove her wrong about the man she was sure was the killer, the man who had been watching Davis's condo, surely waiting for the little girl to appear. Waiting so boldly, right there on the street.

She was lost in thought when Detective Davis and the child did appear suddenly, at the back of the bookstore, coming in from the stockroom, through the back door. Maybe Davis had parked her unit in the alley. The little girl clung close to Juana as the two joined the children crowding in around Charlie's table, where stacks of books waited for Charlie to sign.

But Charlie wasn't there, she had not arrived. Up on the balcony, Kit was starting to worry about her when suddenly there she was hurrying in, all out of breath, and causing a little stir as she headed for the low, round signing table just inside the archway to the bookstore.

Charlie might have hurried, Kit thought, *she might have a few red hairs out of place, but she looked beautiful.* She was wearing the simple gold sheath and the topaz choker Wilma had given her, and her red hair was piled high, strands escaping as usual from the clip that bound it. When all the children had gathered around the table, and Charlie had greeted them, the children sat down on the floor pillows that Sicily had piled and scattered all around, and Charlie told them about the story she'd written, and why she'd wanted to write it. Davis's little charge sat among the youngest children; the detective took a chair near her, with her back to the wall, where she could see in all directions.

And as Charlie told about the little stray kitten who had no home and no mother, Kit squirmed farther out between the balcony rails, listening. Charlie told how the kitten had tagged along with a wild band because she was afraid to be alone in the wild hills, and how mean those cats had been to her. *That's me*, Kit thought. *That really did happen. That's me in the story and in the pictures.* And though she could never tell anyone that secret, Kit nearly burst with the excitement of starring in a real book that so many humans would read.

But then, as Charlie talked with the children, she glanced above their heads to the balcony, looking straight at Kit, and she gave Kit the faintest toss of her head. Clearly this meant, *Come down, Kit, come here and join us.*

Kit looked at her questioningly, and when Charlie gave a tiny nod, Kit flicked her tail and surged down the stairs and fled through the café, dodging table legs and children's feet, then padding diffidently between the seated children.

"She's my little model," Charlie said as the children reached to stroke her. "A friend of mine trained her, and she's a very smart little cat." The children shrieked with delight when Kit leaped onto the table beside Charlie, and they all rose and flocked around, reaching to pet Kit.

"Is the story real, then?" said a blond little boy.

"It's a made-up story," Charlie said. "Made up from

what I imagined a homeless kitten's life would be like. But it's based on this little cat, she is indeed my model." She smiled at the children. "I had to imagine how she would respond to the things that happened to her. No two cats are alike, you know, any more than are people."

"But how did you *know* what happened to her, if it was all made up?" asked a solid-looking little boy.

"I did a lot of research into the habits of stray cats. Into things that do happen to them, and how they are able to survive. Often the strays live in colonies, for companionship and safety. *Made up* is sometimes best when you base your story on fact, on what really could be. I tried," Charlie said, "not to put anything in that could not have happened, that would be impossible. You take all the facts of what *could* happen, and then you weave stories around them. Does that make sense?"

The children thought about this, and nodded that it made sense to them. They talked about imagination, and where it came from, and then Charlie began to sign their books. And Kit thought, as dozens of little hands stroked her, that she didn't mind *these* little strangers petting her. Not like strange grown-ups on the street. And she thought, watching Charlie, *She's signing my story! She's signing* Tattercoat. And Kit nearly burst with joy.

But as the little nameless girl rose to pet Kit, Detective Davis rose, too, and stood directly behind her, carefully watching the room. The gallery and café were filling up now with adult guests, and Davis was growing edgy. And Kit realized that cops in plain clothes were mingling with the crowd, that there were maybe two dozen officers she knew, wandering around like ordinary villagers. She hadn't seen them come in, she'd been so engrossed in Charlie and the children—and in her own starring role—that she'd missed this vital infiltration.

Beside her, Charlie, signing books, was watching the officers, too. Kit thought Davis must have told her that the killer might appear, because Charlie was as alert as Max's people. She was ready to move, to get the children out of the way. *Oh, my*, Kit thought. *What will happen? What will happen now? Oh, but Davis won't take risks. She wouldn't . . . These officers wouldn't . . .* Kit stood on the table beside Charlie, shivering so hard she barely felt the children's hands smoothing her fur. Was this the only way? When she'd told Davis what she'd seen, did Davis think this was the only way to trap the killer?

Trying to watch the whole room at once, Kit was so shaken she didn't realize that Joe Grey and Dulcie had slipped in and were watching, too. Not until she caught a movement from the far balcony, where Joe and Dulcie were now looking out between the rails—at her, at the cops, at the children gathered around Charlie's book table, and at the little silent little girl.

BELOW THE TWO cats, waiters were carrying trays of champagne among the crowd; and in the gallery, already five pieces had "sold" stickers fixed to their title cards. One was a drawing of Joe standing on a rock above the sea looking as big and powerful as a cougar, and Dulcie was sorry to see that one go, she had longed to have it for her own, to see it in their living room hanging just beside Wilma's desk. But then Joe nudged her, and she realized something was happening. A tension radiated from Charlie and Kit, and from Juana Davis. All three looked wary, and ready to move. And when Kit looked up to the rail at them, she looked so alarmed that Dulcie and Joe tensed, ready to run—or attack. And there were so many officers in civilian clothes mingling with the crowd, every one of them on the alert. Dorothy Street and the teachers were rounding up the children to head for the school's buses, hurrying them along. And Officer Sand and several more officers had moved closer around Davis's silent little charge.

Then, as the Patty Rose children streamed out to the street, Cora Lee and Mavity came in with young Lori Reed; and behind them came Gabrielle and Donnie, Gabrielle overdressed as usual, in a green satin gown spangled with glitters and a tangle of mirror-bright necklaces draping her low décolletage, and a pale fur wrap around her shoulders. She held her left hand up to her throat, where her diamond engagement ring would not be missed. Donnie was more tastefully turned out in a dark sport coat and dark tie, pale blue shirt, and cream slacks.

The silent little girl, standing with Davis at Charlie's table, looked up between the officers who surrounded her—and suddenly she spun around, trying to pull away from Davis. Davis held her tight, pressing the child against her. The child's face had drained of all remaining color. Her little body was rigid.

"Poor little . . ." Dulcie began.

But Joe Grey was racing for the stairs.

Dulcie sped after him, dodging between high heels and polished oxfords, between pant legs and long silk skirts. Ahead there was such a crowd of officers they could see nothing but pant legs. Sneaking through behind the crowd, they crept beneath Charlie's table.

The room had gone silent. Officers crowded around Donnie French, harshly pushing Gabrielle back. The little girl, backing against Davis, was staring at Donnie, trying hard to speak.

"Tell me," Juana said softly, kneeling, holding the child close. "Who are you afraid of?" The child pushed harder against her. "Tell me," Juana said. "It's important. Did someone frighten you? Who are you afraid of? What did he do?"

The crowd was silent. Not a whisper, not a sound.

The child clutched Davis as if she could hide herself. "Please," Davis said, turning her gently around to look into the crowd again. Most of those surrounding her were officers, only a handful of civilians. The child, pushing back against Davis as if she could vanish, looked up at the wall of faces, and swallowed. Then, softly, she whispered, "Him." Her little voice was faint. "Him," she whispered, pointing into the circle of officers—pointing at Donnie French. Donnie's face changed from quizzical to cold, to an expression that was icy with fear. He spun around, seeking a way out. As Davis picked up the child, two officers jerked Donnie's arms behind him. Moving swiftly, they cuffed him. Shielded by other officers, only a few guests could see what was happening. Across the bookstore, the guests who had turned away from the cash register were held back by Officers Brennan and McFarland.

Detective Davis, carrying the child, approached Donnie. The little girl fought to tear herself away, out of Juana's arms.

"Tell me why you're afraid," Juana said clearly, "and then we'll get away from him."

"Gun," the child whispered. Her dark eyes were filled with fear—but then suddenly with something more. Suddenly the little girl looked around at the officers who confined Donnie, at the encouraging looks on their faces, and she seemed to take heart. Eleanor Sand nodded at her. Jimmie McFarland gave her a thumbs-up and a wink, and the child seemed to come more alive. Now, as she faced Donnie French, her dark eyes blazed not with fear but with a rage far stronger than fear.

"He shot a gun at my daddy," she said, her voice little and thin. "He was my daddy's friend and he shot him and killed him." She twisted away from him, hiding her face against Davis, but in an instant she turned back. "*He* killed my daddy!" she screamed, and she kicked and fought Juana, trying suddenly to get at the man, burning suddenly to strike him and hurt him.

"What is his name?" said Juana.

"*James Kuda James Kuda James Kuda,*" the child screamed. She stared at him, shivering. Donnie stared back at her, his blue eyes filled with rage, and then the child collapsed against Davis, clutching her and weeping, weeping as if all the tears of her young life—over the death of her mother, the drowning of her siblings, and her father's grisly murder—were suddenly released. Weeping and shivering in a paroxysm of near hysteria. It was at that moment that Max arrived, his jeans and windbreaker wrinkled and muddy and smelling of seawater.

Charlie didn't see him, where she stood by the far bookshelves with her arms around Cora Lee—whether to comfort Cora Lee or to hold her from interfering in the killer's arrest, the cats couldn't tell. But even as the chief walked in, someone *was* interfering, loudly. A dervish of green and spangles was jerking at two officers, trying to shoulder between them, hitting and swearing at them.

"Stop it!" Gabrielle screamed, pounding Officer Crowley's barrel chest. "Stop it! Get away from him!" But as she tried to free her fiancé, Officer Cameron grabbed her and pulled her back. Gabrielle fought Cameron, tried to fight them all. "Leave him *alone*! He's my *fiancé*. He lives here, he's Cora Lee's *cousin*! What is this? What are you doing to him? That child is lying. You can't arrest a man on some child's wild lie. Leave him alone, you can't . . ."

Cameron jerked her out of the way. "Stop it, Gabrielle. This is police business." When Gabrielle tried to swing on Cameron, the officer jerked her arm behind her. "Keep it up, lady, if *you* want to spend the night in a cell."

"I'm going to the mayor!" Gabrielle shouted. "You can't arrest an innocent man for some wild children's tale!" As the officers moved the prisoner away, Gabrielle broke away from Cameron, snatched her keys from her purse, and headed for the door.

35

JAMES KUDA SAT in the back of the squad car behind the wire barrier, highly amused by Gabrielle's rage. If she followed through with her threats, talked to the mayor and hired a lawyer, that would keep her busy for a while, hopefully keep her from nosing around. The car smelled of new leather. Pretty fancy upholstery for a cop car. These cops had it made, in their upscale tourist town with its big money. Well, he'd gotten a bit of it. Would have walked away with more if he'd played his cards closer. Though that would have been hard, in a little burg like this. He just hoped what he did get, stayed hidden, that Gabrielle didn't go poking around, that she'd spin her wheels trying to defend him, go to the mayor, keep her mind on that for a while, while he talked his way out of this. He always did. Easy enough to go for accidental death or self-defense.

If they did make him, which wasn't likely, it would be only a few years, and the money would be there when he got out—and plenty more stashed from past *relationships*, as the ladies like to call them.

First thing, get a good lawyer. Gabrielle would help him with that if he could keep her blindsided. She'd never believe it was anything but self-defense, and not likely she'd go poking around in her computer for another couple of months, not until it was time to do her taxes or maybe even June when she'd roll over her CDs. His women seldom turned against him; they liked the sweet talk too much, and liked his sweet, loving ways.

Too bad he'd had to do Donnie, but there was no other way. Too much back in Texas that Donnie knew. Had to admit, he'd let his guard down, there. As loyal as Donnie was, in the beginning, that sure went sour. That was one of the reasons Donnie had wanted to come out to the coast. Make a new start, get away from him before the Texas cops came nosing around and caught Donnie up in the loop, too.

He had to hope these village cops *were* the soft-living type, with their minds on their fancy cars and on socializing, hope they were like New Orleans cops, partying on duty, taxiing big-name civilians around to the fancy restaurants in their squad cars.

Shackled in the backseat like some dangerous ex-con, he squirmed as the unit pulled in between two chain-link fences and parked in back of the station, next to their two-bit jail. How had this happened, that he got caught? Who blew the whistle on him?

It wasn't that kid, scared all the time—until tonight. No, something had happened before that. He'd kept out of her way, made sure she didn't see him, so it had to be someone else that made him. He just couldn't figure out who.

Earlier tonight, when he saw that detective's lights go out, he could have sworn the woman and kid had gone to bed, that she wasn't going out again, wasn't going to the damned party, and that had been his mistake. But it was Gabrielle's fault, wanting to hit every party, get dressed up fancy, show off her diamond ring and her boobs.

Could that kid have seen him, sometime earlier that he didn't know about? Seen him, and pointed him out to that detective Davis? And then the detective had set him up, brought the kid there to the opening. Someone had done a number on him, they'd had half the damned force there in civilian clothes. Now, he'd better be thinking what to do about it, how to slip out of this one.

But maybe, after all, Gabrielle had the right idea. One little kid. What kind of witness was that? A good lawyer, knowing the kid's background, could easily prove that, seeing her mother die, then most of her family drown, she was real screwed up, emotionally unstable, as they called it. If that kid was all the prosecution had to go on, a good lawyer could make Swiss cheese of their case.

Maybe he *should* have killed the kid when he had the chance. Had he turned soft? But he didn't want a kid's death on his record. With an adult, he could go for self-defense. But a kid? No way; they'd send him up good, for a kid.

The uniform swung out of the car, pulled him out, shoving his head down so they wouldn't crack his brain and face a lawsuit. He should have cut out earlier, before the party. He knew that party was a bad idea. Should have given Gabrielle some excuse that would buy him a few hours, tell her there was another job offer up in the city, that he didn't want to miss it. At least he'd wiped the account pages off the computer, told her he thought there'd been a power surge. Surge arresters didn't catch them all; he'd told her enough about that, early on, to leave her comfortable with the explanation.

But now the cops would call Donnie's sister-in-law. And Cora Lee would, too. Louise was the kid's only remaining family, outside of Cora Lee. He just hoped Louise hadn't found Cora Lee's letters that never reached Donnie, that he should have burned. Why was it he liked to save things? He'd hidden them real well, though—little mementos of past accomplishments.

No, she'd never find those letters where he'd stashed them. Kicking himself for letting his guard down, later he stumbled through the cell door, shoved by the fat cop, stood surveying the filthy bunk as he heard the lock click behind him. He should have run. Should have burned the letters . . . Should, should, should . . . All his careful planning down the drain. And, sitting down alone in his cell, James Kuda put his head in his hands, trying to figure how he *was* going to get out of this one.

IN THE BOOKSTORE, the cats, at the first sign of trouble before the pseudo Donnie French was arrested, had leaped to the top of a bookshelf where they could see what was happening and were out of the way of fast-moving feet. Joe and Dulcie were as surprised as their human friends at what was happening. Only Kit looked smug, watching the action with a cool little smile twitching her whiskers. Dulcie and Joe looked hard at her.

"You better tell us," Joe said, trying not to smile. "What have you done, this time?"

"I got the killer arrested," Kit said, failing to look modest. But too much was happening below them for her to explain. As the killer was cuffed and Gabrielle tried to interfere and then headed for the door, it was Charlie who stopped her, grabbing her shoulder, spinning her around and snatching her keys.

"Leave it, Gabrielle." Charlie's green eyes blazed, her cheeks were flushed and her red hair was all coming loose. "Let the police sort it out. Let it be, until you're calmer."

"Those cops are making a huge mistake," Gabrielle snapped. "All they want is another statistic, someone to arrest! I *won't* see Donnie locked in that dirty jail! If Harper does that . . . The police can be sued, and I intend to talk to the mayor. *And* to get a lawyer in the morning."

It was then that Max stepped in, took Gabrielle quietly aside, and asked her when she had last checked the balances of her savings accounts and CDs. Her rage at Harper exploded. She tried to hit him, and screamed insults in his face. Max held her wrists until she calmed. "Listen to me, Gabrielle. Did he use your computer? Didn't you tell Charlie he made some repairs and loaded some programs for you?"

Gabrielle didn't answer. Her sullen rage would not let her look at Max.

"Didn't you tell Charlie that Donnie was a wizard with the computer, that there was nothing he couldn't fix, that he had straightened out your online problems and made some of your programs easier to manage?"

Gabrielle was white and still.

"Go home, Gabrielle. Check your online accounts before you come charging into the station saying things you might regret."

Gabrielle looked at Max, pulled away from him, and sat down at an empty table, glaring sullenly. Max turned away and left for the station, pausing to kiss Charlie. "I won't be long. With Dallas in the hospital, I need to—"

"What happened?" Charlie said. "How bad is he?"

He looked down at her. "It's a shoulder wound. He was chasing the three who hurt Ryan."

"I didn't . . . I talked with Mabel. But maybe she didn't want to tell me, just before the party?"

"Shot him twice in the shoulder, but they missed the bone. He's out of surgery and in the room next to Ryan's. They have a guard at their doors." He kissed her again. "I won't be long. Are you going to take Cora Lee home?"

She nodded. "She'll want to call Donnie's sister-in-law, in Texas."

"I'll swing by there when I'm finished; we can leave your car, and ride home together."

And as Sicily pitched in to try to resurrect the party, to try to ease folks and cheer them, Charlie returned to Cora Lee, who sat alone in a far corner quietly weeping for her murdered cousin.

36

LEAVING THE GALLERY after James Kuda was arrested, Detectives Davis and Sand headed for Juana's condo with the distraught and frightened little girl. In the apartment, Juana turned on the lights and lit a fire while Eleanor gave the child a quick warm bath and put her into pajamas. She sat on the couch holding her, a warm quilt tucked around them. Juana made cocoa, put Christmas cookies on a plate, and carried the tray in by the fire; though she was concerned about their small charge, she was so encouraged that the child could speak and that her spirit had rallied. As horrifying as the sight of the killer had been, this little girl had stood up to him. Healthy anger, Juana thought, had wonderful curative powers as the child fought her way out of a grim darkness. This little girl didn't shrink for long, when she faced the man who'd shot her daddy, she was mad as hell, and that, in Juana's book, was healthy progress.

The child, now warm and cozy under the quilt, snuggled up to Eleanor, and gulped down her cocoa and cookies as if she were starving; when Juana took the empty mug from her, to refill it, she reached up suddenly to her.

"What?" Juana said. "You want the mug back?"

A shake of the head. *No.*

"You want to get up again?"

Another shake. "No," she whispered. Her white little face was still blotched from crying, and her expression was so needy. "Corlie," she said. "My name is Corlie."

"Thank you," Juana said, sitting down beside them. "That's very special, to know your name. And do you have a last name?"

"My name is Corlie Lee French," she said in such a soft whisper that the detective could barely hear.

"Corlie Lee French," Juana said. "I like that."

"That man . . ." she whispered, looking bleakly at the officers.

"Did you know him?" Juana said softly.

"He was my daddy's friend!" she said in a fast, shivering breath, and hid her face against Eleanor. Eleanor was quiet, holding her—until suddenly a car light blazed across the top of the drawn draperies, and remained there, unmoving.

Tucking the child down on the couch beneath the quilt, the officers rose and moved to the drawn draperies, standing at either side to look out through the crack where draperies met wall. Though Donnie/James Kuda was headed for jail, they didn't know whether someone else might be involved. They didn't know yet whether the Wickens were part of this, or whether the two cases were unconnected.

Earlier in the evening, when the snitch had called her, Juana had turned out the lights and then called the department, quickly putting officers in place. Looking down at the street from the darkened window, she had seen the man standing in the shadows just as the snitch had described, a dark presence beneath a tangle of vine against the black windows of a closed shop. She had seen no one else on the street, until a shadow came slipping along an alley.

But the shadow was one of their own, an officer she'd just put in place. She saw, one street over, another darkly clad officer move into position. Satisfied but wary, she had watched until, half an hour later, the dark figure against the building gave up his vigil, maybe deciding Juana was in for the night. She had watched him step out from beneath the vine and slip away up the street, and had listened on the police radio as the two officers followed on foot to where he got into a tan pickup a block away. She had watched the officers' unmarked car move out a block behind him. And then, on a secure line, she had set the rest of the plan in place.

Soon the officers tailing the pickup had a make on the truck's plates, giving a recent transfer of title to one Donnie French. Cora Lee's cousin Donnie, just as the snitch had said. Thinking, then, that this man was the real Donnie French, she had felt a wave of bitter dismay for Cora Lee, who had been so very happy to rejoin her family.

Hoping that Donnie thought she and the child were tucked in for the night, and hoping that he was headed for Charlie's opening, she had helped little Corlie dress, telling her it was a game. "We'll get dressed in the dark. Can you do that?"

The child had known something was up, but she'd dressed quickly and obediently. She had seemed, then, as if she wanted to speak, Juana thought. But she hadn't, she'd been still and silent as they slipped down the back stairs, where McFarland had a car waiting.

Sitting in the passenger seat holding the child, Juana had asked her, "Do you remember Officer McFarland?"

No sound, no answer; but a small little hand had reached over to the steering wheel, to touch McFarland's big, warm hand.

CHARLIE, TOO, LIT a fire on the hearth, a comforting fire in the seniors' house, while Lori made cocoa—both friends employing the homely gestures of caring and nurturing, to try to ease Cora Lee. Cora Lee, seated near the fire, tremulously picked up the phone to call Donnie's sister-in-law. Before dialing, she looked up at Charlie.

"Would you mind if I turn on the speaker? I'm so befuddled. I'd like you to hear, too, to help me keep things straight. Oh, Charlie, I dread so to speak to her. Louise and Donnie were close after Barbara died." Cora Lee had found Louise's number in their downstairs apartment where James Kuda had been staying.

Now, calling Louise in Texas, reluctantly waking her, she told Louise that Donnie was dead, that he had been murdered, and that his little girl was safe. "I had thought that all three children had drowned . . . One child survived, then?"

When Louise was at last able to talk, and to make some sense, she assured Cora Lee that Donnie's smallest daughter, Corlie, had indeed survived the storm and that she had been with him on their flight to California.

"Corlie was the only one of Donnie's girls to survive the collapse and flooding of the school, the only one of the three who could be reached in time."

It took a long time for Louise to tell what she could piece together of James's Kuda's deception. Donnie had known Kuda for years. "James Kuda was in and out of prison," Louise said. "I didn't like having him here, I thought him a bad influence on Donnie. He was staying with Donnie, here, until he got on his feet, as he put it. But he . . . Well, he is charming. He did a lot of repairs to our house, and he . . . he looked so much like Donnie looked before he lost his hair that . . . Well, I guess I softened to him. Softened too much," Louise said bitterly.

She was quiet for a few moments while Cora Lee tried to comfort her. "You didn't know, you couldn't have known . . ."

"They named Corlie for you," Louise said. "Corlie Lee, because when you were kids . . ."

"He called me Corlie," Cora Lee said, wiping a tear. Then, "His was such a late marriage. I was so glad for him— it did seem strange to have young nieces when I should, at my age, be talking about great-nieces. And now . . . Now we have only little Corlie."

It took some time for Louise to find Donnie's original letters hidden in the room where James Kuda had stayed. She called Cora Lee back, and then faxed them to her: the letters to Cora Lee that James had always taken to mail for Donnie when he went out early to bike or to run, the letters that were never mailed—that had been replaced by Kuda's versions: letters giving a new flight time, many weeks ahead of when Donnie had been scheduled to arrive in San Jose, rent a car, and drive down to Molena Point.

"Kuda left here six weeks before Donnie was to fly to California," Louise said. "He told us he was going back to New Orleans for a while, to help with the flood cleanup." Then, "Why?" she said. "Why did he kill him?"

Charlie looked up when Max arrived, and beckoned him in, and in a minute Cora Lee handed him the phone.

"I'll be talking with the Texas Bureau of Investigation in the morning," he told Louise. "If you would close Kuda's room, don't search further or touch or change anything. They'll have a man out there to go through everything and take evidence. We'll run his record, but please tell them whatever you can about his background."

Louise said, "They may find quite a lot. I heard them talking one night, Donnie and James. They stopped when I came in the room. I never . . . Well, I didn't ask Donnie about it, later. I was afraid of what I might find out about Donnie, too. Donnie wanted Kuda there, and he'd been through so much . . . I didn't want to fight with him. Any kind of stress was hard on him, but squabbling was terrible for Corlie. Corlie . . . She was in the hospital room, in her mother's arms, when Barbara died. Her mother holding her, when she died. That took the life right out of the child.

"She didn't cry for her mother," Louise said. "And she did not speak again."

37

In the car driving home, snuggled beside Max, Charlie was silent, thinking about Cora Lee. She listened as Max told her about the wreck down the coast, and that they thought they might have the missing body of the real Donnie French, of little Corlie's daddy.

When Charlie didn't speak, Max drew her close. "Sorry I missed the party. Sorry I broke my promise to get dressed up—and not smell of mud and seawater."

"I didn't marry you so you'd dress up and smell nice. I think you smell just fine. But I did miss you."

"I understand that before the excitement, it was a great party."

"Sicily did herself proud. I can't believe we sold over two hundred books, besides the seven framed pieces." She had sold the drawing of Joe Grey, too, standing like a cougar on the sea rocks, and that sale pleased her. That was to be Dulcie's Christmas present, Wilma had told her in a whisper.

But no pleasure could mean much compared with the raw pain they all felt for little Corlie. Even the satisfaction of seeing James Kuda in custody was so small, measured against the distress he had caused—the child's terror and desperate rage, and Cora Lee's shock at the death of her real cousin; that pain gripped Charlie too deeply to feel joy in much else. She hardly noticed when they turned down their long lane and through the new gate into the fenced yard, was barely aware of the barking of their two big dogs. So much hurt, at Christmas, that she felt almost guilty at their own happy home and warm, good marriage—as if she and Max had too much, while Cora Lee and that little girl were so hurting. She got out of the car quietly, without speaking. As Max opened the door to the mudroom, she leaned against him.

"What?" He held her away, studying her face. "You can't take on all the world's pain."

"I don't take it on. It just . . . I guess that kind of hurt is catching, something bearing down that I don't know how to sidestep."

"Don't let it steamroll you," he said, holding her tight. "Sometimes you can help more by stepping back."

She tried to think about that; and she was grateful for his strength and good sense. But then later, in bed, clinging close, she said, "What will happen now? What will you do tomorrow?"

"Soon as we can get a warrant we'll search his room, pick up latents, fiber samples. You know the drill. And we need a top computer technician. I expect we'll call the Bureau." He turned on the pillow to look at her. "You're asking a lot of questions. You planning a life of crime?"

Charlie smiled. "I don't think I'm emotionally detached enough. I'd die of fright before I got caught." She nuzzled into his shoulder. "Guess I'm just trying to ease my distress for Cora Lee. To not dwell on the sense of betrayal she must feel, and the guilt for bringing James Kuda here."

"She didn't *bring* him here, Charlie. She was scammed. It happens. And as for Gabrielle, I wouldn't cry too hard. She was more than eager to catch a man, and that can be asking for trouble." And before Charlie could answer, he was snoring.

Sighing, she stared up through the skylight, too distressed to sleep but too tired to stay awake. Tomorrow was Christmas Eve, and it would not be at all the comforting and restorative finale to a busy and often stressful year that she had hoped for.

Loneliness and pain, at Christmas, seemed so much more destructive than at any other time, so much more invasive.

Tomorrow is the day of the contest awards, she reminded herself. She tried to think only of that, tried to put herself to sleep visualizing Lori and Dillon stepping up to the judges' table to accept the first prize and to hold the check and grin. If she imagined that scene hard enough, made it real enough, then it had to happen.

ON CHRISTMAS EVE morning, a bright sun angled into Gabrielle Row's room at the back of the tall, rambling house. Hers was a large, spacious rectangle with long windows overlooking the backyard and canyon, its own bath and dressing room, with the smaller alcove furnished as an office/sewing room, where she still produced a few exclusive gowns for her old clientele. Her desk stood in one corner, and already, at eight-thirty, a Bureau agent sat at the computer flashing codes and diagrams on the screen that meant nothing to her. Agent Mel Jepson was young, dark-haired, and sleekly groomed, dressed in a dark suit and tie. He was pleased that only one-fifth of the hard drive was in use, that no one else in the household used her computer, and that she had not turned it on, herself, since she last made a cash transfer, two days ago.

She'd told him that yes, James Kuda had had free access to her room. It being adjacent to the kitchen, she said pointedly. And yes, she had been out yesterday afternoon for two hours having her hair done, and as far as she knew, Donnie—Kuda—had been working in the garden. All of this information seemed to please Jepson.

"I'm not sure I can pull the programs back, but we have a good chance, getting to it so soon, and you may not have used it since it was tampered with. Good, too, that there's very little on the hard drive." Jepson was so young that Gabrielle had at first wondered if he was competent, but he seemed well acquainted with the systems. He had a soft way of speaking but a keen, intense way of approaching the computer.

Molena Point officers had already dusted the room for prints, and had lifted fibers and various minute particles, retrieving evidence that would show whether anyone besides Kuda, and Gabrielle herself, had tampered with the equipment.

"It's a computer glitch," Gabrielle had snapped when

Jepson had first questioned her. "Something happened when the power surged, the document was just lost, that's all."

"Really?" Jepson had said. "Can you be sure of that?" He had looked evenly at her. "I'll do my best with this. It will take, at the least, several hours. If I can bring the programs back, I'll be contacting the banks themselves to corroborate what we have."

Gabrielle had turned away and left the room. For a while, as Jepson worked, she had angrily prowled the house—letting anger mask her shakiness, mask her fear that indeed her money was gone. Mask the fact that she might have lost everything, that she could be destitute.

Trying to put down the helplessness such an invasion of her personal life left her feeling, and to put down her rising fear of a penniless future, she had wanted to scream and weep and attack something or someone, and had, when Cora Lee came into the living room, turned on her with rage. But then, when Cora Lee had finally calmed her down, Gabrielle could only say, "The programs are gone, the spreadsheets gone."

"Oh," Cora Lee whispered, blanching. "Oh . . . Oh, Gabrielle. Was Harper right?"

"If it *is* true, if Donnie *is* an impostor, it's your fault! Yours, Cora Lee. *You* let an impostor into the house, *you* invited a criminal to move in with us! You let him take me out, let him make promises to me, and you didn't . . . You didn't even . . ."

"I didn't *know*, Gabrielle," Cora Lee said, at first shaken, but then her voice going low and even. "I did not know, Gabrielle. And it was you who let him take you out, you who let him make promises."

"I don't believe you really didn't know your own cousin. How could you not *know* him? You grew up together. How could you not recognize your own cousin!"

"Gabrielle, it's been nearly fifty years! He looks like Donnie, like our childhood pictures. I have pictures in my room, I'll show you—"

"What kind of fool do you think I am? And what kind of friend are you, to let this happen? I trusted you, Cora Lee! And look what you did to me!"

Cora Lee looked at her and turned away. *Christmas Eve,* she thought, going slowly up the stairs to her room. *Christmas Eve, and look what has happened to our lives.*

ACROSS THE VILLAGE in the hospital, Ryan and her uncle Dallas were enjoying breakfast in Dallas's room. Dallas, no longer in ICU, was waiting for the doctor to release him. They were sharing nonhospital pancakes and sausages and had their own pot of coffee, thanks to the changing of the police guard and a rookie who had been happy to go for takeout.

"How come you get to go home," Ryan said, "and they won't let me out?"

"You were hit in the head, Ryan. Even your hard head can take only so much. Maybe this afternoon, once you've seen Dr. Hamry again."

She touched her head gingerly. "I want to know just how bad it really is."

"He told you. Simple concussion, but I insisted on both CAT scan and MRI. He says it's *going* to hurt for a while.

He'll tell you what to watch for, when and if to call him. He doesn't want you to be by yourself for a few days, wants someone with you."

"If there are no complications, I don't see—"

"Clyde wants you over there, wants to take care of you."

"Like a mother hen," she scoffed. But she did not dislike the idea.

He put down his fork, looking intently at her. "Clyde's good for you. Why don't you two get married?"

Ryan stared at him. "What kind of question is that? You never ask me that kind of question. You think I need someone to watch over me?"

"He hasn't asked you?"

She began to eat again, quickly finishing her pancakes. Dallas studied her for a moment. "Ask *him*, Ryan. You're not shy."

"Has it occurred to you that I might not want to get married again? That I might like my single life?" It wasn't like Dallas to nose into her private affairs, he was always laid-back, never nosy.

Well, they were both edgy, fighting pain. She knew that his gunshot shoulder hurt, despite the painkiller.

"I'm sorry," he said. "Your head hurts."

"The doctor said the headaches would go away. I wish to hell they'd hurry up."

Dallas grinned. "The subject of marriage really is none of my business."

"I will be staying with him," she said stiffly. "He did ask me that. He said I can sleep on the pullout in his study, so if I need anything in the night . . ." That made her smile. For a moment she wondered how it would be to live with Clyde in one house, falling over each other, each wanting to keep their own space.

But it wasn't just the constant togetherness. There was another reason why she could never do that, why she could never marry Clyde. The same reason, she was certain, that kept him from asking her, despite how much they cared for each other.

It was a matter she would find impossible to discuss with him, a secret that he would not want her to know. And yet, if she *was* right, a secret that would eat at her until she broached the subject, and got him to talk about it.

38

DILLON THURWELL, HAVING just arrrived at the seniors' house, dropped her jacket on a kitchen chair, sat down, and watched, fascinated, as Lori Reed poured orange juice over her cereal. "You do that a lot?"

"Do what? Put . . . ?" Lori looked down at her bowl. "Oh . . ." She swallowed back a word she wasn't supposed to say, and stared up at Dillon and Cora Lee. They were both grinning. She didn't know whether to laugh or scowl at her own stupidity.

Cora Lee put her arm around the twelve-year-old. "We're all distracted, with everything that's going on, and with the judging in just a few hours."

Dillon studied Cora Lee. "Did something else happen? You two look . . ." Dillon glanced in the direction of the drive. "That big black car out there . . . Do you have company? What's going on?"

"It's a long story," Cora Lee said. "Lori can fill you in while I dress." The time was ten-thirty. The awards ceremony would start at noon, to be followed by a buffet picnic, courtesy of Jolly's Deli.

Dillon watched Cora Lee head for the stairs, then looked at Lori.

"You left early last night," Lori said. "Before the excitement."

Dillon poured herself a glass of milk and sat down again, snagging a handful of dry cereal to munch. Lori got up and moved to the sink, started to dump her bowl, and then tasted it. Turning, she set it back down on the table, and with her typically stubborn turn of mind, she ate her breakfast as she'd fixed it. In between bites, she filled Dillon in on the events of the previous evening, on Corlie's first words, on the child's damning identification of the killer.

Dillon was quiet a long time, thinking about the man they'd thought was Donnie French, the man they'd both liked because he was fun and was so eager to help everyone. They thought about the real Donnie, whom they'd never known, standing there beneath the village Christmas tree with his little girl in his arms, and that man they thought was so nice, that man shooting him.

"Donnie's sister-in-law is flying out from Texas," Lori said. "She called back last night, after Cora Lee talked with her, to say she got a cancellation, a night flight. That she'll be here in the morning—Christmas morning, to be with Corlie and Cora Lee for Christmas.

"She's bringing the letters that Donnie wrote to Cora Lee, that she never got. And bringing Cora Lee's letters to Donnie that Kuda snatched out of Donnie's mailbox."

Dillon's dark eyes flashed with anger. "There's more,"

Lori said. "Yesterday evening Dallas was chasing those Wickens, who hurt Ryan, and one of them shot him."

Dillon went pale. "He's not . . . He . . ."

"He's all right, it was his shoulder, didn't hit a bone. He's in the hospital, he was there when we went to see Ryan, before the opening, but no one said a word in front of Ryan. Maybe they didn't want us to know, either. Didn't want to upset us more than we were."

"We're not little children," Dillon said. "I'd rather have known, even if there wasn't anything we could do." Earlier, up at the school, when they heard sirens, the girls had come running to see what was going on. They had stood watching as Ryan, strapped to a stretcher, was lifted into the emergency van. Later, when Ryan was out of ICU, Dillon's mother had taken them to the hospital for a brief visit. Clyde was there sitting with her. She was disoriented and dizzy. Clyde had smuggled in his gray tomcat, who was lying on her bed, and they thought that was cool.

Lori finished her cornflakes and orange juice, pronounced it delicious enough to send the recipe to the Kellogg company, and rinsed her bowl. Cora Lee returned, looking snug and comfortable in soft corduroy pants and jacket the color of caramel, suede boots, and a suede cap. Heading out to the car thinking about the award, the girls swung from incessant talking to dead silence. Cora Lee, starting the engine, checked herself from saying that the world wouldn't end if they *didn't* win. She was praying hard that she'd see them walk away with the prize.

But whatever happened, she had no doubt that their bright and innovative playhouse would sell at the auction for a nice price. That thought, however, wouldn't calm the girls' competitive spirits.

And that's as it should be, Cora Lee thought. Even if they didn't win, the creative high of that long, demanding project wouldn't vanish. The girls would be down for a while, but the joy of conquering what they'd set out to do, of making something beautiful that others would treasure, would still be a part of them, as would the thrill they got from competing against tough competition. Losing couldn't take that away. *I should know,* Cora Lee thought. *I've lost enough times—but I've come out on top just as many times.*

And Gabrielle? she thought. *Will Gabrielle bounce back and come out on top again, too?*

She had left Gabrielle to lick her own wounds. But Gabrielle should feel somewhat comforted, with the Bureau man there; if anyone could bring back those files, Cora Lee thought an FBI technician surely could do it.

And if the money was gone, Gabrielle had a roof over her head; she wasn't starving, and they'd all do the best they could for her. *But right now,* Cora Lee thought as she turned up Ocean Avenue, *the sun is shining, the judging is about to start, and tonight is Christmas Eve—tonight is concert night.* Tonight she must forget everything else in the world and give herself fully to the music.

But then tomorrow, she thought feeling suddenly heavy and dead, as if her heart had stopped, *tomorrow Corlie's aunt Louise will be here. And, too soon, Corlie will go home. We'll have Christmas together, and then Corlie will be gone again, headed home to Texas . . .*

Turning in to the school's gate and waiting in line to park the car, she sat still and rigid, caught in the painful realization that she'd tried to avoid. She would soon lose little Corlie, too. Lose all that was left of Donnie.

Dillon spoke, but Cora Lee hardly heard her. She sat swallowing back sudden tears, trying to get hold of herself, trying to come to terms with this additional, painful loss that seemed too much to bear.

39

THE ALLEY BEHIND Jolly's Deli, with its fancy brick paving and tiny shops, smelled of roast turkey, though it was not yet Christmas day. The shops' stained-glass windows glowed with Christmas candles and bright decorations. At the back door of the deli, beside a potted poinsettia, stood an empty plate, its surface licked glossy clean. Three satisfied felines sat before it, happily licking their paws and whiskers.

Dulcie and Kit had spent the morning crouched in the oak tree behind the jail, pummeled by cold wind, eavesdropping on Leroy Huffman and Ralph Wicken—while Joe enjoyed a comfortable two hours lounging in Juana Davis's office watching Max Harper on Davis's TV monitor as he interrogated Betty Wicken.

Afterward, the three deployed to Jolly's alley, following the scent of roast turkey—turkeys had been roasting at Jolly's for days, for deli slicing and for the Patty Rose picnic, and each morning George Jolly saw to it that the village cats got their share of generous scraps carefully boned and arranged on the nice white plates that he kept for that purpose.

Now, full to bursting, the cats had a leisurely bath and exchanged the morning's intelligence.

"All they did in that cell was argue," Dulcie said, "and Ralph whined a lot. Leroy said Ralph messed up the heist by calling attention to them with his fixation over little children, and Ralph said it was the blue van that did them in, that the van had been a stupid idea. I don't see that we learned much that could be of use to the department. Except—"

"Except," Kit interrupted excitedly, "Leroy Huffman *did* kill that girl in Arkansas. Evina's niece. Ralph said if he hadn't done that, killed that girl and then run, no one would have followed them, that Evina wouldn't have followed them out here, and they wouldn't be in this fix now, so it was all Leroy's fault." As cold as Kit and Dulcie had been on that oak branch outside the jail window, it was always satisfying to listen to a couple of no-goods laying the blame on each other.

"I wonder," Dulcie said, "how they found out Evina was watching them."

"Betty Wicken saw her," Joe said. "She finally told Harper—she glimpsed Evina twice in that downstairs window. Didn't pay much attention the first time, then later caught a glint that looked like binoculars or a camera. She called Leroy to come look, and of course he knew her. That was just yesterday.

"And," Joe said, "Harper got her to tell him how she knew about the mural. He told her the more she cooperated, the easier it would be for Ralph. She really cares about that little-scum brother of hers. Max said he had enough on Ralph to lock him up for the rest of his life. I'm not sure he does," the tomcat said, smiling. "But he made her believe it. She went on a long time about how hard she's worked to keep Ralph away from children."

"How *did* she know about the mural?" Kit said, licking a smear of turkey from her whiskers.

"She worked there," Joe said. "She worked as a housecleaner for the Patty Rose Home, early in the fall. She cleaned up the old studio after the Home bought it."

"But the mural was hidden," Kit said. "How . . . ?"

"Some old book about Anna Stanhope that Betty read when she worked in a gallery in Oregon. It said Anna had completed a mural that had never been on exhibit or listed with any collector. Some collector had looked for it, years ago, on the Stanhope estate. Betty got curious, came down here, and got a job there so she could nose around. She said she pried off a part of the wall, and then patched it."

"She told Harper all that," Dulcie said, lying down in a patch of sun, "to protect that no-good brother?"

"She did," Joe said. "Well, Dorothy Street will soon have the mural back where it belongs."

"I wonder," Dulcie said, "will they install it in the school, in the main hall? Or sell it to pay for work on the new classrooms? A valuable mural that the school never knew they had."

"I thought you were the art lover. When did you get so money conscious?"

"When I saw how hard Dorothy works to support the school. You think this playhouse contest is just for fun? She's hoping that enough of the builders will donate their houses to the school as tax write-offs so when they're auctioned, the school can add to the trust fund. You know she has a long list of homeless children waiting."

Joe did know. It was hard for the state to adopt out older children when, say, something had happened to their parents. Joe yawned. Full of turkey and warmed by the morning sun, he was thinking of a short nap when Dulcie nudged him. "They'll be gathering for the award."

Kit was already scrambling up the jasmine vine to the roof, and by the time Joe flipped over and raced up behind them, she and Dulcie were gone, flying across the peaks. This was Lori and Dillon's big day, and no one wanted to miss it.

They arrived to see the grounds nearly as crowded as when the playhouses were being assembled, but totally different. No trucks or forklifts, now, lumbering among the gardens. No racket of tools and engines. Only Christmas carols from a sound system on the mansion's balcony, the shouts and laughter of children, and, risen overnight like a Lilliputian city across the lawns and among the gardens, dozens and dozens of bright and amazing playhouses. The cats wanted to explore every one, running in and out as the children were doing, climbing and laughing.

"There's Corlie," Dulcie said, watching the child scramble into a castle tower six feet off the ground. This was the first time the cats had heard her laugh. Juana Davis and Cora Lee stood smiling up at her; but beside them, Lori and Dillon looked wilted. This castle playhouse was far larger and more elegant than their house, and it had not only two crenellated stone towers but a stone wall with arrow niches and a drawbridge that left the girls looking sour and defeated.

"It's overdone," Dulcie said. "Can't they see that?"

"Come on," Joe said. "It's impressive. You have to be realistic."

"I like theirs better," Kit said loyally.

The crowd began to move toward the balcony of the mansion, where Dorothy Street stood with two men. "We'll know soon enough," Dulcie said nervously, watching the girls as they hurried toward the balcony and up the stairs where the contestants were gathering. Davis and Cora Lee followed, walking slowly with Corlie between them; and as the cats scrambled into a pear tree, they saw the girls appear at the back of the balcony clutching each other's hands as Dorothy Street moved the microphone.

The thank-yous and introductions took a long time, and made Lori and Dillon, as well as the cats, fidget with impatience. When at last Dorothy announced the winner, the local contractor who had built the grand castle, and when she turned to beckon him forward, Lori and Dillon turned away from the crowd, long-faced. Cora Lee hurried up the stairs to be with them; but the cats slunk away into the bushes, their own hearts heavy, too.

"I was so sure," Dulcie said.

"*They* were so sure," Joe said sadly, but with a hint of feline disapproval. He might have said the girls had counted their catch too soon. Wisely, he kept his mouth shut.

"There's still the auction," Kit said hopefully, lashing her fluffy tail. "That castle's all for show. The kids all liked Lori and Dillon's bright house better, with all its decks and holes and ins and outs. I bet it sells for a bundle." And she scowled out of the bushes, at the winner, her ears and whiskers plastered to her head, her yellow eyes glaring.

40

THE STAGE OF Molena Point Little Theater was framed with evergreens, and five Christmas trees stood tall behind the white-robed choir; Cora Lee French, the evening's soloist, was brightly robed in Christmas red.

Cora Lee had reserved, for her friends, a spacious box looking down over the audience to the stage. Only the three cats were seated higher than any human, up among the shadows near the ceiling, comfortably sprawled along a rafter, warm and snug in their exclusive aerie.

In the friends' private box, little Corlie French sat at the front with Lori Reed, Detective Davis, Captain Harper, and Charlie. Charlie was dressed in emerald velvet, her red hair piled high and caught with a holly sprig. Ryan, seated behind her, wore white fleece and sported a white bandage wound rakishly around her head. Clyde sat on her left, Dallas to her right, his sport coat lumpy with his own hospital wrappings. Wilma, the senior ladies, and the Greenlaws filled the last rows, dressed in a rainbow of Christmas colors. The cats, looking down past their friends' box, could see the top of Dillon Thurwell's red head where she sat with her parents. None of the audience looked up among the rafters to discover three cats perched above them—or almost no one.

Wilma looked up once, and grinned; Charlie and Clyde looked, and then Ryan glanced up but immediately looked away again, as if shifting position to ease her aching head. The cats watched her warily.

"Do you think she knows?" Dulcie whispered. "Oh, she couldn't."

"Don't go imagining things," Joe told her. But, watching Ryan, Joe felt tense and uncertain, too. "She can't know," he said reassuringly. "Ryan isn't . . ." But then, recalling his argument with Clyde, he shut up and said no more. Had Clyde *told* Ryan? Oh, hell, he wouldn't do that.

But, thinking of this, Joe crouched there on the rafter in the darkened theater, silent and uncomfortable, wondering.

Dulcie looked at him, frowning, but then she turned away, giving herself to the music, to the Christmas hymns and carols that had been beloved by humans for so many centuries. Whatever Ryan *might* have guessed, she thought, there was nothing they could do about it, and her little niggling worry lost itself in the cascades of magnificent Christmas music, in the joyous paeans to a power greater than anyone on earth could really understand. She didn't speak, and there was not a sound from the audience below her. And when at last the concert had ended and the stage lights went up, still everyone sat hushed, bathed in the afterglow.

And then applause rang through the rafters so violently

that the cats spun around on their beam and raced away, back into the lighting booth, escaping the deafening thunder. Running through the dim and shadowed booth, leaping tangles of cable and wires that seemed as threatening as land mines, they fled out through the window they'd left unlatched, to the cold silence of the roof—to the almost silence.

They listened as the soft echo of applause died below them, and as one last hymn began in a curtain call for the chorus. More applause. And then one more, lighter Christmas song, a merry and warming solo by Cora Lee. And then they heard the hustle of the crowd rising and moving out to the lobby; and the cats headed for Kit's house, for the Greenlaws' Christmas party.

Trotting quickly across the cold rooftops, they said little, each small cat still caught in a wonder beyond anything that even these special cats could conjure. Caught in the glorious noise of mankind, which far outstripped the ugliness that seemed, too often, to overwhelm the world of humans.

Pausing in Kit's tree house, the cats sat for a little while watching the Greenlaws' guests arrive, looking down through the windows, enjoying the bright Christmas tree and the lighted candles, the laughter and the good smells, basking in the tangle of familiar and happy voices on Christmas Eve. Lori and Dillon had arrived, Dillon with her parents, Lori with Cora Lee and little Corlie and Mavity. The two older girls, already eating and laughing, seemed nearly recovered from their painful disappointment.

A disappointment of the ego, Dulcie thought, smiling. *Not of the pocketbook.* The cats, after the awards ceremony and the buffet picnic and the very satisfying auction, had padded close behind Cora Lee and the three girls as they came down the stairs and headed for Cora Lee's car, Lori and Dillon holding Corlie's hands, one on either side.

"That was," Cora Lee had told them, "the best Christmas present *I* could have had, to see your house sell for the highest price of them all." She looked down at the girls. "You received nearly twice the amount of the prize money. And what thrills me most is to know where your playhouse will be donated."

"But," Lori said, "we didn't *win.*"

Cora Lee paused by the car, turning to look sternly at her. "You did next best. Your house did better, if you want to look at the financial gain. Think about that, Lori. Your house sold for far more than the winner received. Doesn't that impress you? You built a wonderful house. You did a fine job on it, and it has given back to you a nice boost for your future, a sizable addition to your college fund. But best of all," Cora Lee said, looking very serious and cool, "is that it will become a part of the San Francisco Children's Hospital." She hugged both girls. "Do you know what an honor that is?" Beside her, Corlie looked up at the girls, her dark eyes bright and needy, as if she very much wanted them to smile.

The cats had watched them drive away, and then, wanting to know what the Bureau man had found in Gabrielle's computer, and wanting to know what new intelligence had come into the station, they went their separate ways. As Joe Grey headed for the station, Dulcie and Kit raced over the roofs to the seniors' house.

They had found Corlie already there, snuggled on the living-room window seat with the two dogs, and they could hear Cora Lee and Gabrielle in the kitchen. Joining Corlie and the dogs, pretending to doze but listening to every word from the kitchen, they soon knew that Gabrielle hadn't even asked if the girls had won, and that she was in no mood to hear the financial good luck of anyone, particularly of little girls.

Mel Jepson had, indeed, been able to bring back Gabrielle's programs, and he had found all four accounts stripped bare. He had, however, also found Kuda's accounts, to which Gabrielle's money had been transferred. The cats marveled at what a skilled computer technician could do. Despite the fact that it was a holiday, Jepson had, with a few personal phone calls, been able to put a hold on the transfer of funds to Kuda's accounts. "By tomorrow," he'd told Gabrielle, "if there are no glitches, the money should be deposited back to you." The cats hoped that would be the case, if only for the sake of the three other seniors. Gabrielle was hard enough to live with, anyway, without this disaster and her resulting emotional furor upsetting the household.

But now, at Kit's house, trotting across the oak limb and in through the dining-room window to join the party, they put aside Gabrielle's misfortune as Dulcie and Joe paused on the sill eyeing the long table where that delectable buffet was laid out—and Kit leaped onto a chair, poised to reach up a paw and snag a slice of roast turkey. This was, after all, her own home. She drew back only when Lucinda spied her and gave her a warning look.

But then Lucinda served up three small plates from the buffet and set them on the windowsill: a Christmas feast loaded with rich delicacies that would put down any normal cat, but did not bother these small gluttons. Not until the cats finished every crumb, and looked up, did they see how crowded the room had become.

All their friends had arrived, even Evina Woods. She sat before the fire talking with Max Harper. The cats heard her say she was flying out in the morning, that Cora Lee would take her to the airport when she picked up little Corlie's aunt Louise. Slipping down from the window ledge and making their way across the crowded room, the cats leaped to the top of a bookcase and settled down to wash, and to listen.

They learned, within the hour, that Dorothy meant to press charges against the Wickens and Leroy for the theft of the mural. That the mural would, indeed, be hung in the main hall of the school. That Max Harper was certain Leroy Huffman would be indicted for the murder of young Marlie James. That Cora Lee was hoping to persuade Corlie's aunt Louise to stay and visit for a while in Molena Point, to keep little Corlie near her. And that Charlie was so wired about the response to her book, and about the reviews it was getting, that she was already toying with several new writing projects. Comfortably sprawled above the heads of the party, the cats napped, and listened, and enjoyed; and they pronounced the party a success, a needed time of healing for all their friends, a time of comforting one another after a week of distress; a time of getting their balance, again, for the new year to come.

• • •

THAT NIGHT JOE Grey slept in his tower, his windows closed against the icy wind, his cushions pawed into a warm nest around him to replace the warmth of a bed partner, and to block out any private conversation from the rooms below.

I better get used to this, the tomcat thought. *This could be the new order of the day.*

But Joe had no notion of what was really coming, and how much he would have to get used to. He awoke to thin daylight and the heady aroma of bacon, and decided it was okay to go down into the house.

Pausing a moment to admire the silvery morning around him, he soon slipped in through his cat door onto a rafter, dropped down to Clyde's desk and then to the Oriental rug. Ryan's foldout bed was empty. Glancing through the glass door to the upstairs deck, he saw her standing out in the cold, wrapped in Clyde's warm wool robe, sipping a mug of coffee. He studied her with interest.

Though she had her back to him, Joe recognized clearly the stance and body language that heralded Ryan Flannery's preoccupation with some new and exciting design problem. Curious, he stood watching.

Ryan had built this upstairs deck atop the carport as part of the total remodel she'd done, which gave Clyde's one-story house a second floor. *Now*, Joe thought, *what's she up to? Are we remodeling again? What? Is Clyde planning to enlarge the study?*

But even as he stared at her slim back, wrapped in Clyde's plaid robe, Ryan turned and looked at him, fixing him with a steady green gaze. Eye to eye. Woman to cat,

in a too-familiar manner that shocked Joe and made him
back away.

"I was just wondering," she said, stepping back into the
warm room, "if the city would let us build a solarium up
here—a kind of studio."

Joe stared silently at her, his heart starting a staccato
beat against his ribs. *A studio? Clyde has no use for a studio.
Why are you telling* me*? Why are you talking to me?*

"Would that be all right with you?" Ryan said.

Joe tried not turn tail and run, or to look terrified. He
sat down and washed his left-front paw. Ryan knelt, pulling
Clyde's robe closer around her, and tried to look him in the
eye. Joe wouldn't look at her; he concentrated on his paw.

"Come on, Joe. Did you think I was out cold when you
made that call to dispatch? To Mabel Farthy? When you
said, 'Thank God it's Mabel'?"

Joe looked at her a long time, his heart pounding so
hard he felt like he had a herd of drunken mice dancing
inside his chest.

"With a concussion," Ryan said, "it takes a while for a
person's memory to come back. The length of time varies.
In my case, it didn't take long."

Joe remained safely silent, deeply occupied with his
grooming. This was terrible. This was a major crisis. Why
the hell wasn't Dulcie here? She'd know how to handle this
woman.

Ryan reached to stroke his ear, but then she drew her
hand back. "Joe, I heard Dulcie say, 'Her cell phone!' and
then Kit raced away. Then, in just a minute, you had Mabel
on the line. You said, 'Thank God it's Mabel,' then, 'Stanhope mansion . . .' and then something about thieves hit-

ting me with a hammer." Ryan smiled. "You told Mabel I was out cold."

Joe abandoned his pretense at grooming and openly gawked at her.

"Well, of course I kept my eyes shut," she said. "I didn't know what I was hearing. Talking cats? I thought I was in really bad shape, having really crazy delusions."

Joe gave her a look that said he understood. But he wasn't willing to answer. He could only swallow, his throat as dry as if he'd just eaten feathers.

"It will take a while for us both to get used to this," Ryan said, rising. "I can understand that." She looked solemnly down at Joe. "Never fear, tomcat. I'll keep my mouth shut. This is not the kind of secret I would ever share with the department. Or," she said, "with anyone in my family." And she turned away and headed downstairs, giving him space, following the enticing aroma of pancakes and bacon.

It took Joe some time to recover sufficiently to follow her. He strolled into the kitchen, where breakfast sat on the stove keeping warm. No one was there but the three household cats eating from their bowls on the rug. From the living room he heard voices. He wandered in, trying to look casual.

Ryan and Clyde were sitting on the floor before the lighted Christmas tree eating chocolates from a box that Ryan had apparently just unwrapped. Ryan looked at Joe, and held out her hand to him. The sparkle of the diamond ring on her finger reflected the colors of the Christmas lights. Third finger, left hand. A ring that had not been there yesterday evening when Clyde brought her home from the hospital, and had not been there a few minutes ago, upstairs, when she knelt talking to him. The empty ring box lay beside the open box of chocolates.

Joe would hear, later, how Clyde had gone shopping before he picked Ryan up at the hospital, would hear all about Clyde's agonized thoughts that had accompanied this decisive move, how Clyde had wanted to ask Wilma to help pick out the ring, wanted a woman's opinion. Or maybe Charlie. Or Ryan's sister, Hanni—except that Hanni's taste ran to pizzazz and dazzle, and that wouldn't suit Ryan. Joe would hear about how Clyde thought, should he ask Joe first, to make sure it was okay? And *should* he buy a ring? Or should he just ask Ryan first, and pick out the ring together? Was he *sure* he wanted to do this? And how would this go down with Joe Grey? Clyde would tell Joe how, when he'd thought about not asking her, a terrible loneliness had gripped him, an emptiness that he had never before experienced.

Clyde did not usually share his dilemmas so freely. Joe would listen patiently to all the mental suffering involved in this commitment; he would hear how, after Clyde had bought the ring, he debated about whether to keep his secret from everyone, in the event that, after all, he would be obliged to return his purchase.

But now the deed was done, and apparently the ring had been accepted, the decision had been made by both parties, and this early Christmas morning, beside the Christmas tree, Joe Grey looked at Ryan, and she looked at him. And the two of them shared a secret that even Clyde didn't yet know. There they were, the three of them sitting beside the Christmas tree. Joe and Ryan looking at each other. Clyde looking from Ryan to Joe, puzzled—and it was then that Rock bounded in through the dog door, from the back patio, skidded through the kitchen, and crashed into them, licking their faces, licking Joe Grey in the face as happily as if the big hound had a new toy for Christmas.

We'll see about that, Joe thought, pushing away Rock's nose with a velvet paw.

But for a long time afterward, that moment would remain frozen in Joe Grey's memory like some treasured family photograph. He and Ryan and Clyde and Rock, on this early Christmas morning, all together before the Christmas tree, frozen in time as permanently as the preserved images from Pompeii—a Christmas memory to last, perhaps, for all his nine lives.

And then Clyde raised his coffee cup in a toast. "Merry Christmas, Joe. Merry Christmas, Ryan. And Rock. Merry Christmas to all of us, to a brand-new family."

AUTHOR'S NOTE

The word hound is used to denote dog, not to imply that the Weimaraner is a member of the hound group; this breed is a member of the sporting group.